COCKROACHES IN THE BILGE

MITCHELL PERRY

PAGE PUBLISHING, INC.
Conneaut Lake, PA

First originally published by Page Publishing 2020

ISBN 978-1-6624-2574-5 (pbk)
ISBN 978-1-6624-2575-2 (digital)

Printed in the United States of America

"*Cockroaches in the bilge!*" would echo down the halls of the home, followed by a wheezy high-pitched chuckle. It would last only a short time, for the captain would run out of air. The home was an old military infirmary now used for the elderly or invalids who have no one to care for them. Usually referred to as the poor nuthouse by the local people of Homeport, Virginia. It was a small port very near Jamestown. In fact, it was Jamestown. It was growing so large and fast, most people confused it as part of the town. It was a gray dismal-looking building outside town on a large hillside. You could look down on town from there as well as see the bay, where the town seemed to flow right down to the water's edge. The building was made of stone. The windows were small and barred. There was no landscaping around the building. It was pretty much left to nature's own beauty. A long drive was not paved, so it was rutted from times traveled in the rain. It ran up to the house at the large front steps, which were shadowed by the half round roof that reached out over the large porch held up by large white pillars. The porch wrapped around the whole building, which gave the tenants an area in which to roll in their wheelchairs or just sit out of the hot afternoon sun. Some patients were ambulatory, but a lot were bedridden. The two front doors were arched and extremely large and heavy built to withstand the forces of war. They were rarely used any more as the back entrance was the preferred way of the occupants.

The captain, as they called him, had been at the home for a few years now. He was found wandering around the streets of Homeport with a jarful of roaches babbling sea jargon. Not too many people

3

paid attention to such thing, for many seafaring wanderers come through the area from time to time off the ships for mental reasons, but they usually move on to larger cities. But Homeport was growing into Jamestown, or Jamestown was growing into Homeport. Either way, the area was changing.

But one day, Captain was found very ill and brought to the home and just never left. He was a mystery to everyone. He seemed to appear out of nowhere; there were many stories about him. "He was an old pirate," "He was an old British naval officer," and so on. No one even knew how old he was. Everyone at the home called him captain, not really knowing his real name. For when he would address anyone, it would be in the form of an order. His scratchy voice would grumble an order as, "Where's me gruel, boy? Be quick about it." Or when he couldn't roll himself over, he would yell down the hall, "I needs me a swab on deck! Needs me a swab on decks!" His voice would echo down the hall. When you would show up answering, "Yes, Captain," he would smile a bit and he would ask, "Aye, mate, gives me hand cumin about, will yas? I've been leeward way too long." Then he'd laugh his wheezing little laugh.

He never talked much. He spent most of his time mumbling to himself and laughing his little laugh. His appearance was of a man you might think of as skin and bones. His weight must have been close to ninety pounds. More bones than muscle. His whole body was badly scarred up. The back of his left shoulder had a scar, and part of his arm was missing, as if it were bitten off or cut out. His jawline was strong and square and sported a white beard. Since he came to the home, he quit shaving, leaving a ghostly white but sparse facial hair. His lips were skinny and ran from deep indents in his cheeks. When he would grin, most all of his teeth were missing. A few hung down, creating a sunken face look below his pointed nose. His eyes, though pale gray highlighted with green, were always sharp and direct. Although he seemed feeble, his eyes never seemed to miss a thing.

Most of the people who worked around the house were volunteers or hired for part time. Forty residents was the maximum bed room they had, and it was full most of the time.

Most lived out their lives at the home, so death was no stranger to the house. Some stayed for quite a while. Others seemed to just pass through as though it was just part of their journey. Mrs. Summit was a permanent resident and caretaker of the house. She came to Homeport with her husband years before to settle in the growing new states, but her husband died shortly after they started to settle. Being a widow and pregnant at the time, she needed some assistance. Having no family in the area, the local church found her the position of caretaker for the old infirmary. Food and shelter would be provided. Also a small income would be provided. She was very grateful for the opportunity and took the job. Because it was state funded, it was a very big challenge to supply the residents with quality care on the meager allotted moneys she was to work with. Mrs. Summit did a marvelous job and supplied a fine upbringing for her son without being a burden to anyone in the community. Mrs. Summit was a stout woman. Not skinny but not fat. She was short, about five feet one. She always wore a drab brown dress and would cover it with a clean apron. She wore her hair up, which was quite long when down, but no one ever saw it down. She always wore it up tight on top of her head. She wasn't a strikingly pretty woman. Her face was a bit homely. Her best feature were her dark brown eyes. It was her smile and her warm heart that made her most attractive. Her hands were rough as a blacksmith's. She never stopped working. Never took a vacation, really. In fifteen years, she never left Homeport. Her voice had a relaxed English accent and was very soft-spoken. She could put any anxious person at ease.

The only other permanent resident was Mrs. Summit's son, Benjamin Fredric Summit. Ben, as they called him, was born on October 15, 1834. Ben was now fifteen years old and was a great help to his mother around the home. Ben had been a great help ever since he was five. Ben wasn't a large boy, not skinny built much like his mother. His eyes were a multicolor of brown and blue. His mother would joke to him how she could tell what mood he was in by the color of his eyes. His hair was jet-black, but his facial features were soft and round. Very much like his mother, he wasn't an overly attractive boy. But like his mother, it was his kindly heartfelt attitude in life that made him attractive. The residents at the house appreciated his hard work and young presence. It was the little thing he did. Like for Mrs. McGregor, if Ben went to town, she would find a reason to call him in, maybe to fetch her shawl. Then the questions would start. They lived memories through his youth.

Ben attended school in town, but his mother educated him further than most other kids, so Ben was very scholarly. His day would start very early with the chores he had to do before school. He would study in the evening under his mom's strict attention. Mrs. Summit knew she was grooming him for a better life, but that also meant he would leave the home. She had mixed feelings about it, for the laborious task of taking care of the home was showing at her age, and Ben was more help than he knew. She couldn't help but wish sometimes he would meet a girl who felt the same way she did about the home. He would stay and work in town, and they would both take over the home. But deep in her heart, she knew that to be selfish, and she couldn't blame him for wanting to get as far away as he could from this place. Ben never complained, and he worked as hard as any man in town.

Ben had never been anywhere but as far as Homeport, but he was well aware of the world and what could be from his mother's teachings. One day, while working in the captain's room, Ben felt a sensation that somebody was sneaking up on him. He turned around, only to find the captain sleeping and no one else in the room. He went back to what he was doing, and that feeling rushed over him again. This time, he turned around, and there was the captain staring at him, eyes fixed sharply on Ben's. He didn't appear to be breathing either. Ben stood frozen for a minute, watching to see if the captain was possibly dead. Ben knew the look of death, and even though the captain wasn't making noises or mumbling to himself as usual, Ben could tell this was not a man whose life had just ended. This was a soul-searching stare. Ben felt as though the captain was looking right into his inner thoughts.

Ben broke the silence by asking, "You all right, Captain?"

A sly grin came over the captain's face as he yelled, "Cockroaches in the bilge!" And then he ended with a wheezy laugh.

Ben just shook his head at the crazy old guy and went about his work. Ben added, "You had me worried, old-timer." That feeling Ben had that day never really left him. For days, that feeling of the captain staring at him kept creeping back.

One evening, while Ben studied in the kitchen by the lantern light, he thought he heard something. He broke his thoughts from his studies and looked around the spacious room. He liked to study in the kitchen because of its size, but it also had the best light. It also had the heat from the ovens that still had embers burning from Ben's mom cooking all day. He surveyed the area with his eyes, looking over to where the well was. He was always surprised at the insight the builders had to put the well inside the compound. That way, the settlers could hold out for a long time if they had to. Ben's eyes looked over the hanging pots, casting long shadows across the wall. He looked at the caldron hanging in the fireplace as the shadows danced behind it. But nothing seemed out of place. He sat back in his big oak chair with big flat arms that was left, he figured, by some important settler at the time the fort was being used. He grabbed up his slate and piece of charcoal to do his studies. He was just starting to concentrate when a voice yelled down the hall, raising the hairs on the back of his neck. *"Man overboard! Man overboard!"*

He jumped to his feet and ran to the hallway, leading to the many rooms the residents stayed in. As he threw the door open to the corridor, the voice got louder and more distinctive as it echoed down the hall. Ben recognized the voice now as the captain yelled, "'Tis mutiny, it is!"

Ben opened the door to the captain's room. "Man overboard! Man overboard!" The captain yelled again, echoing down the hall.

"Captain?" Ben asked.

"'Tis about time," the captain said with a growl in his voice.

It was dark in the room, so Ben quickly lit a lantern. The room illuminated a soft yellow glow. And there on the floor was a huddled little mass. Realizing it was the captain, Ben ran over and grabbed the captain by the shoulder, asking, "You okay, Captain?"

The captain rattled off and mumbled, "The wind came up, and I tried to lower some sail, but the boom came about and dropped me overboard."

"Well, you'll be all right now," Ben assured him as he helped him to his feet.

The captain snapped. "Whose on watch? I could have been lost at sea!"

Ben said, "Oh, I'm sorry, Captain. I was studying in the kitchen. I couldn't hear you."

As he sat him on the bed and swung his legs around, the captain grunted as he positioned himself. "That's all right, Ben," the captain said, patting Ben on the shoulder.

Ben looked up with a shock. He had never heard the captain use his name or anybody else's name before, for that matter. Ben looked at the captain, whose eyes were clear as the sea, and Ben felt that feeling again. It wasn't scary. It just felt like the captain was looking right into his very thoughts. As fast as a snake strikes, the captain reached up and grabbed Ben's shirt collar on both sides, filling his fists with Ben's shirt collar. He then pulled Ben's face right up to his. Ben jerked back as a reaction, but the old man had more strength than Ben gave him credit for. They were staring eye to eye, and Ben was trying to pry the old man's grip away but was unable to. Try as he might, he could not break the grip of the feeble old man.

The captain laughed, and as clear as any intelligent man, as sound mind as any man, the captain spoke quietly under his breath, "Ben, you're a good man, honest at heart, and a hard worker. You deserve more from life, Ben, and I can give it to you." Ben was still hanging on to the captain's hands and pulling back as hard as he could. He was spellbound by the captain's clarity. He listened to his every word. The captain could see he had gotten to the lad, so he added, "Pull up a chair, boy, and I'll tell you a tale."

Ben, stammering to speak, squeaked out, "I can't. I've studies." The captain let go with his right hand and reached behind the back of Ben's head. He grabbed a handful of Ben's hair and pulled Ben's head back, forcing his chin up. He pulled with the strength of a large healthy man. Ben let out a yell. "Ouch! Captain, please, you're hurting me."

The smile disappeared from the captain's face, and a stone-cold serious look overtook it. "Look, swab." The captain was growling "I don't have much time, and I certainly don't know of anyone more deserving of this story. Now sit down, and that's an order from your captain!" And with that he pushed Ben away as he let his grip go.

Their eyes never lost contact, even as Ben reached over by the nightstand to retrieve a small cherrywood chair. Ben felt hypnotized, like the captain had his attention. He was being held against its will. He pulled the straight-backed chair up to the bedside and slowly sat himself down. Just as Ben sat, the captain sat straight up in the bed, cross-legged Indian style with his hand on his knees. A smile crept back to his face as he started his story.

"I was born in Athens, Greece, back somewhere around 1748 to a street whore. I stayed there till I was ten years old. Then one day." The captain was talking, and Ben was listening, but he was amazed at this skinny near-death old man sitting straight up in the bed, full of excitement. Life seemed to feed back into him as his story continued. He was actually radiant with it. With his hands and gestures, he bounced on the bed to make his points of the story. "Are you paying attention, boy?" the captain asked as he leaned forward on his legs, putting his face in Ben's.

Ben's eyes got big, and he answered, "Uh, yes, street whore 1748, makes you about one hundred years old."

The old man snapped back, "One hundred and one." Ben felt a little stupid at that simple math blunder but was a bit surprised at the age of the old man. The old man said, "Hey, boy. You know what we need?"

"No, I don't," Ben answered.

"We need some rum," the captain said, raising his eyebrows. "Got any about?"

Ben was caught off guard at the question, and he stammered, "Uhhm, I think my mom has some in the pantry for cooking at Christmas."

"Argh, what a waste," the captain barked. "Quick, boy, go get it. Bring it here. Hurry, we don't have much time."

Ben felt real uncomfortable about the idea and hesitated then said, "I'm not sure if you should have any."

"Why, because of my age?" The captain growled, closing one eye and continued, "You know, boy, at one hundred and one years old, I've lived longer than most presidents of this here United States. Well, hell, I've lived longer than most human beings on this earth! So I'm pretty sure that a boy of your age knows what's best for me, but what your missing here, son, is I'm not askin' your opinion. I'm given you a direct order, from your captain." Ben sat for a second, trying to make sense out of what he just heard. The captain barked very loudly, "Go get the damn rum, boy!"

Ben found himself jumping to his feet to go get the rum. He found himself running down the hallway, and as he got to the kitchen, he was surprised at himself for letting that old man boss him around like that. *Giving me orders*, he thought. *Giving me orders. He's a self-proclaimed captain. I don't know if he's a real captain or not.* The whole time he was arguing with himself, he was obediently getting the rum out of the cupboard. He reached behind two large bottles of vinegar and pulled a half-gallon container, a jug of sorts with a small round circle off the top one could stick his finger in. It was the rum. Ben ran it back down the hall to the captain's room. Ben quietly closed the door behind him and brought the jug over to the captain.

The captain, still sitting up, reached out for the jug, saying, "That a boy, Ben. You're a good mate." The captain grabbed hold of the cork in the top, which had been in there for months. He tried but could not pull it out.

Ben reached up and said, "Here, let me try."

The captain swung the jug away from Ben's hand. "I'll get it, boy. Just sit back down," the captain barked, and he grabbed hold with his back teeth, twisting the jug with both hands until he heard the hollow thud of the cork as it pulled out. The captain spit out the cork onto the bed, saying, "Oh, yeah." Then he laughed to himself a bit and passed the open jug under his nose, taking a deep sniff. The captain mumbled to himself, "Ahh, 'tis heaven, it is."

Ben perked up and said, "It's been aged a while."

Captain swung the jug to his lips, taking three deep swallows, coughing a bit. He growled out the words, "Oh, that's good."

Ben never understood why people liked rum. He tried it once but did not find it very appealing. The captain was wiping the extra off his lips with his forearm. He bounced it hard on the bed then pushed it at Ben, saying, "Here, boy, take a swaller."

Ben put his hand up, trying to be polite. "No, thank you. Really, I'm fine." Ben's mom always told him the demon rum was only for vagabonds, crooks, pirates, and crooked politicians.

The captain persisted, "Come on, boy. Only real men drink rum. A couple of swallows won't hurt you."

Ben, still trying not to have to drink any, said, "I really shouldn't."

The captain pushed his button once more. "Oh, mate, you can tell you've been raised by your mother."

This was always a sore spot for Ben. Ben started to argue. "That's not why I don't want any. It's not good for you."

The captain let out a laugh and spat out, "Boy, did you know in many countries, it's used for medicinal purposes? In fact, that's how it was invented. As a matter of fact, I'm feelin' better already."

Ben couldn't argue that he was looking better. Ben was tired of the argument, so he reached out and grabbed the jug from the crazy old man. He mimicked the old man, passing it under his nose and taking a sniff. He didn't find it as appealing as the captain did. His nose wrinkled up as he tried not to choke on just the smell. He raised the jug to his lips, taking a large swallow. The captain was bouncing Indian style on the bed with a smile so big you couldn't see his eyes. They were squinting so tight. The rum hit Ben's lips, and he immediately let out a cough, spilling rum down his shirt, his tongue hanging out as Ben tried to catch his breath.

The captain, laughing and bouncing on the bed, said, "Boy, next time, take a smaller drink. Now give me that before you waste it all." He reached over and took the jug from Ben, who was only nodding as he gasped for air and was glad to hand over the jug. "Besides, I need you to remember what I tell you," the captain said as he snapped the jug from Ben's hand. Ben could feel the rum warm in his chest. In fact, he could feel it rushing through his whole body. "Now where was I?" Captain asked as he fluffed his pillow behind him, leaning it up behind himself then resting backward on it with the jug resting between his legs.

Ben tried to answer, still coughing a bit. "You were just being born. Yes, to street whore."

The captain interrupted, "I was ten years old, and as many poor children in those times, I was sold to a pirate ship for slave work. I was sold to a Captain Farrow, also known as Bloodthirsty Bob, notorious pirate of the time. His real name was Robert Farrow. He was a lieutenant in the British Navy, a much-decorated sailor. He gave it up for greed. Piracy was rampant in the open seas, and he just loved the lawlessness. He commandeered, in a mutinous manner, a large English warship, brutally killing several hundred men using a small band willing to follow him. Thus his name was given as Bloodthirsty Bob. Captain Farrow was a tall lean man and a well-trained soldier in fighting, fencing, shooting, anything that had to do with killing someone. He was much practiced. He also was touched in the head a bit. He always wore the finest garments and a large captain's hat. He had a beard that he kept trimmed. When he was aboard ship under way and behind closed doors, he was bald. But when he was out in town or on decks, he wore a powdered wig he claimed he stole from a king. I met Captain Farrow the way most people do—violently. Upon completion of his business with my mother, I happened to come in and run into Captain Farrow. He grabbed me by my hair on the back of me head just like I did you a minute ago. Gets your attention, don't it, boy?"

Ben could only nod an agreement, spellbound by the story.

* * *

He spun around and yelled at my mother, "I'm takin' the boy!"

My mother jumped up, yelling, "You're not taking my boy!" For the first time, I thought she had really cared about me. Then she added, "He's worth at least a hundred gold pieces at the market."

Captain Farrow grabbed some coins out of his pocket and threw them at her. "Here's fifty. That's all he's worth."

My mother gathered them up, not even a goodbye as the captain marched me out of the house and down the street. I cried silently as he marched down the cobblestones, past merchants selling vegetables and pots and pans, clothes and pottery. His shoes clopped as he dragged me. my little legs barely keeping up with his stride. As we reached the docks, it was very busy. I looked back once more to my old street, knowing I would never see it again. When Captain Farrow talked, it was with elegant precise English. He kept calling me roach boy.

"Come along, roach boy. Quit draggin' your feet," he said as he pulled me along by my arm. My heart was beating. I spoke some English but spoke Greek for the most part. Confused and scared, I tried my best to keep up with him. I can still see his shoes clipping along on almost a run, big shiny buckle on top, and he had long stretch socks that went up to his knees. His pants were green velvet. His dress coat was of the same material but decorated with silver. He had a large belt that had a pistol tucked tightly in. I tell you, Ben, if I knew now what I knew then, I would have grabbed that pistol from his belt and killed him right there. But I was too afraid, so I dragged along. His shirt was white and ruffled. His sleeves hung out, and they were ruffled also. Both hands had rings on almost every finger. On the back of each hand was a tattoo of a skull and crossbones. As we walked down the pier, all eyes looked elsewhere. No one dared to look at Captain Farrow in the eyes. We approached a skiff filled with goods, kegs of rum, flour bags, gunpowder, and smoked hams. As we approached, four sailors snapped to attention as we came marching down the gangplank that led to floating slips filled with fishing boats. The skiff stuck out among the group, being very tidy and polished.

"Shove off, Mr. Riggs, and keep your eyes on the roach boy here," the captain ordered.

"Aye, aye, sir," the sailor answered.

The captain threw me off the dock onto a sack of flour. The captain stepped one foot onto the rail, and Mr. Riggs offered a hand to steady him as he stepped aboard. The captain made his way aft and sat down. With that, Mr. Riggs started giving orders to the other sailors. One sailor jumped onto the dock and untied the bowline while Mr. Riggs untied the stern. The other two sailors readied two large oars. I had been to the waterfront many times and dreamed of going on the ocean, seeing the world, but not on a pirate ship. My heart pounded as I lay there on the flour sacks. I hadn't moved a muscle from where I landed. Mr. Riggs hollered the order and made me jump. "Oars ready."

The sailors answered, "Oars ready, sir."

And the oars clunked into place. "Cast off" was the next order. The sailor at the bow gave a big shove and hopped aboard the tip of the bow, coiling his lineup. He stared at me for a second with a sly smile. "Row," came another order from Mr. Riggs, and I jumped again.

The waters were calm, and the boat rushed into movement as the two sailors in perfect unison reached and pulled at the oars. The oars made a slight splashing noise as they met the water. The boat glided across the water with ease as the two strong men worked. These men were not dressed as pirates as I would have imagined. They were in English uniform dress. Billowed pants, clean white shirts, and small round caps with a small tailed ribbon perched on their heads. No one spoke a word. Just did what they were ordered to do. The captain had made himself comfortable and drew a pinch of snuff out, inhaled hard through his nostril, and then pinched his nose tightly as if trying not to sneeze. He let out a relieved sigh then asked, "Mr. Riggs, what do you think of my new boy?"

Mr. Riggs stood at attention, hands behind his back, and answered, "Well, sir, he's small enough. I think he was a fine choice, sir."

The captain pointed a lazy finger at me and said, "I hope this one lives longer than the last one."

Now I was really scared and started to shake. *Small enough for what? Live longer than the last one? Doing what?* I wondered quietly to myself. *How long did he live?* All the sailors laughed, including the captain, at that comment. I tell you, Ben, if I had known what was to happen next, I would have jumped ship right there and drowned myself. We rounded outside the protected bay, and as the sea got choppy, Mr. Riggs still stood, hands behind his back as we made a course to a British warship anchored off in the distance. As we neared the ship, you could see sailors rushing around, doing their jobs.

As we approached, I heard someone on decks yelled, "Captain's returned! All hands ready!" The two sailors rowing gave extra strong pulls on the oars, pulled their oars out of their places, and stowed them across their knees. The skiff glided up alongside the massive ship, and the bowman grabbed a line dangling off the side.

"Drop the boarding ladder!" Mr. Riggs yelled. Immediately a rope ladder dropped over the gun rail to the waiting skiff. The captain stood and grabbed onto the ladder. Mr. Riggs helped the captain up as far as he could reach. As soon as the captain was up safely, Mr. Riggs followed. Once Mr. Riggs reached the top decks, I heard him giving orders. "Ready the cargo net." The men were already waiting for that order. So it didn't take long before the net was lowered to the side. It was laid out flat in the center of the skiff while the two oarsmen loaded supplies into it. Then one grabbed me by the pants and threw me on top of the pile.

"Haul away!" the biggest one yelled, cupping his hands around his mouth and yelling up to the men above.

A faint yell was returned. "Haul away!" The net started to close up around, and with slow but steady jerks, the supplies and I rose into the air. It went up the side of the ship past the main decks. It kept going up to the first set of spreaders, where there was a sailor waiting to tie another line on to help pull the load over the hatch leading belowdecks. As I came up, he grabbed the net and saw me. It surprised him. "Oh, a bilge rat. Have a nice day, mate."

As he finished tying his knot, he then waved his hand, and the whole bundle swung fast and sharp across the vast ship. I grabbed hold of the net and screamed like a girl. It came to an abrupt stop right above an open hatch midships. They started to lower the net, and as I looked out over the water, I saw my little town in the hazy distance for the last time in my life. Tears ran down my cheeks as I passed the main decks down to the darkness of below. The ship was bustling with sailors doing their jobs. The ship was a beauty, the old

English warship, long sweeping lines, cannons positioned off both sides, high rails that flowed from the stern that gave way to a towering bridge to the up reaching bow. Three massive masts were stepped evenly in a row and raked back a bit. I noticed Captain Farrow on the bridge talking to what appeared to be other officers standing around a large wheel. That old boat was so shipshape it sparkled.

As I lowered belowdecks, I looked back at Captain Farrow one last time for, I didn't see the captain for a long time after that. As I passed the decks and dropped into darkness of the bowels of the ship, the fresh air changed to a musty smell. The net settled lightly on the planks belowdecks, and sailors were there, quick to untie and ready the cargo. Mr. Riggs was there. He grabbed me by my hand and promptly stood me up. I had been through so much already this day that I almost found it hard to stand on my own. He grabbed me around my shoulder.

"Easy sailor. Come with me, roach boy." And he guided me down through the goods below, stacks of stored foods, and ammunition. I passed a few sailors working away, and we came to a bulkhead. We stepped through a portal that led to long rows of bunks stacked three high. Each one was made exactly like the other. A few had people sleeping in them. Then a small stairway that led to another row of bunks. As I stepped down to another level, the air got a little staler, and the sound became muffled. I had a feeling I had just dropped below water level. At the end of the row of bunks was a small door about chest high. We stopped there, and he handed me a jug that he had been carrying. He pushed it into my chest.

Mr. Riggs opened the little door, turned to me, and said, "We have a roach problem on this ship. The captain doesn't like roaches. In fact, he despises them. Your job is to go into the bilge where they go during the day and catch as many as you can. You will be fed by how many cockroaches you gather each day. I will come down to this door two times a day at the same time. Once in the morning, once at night. Each time I will blow this whistle." He was holding a boatswain's whistle up. He then put it to his lips and blew a high-pitched whistle and a certain rhythm. Three sharp blows. "I will give you one minute to show up. Once you show, I will check your jug, and I will send someone down with the appropriate food for work done. Do not keep me waiting. That one minute is the allotted time. If I don't see you, I will leave, and you will go hungry. Do you understand everything I have just told you?"

I just nodded yes. He then reached up and opened the small door and stood staring into space as if at attention. I looked into the black hole and then at my jar and back into the hole, and then I looked at Mr. Riggs. He bent down, looked me in the eye, and said, "I don't have much time, boy. Get in or I'll put you in." I nodded again and started to climb in. There was a horrible smell. The ribs of the ship were wet and slimy under my feet. I climbed in farther and turned to Mr. Riggs. He smiled and said, "You're a good man, roach boy. Do a good job." I once again just nodded. He started to close the door but stopped short. He added, "If you see the other boy in there, bring him out, will you?"

I just sat there, staring at him. Just as the door was about to shut, I grabbed the door and stopped it from closing as the dark started to close with it. I managed to squeak out, "What about a light?"

"Cockroaches run from the light, boy." And he pulled my hand off the door and it closed with a click. All I could do was sit there and stare at the only crack of light piercing through the small door. In total silence and complete black, I sat holding my jar. The air smelled horrible after a while. I tried the door, but it was latched from outside. I could hear rumblings, a few voices, and small scratching in the darkness farther into the bilge. It seemed like days had passed when I heard three sharp whistles and the door swung open.

"Prompt. I like that," Mr. Riggs said. I recognized his voice, and the lantern's light hurt my eyes. If he hadn't spoke, I wouldn't have known who it was. I barely made out his frame, and he reached in to take the jug from my hand, saying, "Let's see what you have here."

"Have?" I asked with question in my voice.

"In your jar, he said sternly." I looked down at my jar, and it struck me I never did anything. I hadn't moved all day! He snatched the jar out of my hands, removed the cork, and looked surprised. "I thought you were better than that," he said, handing it back to me. "Good night, roach boy," he added as he shut the door.

I woke up. Something inside me snapped. I realized he wasn't going to feed me. No roaches, no food. I had done no work. No pay. I was already hungry, which made me realize I might starve to death if I didn't catch some of those damn bugs. I started to move farther into the darkness, feeling my way. The bilge was slimy and slick under foot, and the walls of the ship came to a sharp *V* in the bottom where the ribs met the bottom. There was about a foot of water in the bottom. I noticed the farther up the walls I felt were dry. As I slipped and slid about, trying to get my footing, I started to lose my bearings as to where I was. I heard the insects scurrying ahead of me in all directions. I started to realize there might just be a problem on this ship. I took a second to sit and retraced my trip into the ship. I then started to realize at best guess I was heading toward the bow of the ship. As I was working my way forward, I bumped into something with my foot. I felt around that general area with my hand. I felt a squishy lump with clothes. A shock ran over me as my heart started beating hard. My hand recoiled fast, and my feet started to peddle backward. Slipping and falling, I dropped the jug. The thought of finding the missing boy was scary enough, but the idea of ending up like him by starving to death was just as scary. I frantically felt around for it, knowing it made its way to the *V* of the ship. I finally found it. I tucked it up under my arm. I slowly felt my way back to where my roommate was resting. I felt from his foot to his belt to his shirt. The smell was horrific. I pulled hard, only to find he was slightly wedged. I grabbed both his legs to pull harder, and as I raised his legs, cockroaches, hundreds, scurried about. I realized this was my food running away. I pulled the cork from my jug with my teeth and grabbed frantically. I started to stuff the jug with them.

The little creatures were crawling all over me as I worked fever-ishly. My forehead started to sweat as I stuffed the jug. Forgetting the creepy part of having my roommate as bait, I sat back against the hull and caught my breath. I then tried to pull him free. I'm not sure, but it wouldn't surprise me if that's not how he died. I had to twist his head just right and pry it out, and as I did, I noticed a small hole with light peering in. That must have been why he got stuck in that position, I thought. He was looking into that hole. The light, as little as it was, gave me a look at my friend. He was much bigger than me, and his clothes were much nicer than mine. He also had a knife on his belt.

I had just started to remove his clothes and the belt and knife when I heard a faint whistle, three sharp blows. My heart stopped. *Was that mine?* I wondered. And then it struck me. One minute. I grabbed the jug and crawled as fast as I could, yelling, "Wait, wait, I'm here! Please wait!" I got just in sight of the light, I yelled extra loud, "Please wait!" I was screaming almost like a girl. The door slowly opened back up.

Mr. Riggs said, "Boy, my time is limited, boy. I told you one minute. I will give you no more warnings." I nodded an understanding. He added, "The proper response would be 'Aye, aye, sir.'" I nodded again. Mr. Riggs said, "I didn't hear you, roach boy."

I managed to squeak out, "Aye, aye, sir."

"Now that's better," Mr. Riggs said, holding out his hand. "Let's see what you got there this time?" I handed him my jug. He took it and looked inside. "That's much better, roach boy." He hurried to get the cork back in. "I'll send a mate with some food in a bit," he said as he marched off.

He left the door open a crack, and I couldn't help but push it open a little more to get a look. The air smelled almost sweet compared to what I had been breathing. I looked around the crew's quarters. No one was in their bunks at this time. The lanterns swinging with the movement of the ship made shadows move around the room. I couldn't help but notice all the bunks were made up exactly the same. Nothing different about any of them.

My concentration was interrupted by a sailor who rounded the corner. He was carrying a burlap bag and a jug. "Aye mate," he said as he approached. "Got some vittles for ye." His voice was cheery, and he seemed in good spirits. He handed me the bag, saying, "This here's your food." Then he handed me the jug. "This here's your replacement jug. Oh, by the way, there is some water in the jug also." I tossed the jug to the side and opened the bag, reaching in and pulling out the bread and some cheese. I felt like a ravenous dog. The sailor smiled big and said, "A bit hungry this mornin', eh?"

I had my mouth so full I could only nod. I swallowed hard and said, "Thank you."

He stopped, quickly grabbed a blanket off one of the bunks, and threw it to me. I caught it with my forearms, making sure not to drop any of my food. I hung it on the door while I finished my meal. As I sat there eating, I realized he didn't shut the door. I sat in the little doorway, enjoying the fresh air and listening to the sounds of the ship. The water against the bulkhead, voices of sailors as they bustled about.

There were footsteps and voices getting louder as a large group of sailors came bounding into the crews bunk area. They were laughing and talking as they came in. One of the sailors who was the loudest looked up and saw me sitting in the doorway. He stopped laughing, and his face grimaced as he started walking toward me. I could see his eyes locked on mine as he marched right at me. He walked right up to me, put his hand on my face, and pushed me hard backward into the bilge. He pulled my blanket down and then slammed the door, saying, "Get to work, roach boy." He grimaced as he closed and locked the door.

I sat there in the *V* of the bilge, now soaking wet. I climbed up the ribs of the ship to where it was dry, wedged my feet up against the ribs, and tried to get some sleep before I would start to hunt again. I dropped off to sleep for a bit. My last thought was hatred for that sailor. Something woke me up, and I realized it was cockroaches crawling all over me. At first, I started to bat them away. Then I quickly came to my senses. I snatched a handful and desperately felt around for my jug. I grabbed it up, pulled the cork with my teeth, and started to fill it with bugs. I crawled up to the door and peered through my small crack. It was dark in the bunk area. The only sound was that of twenty or so sailors snoring and breathing hard. Every once in a while, one would yell out something in his sleep, and someone would yell for him to shut up.

I must have drifted off back to sleep. I heard a noise that jolted me awake. When I opened my eyes, the lantern lights were showing through the door crack. I got closer to peek, and the sailors were all getting up as someone started to yell, "Get up, you lazy dogs! It's your watch!" Then something blocked my view as the door swung open. It was Mr. Riggs. He had his whistle in his mouth and was just taking a breath to blow when he realized I was right there. His eyes got big as he said, "That's much better, roach boy. Much better. I'm glad to see you taking this seriously." He whisked the jug from my hand and turned to walk away.

I quietly said, "Aye, aye, sir." He left the door open again. I sat there, wanting to jump out and grab my blanket back, but I was too afraid.

* * *

Ben sat in complete amazement. This old man was rattling off a story with complete recall and detail. Ben could do nothing more than listen to this story. Whether true or not, it was told with such detail and enthusiasm. He was spellbound as the captain continued talking.

* * *

I knew that if I was going to survive in the bowels of that ship, I was going to have to be smarter, use my head more. I kept daring myself to jump out of that door and run. This was where smarter came in. *Where are you going to run on a ship in the ocean?* I sat back, figuring I was stuck here for now. Just then, my friendly sailor came down with my meal. I understood English, but I didn't speak it well. He greeted me with a cheery "Morning, mate." I nodded. He handed me my food and jug. "See's you around supper time," he said as he bounded off to get topside. Once again, he left the door to my space open. I sat eating my food and drank my water. As I sat there, I reminded myself of being smarter. I noticed each bunk was made of four-inch slats tucked neatly together for support. Then an idea hit me. No one was in the bunk quarters. I bounded out of the door, ran to each bunk as quickly as I could, and grabbed a slat from each foot end from every bunk, being very careful not to disrupt the bedding. I ran the slats over to my door and thrust them in. My heart was pounding. I had no idea what would happen to me if I were caught. After I had grabbed enough slats, I thought I was in as much trouble as I could get in, so I ran over, grabbed one of the lanterns, and stole the blanket off the mean sailor's bunk and ran back into my hole. I then closed the door myself, but it was not locked this time. My breathing was hard, and I thought my heart was going to beat right out of my chest. I started to laugh to myself a little. It reminded me of home, when you could successfully swindle someone for a little money. I gathered my newly acquired bounty and made my way far enough into the hole so the lantern couldn't be seen from the doorway. I laid the slats across the *V* of the bottom of the ship, giving me a flat place to lie down and kept me out of the water. I was excited now. Maybe I could get some real sleep. But first thing I needed to do was fill my jug, so off to work I went.

I reached for my friend. I quickly went to work, filling my jug with bugs. Then I went to work getting that boy unstuck. It took a bit of work, but I finally got him loose. I dragged him to my perch, where I traded his clothes for mine. His were much nicer than mine, and the belt and knife would come in handy. I pulled him right to the door and went back to finish my meal. Halfway through my meal, I realized that I had just removed my bait for those hideous bugs. So I saved a little food to put out for bait. Having done all my work with time to spare, I went down to the door. I pushed it open. I looked around and found no one there. I called out, but no one answered. I hopped out of my door and walked cautiously past the rows of bunks. I was trying to find one person to help me get my roommate out of my bilge.

I passed through a bulkhead and into a storage area and ran right into the mean sailor, who pushed me in the hole the night before. I looked up and couldn't seem to move. He was just as surprised as I was. He reached down and grabbed me by my hair and, with one arm, lifted me off my feet. I instinctively grabbed his hand, trying to keep the pressure off my hair. My feet were kicking in the air. It felt as though my scalp was going to rip from my neck to my eyebrows. I was squealing like a girl, trying to pull myself up to his hand to take the pressure off. He raised me up to his face level and sneered into my face and scowled. "Trying to get away, eh, roach boy?"

"No, no, I wasn't." I was barely able to get that out of my mouth as tears swelled up in my eyes. I managed to get the words "Roach boy out. Roach boy out need help."

Just then, my friend who brought me my food came around the corner. He yelled, "Hey, what are you doing? Put him down."

The mean sailor said, "I caught him trying to escape." He was shaking me a bit as he talked. My friend's face got angry.

"I said put him down, mate."

The mean sailor laughed and added, "I'll put him down, all right. Down under the keel."

My friend who was much smaller grabbed the sailor by the arm and sternly said, "Put him down. I won't ask you again."

With that, the sailor dropped me, and before I knew what had happened, the big sailor pulled a knife from a sheath on his side, pushed my friend up against the bulkhead, put the knife to his throat, spoke into his face very close, and asked, "Are you crossing me, mate?"

I was just about to jump up and do something about my friend when Mr. Riggs came around the corner. He stopped in his tracks and quickly assessed the situation and said, standing with his hands behind his back at attention, very military style, "Mr. Jackson, I am afraid I do not see playing with knives is very productive, so turn that sailor loose and go about your job."

The mean sailor started to say, "But, sir, I—"

But he was stopped short by Mr. Riggs's interruption. "Mr. Jackson, I think you're confused. That was an order, not a request."

The sailor responded, Aye, aye, sir. Sorry, sir." He reluctantly let go and slowly pulled his knife back to its sheath.

Mr. Riggs stepped up to the mean sailor and put his face right up close to the sailor's and said quietly, "If it wasn't for the fact you were such a strong fighter, I would have you walk the plank. I don't like you, Mr. Jackson, and I want you to find a way to keep your temper in check on board this ship, understood?"

The sailor. Jackson, stood at attention but did not look into Mr. Riggs's face but answered, "Aye, aye, sir."

He turned to the other sailor. "Perhaps you could enlighten me to what is going on here?" he asked sternly.

Sailor Goodin answered, "It was nothing, sir. Just a slight disagreement as to how roach boy should be treated, sir."

Mr. Riggs answered, "He shall be treated like a crew member. No better nor worse, and to help you two to remember, you shall both be given three lashes tonight. Now get back to work."

They both answered, "Aye, aye, sir" and went about their way.

He then turned to me and asked, "What are you doing above decks?"

I explained in my best English. "Dead roach boy by the door," I told him."

"I'll send someone down in a minute. Now get back to your hole."

I jumped to my feet, saying, "Aye, aye, sir." and ran back to my perch. I climbed in. My roommate looked a lot more gruesome in the light, so I moved farther back to my bed area to get away. It was only a minute before someone at the door yelled, "Hey, where's the stiff?" I was surprise to hear someone so fast. Mr. Riggs was a man of his word. I slipped down to the door, and there were two sailors standing there.

One asked, "Ey, mate, where's the dead one?" I pointed to where you could see his feet.

The other sailor said, "Whew! That's a rotten smell." The other sailor poked his head in to see. He jumped up to bend his waist just enough to grab the boy's feet. He slid him out fast. He hit the floor with a solid thud. Then one sailor grabbed his arms while the other grabbed his feet and started to walk away.

I yelled, "Thank you. It will smell better in here now."

Then the front sailor, twisting his neck around, yelled back, "This tub will always smell of death, boy!"

I felt a little better having him out. I went back to my perch I had built, lit my lantern, and just sat for a while. My jug was full. I was waiting for Mr. Riggs. Things were looking up. I put my new clothes on, strapped my belt and new knife on, grabbed the lantern, and went exploring. Each area of the ship had different sounds. I was getting very comfortable with knowing where forward and aft, port and starboard were. At one point, I could smell something good for a change. I made my way toward it, then I saw a light piercing into the bilge, more powerful than my lantern. As I got closer, I noticed a large crack in the wall. I got closer. It was floor level into the galley. I saw men hurrying about, cooking away, pots banging, men yelling. The smell was heavenly, and I just lay there, taking it in. I also started to get hungry, and as my thoughts roamed, it dawned on me that my bait for my roaches just left, and they were my meal ticket. I then deiced this would be a good place to put my bait. Seems it was close to the kitchen. So I scrambled back to my perch and grabbed my leftover bread. They fed at night, and the kitchen would be the most logical place to go. I crawled back to the crack and put my bread and a small piece of cheese by the crack. I then went back to the perch and slept. Mr. Riggs woke me with a start. I grabbed the jug and scurried to the door. Mr. Riggs was there, waiting. I presented the jug to him.

"Thank you, Mr. Roach. It's good to see you being prompt. I like that." He opened the jug and looked in and added, "You seem to be doing a fine job also." With that, he walked away. He stopped and turned around. "You keep it up and I'll see you get something special for dinner." Then his face became stern, and he added, "I see you on decks without permission, I can't guarantee your safety. Do you understand, boy?" His stare into my eyes let me know I had pushed a limit for him. I felt like he was staring into my soul. He had a way of making you feel like he could read your mind, all your secrets revealed. I almost blurted out that I had taken a lantern and blanket but stopped myself. He pushed a new jug into my chest and pushed me into the hole. This time, he shut and secured the door.

I crept to my perch and found my lantern had burned out. With no flint or fuel, I would have to do without it for a while. In the darkness, I heard a noise, a screeching and yelling. Coming from the stern of the ship, I made my way toward the commotion. In the darkness, I saw a small light beam on the floor coming from same place as the noises. As I looked in, I could see into Captain Farrow's cabin. There was the captain standing on a table, yelling about the cockroaches. Mr. Riggs came in and calmed the captain down. The captain started to yell about having that new roach boy shot and made to walk the plank. Mr. Riggs jumped across the room and stepped on something. It made a loud crunch.

Mr. Riggs was saying, "I got him, Captain. I got him, It's okay. You can come down now."

The captain, still hesitant, was asking, "Are you sure? There aren't any more?" Mr. Riggs assured the captain it was fine and convinced him to come down.

He was sniveling, standing in his nightshirt, and then he started back with a very nasty attitude, "Why can't that roach boy do his job? I want him flogged. Ten lashes, Mr. Riggs. Ten, do you understand?"

Mr. Riggs assured him it would be done. My heart jumped a beat. *Flogged for what? I've been doing my job*, I thought. It was not fair why. I stopped myself right there. I wasn't doing my job right then, so I scrambled to go check my trap. As I reached the galley crack and where my bread was, I could see the multitude of creatures all around my bread, crawling in and out of the hole. *It's working*, I thought as I removed the cork from my jug and started to grab the roaches frantically. Within minutes, I had stuffed my jug full of roaches. They had all scattered after that commotion. Only a few lingered. The crack in the wall drew me closer. I peeked into the galley. Two barrels had been placed in front of the crack, and I couldn't see very much, but the smells, oh boy, the smells were heavenly. I wanted more, so I quietly and carefully took my knife and started to carve at the crack. I was starting to see more of the galley. I put my nose up to the crack and took in a couple of big whiffs. I must have made too much noise because a pan hit the wall right by my nose. It didn't hurt, but it sure startled me.

I heard a sailor yell, "It's a damn rat! Did you see the size of him?"

I had jumped back and just in time, for someone jabbed a butcher knife into the crack and shook it about. I thought how funny it would be to grab it from his hand and turn it around and shake it back at him, but I figured it best not to let them know I was able to see into the kitchen. I waited for him to leave the crack, grumbling about bug and rat-infested tub, referring to the ship, I guess. Then I quietly went back to my perch to wait for Mr. Riggs.

* * *

The old man stopped talking for a second, took another swallow of rum, and gestured to Ben as if to offer him a swig. Ben politely waved his hand as to say no. The captain wiped his lips off with his frail arm and continued with his story.

* * *

I was getting real good at sleeping on that perch. I never heard the door open, but I sure came to attention when Mr. Riggs blew that whistle. Scrambling to the door, I handed him my jug. He looked inside the said, "Nice job, roach boy. Someone will be right back."

As usual, there was someone, and it was my friend. This time, he had a nicer meal of bread with cheese and an apple. As he turned to leave, I quietly said, "Thank you for your help with that large sailor. I'm sorry if you had to be whipped for it."

"It's all right, mate," he answered back. "He'll get his one day, you'll see. He's a problem, always makin' trouble. 'Sides, me back is so scared and calloused. Won't even know what hit me."

"Well, thank you just the same." He grinned and walked away. I started to put my traps together. This time, I thought I would put a little bread and cheese in the jug, then wrapped a piece in a cloth as before.

I was just about to go set my traps when I heard a voice in a low whisper say, "Hey. mate, where are you?" I made my way back to the door, only to find that sailor again. He reached into his shirt and pulled out a candle and flint and a piece of salted pork.

I asked, "What's this for?"

He smiled and answered, "I had your job once. It ain't easy."

I thanked him again and again as he walked away. I went back to my perch and dropped my supplies off. Then I went to find the kitchen crack to set my traps. Once there, I laid my cloth with a small piece of bread on it and laid my jug on its side with bread and cheese in it. I could hear those insects crawling all around me as they scurried away. I laughed to myself, thinking this was going to be a good night. I couldn't help but look into the crack and smell one more time before I left. The galley was quiet and dark. *It must be late*, I thought. There was a crack in the boards a little farther down, so I took a look. It had a much better view, so I took my knife and went to make it a little bigger. As I started to carve at the hole, the board moved. I wasn't sure if what I saw was real, so I pushed a little harder. The whole board moved under pressure. I pushed a little harder, and it broke loose with a loud crack! I jumped back into the darkness and, with my heart pounding, waited to see if anyone was going to investigate. No one stirred. The kitchen was a tomb of silence. Sliding back to the loose board, I carefully looked around. I pried at the only corner that was stuck with my knife, and the board came out. I was paralyzed with excitement, looking into that gaping hole into the kitchen. "What have I done?" I asked myself under my breath. "I could be whipped for this if caught. Hell, they may even kill me for this."

After a few minutes, I had convinced myself that I really didn't have much of a life at this time. So I squeezed through the hole. It was under a shelf, so I slid out from under the shelf, and there I was standing in the middle of the galley. Large pots and pans were swinging with the rhythm of the constantly swaying ship. I knew I shouldn't spend too much time there, so moving quickly, I rummaged around for supplies. I found some lamp oil, two jugs like my roach jug, helped myself to another apple out of the apple barrel. I also came across a veil of peppermint oil. I wasn't sure what I would do with it, but it smelled good, something that bilge didn't do. I went back to my little crawl space and put my bounty of stolen goods inside. I sat for a while, trying to figure out how to put the plank back without anyone knowing. I was looking for a nail, but that would be loud. Besides, I might want to find my way back into the galley someday. Finding a towel, I tore it into four pieces, and then I tied a small knot in the end of each one. Carefully, I climbed in the hole under the lowest shelf. I laid my towel pieces onto the board, two on the bottom and two on the top. I left the knots on the outside and used them to wedge the board into place by pulling on the rag pieces. It fit itself back securely into place. I was feeling very proud of myself. After unloading my stores at my perch, I went back to the hole in the captain's quarters. It was dark, and he was snoring very loudly.

I sat back for a minute and listened to the sound of the ship creaking as she moved with the ocean's waters. If I listened close enough, I could make out the sound of water rushing past the hull as we sped along to an unknown journey.

Running along the cobblestone streets barefoot and free, I was having so much fun then. My mother grabbed me by the shoulder. "What are you doing?" she snapped angrily.

I answered her by saying, "Just playing, Mother."

She shook me. "You have a job to do. Why aren't you doing it?"

With that comment, my eyes opened. I must have fallen asleep. I awoke only to find cockroaches all over me. Salted pork was in a pocket I had forgotten about. I bunched my shirt tight to keep them in and scurried forward to get my jug. Once I filled that jug, I went to check on my other trap. I found it to be just as productive. Baiting the jug was much more resourceful. I made my way back to my perch to eat the pork and my apple I had acquired. Not much time had passed before I heard a sailor yelling from the crew's quarter, "Shift change! Get up, you swabs!"

I heard the men stir, grumbling and laughing. I made my way to the door and was peeking out to see the men getting up when an object just missed my head and stuck in the door with a thud! My head turned quick to see what it was. It was a knife. A large knife was stuck in the door. Then a voice I recognized yelled, "Enjoyin' the show, rodent!" I turned back to see that mean sailor pushing people out of the way and coming right for me.

Reaching up, I pulled the knife from the door. When he saw me take his knife, he sped up, and with a growl in his voice, he yelled,

"Drop that knife or I'll cut you up for fish bait!" Jumping back into the hull and scrambling quickly out of sight, I could hear that sailor still yelling, "You little wharf rat! I'll skin you alive when I get my hands on you!"

My heart was pounding, and I knew I had just made a serious enemy, but I couldn't help but smile. I was far enough back in the area. He couldn't see me, but I could see his face, and he was seriously angry. The smile dropped from my face as he jumped up and started to crawl into the doorway.

"You little scallywag, I'll skin you alive," he growled as he started to climb in.

I was just about to start crawling farther in, but I heard someone yell, Get out of there!" I was pulled back a bit. It was Mr. Riggs. "A flogging wasn't enough to train you to leave that boy alone? Looks like I will have to find another way around to teach you, and it won't be pleasant! I don't like you, Jackson. You're trouble."

Jackson tried to interrupt and tried to explain that I had his knife, but Mr. Riggs wouldn't hear him out. He told him to report to the brig and he would deal with him later. Finally, Jackson stopped arguing and went to the brig. Mr. Riggs said in the darkness of my hole, "I think it best you avoid Jackson at all cost, roach boy."

It amazed me that even though he couldn't see me, he knew I was there. I crawled forward, saying "Aye, aye, sir."

He asked, "Do you have something for me?"

It took me a second before I answered, "Yes, yes, I do." I reached down and brought up my jug. He took a look inside. "Fine job you're doing. That's why I keep sparing your life."

I was feeling smart about then and said, "I thought you just liked me."

He spun a glare at me that shot a cold shiver down my spine and said, "It's not my job to like anybody, roach boy, so don't push your luck." It was said so coldly and honestly, it took the fun right out of the day.

A few minutes went by, and my friend came down with some food. "Here, boy," he said, handing me a jug and a small burlap bag with bread and cheese.

"Thank you," I said in a depressed manner.

The sailor asked, "What's wrong, my little friend? You're eating well, so you're obviously catching plenty of roaches."

"Mr. Riggs doesn't like me," I answered, pouting.

He laughed. "Is that all? Hey, mate, he don't like anybody. He has some magical rule book in his head, wrong and right, and he works for the ship. Nobody else. Only what's best for the ship. So don't take it so personal."

"Thanks," I said, feeling a little better. He turned to leave. I asked, "What's your name?"

"Cecile Reginald Augustine Goodin," he answered. "But everyone calls me Reggie."

"Well, thanks again, Reggie."

He turned waved goodbye and added, "You're most welcome, Mr. Roach."

I sat back. *Mr. Roach* made me laugh a little, and I liked the sound of it. Almost gave me a little respect. Weeks passed by, and I had a routine going. I was hunting at night every so often, slipping into the galley to replace my stores. I had gathered quite a collection of jugs, about twenty altogether. The captain's state room was on my frequent visits, as were a few other interesting peepholes. Mr. Riggs was pleased all twenty jars were full. He never had to wait. The cockroach population was starting to diminish. I did stay out of sight of the door unless Mr. Riggs was present just in case, for the mean sailor would poke his head in every once in a while and yell things like, "You'll have to come out some time" or "Roach boy, I have a treat for you. Want to see it?" But even if he disguised his voice, the way the light shone in the door, I could always see him before he could see me in the shadows.

One night, while making my rounds in the galley and rummaging around, I found me some salted pork for bait, some vegetables, and oil for my lamp. I had gotten quite used to making myself at home. I even called it my day to go to the market. It reminded me when I was young, walking to the market with my mom. She was so beautiful that shopkeepers would give us free samples to impress her. I also remember shopkeepers' wives coming out and scolding their husbands for taking such interest in my mother. As soon as I would start to get homesick, I would then remember she sold me to pirates! On this evening, as I was at the market, I heard some voices coming toward the galley. This was not usual, so I panicked and jumped under the shelf. The voices came right into the galley. I was glad it was dark, so you couldn't see me under the shelf. I didn't want to move into the hole for fear they would hear me. So I eased back ever so slowly and quietly.

Someone said, "It's here in this locker."

All I could see were feet and legs about knee high. As I inched my way to the hole, the next voice froze me cold right to my soul.

Mr. Jackson demanded, "Give me the key!"

My body ran a shiver of cold down my spine. I found it hard to get a breath. If that mean sailor was to see me, he would surely kill me on the spot.

The other sailor replied, "I can't do that. No one is allowed in the rum cabinet without perm—"

He didn't' finish that sentence. A loud crack split the air, and he came crashing to the floor. His head hit the floor right next to mine. My eyes got as big as a dinner plates, fearing he would say something.

His attention was fixed on Jackson as he pleaded, "No, Jackson, you said Mr. Riggs sent you to find the cabinet, not get in it. I need orders form Mr. Riggs himself to open the rum cabinet." He was holding his hand up as if to ward off another blow. When I saw the blain pin come swinging down toward his head, he deflected it.

Mr. Jackson said, "I've got your permission right here."

He deflected that blow. He turned his head. His eyes got as big as mine as our eyes met. Unfortunately, that hesitation cost him his life, I'm afraid, for the next blow was squarely on his forehead. The others were because that mean sailor was just that mean. He bent down as he fumbled through that poor sailor's clothes and flopped him around as he looked for the key. My heart didn't beat, and I didn't take a breath for fear he would spot me. He couldn't have been more than fifteen inches from me as he grabbed that sailor by the shirt collar and shook him, vigorously demanding, "Where's that damn key?" Then he slammed his head to the floor. He then got up off his knees and fumbled around the galley until he found what he was looking for.

I heard banging, then a cupboard opened and the clank of bottles, then silence. I sat in dark, staring at that poor sailor doing his job and dying for it. I was confused what to do. I couldn't tell anyone what that mean sailor had done, or they would know I had been in the galley at night. It could be the death of me, to tell the truth. I slid into my hole and pulled my plank into place with my knotted rags. I started to go back to my perch and put away my supplies. As I did, I looked at that mean sailor's knife. It hit me, the answer to my problem. I took the knife with me as I headed for the galley. Opening my hole, I crawled in carefully. I looked around to make sure I was alone with the poor fella on the floor. I closed my eyes and planted the knife in his chest. The pressure made him groan a little and sent me peddling backward fast. I sat under my shelf, staring at the sailor and wondering if he was dead or not, and now I made it worse. After a long silence and him not breathing, I realized he was surely dead.

The galley crew started early, and I knew they would come in soon. I put my plank back and sat, waiting to see them find him. I didn't have to wait very long when I heard them. The first one to see him said, "Hanagen, what are you doing? Get up, man. You can't be layin' in my galley. Hanagen!" His voice was a little louder. Then his voice changed completely as he rolled him over. "Hey, I need some help in here!" he yelled.

Soon there were many sailors coming to see. I scurried up back to my perch then up to the captain's quarters where Mr. Riggs was just briefing the captain of the situation.

"It appears, Captain, we had a break in to our rum closet, and in the process, a sailor was murdered," Mr. Riggs reported, as calm as ever.

The captain, however, was not as calm. He jumped up and paced around, yelling, "I want this man found and keelhauled, Mr. Riggs! And I want it today!"

Mr. Riggs stood, unchanging in his emotions. "There is a good chance, sir. He left his knife in the body, sir, and as soon as we figure out who owns it, I do believe we will have our man."

The captain, still pacing the floor, ordered, "Assemble the men to the main deck immediately."

Mr. Riggs answered, "Already taken care of, sir."

"I'll get dressed proper and be right out," the captain said, waving his hand as to shoo Mr. Riggs out the door.

"Aye, aye, sir," Mr. Riggs answered then left.

I started back to my perch when I heard the whistle. I stopped for a second then hurried to the door. I met Mr. Riggs, waiting and looking at his watch, and handed him my jug. He took it then said, "Come with me. There is something you need to see above decks, boy."

The thought paralyzed me. I didn't want any part of condemning the mean sailor. He'd know how the knife got there. What if he recognized the knife but they'd think it's someone else's and he's free? He'd know I framed him.

Mr. Riggs broke my trance by saying, "Come on, boy. We don't have all day."

When Mr. Riggs walked, he moved right along. His pace was fast, and I had to half run to keep up with him. He yelled at me a couple of times to keep up as I followed him above decks. As we came into the daylight, my eyes hurt, and I could barely see after being in the dark for so long. Mr. Riggs grabbed me by the back of the neck and shoved me down behind a large coiled hawser line.

The ship was a chorus of voices, yelling and talking. I just sat quietly, looking at the blue sky and smelling the fresh air of the ocean. I couldn't see much yet. As I looked around, I could see only outlines of people as my eyes adjusted. I stood up once to look over the rail and look at the ocean. What a sight. It went on forever. Mr. Riggs had pushed me low for a reason, so I sat back down. The warm sun on my skin felt good also, so I just enjoyed my time above decks. My eyes were getting adjusted, and I peeked above the line I was sitting behind to see more of the decks. As I looked around surveying the layout and getting my bearings as to where I was when crawling around under the belly of the ship, my eyes caught sight of the mean sailor. He was standing fairly quiet in a corner with his arms crossed. He hadn't noticed me, and I sure didn't want to take that chance, so

I hunkered down behind the line again. The captain strolled by me, looking out over the crew. And as he stepped up to the wheel, a sharp blow of the boatswain's whistle brought the whole crew to silence.

Mr. Riggs started speaking. "Gentlemen, we have assembled to remedy a problem we had last night. It is a problem that the captain and I will not tolerate, and we will get to the bottom of today. Someone broke into the liquor locker and then killed seaman Hanagen. This behavior cannot and will not be tolerated!" The captain stood with his hands on his hips, scanning the crew as Mr. Riggs talked. "We have only one piece of evidence to go by." He held up the knife, showing it to the crowd. I couldn't help but peek over the line to see the look on Jackson's face as Mr. Riggs announced it was found in the chest of seaman Hanagen. The look on that mean sailor's face was priceless. It was then while staring up at the knife that he spotted me.

The crowd had begun to mumble quietly as they all discussed whose knife that might be. Jackson pointed to me and, making a scowl on his face, took his finger and ran it across his throat as if to say he would cut my throat. I slid back behind the line and saw Mr. Riggs as usual had not missed anything as he looked at me in a very curious manner then back to Jackson.

"Anyone who can identify this knife and reveal the killer will get ten pieces of gold and a dinner with the captain."

I peeked over the lines again as the crew mumbled among themselves. I saw Jackson inching away from the crew, making himself less obvious. Someone had to know whose knife that was, I was hoping, because if he wasn't caught, he would certainly hang me if he found me for setting him up.

A huge man stepped forward, very muscular with scars on his face, and asked, "May I see that closer, sir?"

Mr. Riggs answered, "Of course, sailor." He handed him the knife. He rolled it over and over in his hands then held on to its blade. He started to hand it back to Mr. Riggs. Then as fast as a finger snap, he turned and threw the knife right through the crowd and stuck in the arm of, Jackson pinning him to the wall.

Mr. Riggs, just as fast before the knife hit its mark, pulled his sword and had the point of it sticking at the base of the throat of that large man. The sailor showed no fear at all as Mr. Riggs said, "Would you mind explaining yourself, sailor?" The crew had gone quiet after the crowed had gasped at the sudden change of events. Then the crowd started to get noisy. Mr. Riggs shouted, "Attention on decks!" He never took his eyes off the man at the end of his sword. The crew immediately got quiet, and Mr. Riggs pushed a little more pressure on the tip of his sword. "Well, sailor? I asked you a question, sailor, and I won't ask again."

"That's Jackson's knife, sir. And the sailor he killed was my brother."

Mr. Riggs dropped his sword and then returned it to its scabbard. Mr. Riggs hollered, "Bring that man over here!"

Mean sailor Jackson was just pulling his knife out of his arm as the order was given, but the men were too fast and grabbed him as he started to struggle to get away.

Captain Farrow interjected, "Slap that man in irons and put him below in the brig."

It took several men to secure him as he disappeared belowdecks. He yelled, "I'll see you in hell, Mr. Riggs!"

Mr. Riggs smiled and mumbled under his breath, "I don't doubt that for a second." He then addressed the men again. "Does anybody else recognize this knife as Jackson's?"

One sailor came forward, saying, "Aye, sir, that's Jackson's, all right."

Another stepped forward and added, "And he was on watch with Rodney's brother." He pointed to the sailor who just had Jackson arrested.

Another sailor stepped forward. "And I relieved him of duties this morning, sir. He was drunk then. He even offered me a drink. He said you issued it to him, sir, for doing a fine job."

Mr. Riggs cracked a small smile on his face and said, "Now we know that didn't happen, don't we? It's not like me to be nice to someone just for doing his job." A small laugh rippled through the crowd.

The captain interrupted. "Discipline, gentlemen. It's what makes or breaks a ship. Just because someone kills your brother doesn't give you the right to throw knives carelessly about my ship. Four lashes tonight for you, Mr. Rodney. As for your brother's killer, he will be keelhauled in the morning." Then he held his hands up. "Thank you, gentlemen. You all may go back to your usual jobs."

"I'll check his locker," he said to the captain and turned on his heels. I started to walk away. As he passed me without even looking at me, he said, "You, back to your hole. You've caused enough trouble for one day." I wasn't sure what he meant by that, but I thought it best not to argue or question his orders. He stopped in his tracks and turned on his heels. He looked at me, sniffing the air. "On second thought, you may have one hour above decks. While up here, you will wash yourself and your clothes. I can smell you from here."

"Aye, aye, sir," I replied. He then bent forward with his hands behind his back, putting his face close to mine. "A proper seaman would stand at attention when addressed by an officer."

It took me only a second to understand. I jumped to my feet, standing rigid as a board. "Aye, aye, sir."

Mr. Riggs smiled and turned on his heel again, adding, "Carry on, roach boy" as he walked away.

I quickly looked around and saw my friendly sailor Reggie. I spotted him swabbing a deck. I made my way over to him. When he saw me, he panicked and threw the mop down. He ran over and pushed me down behind some coiled lines.

"What are you doing above decks?" he asked, looking around to see if anybody saw me. I tried to stand up to explain myself. He pushed me back down, holding onto my head.

I pushed his hand off and quickly said, "Mr. Riggs told me to get myself washed up. I have an hour above decks."

The panicked look on his face left, and he could only say, "Oh, well then, come with me." He held out his hand and grabbed mine. He pulled me to my feet. "Come on, boy. Let me show you how." I started to follow him. He said, "You do smell a little ruff."

We walked over to the bucket he was mopping with, and he picked it up and poured it over my head. "I'll show you where to get more." I was spitting that dirty water out of my mouth, thinking that did feel pretty good. He tied a line to the bucket and threw it overboard. I was laughing to myself, watching the antics of this sailor. And whoosh, he did it again.

I grabbed the bucket out of his hand and said, "I think I got the idea."

He laughed and said, "Well, ain't we the fast learner?" He went back to scrubbing. And as I threw the bucket over the side, he said, "Be careful, boy. Don't use all the water. We have a limited supply." He laughed at his little joke and went back to work.

At first I wasn't sure what he meant, but as I turned and looked out over the horizon, there was water as far as the eye could see. I understood the joke. It felt great to be above decks, and it was nice to be around him. I felt a part of the ship. Washing felt good too. I spent some time walking around above decks. I went to the bow and watched the front cut the water. I sat back and let the sun dry my clothes. I caught a glimpse of Mr. Riggs as he walked by on deck. I felt a rush of panic. I had no idea how long an hour was. Rushing down below, I scurried into my hole. I climbed forward to the galley peak hole. The smells made my mouth water. They were preparing the dinner they were to have with the sailor they were going to flog. I found that odd, to beat a man then have dinner with him, but that's the life of a pirate, I assumed.

I fell asleep for a little while. Something woke me up, and as I moved back to my perch, I heard the whistle. I scurried to the door where I had many jugs waiting and found Mr. Riggs waiting. I handed him one, and he looked inside.

He praised me for my work then said, "You do fine work, and you are pretty intelligent for a street kid. I like a sailor who can take orders but can also think on his own. Let's test your intelligence while underway starting tomorrow, shall we?"

I just nodded, not having a clue what he was talking about. He turned and left while I sat back waiting for dinner. It was nice not having to worry about that mean sailor, so I sat by the open door and waited. Soon Reggie came, happily bouncing along with my bread, cheese, and water.

As he handed me my food, he asked, "What's your real name, roach boy?"

Hesitating for a second, I thought how no one ever cared what my name was before. When you're the offspring of a whore, nobody cares who you are.

I answered him, "Roach boy is just fine."

He smiled. "Good day, Mr. Roach." And he waved goodbye.

"Hey, Reggie!" I yelled. "What's that keyhold thing they're going to do to Jackson?"

Reggie laughed as he answered, "It's not keyhold. It's keelhauled. They tie a line to each leg, then they throw him off the bow of the ship. Then each man walks down the side of the port and starboard side of the ship. The man is dragged across the bottom of the ship." His eyebrows were twitching as he spoke. "'Tis not a pretty sight, boy."

I thought for a second then asked, "Anyone ever live through it?"

"I've never seen anybody live through it. And even if they do, the lines are tossed off, and you leave them in the middle of the ocean, bleeding. I don't think it would take much to finish you off," he answered, doing that eyebrow twitch again. "Sharks would come from miles around. You'd be better off taking some deep breaths as you went under. At least that's what I'd do," he quipped and turned waving. "Gots to get back to work. See ya, boy."

* * *

The old man stopped talking for a second and looked at Ben with a distant look in his eye. "I bet that's the first man I ever killed, and I never laid a hand on him." He laughed a small cynical laugh and took another sip of rum. Then started into his story again.

* * *

I finished eating, and while checking my traps, I happened by the captain's quarters. I heard him talking to Mr. Riggs. They discussed that evening's meal and a few other pleasantries. Then the subject changed to a serious note about a French trade ship making its way from South America. They should intercept her in about nine days if she's still on schedule. They mentioned if she wasn't flanked by any warships, this would be easy pickings.

The captain said, "Set the course, Mr. Riggs, and come what may."

Mr. Riggs asked, "Will that be all, sir?"

The captain replied, "Yes, that will be all. Thank you, Mr. Riggs."

I heard Mr. Riggs leave, and the captain sounded like he was rustling papers. I got bored and went down to get some sleep on my perch. As I sat there, I couldn't help but think about me on a pirate ship in a battle on the ocean. I fell asleep and dreamed some wild dreams.

My wild dreams were interrupted as I was awakened by being launched off my perch and tossed around in the bilge. Working my way to the hatch door, I looked in the sleeping quarters, and no one was to be seen. All the lanterns were swaying radically, and the ship was pitching to and fro. Scurrying back to my perch, I wrapped all my precious belongings into my blanket and stowed them securely up high. Not knowing what was going on, my gut was telling me the seas were getting rough. That meant that more water would be in the bilge. Getting bounced around mercilessly, I took a big chance and ventured out of my hole into the crew's quarters. The ship rocked and pitched under my feet as I got tossed around. I decided to take my chances up on decks. As I worked my way topside, the noise of wind and ocean became louder. Part of me wanted to stay below and hang on for dear life, while the other wanted to go see this amazing storm. Curiosity overtook me. The first sailor I ran into was hurrying to do some job. He was dripping wet coming down a companionway stairwell.

I asked, "Where's Mr. Riggs?"

He answered, "Up at the bridge, but be careful, mate. Keep a sure hand on something. It's getting pretty wild on top." Just as he said that, he was dumped on by a large amount of water. It came crashing down on him from the opening above. The miniature tidal wave swept over him and hit me about knee level, knocking me off my feet and sliding me a few feet backward until the water dissipated down the hallway. He helped me to my feet and ran off to get whatever order he was given taken care of. I have to admit, I was a little scared, but then again, I wanted to see a storm at sea.

All my short life, all I've heard were sea stories, and now I was living one. As I made my way to the upper deck, I stepped outside to see a wall of water at the bow. Then the ship started to climb. The ship started to raise high in the air, and the deck below my feet pitched me backward. I stood stunned at the sheer mass of the wall, then the wave enveloped the bow. Those sailor's words ran through my head: keep a tight grip on something. I grabbed the stair railing, lowered my head. I let the wave wash over me and take my feet out from underneath me, but I hung on for dear life and was dropped to my knees as the wave passed.

I started to make my way toward Mr. Riggs as I looked about at the sheer mass of the waves all around the ship as she pitched and rocked. The sky was black. It looked like we had been hurled into a vast hole of darkness with waves crashing around us. The wind was so loud, and the waves crashing were deafening. Lightning would light up the sky at that moment. You could see men in the rigging, taking sails down, securing parts of the ship so it didn't tear itself apart as she pitched wildly. Orders were being yelled and repeated like a fire brigade. They passed buckets of water. I was standing, watching the entire goings-on.

Someone grabbed my shoulder. A sailor yelled in my ear, "Mr. Riggs wants to see you up on the bridge now!"

I snapped an "Aye, aye, sir."

The sailor's face broke into a big grin. "I ain't no sir, mate. Now get your ass up there and hang on tight," he snapped back at me, staggering to get a foothold and shaking his head.

My thought was, *What, does everyone think I'm stupid? Why do they all keep telling me to hang on tight? It's not like you have a lot of choice in the matter.* I almost had to crawl to get up to him. When I reached him, he was holding on with one hand on the rail, the other to the top of his sword. Two men behind him were hanging on to the wheel, trying to keep control of the ship.

Mr. Riggs was yelling orders. "Hold her steady, boys. Don't let her broach! Hurry and get those squares down before they drive us into the sea!" Mr. Riggs was a sight to see. He was calm, and his commanding presence made you understand why he was in his position and why the men had such great respect for him. He yelled, "Well, roach boy, you are either so inexperienced you don't know any better or you're half-crazy or…" He hesitated for a second. "You were taking on so much water that it flushed you out of your hole?" His eyes were burning a hole in me as he stared at me. "Well, which is it?" he asked sternly.

I blurted out, "I would guess half crazy."

"Well, sir, I guess that makes you a sailor," he snapped back with a smile on his face. The two men at the wheel just laughed out loud. "As long as you're up here, you might as well make yourself useful. Do you see those six men standing midships starboard side?" he asked.

"Yes, sir!" I answered, yelling to be heard.

"Tell them I sent you to help in any way you could. After all, they're about to pump the bilge. I would think you wouldn't want your lantern or blankets to get wet now, would we?"

I was swept with a moment of embarrassment. *How did he know?* I thought. He didn't seem upset, and I thought it best not to inquire at this time, so I just answered, "Aye, aye, sir." I went about making my way across the decks.

The waves were relentless as they swept across the decks, but I hung on tight just as everyone had suggested. When I got to the sailors, I was glad to see Reggie with them. I explained I had orders from Mr. Riggs to help as needed. They all looked at a sailor who seemed to be in charge. He nodded and yelled, "We need to get belowdecks to the stern!" He was motioning to leave.

We all followed in single file line, hanging on to the rail, burying our heads as the waves crested the rails. I was second to last, and Reggie was behind me as the waves hit. He would push me forward to help me stay. One rogue wave hit so hard, the leader of the line lost his grip, knocking into all of us. We lost our grip with the weight of all the men. We were riding the wave across the deck. I managed to grab a coil of line to stop myself. Reggie wasn't so lucky. The wave crested over the rail and took Reggie with him.

I heard someone yell, "*Man overboard!*"

At that same moment, the ship's bow raised up. As we started to climb the huge wave, Reggie disappeared from sight. As we came back down, I saw Reggie's arms flailing, trying to get back to the ship. Some men threw him some lines, but the wind blew them too short. I was a good swimmer, so I wasn't afraid of the water. Without thinking, I took the line that had saved me from going over and tied it around my waist. The ship was at its lowest point to the water. I handed my bitter end to a sailor who had just pitched his line to Reggie.

I said, "Pull me in when I reach him." I jumped over the rail and stated swimming toward Reggie. I lost him as I swam toward him a couple of times. I could see panic in his face until I reached him. Then we held on to each other, and relief came across his face. The sailor started to pull us in, and several others joined him. We were moving fast through the water.

Reggie said, "Just what you needed, boy. Another bath."

As the ship dropped to the low side, we were pulled aboard. The sailor who was in charge of our little work crew said as he pulled us up, "If you two are done messing around, we'll get some work done." Everyone had a good laugh at that as we made our way below. As we gathered down below where it was a little quieter, Reggie started to thank everyone. But in true sailor form, they said things like, "Reggie, we didn't mind you going overboard, but if we lost the kid here, we all would be in trouble. You just came along for the ride." It was their way of accepting his thank you and letting him have his dignity. We all had a good laugh and then went about pumping the bilge. We bailed for about two hours. In that time, the seas had calmed down. We bailed for about another hour when orders came back to stop. My arms were tired, and my back hurt, but I wasn't about to complain. We started to go above decks, and I passed the alleyway to my hole, so I thanked all my comrades. They ruffled my hair and patted me on the back as they all went topside.

Reggie stayed back, and as the other sailors were out of sight, he said, "Hey, roach boy, come with me for a minute." He waved his arm to follow him. I did as was asked. We made our way to his cabin room. It slept about six men but had a little more room than the other sailor's quarters. He reached into his locker and pulled out a thin stick and handed it to me, saying, "This is for saving me, mate. 'Twas much appreciated."

I wasn't sure what to do or say, so I answered him, "It's all right, mate. I figured it was returning the favor for saving me from that mean sailor so many times and feeding me. Besides, I don't really need a stick."

Reggie laughed out loud. "It's not just a stick, It's a flute." He put it up to his lips and played a happy little tune. He then pushed it into my hand, saying, "Here, please take it."

I tried to hand it back to him, saying, "I don't play it."

He pushed my hand back at me. "I makes them in me spare time. I have many. Please try. It makes a lot of wasted time go by."

I thanked him and started to head for my perch. I took a short-cut to get back as I played with the new toy that was given to me. I rounded a corner. There, in a small cell with bars, I came face-to-face with the mean sailor. He was just as surprised to see me as I was him. He was sitting on the floor, his knees against his chest. His arms were wrapped around his knees. He must have had his head resting on his knees. As I rounded the corner, he raised his head and our eyes met. His face was filled with rage. He bolted to his feet and thrust his arm through the bars, reaching for me. I jumped back just as fast as he jumped up. My back hit the wall behind me as I dropped to the floor, just out of reach from his grip. My feet were sticking straight out, and he dropped to his knees, pulling his arm back in and thrusting his arm through to grab my legs. I pulled them back just as he laid his hand on me. He was growling like an animal as he spoke, straining to reach me.

"You little scallywag. You set me up. I swear on me mother's grave, if I get out of this, I will kill you. A slow painful death, I promise you."

I was speechless, trying to slide out of his reach. I managed to slide out of reach then took a good hard look at that part of the ship so I didn't make that mistake again. I found my way back to my hole and my perch. I sat down to sleep a bit. The whistle was sharp and loud. It awoke me. I snagged a jug and made my way to meet Mr. Riggs. He took the jug, looked inside, and commended me on another job well done.

He stood, looking at me for a second. He then asked, "Can you read, roach boy?"

My answer was simple. "No, sir," I answered. "Can't write either," I added.

Mr. Riggs just smiled. "Yes, that would make sense," he quipped. "You are intelligent enough. You think fast on your feet. After seeing your brave actions yesterday, risking your own life to save that other sailor, I would say you're as brave as any man on this ship. I think you have potential to train to be a fine sailor. If you do well, you may find yourself out of the roach collecting business. Tomorrow you will meet me at my quarters at 0900 to begin training."

"Aye, aye, sir," I answered. Then I asked, "Sir, how will I know it's 0900?"

"I come down here every morning at 07:30 to retrieve the jug. Then Mr. Goodin comes down to deliver your meal. After that, report to the bridge like you did the night of the storm." With that, he turned and left.

I was a little excited at first, then I started getting a little nervous, thinking, *What if I don't do well? Flog me, keelhaul me?* I sat and played my flute for a while. Reggie was right. It did waste the time and made you feel good. At one point, I would play a note that didn't appear to make any noise. I could feel it though as if it were. Every time I made that same mistake, I could hear the roaches in the jug make noise and move around excitedly. I pulled the cork out of the top of one and watched as I made the noise with the flute. They would get all excited. I finally grew tired of the game and drifted off to sleep. The whistle woke me up from my slumber. I made my way to the door, and Mr. Riggs was standing as usual, waiting. I handed him my jug, and he looked inside, praising me for my work.

Then he said, "Don't forget. Today is the first day of school. Don't disappoint me."

"No, sir, I won't," I answered, hoping to myself I wouldn't. Soon Reggie came down and delivered my breakfast. He asked how my flute playing was going. I told him I was enjoying it a lot, and the roaches liked it to.

He stopped and looked at me funny then said, "I think you've been in the hole too long, boy."

As I ate my breakfast, eagerly waiting my first day of school, an odd noise bounced under me, running the length of the hull. I assumed we had run over something like a tree.

* * *

The captain stopped talking, looked at Ben with a strange look in his eye, took a sip of rum, and said, "I figured out later what it was. My hated enemy had just been keelhauled." Captain sat back with a wry smile and continued his story.

* * *

I finished my breakfast and went topside to meet Mr. Riggs. Many sailors looked familiar now, and they all greeted me with a "Morning, swab" or a "Hey, boy" I was starting to feel at home here, like I belonged. Every time I came above decks, it took a while for my eyes to adjust.

As I bounded up the companionway leading to the wheel, I ran right into Captain Farrow. He let out a yell. "Argh, what have we here?" He grabbed me by my shirt collar and hollered to Mr. Riggs. "We've a stowaway on board."

Mr. Riggs was quick to respond, "No, sir, that's the new roach boy you commandeered in Greece, sir."

The captain pulled me up and took a close look at my face and said, "So it is." He hesitated as he looked at me then added, "Well, if he is still alive, why isn't he belowdecks doing his job?"

Mr. Riggs answered, "He is only above decks as to my request, sir."

"As long as it is by your request, Mr. Riggs, then so be it." He dropped me and pushed me aside like an old sack and continued on his way. He stopped, spun on his heel, and put his face right in mine, saying "You had better watch where you're going, boy, or I'll crush you like a roach that you are."

I nodded yes and somehow squeaked out an "Aye, aye, sir."

He was definitely someone to fear. Just the way he looked was scary. His face resembled a skeleton with sunken eyes. Dark circles surrounded the green bloodshot portals of his mind. His face was with chiseled skinny cheekbones, his hair jet-black, wildly flying out of his large brimmed hat. The creases in his brow made him look angry all the time, but when he was angry, they would get deeper, and his eyes would get smaller, making him look as if he had none at all. His thin lips pursed in a permanent scowl. As he strolled away, I couldn't help but watch him. It was Mr. Riggs's voice that got my attention back.

"Come along, boy," he said as I followed. I couldn't stop looking back, making sure the captain wasn't following me or watching me. Mr. Riggs said without even looking back, "Don' worry about him, boy. You stay out of his way and out of sight. He won't even know you're on board."

It was creepy how Mr. Riggs could almost read minds, always knowing what was going on around the ship. We came to his cabin. It was smaller than the captain's but every bit as elegant. He pointed to an oak chair that swiveled but was anchored to the floor. From here, you could spin around to face the center to the cabin or swivel back to face the chart table. I was to learn very soon that the chart table was an area that you laid your maps called charts on to plot your course. I was facing the center of the room. As I sat, I was instructed.

Mr. Riggs sat back against a desk to one side of the room, gripping the top with his hands by his side. "You speak English pretty well, but you also speak Greek, is that correct?" he asked in a matter-of-fact voice.

I answered sharply, "Yes, sir."

He smiled a sly smile. "That's a good sign of intelligence," he said, shifting his weight to one leg. "This, my friend, is your lucky day," he started out. "This is your classroom one hour a day. You will come for your assignment and learn to read, write, do math. That is if you do well. If you flounder at these studies, you will go back to living in the bilge. Understood?"

I nodded approval but also said, "Yes, sir, I understand."

He snapped to his feet, saying, "Good. Let's get started." He handed me a slate, very much like the one you use, Ben, and he turned me toward the chart table. And for exactly one hour, we worked on the alphabet sounds and how to write them. After one hour on the button, he stopped and said, "Get back to work, sailor." I laid my slate down, but he said, "Take it with you. You can practice in your hole." And as I walked out, he said, "Good job, roach boy. I knew you had it in you."

I felt taller that day as I walked with pride back to my hole. Someone was actually proud of me. I went to work gathering roaches. Then after I had filled another jug, I went about playing the flute. I found a couple of the roaches reacted to the silent note more than others. I laid a small piece of salted pork down as I played with my friendly bugs. They would eat at it once in a while. Then I would play the note and they would dance about. I soon heard my own three sharp whistles. My training sent me scurrying to the door with jug in hand. Mr. Riggs looked inside, praised me for my work, and I awaited my dinner. As I sat there waiting, I wondered if I conditioned my bugs to come to eat when I blew my flute. It would be a lot easier to catch. Soon Reggie came by, said he had a couple of special scraps from the captain's table for me. I asked him how he came about getting them, and he told me he was the cabin boy for the captain.

I asked, "What does that mean?"

"I takes care of the captain's needs."

"How did you come to get that job?" I asked.

Reggie stood there for a second, pondering my question, then said, "I don't know. Me thinks it's because I'm not afraid of the captain."

I added, "He is a bit scary at times."

Reggie shrugged his shoulders, saying, "I've seen a lot more scary things in my time."

He got my attention. "Like what?" I asked.

"Like Mr. Riggs when you don't get your jobs done. So I best be going." He started to leave.

I said, "Thanks again for everything, Reggie."

He turned back and said, "Thanks for saving my life."

I smiled and said, "You would have done the same for me."

He waved his hand in disgust at me and said on his way out of sight, "I wouldn't bet on it, mate. I wouldn't bet on it."

I went back to my perch, ate my meal, proceeded to get a roach out of the jug, and play my flute. He would dance around a bit, then I would give him a small bread crumb with a taste of peppermint on it. He would start to leave. I would play a little, and he would come back for another bite. This went on for a while until he must have had enough to eat and didn't come back. I, too, was tired and finally fell asleep. When Mr. Riggs awakened me the next day, I gave him my jug and asked if we were still having class today. He assured me that we would have class every day unless told otherwise. Reggie did as promised and brought me some extra fruit and vegetables. After I ate, I ran to my studies. This was the way of things for days on end. Mr. Riggs seemed impressed with my learning abilities, and I enjoyed it also. He wouldn't let me talk like the other sailors. I was to use only proper English. My roach training was going well too. When I played the silent note on my flute, several would return for a treat. The best part was when they returned, they brought others with them. I would capture the others and release the trained ones.

It was one evening while training my roaches that I heard a lot of commotion. I went to my door to peek into the sailors' quarters. Everyone was rushing about. I asked a sailor, "What's going on?"

He answered, "We're going into battle!" And with that he turned and ran out. I sat back for a second, thinking the word *battle*.

Another sailor who heard the conversation stopped long enough to say, "The English trade ship we were looking for is here. We finally caught her, and she is supposed to be loaded with gold." He laughed and slapped me on the shoulder. "Now's your chance to become a real pirate, boy."

With that, he turned and hurried above decks, just as Reggie came around the corner. They both bounced off each other. Reggie saw me sitting in my doorway. He yelled, "Roach boy, Mr. Riggs says to get out of the bilge area but stay belowdecks about midships!"

I instinctively answered, "Aye, aye, sir" as I leaped out of my hole.

He put both hands on my shoulder and said, "See you after the battle." And off he ran. I stood there for a second, thinking I want to see the battle. Besides, I'm no more a pirate than the roaches I catch every day. I laughed to myself. Then an idea hit me. I went to the midships where the cannons were. That way, I could watch and be belowdecks as ordered. So I made my way to the cannons. When I got there, men were running about, very busy. When I first entered the area, I immediately was in someone's way, and he pushed me to a corner, saying, "Out the way, boy. Not a good place to be."

I felt a little embarrassed and found me a spot out of the way where I could see through one of the cannon portals. And as if conducted by an orchestra leader, everyone fell silent. The only sound you could here was the water rushing past the hull. Soon I heard Captain Farrow's voice, very faint. "Full to port." It was answered by another sailor and another. Each area had its own person to repeat the orders. Ours quickly yelled, "Coming to port!"

We felt the ship come hard about then. Many orders followed. Most were upper deck to trim sails and ready approach to the merchant ship. Our person then yelled very loudly, "Cannons ready?"

Several men, one from each cannon, returned, "Cannons ready!"

I heard another sailor pass the answer to the captain. I had to lean down to see out of one of the cannons portals. At first, all I could see was the ocean, then the stern of a large ship started to come into view. I could see men on the decks, waving to us as if to welcome us. Then I heard a faint command: "Fire when ready."

It made its way down to our deck, and the gunner sergeant said, "Ready your flint!" All eyes were watching him. One sailor turned to me and made a gesture for me to cover my ears. Then the order "Fire!" rang out. I had my hands over my ears. The blast, one right after the other, was swift, but the first blast sent my hair flying back, and the concussion made my ears ring. I hunkered down and covered my ears tighter. As all ten guns were fired, I could see the men on the other ship stop waving, and they had shocked looks on their faces as they quickly tried to get out of the way of flying cannonballs. Pieces of the ship exploded as they hit. One round hit the mizzen mast and sent it and its sails crashing to the deck, and as the last of the ten cannons was done firing, cannons were rolled back. Powder was put in, packing inserted and tamped into place, then a cannonball rolled down the muzzle and tamped to make sure it was in its place.

As the ship rolled from the waves and she started up level, the gunnery master said, "Aim for their cannon ports, men! They should be just about to open!" They were waiting for just the right time to order fire. The men locked the cannons into position, and as the ship came level, you could see the cannon ports on the other ship just start to open just as the sergeant had said they would. The sergeant yelled the order to fire. And once more, the cannons boomed with a loud noise, and smoke filled the area with choking aftermath of the gunpowder.

I sat with my ears covered, peeking as hard as I could to see the damage. I watched the innocent men on the ship be torn apart as the rounds hit the cannon ports. Out of nowhere, the sergeant grabbed me by the shoulder and yelled in my ear, "Did you see what happened to that ship, lad?" He was angry in a way. "Get your ass out of here. Find somewhere safer."

I could tell this was not the time to argue, so I left grudgingly. Making my way down a passageway, there was a noise as loud as I have ever heard. At the same time, the ship listed hard to starboard, throwing me off my feet. I almost hit the ceiling. There was a lot of commotion, men yelling, and gunfire. There was a cabin door where I landed, so I ducked inside. It was a nice size cabin with bunks for sleeping and one small porthole that looked out on the portside to give me a great view of the other ship. I stepped up to it and saw Captain Farrow on the other deck of the other ship.

He was the happiest I had ever seen him. He was killing men left and right, wielding his sword in grand fashion, grinning from ear to ear. The battle was pretty gruesome and went on for twenty minutes. It seemed like hours as I watched some of the nicest sailors I knew brutally killing and maiming men with no remorse. As the battle settled down, I decided to go above decks. So I made my way up but ran into a group of our men bringing wounded on board. I made myself small against the wall as they passed. Michael, a friend of Reggie's, was carrying one in.

As he passed me, he said, "Come on, roach boy. We could use your help."

I followed him to the galley where the two cooks were lining people up for help. Most of the ones brought into this area were in pretty bad shape. The two men were directing who was to be laid on which table. Most of the men that were injured were tended to on decks. These men needed…well…

* * *

Ben could tell the old man was looking for the right word, and he found it: meat clever surgery.

* * *

I stood in somewhat of a shocked trance till one patient grabbed my arm and faintly asked, "Could you get me some water, swab?" His head was wrapped with a bandage. It was already starting to bleed through. His right leg was missing from just above the knee.

All I could do was answer, "Aye, aye, sir." As I walked slowly away, I couldn't take my eyes off his leg, lifting and kicking about. As I reached the companionway, I turned to go fetch some water. I turned and ran right into Mr. Riggs. I looked up to see it was him, saying, "Sorry, sir."

He put his hand on my shoulder, saying, "It's quite all right, son."

"Permission to get some water, sir...for the wounded?" I said, explaining my meaning better.

He answered, "Yes, that's a fine idea. Carry on."

As he passed me to enter the makeshift infirmary, I saw four men hold a sailor down as the cook cut the rest of his arm off. The other one was ready with a hot iron to burn the wound shut. I was really ready to go get some water as the man screamed with pain.

Men were running about ship, all still excited about the battle stories being told and parts reenacted. I stayed close to the bulkheads, making myself small and inconspicuous as possible. One man was talking about the amount of bounty coming off the ship and how they would all be rich. I was excited about the battle at first, but once you're in it, it's another story altogether. The senseless slaughter of many for greed.

* * *

The old sailor looked blindly at the floor and took another sip of rum. Then just like that, his head shot up, and without missing a beat, on he went with the story.

* * *

So I made my way to the galley and fetched two pails of water. I made my way back to the infirmary and went to the sailor they all call Doc. I showed him the water and asked if there was anything else I could do. He took one look at my face. I surveyed the room at the maimed and deformed bodies, some moaning, some screaming, some very quiet as the pool of their life's blood dripped to the floor. He said, "No, but thank you, son. I think they could use you above decks better."

That was a fine idea to me. It was a bit too gruesome for me in there. I hesitated and asked, "Do you know where Mr. Riggs went to, sir?"

He looked up from the bloody mess his hands were in and said, "Sorry, boy. Didn't see him go."

I thanked him again and quietly made my way out. I asked the passing sailors if they had seen Reggie or Mr. Riggs, but none of them had. I made my way to the main companionway that led above decks. I stood below, staring up. I could see the leaning mast of the other ship. I was hesitating going above decks, not sure if I wanted to see what was above. Smoke rolled by the companionway. I could make out a few men hanging in the rigging, lifelessly swinging in the breeze. I took a deep breath and made my way upstairs. As I stepped onto the deck, the devastation around was a bit surprising. Men were running around. The whole scene seemed chaotic, but everyone seemed to be doing their job.

"Roach boy!" someone yelled behind me. I about jumped out of my skin. The yell was followed by a heavy slap on my back. "Well, boy, you made it." I recognized that voice. It was Reggie. A rush of relief came over me.

I spun around and said, "I've been looking all over for you."

He smiled big. "Were you worried about me? Don't worry about me, roach. I've been swashbuckling since I was born. I come from a family of twelve. I had to fight just to eat." He laughed a little. I told him I was looking for Mr. Riggs to get some orders. He said, "Just come with me and help me carry some bounty."

I tagged along as he told me his recollection of the battle. We came to a plank bridging the two ships and men were coming and going from one ship to the other. Reggie looked back at me as he stepped up onto the plank. The two ships were rocking and not together.

"Don't fall off, whatever you do." He pointed down to the turbulent water where there were a couple of bodies being whipped about by the waves between the two ships. I nodded an understanding and prepared to make my way across the moving plank. We both made it with little effort. It looked harder than it really was. As I stepped to the other ship, I was surprised at the size of it. As I surveyed the surrounding ship, I saw men tossing dead men overboard. Others were gathering lumber lines and other useful hardware. I watched as a few sailors cut a sail loose, and as it floated to the decks, I saw Captain Farrow midships on the portside. He was sitting at a small table. There was a line of men standing with their hands bound. I stopped walking as I tried to make out what he was doing.

Reggie noticed my curiosity and leaned toward me and whispered, "He's recruiting." I still looked confused as he explained further. "Each man from the other ship is asked to join our ship. They can join or swim." I still looked confused, so Reggie said, "Watch." And he pointed to the spectacle.

Captain Farrow was sitting, and he was talking to the sailor who was being held in place by two of our sailors. Captain Farrow was done talking. The sailor shook his head no. Captain Farrow pointed to a plank that was attached to the deck and led out over the open ocean. The two sailors pushed him, kicking and fighting over to the plank. They picked him up until his feet were on it, then shoved him hard out on to the plank. The man tried desperately to regain his balance but ended up falling in with his hands still tied.

Reggie said quietly, "It's called walkin' the plank. You either sign on as a crew member of this heathen ship or you swim for your life."

I looked at Reggie and asked, "Why don't they just say yes and jump ship at next port?"

Reggie patted me on the shoulder and explained, "You see, boy, they may say yes, but we only take them on if we has a job for them. 'Tis truly unfortunate that we never have a position open. It's just a game the captain plays to amuse himself." I just nodded. I was starting to figure out Captain Robert Farrow.

* * *

The captain stopped for a second and added, "That's the funny thing about the sea, Ben. Nothing is always quite what it seems. Then he continued on with his story.

* * *

So Reggie took me up to the captain's quarters of the commandeered vessel, but he was the only one who was allowed to ransack a captain's cabin, so he lined me out with a couple of sailors to help empty the cargo area. The gold was there, just as everyone had thought, but it was too heavy for me to carry, so I got to carry small crates of chickens. The day dragged on. I was getting pretty tired, and I had lost track of time.

I ran into Mr. Riggs. Panicked, I said, "Sir, I'm sorry I wasn't there with my jugs."

"That's quite all right, boy," he said. "I could see you were busy enough with more important duties. Why don't you go get some dinner with the crew? And I think we will take a holiday from our studies tomorrow also."

I only answered, "Aye, aye, sir."

And he went on to his duties. Dinner with the men! Wow, I was so excited. I couldn't wait. I ran to the galley and then slowed to a walk just before I entered. I casually walked around, looking for a proper place to seat myself.

A sailor finally said, "Hey, roach boy decided to join the men."

"By orders of Mr. Riggs, sir," I snapped back.

He laughed. "Ordered, ey? Well, sit down and fill your belly. It's been quite a day." He pulled me down to the seat next to him. "By the way, boy, I'm not a sir to you. I'm a mate."

A big pot of some stew was passed around with a plate of bread, cheese, and fruit. I ate until my belly hurt. I sat listening to battle stories. All the men were still excited. Someone woke me with a start. It was Reggie. I must have fallen asleep. I still had a half-eaten apple in my hand. Most of the men had gone already.

Reggie said, "Maybe you had better go to bed, roach boy." I looked around the room, very groggy, and made my way back to my perch.

My dreams were made up of vicious nightmares I'm sure from what I had witnessed that day. When I awoke that next morning, the ship was very quiet. Everyone had slept a bit more than usual. Having no studies that day, I played with my roaches for a while. Some were getting very talented, walking a tight rope, climbing through an obstacle course, and one could almost play jump rope. They would all go back into the jug when I blew my whistle. I had so many jugs, I was having a hard time finding wild ones anymore. My scouts weren't bringing them back. Luckily, they were breeding in their jugs, or I would start to run out of bugs to give to Mr. Riggs.

Days passed, and Mr. Riggs was pushing me to learn more and more. I was getting it and doing well, everything from reading, mathematics, science, and geography. One day, while studying, I heard a faint yell. "Land ho!" Then I heard much commotion as someone on decks yelled it. I poked my head out to see what the disturbance was. I then heard Mr. Riggs yell, "All hands on deck!"

I came out on to the main deck. A lot of men were on the starboard side, looking out over the rail. I found me a spot to peek. I could barely make out the faint dark blue line. Clouds were encircling it. I realized then what land ho meant, and it looked like we were heading for it. I had no idea what land we were at, but within thirty minutes, we were there. It was a small island which seemed to be floating in the middle of the ocean. The orders came: "Drop anchor!"

And a man yelled back, "Dropping anchor!"

Then there was a sound of large chain rolling over the massive winch with a loud splash as the anchor hit the water. Many orders started to fly as men all busied themselves, taking care of their jobs. They were tying lines, dropping sails, lashing them tight so they don't take on any wind. I could see the island now. Its rock walls were looming out of the ocean, dripping with green vegetation. Inviting us to come ashore was a white sand beach, while monstrous waves beat against the walls. A pale green mist moved ghostly among the dark green canopy above. I was entranced in the wonder and then felt a hand on my shoulder.

Mr. Riggs spoke. "Ever see anything like it before?"

I looked back at the island. "No, sir," I answered. "Never."

He said, "It's quite a sight." And he went about to see if the ship was being put away correctly. I thought I would follow him a little just to learn what was done when anchored. I took two steps behind him, and he said, "Get back to your studies, boy."

I just hung my head and answered, "Aye, aye, sir." I stopped once more to admire the view. It was one I would never forget.

That evening, two crews were chosen to go to shore the next day. The next morning came, and as I went topside to do my studies, I saw Reggie. He was organizing two boats to go ashore. I stopped and asked him if I could be part of the crew to go ashore, but he told me that this would not be a good trip for me. It was a special crew that goes ashore. I couldn't help but notice that the crew he chose was made up of men, not real intelligent but good strong fighters, and two were from the ship we had pillaged days before. When I got to Mr. Riggs's cabin, he told me from now on, I was to just bring my jug with me and put it in the cabin and take a new one when I went back to my area. I was also to eat with the crew from now on. As I did my studies, I noticed the crew was loading the skiffs with the bounty from the merchant ship.

Mr. Riggs had me on a strict schedule with regular bathing, studies, and work routine. He even gave me some quality clothes that I'm sure were from some small sailor that was aboard the merchant ship and no one else could fit. Mr. Riggs also made it clear that I could go ashore tomorrow but not today, not with this loading party. After the loading party had loaded up, they dropped the skiffs overboard and prepared to row ashore. I couldn't help but watch, so I went to the rail. I watched as all the men rowed.

As they reached the shore, a deep voice from behind me said, "They're going to hide the treasure." I turned around with a start to find that big sailor who stuck ole Jackson in the arm with his knife. "Don't get too excited to see this island, boy. They don't let many see the islands that they hide their treasures on."

The surprised look on my face matched my question: "There's more than one?"

He laughed a hearty and deep laugh and said, "There's many, son. Many. Now let's go get some lunch." He pulled me by the shoulder and ruffled my hair.

After lunch, I went back to my studies. After several hours, I went to the cabin door and looked out to stretch. I could see the small skiffs on the shoreline moving up and down as the surf rolled in and out. Then I saw the landing party just coming out of the forest. The two men from the commandeered vessel who elected to stay on as crew were being grabbed and pushed down to their knees by several crew members. I then witnessed Captain Farrow walk up to one, and as far away as I was, I saw Captain Farrow pointing something at the sailor's head. Then I saw a puff of smoke. The man dropped hard to the ground. And after a few seconds, I heard the fatal boom of the pistol. The other man struggled harder after that, but to no avail. He, too, was executed. I stepped back into the cabin. I was afraid they would see me witness such a crime. I wondered what the two men had done to be given such a harsh punishment. I went back to my studies, but I don't think I learned much. My mind would not forget what I had just witnessed.

When the landing party returned and all were back aboard ship, I found Reggie and had to ask him. He more or less laughed and said, "Those two men from the other ship were kept for one reason—to dig a hole for the treasure to be buried in. They are the only two that accompany Mr. Riggs and Captain Farrow to the location on the island. First they have the whole crew walk around the island, making tracks in the sand and dirt. Then they make the rest of the crew go back to the skiffs. Then they take the other two sailors only, record where the treasure is buried, then eliminate the only witnesses to the whereabouts of the treasure."

I stood for a second then looked back at Reggie and said, "Mr. Riggs is so military and disciplined. That kind of behavior doesn't seem like him. I mean, he doesn't seem to enjoy the killing part as much as Captain Farrow does. Mr. Riggs also seems smarter."

At that point, Reggie grabbed me up fast, threw his hand over my mouth, and with a very serious look on his face, he held me hard against his chest as he looked around. "I like you, roach boy, but comments like that heard by anyone and you could end up like those two sailors today. Don't count ole Captain Farrow out. He taught Mr. Riggs everything he knows, and he gets pretty defensive about his intelligence and his bravery or how strong he is. And Mr. Riggs, he may not be as eager to run a man through with a sword, but he has no problem with it if it's done to someone. Mark my words, boy.

If the captain heard you talk like that, he would cut out your tongue. You got that, boy?"

I had never seen Reggie so worked up before. I nodded as an understanding, and he took his hand away from my mouth.

Captain Farrow and Mr. Riggs went straight to the captain's cabin. I went below and went to my peek hole to the captain's cabin. They were speaking very quietly. Mr. Riggs pulled a sliding panel on the wall open. Then he pulled what looked like a rolled chart from within the hole. Mr. Riggs rolled it out on to the table. They both had their backs to me. I couldn't hear what they were saying, but when they were done, Captain Farrow said, "We seize any more ships, we'll have to get a bigger map to chart it on."

They both laughed as Mr. Riggs put it back into the hidden panel. I thought, *That's the treasure map.* I went back to my perch, thinking about getting a look at that map. But there wasn't an easy way. Captain Farrow only allowed Mr. Riggs or Reggie into his cabin. I was doing tricks with my roaches when it came to me. I would slip a small piece of bread with a drop of peppermint on it through my peek hole in the captain's cabin. I would turn the roaches loose after the captain started to scream and jump up on a chair. Mr. Riggs would come to help him. I would blow my flute, and they would return to me. Mr. Riggs would see no problem. Soon he would have to let me in to see if I could find them. I laughed to myself at the clever plan. The next night, I started my plan. It worked almost too well. I poked a small piece of bread with the drop of peppermint through the hole. I turned the roaches loose. It only took a couple of seconds before the captain started yelling. He jumped up on his table. I went ahead and blew my flute, that certain note that can't be heard by human ears. All the trained roaches came back through the hole where I had food waiting for them. Mr. Riggs came bounding in right on cue. The captain was yelling about a roach invasion and to get it cleared up immediately.

Mr. Riggs looked around and found nothing. He picked up furniture and papers. He finally got the captain to calm down and showed him there were no roaches. The captain retained his composure and thanked Mr. Riggs sincerely. Mr. Riggs, once satisfied the captain was all right, left. It worked so well, I threw a new piece of bread and sent in a new batch of roaches. It didn't take long before the show was on again. I was having quite a bit of fun with the whole thing. In came Mr. Riggs, a little shorter tempered this time. He was promising he would look into it in the morning, but he couldn't find anything at this time. Once he calmed, the captain down he left. I gave him a little longer. The next time, the captain was nervously looking at the floor as he tried to get ready for bed. As his attention went to the other part of the room, I sent in the third wave. This time, he went totally crazy. He pulled his pistol as he yelled while standing on his desk and shot at one on the floor. Mr. Riggs came bounding in. He insisted that the captain stay in his cabin for the night so they could all get some sleep. Mr. Riggs spent about a half an hour looking over the floor for roaches. He finally put out the light and went to sleep. I, too, went down to my perch and went to sleep. I got up with the morning crew. We had breakfast, then I took my jug of roaches to Mr. Riggs. He looked inside and said, "Mr. Roach, I have a problem and I need your help. The captain has seen roaches in his cabin again. It hasn't happened for a long time. I couldn't find any sign of them in his cabin or on the ship, for that matter. But you seem to keep the jugs full, so I need you to go with me to his cabin and work your magic and find these pests."

I could only answer, "Aye, aye, sir."

He turned on his heel. "Come with me," he said curtly, and we marched off. I could tell he was upset because I had to run to keep up with him. We marched up to the captain's cabin. He knocked three sharp knocks and threw the door open. "Get in there and do your magic," he said. I went in scurrying about, looking under everything in drawers. As I passed the hidden panel, I made sure not to look at it. Mr. Riggs was watching my every move. I knew we wouldn't find any roaches. I planted them. But I continued my show, and after a prolonged time crawling on my knees, I stood up and shrugged my shoulders at Mr. Riggs and shook my head no. He muttered under his breath, "Damn it, I knew it."

I took the opportunity to say, "Maybe at night, sir, they will come out."

He sighed and said quietly, "You're right, son. I'll speak to the captain. Now get back to your studies."

I quickly went back to my studies as ordered. I stopped to have breakfast. I rarely missed a meal anymore, and if I did, I had my plank I could squeeze through to help myself. I was feeling pretty confident. I had a run of the ship anytime I wanted, and now with any luck and if my plan worked, I would have a map of Bloodthirsty Bob's treasures. This adventure was a bit scary. I worried about it all day. Then it occurred to me. You don't steal the map outright; you copy it!

As I finished with my studies, I took some extra paper and ink and a quill with me. As for the next few days, I made sure the captain had roach sightings. Mr. Riggs was getting desperate to find an evening that the captain would let him use his cabin for the night. The captain was getting very irritable and was punishing everyone in his path for very minor reasons. Morale was starting to get low. The men's attitudes were starting to show, and he knew that in the pirate world, this could easily lead to mutiny. He suggested a rum drinking feast on shore. The captain thought it was a grand idea. It was a small celebration before we lift anchor and head to a more populated city where the men could spend their share of the treasure, and they could listen for any information about merchant ships carrying large amounts of payroll.

Mr. Riggs was very good at that. He would pose as a merchant trader and look for seamen to hire for his vessel. Setting up shop in a local tavern, he would buy drinks for any sailor interested in work then talk to them about the ships they had any experience on what they were accustomed to hauling. You put enough rum in someone and be kind and they'll tell you anything. Mr. Riggs informed me that it was decided, and I would have a chance to look for roaches that night. The crew had been on the beach all day, readied a firepit, an caught a wild boar. Two kegs of rum were taken ashore, and the festivities were starting to grow as more and more sailors went to shore. It wasn't long before you could hear the celebration on shore. An occasional pistol shot could be heard. As the sun got closer to going down, most of the crew had gone to shore. The bonfire was very visible now. I had hidden paper and pen in my clothes and awaited the go-ahead to look for roaches in the captain's cabin.

My heart started to pound in my chest when I heard Mr. Riggs blow the whistle. I came immediately with a jug in hand, roaches already in it. I was a little disappointed that I wasn't going to shore, but my quest was much more important.

Mr. Riggs said quietly, "Let's go, boy, and get this done. We only have one chance."

I answered a direct, "Aye, aye, sir." And off we went. I hopped down out of the perch and grabbed my jug. We went topside and right to the captain's cabin. He opened the door. I made my way in. Just as I passed him, I dropped two very small crumbs of bread, each with a tiny smell of peppermint on them right by his feet. I started to rummage around like I was looking for something, then I turned a small handful of roaches loose and waited a second. They headed straight for Mr. Riggs. I waited till they got right to his feet, and I yelled, "I have some here!"

He then looked down, and under his breath, I heard him say, "I'll be damned...there's some here as well." I quickly blew my flute so he didn't start to squish them with his foot. And they all started back to me. I went around the room, rummaging around and releasing roaches every once in a while and then calling them back. Mr. Riggs stood fast at the door, a problem I didn't anticipate. I was trying hard to figure a way to get to the map and copy it, but where he was standing was impossible. All of a sudden, a sailor came running up, out of breath.

"Mr. Riggs," he said, "you must come quick. There's been a horrible accident on shore!"

Mr. Riggs looked sternly at the sailor and asked, "Accident? What kind of accident?"

"Please, sir, Captain Farrow is requesting your help. There's been a bit of a fight."

Mr. Riggs stomped his foot. "Damn that rum," he said. "That man is getting on my nerves lately." Then he yelled back to me, "Roach boy, get those damn roaches out of his cabin. I'll be back, and I don't want to find any, understand?"

I answered with a very confident "Aye, aye, sir." My heart was beating so hard. I could feel and hear it. I dashed over to the door and watched as they loaded onto a skiff headed for shore. I ran over to the hidden compartment and slid it open. I pulled the rolled parchments out and dropped to the floor. Looking at the scratches and markings, they didn't mean much. They were almost written in some kind of code. I worked fast, copying as fast but as accurately as I could. I had to stop every once in a while to see if I heard anyone coming. I finished copying it and rolled it back up, making sure it was rolled the same way. I put it back the same as I found it. After all, Mr. Riggs was very sharp about details, and I didn't want him to suspect a thing. I called the roaches and made sure they were all put away. I then went below and got a jug of untrained roaches to give to Mr. Riggs.

I went back above decks and watched from the railing. There was a lot of commotion on shore, a lot of yelling, a few gunshots. It was too far to hear anything, and I couldn't see much either. I could make out two skiffs leaving shore, so I went back and sat just outside the captain's cabin door and waited. Mr. Riggs came aboard, barked a couple of orders to the crew, made his way to the wheel, and addressed some sailors there. Then he came to me.

I jumped up with an excited expression and said, "I found some."

In a very somber voice, he answered, "Yes, but it doesn't matter much now. Thank you, roach boy. Put it with the others and then assemble on decks, please."

I just answered with a quiet "Aye, aye, sir." I went ahead and put my jug with the other roaches. There was something wrong. Mr. Riggs was like I had never seen before, and as the men came in on the skiffs, they, too, were in a mood like his. I knew something had happened ashore, but what? Something had gone wrong at the celebration, but no one was talking.

Reggie was coming aboard, so I asked him, "What happened?" He pulled me aside and told me the story.

* * *

The old man stopped talking for a second, leaned back upon his pillows, and took a sip of rum. He reached out and put his hand on Ben's shoulder, who was intently leaning on the bed with both elbows and his head rested in his hands in a trance as he listened to the story he was hearing. The old man winked one eye and said, "This is where it gets interesting, real interesting, Ben." He took another sip of the rum and laughed a small chuckle. He mumbled, "Real interesting." He sat back up Indian style on the bed and continued.

* * *

So Reggie told me that Captain Farrow was getting very drunk as were many of the men.

"Captain Farrow started to brag about what a great knife fighter and swordsman he is. Then he started to challenge some of the men, but no one wanted to take his challenge. He's a ruthless fighter, and every man knew he wouldn't stop until someone was injured or dead. He grabbed Arthur, you know, that big sailor the one with the tattoo of the lady on his right arm?" he asked in his story, but I knew exactly which sailor he was talking about. I had seen that tattoo several times. It was the most detailed tattoo I had ever seen. The old man wiggled his eyebrows at Ben and continued Reggie's story.

"Well, Arthur was big, all right, but not much of a fighter. Captain Farrow stabbed him once, and he let out a thunderous yell. He knew the captain would kill him, so he grabbed the captain in a bear hug, trapping his arms. Arthur kept yelling, 'Please, Captain, I don't want to die!' The captain kept yelling as best he could, 'Put me down, you coward! Fight like a man!' He only got to yell that once. As everyone else started yelling, he squeezed harder. He had his eyes closed. Everyone was yelling things at him. 'Put him down! Die like a man!' someone yelled. Pretty soon, the captain stopped wiggling and went limp.

"Someone yelled out, 'The captain's dead!' Not too many men heard him for all the yelling. but the ones that did tried to stop it. One man thrust his arm between the two, trying to pry them apart, but he was unable to get his arm between them. Another saw the problem and tried to help pull the two apart but couldn't budge the giant. One man hit him in the head with a large branch, but it did not faze him a bit. Everyone was starting to realize the captain wasn't breathing. That's when a drunken fool stepped up and yelled, 'Let him go, you yellow coward!' And then he shot Arthur in the back with a musket. Well, at that close range, if the captain wasn't dead before, that didn't help, for the musket ball went right through the both of them. Then someone shot the drunken fool for being stupid. Then someone shot him for shooting the shooter. Finally, I yelled to everyone to stop while we had a crew left. We all stood there in silence, trying to put together what just happened. That was when we decided to get Mr. Riggs. He's in charge now. I was stunned for a second then—"

I spurted out, "You mean the captain is dead?"

My question raised Reggie's eyebrow. "Did you not just hear my tale I told you just now? Yes, he's dead."

I asked, "So that makes Mr. Riggs captain?"

"Aye, boy, that's how it works, and there isn't a more deserving fella." The whistle blew and ended our conversation as we went midship to gather for Mr. Riggs.

Mr. Riggs stood in front of the wheel, his hands clutched tight behind him. He had changed clothes. He had on a suede green overcoat with pants to match that went to his knees and stretched white socks that went from knees to his highly polished shoes. His hair was pulled back in a tight ponytail. He was always clean shaven, and today he looked the proper English gentleman. He had on a host of medals, which made him look a proper English officer. All the men were gathering and talking. Mr. Riggs held up one hand.

"Please be quiet. I need your attention, please." The men quieted immediately. He started to speak. "As most of you know by now, we will have some changes aboard this ship. Our beloved Captain Farrow is dead." With that news, the crew started to talk among themselves, and a low murmur was heard. Mr. Riggs held up his hand to silence everyone, and they did. "The changes will start with me." He hesitated for a moment, knowing changes aboard any ship could cause a crew to mutiny. He continued, "I will assume the responsibility of captain. At this time, I would like to promote Mr. Reginald Goodin as first mate." The crew started to murmur again among themselves. Mr. Riggs held up his hand again, asking for the crowd to quiet. "You will get your chance to speak. For now, whatever your duties are, you will continue to do them. We will remain anchored here for three days. During that time, anyone wishing to come to my cabin and voice their approval or disapproval may do so with no repercussions. You may speak your mind if you are civil and respectful. Three days, gentlemen, before we pull anchor. Please go about your duties. Mr. Goodin and Mr. Roach, would you please come with me?" He turned sharp on his heels and headed for his cabin.

Reggie and I were almost at a run to keep up with his brisk walk back to the captain's cabin. Reggie's face still showed disbelief and shock as he had no idea Mr. Riggs even liked him, let alone think he was competent enough to call him the first mate. But he seemed to walk a little taller, and his pride was starting to show as we got to the cabin door. As he went by, many crew members, most all, nodded and smiled their approval, for Reggie was well liked by all the crew. That I could tell. As the men started to go to their duties, the silence that had gripped the ship had started to disappear, and the ship started to sound like itself again.

As we entered the cabin, Mr. Riggs was already at the desk, his head was down. and he was heavily holding his body on his closed fists on the top. As we walked in, he raised his head and said, "Please, gentlemen. sit down." He pointed to some chairs in front of the desk. As we sat, he also sat. He had a bottle in front of him and three goblets. He filled each with about a quarter full. He handed Reggie and I a glass and said, "May I congratulate you gentlemen on your promotions. You are both knowledgeable and well-respected men aboard this ship and feel you will both do well. But if either of you chooses not to accept your position, I will understand, and you can go back to your old duties."

Reggie jumped to his feet at attention and said, "Sir, it would be an honor to serve under you, sir. I have great admiration for you, sir, and would be faithful to your ship and duties, sir."

Mr. Riggs gave a slight smile as he replied. "I know you would, Mr. Goodin, and that is why I chose you, but please sit down. We have much to discuss. As for you, roach boy." His voice changed to a serious tone. I jumped to my feet at attention, as did Reggie. "You are a challenge to me. Your intelligence is impressive to me. You had for instance one enemy aboard this ship, and you managed to have him killed by setting him up with his own knife, and you never had to lay a hand on him." Reggie was looking at me from the corner of his eye but trying not to look directly at me. Mr. Riggs sat forward on his elbows, clasping his hands. He cocked his head to the side and squinted one eye. He continued, "So not only are you smart but also you still have that street survival instinct about you. So the position I am about to offer you would mean I would have to have your faithful alliance to me and my ship. At times, young man, I get a feeling I shouldn't trust you, and yet you seem very trustworthy." I could feel guilt running through my veins with every beat of my heart. I wanted to speak right out and apologize for stealing the map. But I smartly didn't, for he would have killed me on the spot. He leaned back from his desk, saying, "So, Mr. Roach, I was thinking of asking you to be my cabin boy, but it would mean complete loyalty and devotion on your part to me and the ship." I just stood there, staring at him and him at me. "Well, boy?" he asked.

I looked surprised and answered, "Oh, sorry, sir. I didn't realize you had asked me yet." It was hard to pay attention. My mind was racing. How did he know about setting up Jackson? What else was he aware of? Was this a test to get me to admit to copying the map? I finally just said, "Yes, sir."

Mr. Riggs sat back in his chair and said, "Good. You have a lot to learn in a short time, but first, what is your real name?"

I answered, "Homer, sir."

Mr. Riggs stared around the cabin. "As in the *Iliad*?" I wasn't sure what he was talking about, so I nodded agreement. "Homer Roach," he said. "What's your last name, son?"

"Gregoreouse," I answered. Then I did something that surprised me. I said, "I think I prefer Homer Roach, sir."

Mr. Riggs let out a laugh and said, "Homer Roach it is, sir."

"Well, gentlemen, we have a lot to discuss, but let me congratulate you on your new positions." Then he raised his glass and we followed. We clinked them together as he said, "Salud."

Reggie answered, "Salud," so I copied his lead. We all took a large swallow. This was not at all like the rum I tasted before. This was sweeter but just as warm going down. It was brandy.

Mr. Riggs said, "Please sit down." He pointed at the chairs. As we both sat back down, he started to explain some things to us. "Captain Farrow was my father." Reggie and I looked at each other as Mr. Riggs stood up and turned to a porthole that looked out the stern. He was looking out on the ocean as he spoke. "I was very much like you, Homer. On the streets of England, uneducated. My mother, too, was a whore. Captain Farrow was a frequent visitor when she became pregnant. He knew I was his child. Soon after she had me, she fell ill to a plague and died. He took me in and brought me aboard the English vessel he was in charge of at the time and made me his cabin boy. Once he had me caught up on my studies, he enrolled me into the British Naval Academy, not under his name but of my mother's. As time went on, we both grew to be very prominent figures in the Royal Navy. Captain Farrow had ties to royal blood, which made it easier for him, and his endorsement of me came to be a problem later as I reached my graduation into the Royal Navy. The background found out who my mother was and said I was not of pure blood, not acceptable for rank of officer in the Royal Navy and expelled me at once. They then discovered his involvement, at which point he was relieved of his duties and court-martialed. He took it pretty hard. We both did. We then set out to make them all pay for what they had done. His thoughts were to kill every British officer. I convinced him to become pirates and financially ruin the Royal Navy by plundering their ships and sinking their fleet. I was to show them that I was indeed worthy of running a fleet and my seamanship was that I was qualified, if not superior!" With that, he slammed his fist hard on the desk. Reggie and I both jumped as he did. Then just like that, he calmed down. That's when Robert Farrow started to lose sight of our objective. He was plundering defenseless vessels and killing and plundering just for fun. I went along only because he was the captain, and I was faithful to my captain. It was the way I was raised, and I didn't want to disappoint my father. Mr. Goodin, this is where you come in."

Reggie sat up. "Aye, sir. What do you need?"

"I want every sailor to be sharp in uniform and have specific jobs. I want every sailor well versed in combat—fencing, archery, artillery, and marksmanship. I will give you a list of guidelines to follow, and in return you give me a list of any supplies you need to get those guidelines met. For now, sir, I want you to get this ship and its men ready for sail in three days, and try not to disrupt the natural flow of things as they are until we get to port. From now on, you will be addressed as Mr. Goodin, even by your friends, and you will address me as Captain Riggs. Is that understood?"

Reggie didn't hesitate to answer with a snappy "Aye, aye, sir."

The captain continued. "Mr. Goodin, if you will leave me and Mr. Roach alone, I have some things to discuss with him. And if anyone wants to discuss anything about the ship or the decisions being made, you tell them they are to address me personally, and together we will discuss them. Is that acceptable to you, Mr. Goodin?"

Mr. Goodin bowed to Captain Riggs and answered, "I see that as very fair, sir, and thank you again for this opportunity to serve."

Captain Riggs bowed slightly from the waist and said, "No, sir. Thank you for joining me in my quest. You are dismissed, sir." With that, Reg...Mr. Goodin turned a snappy turn on his heels and left me and the now Captain Riggs alone. As Mr. Goodin left, Captain Riggs clasped his hands behind his back and paced a few steps back and forth. He turned to me and asked, "Do you know why I chose Mr. Goodin as my second-in-command?"

I sat, a bit uncomfortable, and then shrugged my shoulders and mumbled, "Uh, I don't know."

Captain Riggs's voice got sterner and louder as he said, "Sit up, boy. Don't slouch. And be decisive in your answers if you want people to respect you. Even if you don't know an answer, say with confidence you don't know or you're not sure. So tell me, what don't you know?"

I sat a straight up and answered, "Well, sir, he is not the most knowledgeable sailor, nor was he the most skilled in combat. Other than that, he does know this ship. All the men like him, and he was faithful to the captain."

Captain Riggs yelled, "That's it, boy! Right there. Faithful to the captain. Not just the captain, Mr. Roach, but to the captain and his plan. Everything else I can teach him. He has the aptitude and the skill, but you can't teach loyalty, Mr. Roach. That, my friend, is either in you or not. Do you have it in you, Mr. Roach? Can I trust you, Mr. Roach, with all my belongings, with all my personal things alone in my cabin at any time, to follow me through my plan to overtake the British Navy? Are you that man, Mr. Roach?" He stopped and stared at me.

I felt like he was reading my mind again, but I sat straight and answered, "Yes, I am that man, sir." I knew I was lying. I had already betrayed him.

He leaned down, put his face in mine, and said, "All right, Mr. Roach, tell me how you set up Jackson, for starters." He then sat back in his chair for my answer. My mind raced for a second. How much should I tell him, and is now the time to tell it all?

I started to answer him, "I planted it, sir, to show he was there."

Captain Riggs sat back in his chair and put his hands up to his face as if to pray and said, "I'm not a moron, boy. I'm already aware of that. Tell me more, like how and why."

I took a big breath and started to tell the truth. Well, most of it anyway. I just couldn't seem to do it. I told him how I had a way to sneak into the galley, how I watched Jackson strangle the other sailor, and how I had acquired the knife when he threw it at me, and I knew it would incriminate him. I told him all about the planks I had stolen to build my perch, the lantern, the fuel oil. The parts I left out were the jugs of roaches I had in storage and the fact I could see into this cabin. And I never mentioned the treasure map I had copied. He was surprised, I think, how much I did tell him, so I don't think he thought I was holding back.

He sat back easily in his chair and then said, "Mr. Roach, I understand your instinct to survive on this ship, but your dishonest and petty thievery must stop if you are to be my cabin boy. And I expect you to be forthright and honest with me at all times. Do I make myself clear to you?"

I started to nod then said with conviction, "Yes, sir!"

He scowled and asked, "Does this mean you will take the position?"

Again, I sounded a resounding "Yes, sir."

He just smiled and said, "Thank you, Mr. Roach. I'm sure we will have a wonderful relationship. Your first order is to tell Reggie that you will help him move into his new quarters as soon as you help me move in here."

I snapped to attention and again and said "Yes, sir." I bounded out the door in search for Reggie. I was so excited to have a position of honor on the ship. I was walking very tall and felt like I was floating across the decks. When I found him, he, too, was excited and congratulated me on my new position. I went below and gathered all my worldly positions from the dark damp bilge. I then returned all my pilfered goods, even the slat boards to the foot of each bunk. Then I went above decks to help Mr. Goodin and Captain Riggs get moved into their cabins.

My cabin was right off the captain's, a very small cubby more than anything, but it had a portal. I could see out the portside and could open for fresh air, something I hadn't had for a while. Most of the men were happy with the change, but only some were concerned that Mr. Riggs wouldn't be as fearless or aggressive as Captain Farrow. I wasn't too sure about that, but he was more calculating and intelligent. The three days passed quickly, and before I knew it, we were under sail again. I was involved with plotting and navigation in general. It was nice. Before, I never knew where we were headed, but now I knew exactly where we were and where we were going. We were headed for a large island they called Cuba, where we would lay up and decide our next destination. The men were excited. Cuba offered everything they were lacking right now—rum, women, and tobacco. The order varied between each sailor, of course.

We had a week of great trade winds. Then as if someone shut off the wind, we were motionless in the doldrums. You want to see the moral of a ship deteriorate fast, sit in calm water for a week. Tempers get edgy. During the day, we were allowed to swim as long as no sharks were visible. At night, sailors who played instruments would bring them out and play above decks. Mr. Riggs allowed the rum cabinet open as long as everyone behaved. As he put it, "Any incident involving alcohol that is not becoming of a sailor on my ship and the rum privilege will be halted." This kept many from overindulging, so it was rationed sparingly, not for fear of running out. Mr. Riggs just liked things to be in control. He felt excessive rum made for excessive behavior, and after the incident with Captain Farrow, most agreed with him.

We sat helpless for six days until the air changed. You could feel it and smell it as the wind started to pick up. Everyone, no matter what they were doing, stopped, and the ship became deathly quiet as the crew all looked in the direction of the wind. Then like a row of muskets firing, the sails ruffled then filled with a bang. The crew cheered, and Captain Riggs was fast about decks, seeing that Mr. Goodin was getting the job done to his satisfaction. All the men were yelling and dancing around, happy and excited. Captain Riggs was, too, I could tell, but as usual, he didn't really show it. The wind carried on all day and through the night, but the celebration would quickly end the next morning as a ship was spotted off the starboard stern. It was just daybreak. The lookout in the crow's nest spotted the ship and yelled below. Soon it traveled all over the ship. Captain Riggs was up already and studying his charts when he heard. He was usually up before daylight just for this reason to see what the daylight might show. I was awakened by Mr. Goodin, who rapped sharply on my cabin door, yelling, "Get up, boy, and get on decks right away!"

I quickly dressed and met with a group of sailors by the wheel. Captain Riggs was looking through a spyglass, and all hands were at their stations and at the ready. It has always amazed me how so many men could all be completely silent. All you heard was the wind, the rushing of the water, and Captain Riggs's voice as he yelled, "Mr. Goodin, what's the crow's nest say?"

Mr. Goodin called up to the crow's nest. "What's ye say, nest?"

When he answered, everyone could hear. "Can't make out who she is. but she's big and fast."

Mr. Goodin turned to the captain and repeated what was heard. Captain Riggs lowered his spyglass and said, "Mr. Goodin, ready the cannons and arm the men."

He snapped to and answered, "Aye, aye, sir." And off he went yelling orders. Big and fast, that was the ship they were on. That's why Captain Farrow and Mr. Riggs stole her. She was built to chase down, capture, and destroy pirates. But since then, the English Navy had been working and building other ships to get this one back. For another ship to be catching them, she would have to be pretty special. He knew in his heart she was not there by accident. They didn't just run into her on this giant ocean by chance. She was hunting them, and they had found her. She won't be filled with treasure and merchant mariners. She'll be filled with trained battle-ready seamen and plenty of firepower.

Captain Riggs started to try sail changes and tacking maneuvers to try and outrun this monster of a ship. But she continued to close in. Captain Riggs ordered Mr. Goodin and myself to his cabin. We assembled in his cabin. He had a concerned look on his face. He started to explain to us, "Gentlemen, this ship that is gaining on us is no normal ship. She is hunting for us, and she intends to catch us and kill every one of us. That was the sole reason she was built, so the battle will be hard, and she will be ready for it. I know this because this ship was the fastest ship out there, and no matter what direction we go, she stays on the same heading. No merchant ship would do that. This will be the fight of our lives, gentlemen. Those who are not killed in battle will be captured and tried and hung. You, Mr. Roach, may be able to live through this now. I have a selfish reason for saving your life, Mr. Roach." With that, he went to the hidden panel, slid it open, and pulled out the map. "This, Mr. Goodin, is written record of all the treasure locations. It's in code. I will go over this with both of you. Then, Mr. Goodin, I want you to take Mr. Roach and carve this into his hide. Then burn this document and throw Mr. Roach into the brig as a prisoner from the merchant ship we just plundered, the *Ingatine*. And you refused to sign on as a cutthroat pirate. If any

COCKROACHES IN THE BILGE

of us survive this battle, we shall meet in Havana, Cuba, in the main square one year from today. You must swear on your life."

We both nodded in agreement. I was a little concerned about the carving in the hide part. He explained the way the maps code read, and with that he said, "Get moving, Mr. Goodin. We've not much time." Then with a stern look on his face, he said, "Excuse me, gentlemen, but I have to inform my men of the same fate." With that, he briskly left the room.

Mr. Goodin pulled his knife out of its sheath and asked. "Are you ready, boy?"

I pulled off my shirt. "As I'll ever be, sir," I replied.

While Mr. Goodin went to work, the crew on deck got ready to battle. Captain Riggs was hoping if they can't outrun the battleship, outmaneuvering was their best bet. Being smaller and more maneuverable, they may be able to do damage to their guns before they get the upper hand. Captain Riggs had explained to all the men the situation and his plan to show their more experienced crew can outmaneuver them. And if they pull off this victory, he would personally see they all get a large bonus. He also explained any man finding his way out of this, if they don't win, should make his way back to Havana in one year and meet in the main square.

* * *

"Funny thing, Ben," the old man said with a smile. "Captain Riggs never mentioned the treasure carved on my body. In fact, he never mentioned the buried treasure at all."

Ben's eyes got big. "That's what the scars are all over your body. I thought you were shot by a dozen shotguns or something."

The old man said, "Be quiet, boy. I'm telling a story." With that, the old man continued.

* * *

So while we were down below, getting carved up like a well-roasted turkey, topside the British ship was closing in. Captain Riggs

75

knew timing was crucial. Turn too soon and the guns will be out of range and the British ship could recover faster and take advantage. Too late and it would leave them no room to maneuver around. Every man sat quiet and poised, waiting for his order. Captain Riggs didn't need his spyglass now to see the ship, but he was using it to see the ship's rigging guns and possibly a look at who was captain of this ship.

One sailor asked, "Sir, should we put up our British flag and confuse them, sir?"

Captain Riggs answered, "No, mate, they're not to be confused. They know exactly who we are."

As the vessel came closer, he was rewarded with a glimpse of the commanding officer. It was Admiral Lindenpoof. He laughed to himself. At the academy, they called him Admiral Littlepoop, for he wasn't very tall, and he had a raging temper, but he was one of the best tactical men in the Royal Navy. There was another surprise he saw as the vessel neared—a cannon mounted on the bow. It was a very large cannon. This usually wasn't done, for the bow of the ship rises and falls so dramatically that it would take a very skilled artillery man to handle such a feat. Nonetheless, Captain Riggs realized that it was a great military strategy. He called out, "Hard-a-port!?" The order was repeated, and the ship swung to port.

Men were working feverishly to get the large square sails to come about and recapture the wind. From a distance, though, it looked like a poetic dance, and it was all performed with a beauty and grace that you would expect from an experienced crew. Just as the ship swung to port, the bow cannon on the British ship fired off. Mr. Goodin and I heard the shot below and knew our time was running short.

A cannonball just missed the stern of the pirate ship, and Captain Riggs chuckled a little and muttered to himself, "Trying to take out my rudder, hey, Littlepoop?" He yelled out, "*Ready the cannons on the portside!*"

The order rang across the ship, and the answer came back, "Port guns ready, sir!"

Just before Captain Riggs could order the cannons to fire, the bow gun on the British ship had reloaded and fired. Captain Riggs yelled, "Fire!" Six cannons let fly. Three fell short, two missed the bow, and one hit the bow, breaking off a stay and sending wood chips flying. The ball from the British ship whizzed with a whistle right past Captain Riggs and just missed the wheel. Captain Riggs laughed again and out loud said, "Getting personal, are ye, Admiral? *Fifteen degrees to port, and tell me when we're ready to fire!*" With that, another boom from the bow of the British ship, and that ball hit midship, bounced across, and took two crew members with it.

A yell came across decks: "*Cannons ready, sir!*"

Captain Riggs yelled, "*Take out that damn bow gun that barge is toting!*"

The order was relayed. The British ship started to come about, facing her starboard side so she could unleash her own gallery of cannons. Captain Riggs knew he had one of the finest artillerymen in the seven seas. And as the ship rocked down into a swell then came back up at the right moment, six cannons went off at once. Two missed the ship, falling short. Three hit the bow and took the gun out. One ripped through the bow sprit, letting loose some major rigging which would slow her down. But just before Captain Riggs could congratulate the crew on a job well done, he knew they had to maneuver away from the broad side of the British ship. As he gave the order to come about, before it could even have the order relayed, the efficient British ship had already fired. Captain Riggs counted twelve balls hit his ship, and as they ripped sections of the ship to splinters, then you heard the booms of the cannons.

Mr. Goodin was just finishing up with me. He put some sort of paste on the cuts then wrapped me in some sort of cotton sheet. "You're a brave man, Mr. Roach," he said, patting me on the shoulder. "Let's get you belowdecks and in the brig." It was very painful, and he helped me stand. We heard the cannons damage below, and Mr. Goodin was getting anxious to get up on decks. He took me down to my cell. He handed me a key and said, "Lock the door, but if we are overtaken, throw the key. If not, you could still get out." He winked at me and said, "See you in a bit, boy."

I just nodded, but I wanted to go above decks and see what was going on. But I had my orders and knew what I was to do. Mr. Goodin grabbed a brass goblet and shoved the map into it. And with the butt end of his sword, he smashed the top closed so the document couldn't fall out and threw it overboard and watched it sink.

Captain Riggs was barking orders when Mr. Goodin arrived at the wheel. He looked at Mr. Goodin and asked, "Finished with your last order, Mr. Goodin?"

Mr. Goodin nodded a yes as he answered, "Aye, sir, and locked up just like you requested."

Captain Riggs laughed and shouted, "You're a good man, Mr. Goodin! Now see if you and I can't get out of this mess."

They had swung back in the same direction as the British ship. She was gaining on them fast. They could see the men on board now. Captain Riggs yelled, "Ready the guns on portside! We'll come about. We're going to take quite a hit. Go around so see that we take out some of those guns."

The order was relayed as the ship swung to port. The British ship also changed her heading, trying to get broadside faster. Captain Riggs wanted to get the first round off at the British ship before they could to hopefully lessen the barrage they were going to take. Although Captain Riggs had a great crew, the British ship was just as good, and their intentions were the same. Both ships got a round off, and although we did severe damage to their arsenal, they still had twice as many guns, and damage to our ship was severe to the port guns.

Captain Riggs let out a yell, "Damn, ready the starboard gun and come about!"

All hands worked furiously, trying to get an edge on this monster ship. As they swung around, the gunners on the British ship were unfazed by the damage done and were reloaded and got off three shots before we could come about. Two took out the rudder, and one blasted the mizzen mast, breaking it in half.

The helmsman yelled, "I have no steerage!"

Captain Riggs laughed at him and said, "That's because you have no rudder!" He reached over and grabbed Mr. Goodin by the shoulder. "Get all the sails down. Use every halyard we have and arm all the men. If they should come close at all, we want to board her. Keep those starboard guns ready, and if she approaches from that side, you blow that bastard captain right off that deck," he said through gritted teeth. As the British ship came up, it came to our starboard side. Captain Riggs was excited. Just what he wanted. He yelled out, "Ready those cannons!"

That was the last order he gave. The British cannons ran so far forward that they started to fire and take out the whole gunnery section of our ship. As they sailed up alongside. they blew the ship apart. Our men never got a chance to try to swing across on a halyard. They stayed far enough away that was impossible to reach. They also had a squad of men with muskets. As they became completely broadside, they systematically picked off all men who hadn't ducked for cover. All that was left of where Captain Riggs was standing was nothing but splintered wood. I could feel and hear the devastation, then it went deafly quiet. Then a loud boom, and the ship racked hard to port. I knew they had pulled alongside and were about to board.

I quickly locked the door and threw the key down the hall. I heard men yelling and screaming, and that, too, soon stopped. I sat in silence for a while. I could hear footsteps running around and a faint voice now and then. The voices became louder, and soon they were in the gangway of the hall of the brig. I could hear voices as they worked their way toward me, checking each cell. I sat on the floor in the corner, my knees up against my chest and my arm wrapped around my knees. When they got to the cell door, they had muskets drawn. They pointed them at me.

"Whatave we eer now?" they said in very thick English accents. I said nothing. My mind was racing. I wasn't sure what to think or do. He pointed his musket at me and said something like, "Don't move by orders of the king."

I had no intention of moving. In fact, I was scared stiff, having that gun pointed at you by some strangers who have already spent most of their day killing.

One of them asked, "Hey, lad, can you speak?"

I knew his question was pointed at me. I made no movement and no sound. The other sailor asked his friend, "Is he alive?"

The other said, "He appears to be breathin'."

"Well, find the key and get him out of there." They started to look for the key, almost stepping on it two or three times.

One of them said, "Ah, forget it. He's sittin' in a damn pirate's brig. He musta done something horrible." They both laughed at that and went on their way.

I sat in silence again, thinking I should have said something, told them where the key was or something. What if they sink the ship and I'm trapped inside? I could die in here. A panicked feeling ran over me. I started looking for a way to retrieve the key when I heard voices again, so I went back to my corner. It sounded like an army thundering in, but it was about six men altogether.

They gathered around the cell door, and an officer dressed fellow said, "Is that him?"

"Aye, sir, that's him," another answered.

The officer yelled, "Hey, boy, are you all right?" I didn't move from my spot. I did look up, but I said nothing. He barked out, "Well, he's not deaf. If there is no key, get a large piece of metal and we'll bend the bars enough to get him out."

One of the sailors standing to the outside of the group said, "Aye, sir, I will get it." As he turned to find a piece of metal, his foot kicked the key. It rang as it bounced down the narrow passage. They all stopped looking at me when they heard the key, and the sailor stopped and picked up the key. He turned with a smile on his face and said, "This piece may be big enough." He handed it to the officer.

"Thank you," he said as he grabbed it out of the sailor's hand. "It does look about the right size." He shot a disgusted look at the two who said they couldn't find the key. If I wasn't so scared, I probably would have laughed as he snatched the key from the sailor. He put the key in the door, told the sailors to fix their guns on me, then he spoke calmly but firmly. "Young man, I need you to get up and come with me." I wasn't sure at that point whether I wanted to go with him. They might just hang me on the spot too. As we stared at each other, he added, "Come, boy. We came to help you, and we don't want any trouble."

I spoke in Greek and answered him, "I don't want any trouble either."

He smiled a small smile and said, "Oh, you don't speak English, eh, boy?"

Another sailor asked, "What's that he said?"

The officer shrugged his shoulders and said, "I'm not sure. Sounds like Greek. Ready your muskets." With that he turned the key in the lock, and the clank of the tumblers fell from their hold. He swung the iron door open slowly as it creaked. "Stand up!" he ordered. I almost jumped up, but I sat staring at him. He pointed to two sailors standing to his left and ordered, "Get him up." They both jumped at the order, rushed in, each grabbed an arm, and stood me up. I groaned with pain, for all those cuts had gotten tender. "Bring him topside" was the next order, and they literally carried me to the top decks.

As we reached above decks, I saw British soldiers everywhere and bodies slain, lying everywhere. They were gathering them up and accounting for each one description and name if it was available. A small group of my shipmates were tied to the main mast. The rest were either dead or close to it. Captain Riggs was right about these men. They chased us down for one reason, and they accomplished that in well fashion. I desperately looked for Mr. Goodin and Captain Riggs, but they marched me fast over to the other ship. I didn't have a chance to get a good look around. The other ship was big. She made ours look especially small, and everyone was extremely disciplined. I was quickly marched down belowdecks and tossed into the brig. There were many cells, and others were in there, but no one I recognized. There were no portals to see outside, and I didn't talk with anyone. It seemed like I was there for a long time before some sailors came down, banging on the bars. Everyone jumped with a startled look as they came down, opened my cell, and grabbed me up again. They walked back above decks.

It was dark out now, and I could see our ship still tied off to the British ship. Most of the bodies had been removed, tossed overboard most likely. Some were hanging in the rigging by their necks with their hands and feet bound. Captain Riggs was right again. They were not gonna let anybody who was on that ship live. There were some more of my shipmates waiting their fate, to be hung. They rushed me, my feet barely touching the ground as they walked with a brisk pace to a large room. A large group of men sat in an organized circle, facing the door as they brought me in. The men looked almost regal with their white wigs on. They all had some sort of books in front of them and an inkwell and pen in front of them. The sailors sat me down hard in a chair which sat in the middle of the floor then stepped back a few steps.

I turned to look at them as they stepped backward, and a sailor yelled at me, "Face forward!" I turned quickly to look at him.

We sat in silence for a while, and then one of the gentleman said, looking over at me, "He's just a boy. I also understand he doesn't speak English, is that correct?" He looked at one of the sailors who pulled me from the brig.

He answered with a snappy "Yes, sir. That is correct, sir. We believe he speaks Greek, sir."

With that, one of the royal looking men spoke to me in Greek and asked, "What's your name, son?"

It surprised me to hear my own language, and it took me off guard for a second. I sat deciding what to do, then I decided to tell the truth. I answered him, "Homer Gregoreouse, sir." But when I answered him, I answered him in English.

I saw one of the royal men sit up quickly and asked in English, "You do speak English then?"

I then remembered what Captain Riggs taught me, so I sat up straight and looked them in the eye and answered, "Yes, I do. I was just not sure what was happening to me, so I remained quiet until I was sure."

One of the men who appeared to be the commanding officer sat back in his chair and put the pen to his lips then said, "Well, son, I suggest that you start to explain how you should find yourself in the brig of a notorious pirate ship."

I swallowed hard and started the story all about how I was kidnapped from my home, put in the bilge to collect roaches, and how Captain Riggs befriended me.

I was abruptly stopped by one of the men saying, "Mr. Riggs was no captain, son. He wasn't even an officer."

"He was, sir," I corrected him. "He was first mate, and then when Captain Farrow was murdered, he became captain."

The news that Captain Farrow was dead was a surprise to all the men sitting at the table. One of the men interrupted, "You mean to tell me Captain Farrow was dead before we got here?"

I answered, "Yes, sir. He was killed on an island by one of the sailors by accident."

Most of the men chuckled under their breath. One added in a quiet voice to another, "All pirates kill by accident."

The main leader slammed a wooden mallet down on the desk and yelled, "Order, gentlemen, please! We have a lot to do, so please, son, finish your testimony."

I finished telling them about the lie I was to tell about being captured from the merchant ship and how they cut me up to say I was tortured. And, Ben, here's where the curse of the treasure comes in. I never told the truth about the treasure. I never could tell the truth about that damn treasure. I was talking so fast and telling every detail that when I finally got to the part about their sailor finding me in the brig, they all sat staring almost in disbelief.

Finally, the main wigged fellow said, "Do you expect this court to believe you trained roaches?" I nodded yes. "The crawly little bug type?"

This time I answered, "Yes, sir."

He sat back and looked at the group as they all started talking quietly among themselves. Then they all sat back, and the main speaker said, "My boy, the court has decided that you were more a victim than a criminal. The reason we hunted this boat down was the men aboard this vessel were a treasonous band of men set out to hurt the British kingdom. Mr. Farrow and Mr. Riggs had a vendetta, and most of his crew had the same reasons, but you, my young friend, are to be set free. There will be no punishment for you, Mr.

Gregoreouse. We will give you passage back to England. From there, you can find your way back to Greece. As aboard this ship, you will work as a deckhand. Do you have any questions, Mr. Gregoreouse?"

I sat up straight and answered, "No, sir, and um, thank you, sir."

The gentleman answered me with a "You're welcome, lad." Then he gestured for a sailor to come over. As he came over and snapped to attention, he said, "Take Homer here to get a uniform and then to the medic to have those cuts looked at. Then have him report to Mr. Harris."

The sailor snapped to attention and gave a stern reply. "Aye, aye, sir." And he turned to me, gestured for me to stand, then said, "Come with me."

I stood and started to follow him out. As I passed through the door, I looked back and thanked the group of gentlemen again, and the main one just nodded and waved his hand in a gesture as to say "get out."

Then they brought in past me Harmon, one of my mates. With his hand bound behind his back, he winked at me. And as we passed, he said under his breath, "See you in hell, boy."

All I could say was "Good luck, Harmon."

He laughed and yelled back to me, trying to turn as they men pushed him forward, "I think I spent that, roach boy!" That's all he got out before they slammed him down in the chair I had just vacated.

We went below, and I was fitted for a uniform. Then I went to see a man who unwrapped my bandages, cursing those damn heathens that had done this to such a young man. He cleaned them up and then put some sort of salve on it and redressed it. It did feel much better, so I thanked him for that. Then I went and met with Mr. Travis Harris, who was in charge of duties aboard ship, who does what and when, and he was in charge of punishments when jobs were not done. He seemed like a nice enough fella.

The sailor left me with him, and I thanked him for his kindness. He patted me on the shoulder and said, "Welcome aboard, mate."

Mr. Harris put me on many little duties. Every time I was done with one, he would put me on another. The men all treated me well, but they weren't as friendly or made me feel at ease as my last crew members. These guys were very regimented in their ways, and relaxing and fun were not part of the daily routine on this ship. I had off duty time, and when I did, I spent it with the helmsman and the navigator. I was working on a plotted course on my own made-up chart when Mr. Traeton Perry happened to look over my shoulder at what I was doing. I hadn't met him yet, but I had seen him around and knew who he was.

He addressed me. "Mr. Gregoreouse, where did you learn your navigation skills?" The fact he knew my name surprised me.

"Captain Riggs taught me, sir," I replied, looking up from my work.

He asked politely, "May I see that?" He pointed to my paper.

I nodded a yes and followed with a "Yes, sir." I handed it to him.

He looked it over. "This is good work. You're right on course." He nodded a bit and handed it back to me. "Carry on, sailor" was all he said and he walked away.

The next morning, Mr. Harris came to me. He said, "Mr. Gregoreouse."

I snapped to attention, saying, "Yes, sir."

He continued, "You're to report to the poop deck immediately and see Mr. Perry."

I put the mop bucket and mop away and ran up to find Mr. Perry. When I found him, he told me I was to work with the navigator from now on. "Mr. Harris is aware and will use you only when necessary for other duties, but for now, you answer to me and the navigator."

"Aye, aye, sir," I snapped. My duties around ship changed. I spent most of my time taking readings and plotting positions.

After several weeks went by, we soon heard a voice from the crow's nest. "*Land ho!*" It was a special sight to see land in the distance. As we grew closer, the men seemed to get more and more excited. I especially was ready to eat some different food, see some different people, and sleep in a bed that doesn't move. As we came into the harbor and up to the waterfront, the city was very large. The docks were alive with bustling people, and many were gathering to come see the British warship. Sails were dropped, and men scurried about. Several skiffs were rowing large lines out to the big ship. Once they reached the monster boat, the men tied her off, and a crew on shore started to haul her into dock. Once secured and a gangway attached, a boatswain's whistle was blown, and all the men assembled in military order.

Admiral Lindenpoof came out. They all were quiet and came to attention. He stood silent for a moment, surveying the crew, then started a speech. "Gentlemen, we were sent months ago on a mission as ordered by Our Majesty the king to rid the seas of unlawful pirates intent on trying to harm the British Empire. We accomplished our goal in fine fashion. I am proud to be the captain of such a crew, and as promised, you will be rewarded for your bravery and loyalty to the crown. You are to be commended for your actions. You will receive twenty days leave, then report back here. I look forward to sailing with you again. You are dismissed."

With that the ship broke out in whoops and hollers, and the men danced around, singing songs, shaking hands, and all the while a line was forming around a table located by the gangplank to the pier. The man at the desk had two large chests by him, a large book in front of him and an ink quill. Each man would walk up, talk with him, and then he would shuffle through the book until he found his name. Then a sailor standing by the chest would reach in and hand out a certain amount of gold coins. The men would sign the book. They would then walk down the plank to join family, well-dressed women with children in tow yelling, "Daddy!" Some would be meeting no one. Off to the closest saloon. I would be one of those men with no one to greet me. I started to feel sorry for myself. I had no use for a saloon or any money, and I didn't even know where I would stay for the night. It was getting down to the last few men, and I had run out of thoughts. I decided to go ashore and see where my travels would take me.

As I tried to go past the desk, one of the large sailors put his arm out and said, "Hold it, boy. You have to sign out."

"Sign out for what?" I asked.

"You have to settle your dues," he said abruptly.

The man at the book was growling. He looked up and said, "Name!"

I looked at him puzzled and tried to answer, "Homer, sir."

He growled again. "Homer what?" he asked with a snide, almost annoyed attitude.

I stuttered my answer as he caught me off guard. "Homer Gregoreouse."

The old grouch fumbled through his book. "Ah, here it is," he said, squinting a bit. Then he blurted out, "Ten gold pieces. Most in your position get twenty, but it says here you joined them for only half the voyage." He looked up at me and squinted his eyes, saying, "What did they do, pick you up in the middle of the ocean?"

I laughed a little and answered. "That's exactly what happened."

The old man growled under his breath as the sailor handed him my gold pieces. "Ten gold pieces is what you're owed." He spun the book around. "If you agree, sign here." He thumped his bony finger on the page where I was to sign. I was confused a little.

"I didn't know I was getting paid," I said.

The man thumped the book again and said sternly, "You want it or not?"

I just nodded and answered, "Um, sure, I guess."

The old guy handed me my coins. "Be back in twenty days." He snapped and then yelled, "Next!"

I went down the plank. There were a lot of people on the dock. Some sailors were still celebrating with their loved ones. Others looked like they might be waiting for theirs to arrive. I just stood there, looking up the dock then down the dock, not really sure where to go. There was a sailor walking with one baby in his arm, two older ones following close behind, and a lady looking adoringly at him on his other arm. Just as they passed by me, the sailor stopped abruptly. I had recognized him from the ship but didn't really know him.

He said, "Homer?"

I turned to him. "Yes, sir," I answered.

"Homer, what are you going to do?" he asked.

I wasn't sure what he meant, so I asked, "Do, sir?"

"Yes, did you find a boat to Greece or are you going to walk home?" He laughed a little at his own joke. His wife and kids were all waiting patiently as he continued his conversation.

"Well, sir, I just started to decide what to do."

He looked at his wife and said, "It's kind of late, boy. Where are you going to stay tonight?" He had a concerned look on his face.

I answered. "I'm not sure, sir. I was just deciding."

He turned to his wife and said, "Dear, this is the lad I was talking about. We found him in the pirate's brig." The wife and the kids all gasped. She covered her mouth, trying not to be so obvious about her shock. "Homer, why don't you come with us? Put some food in your belly and a nice place to sleep and make your decision in the morning." He bent down, putting his hand on my shoulder with a sincere look on his face.

Strangers being friendly was not common to me. Where I grew up, you just didn't open your home to strangers. I had heard of people like these but never met any.

I started to say, "No, thank you, sir. I don't want to be a bother."

His wife pushed him gently out of the way, and she bent down face-to-face with me and said in her sweet soft voice, "Homer, I don't think he's asking. I do believe that's an order. Now come along." She grabbed her kids by the hand and stepped right along.

* * *

"That, Ben, could very well have been the first time I fell in love with a woman." The old man sat back and took another sip of rum. "Ben, that woman was an angel dressed in that bright yellow dress, deep dark brown eyes with flowing soft hair to match her eyes long curls draped out of the matching yellow bonnet. Her face was soft, her touch was soft, her voice was—"

"*Soft!*" Ben interjected, wanting to get on with the story.

The old man gave Ben a discouraged look then said, "Yes, soft." Then he handed the jug to Ben.

Ben wrinkled his nose. "No, thanks. I'm fine." He held his hand up in a defiant gesture then asked, "So what happened?"

The old man sat back forward and began the tale.

"Well, I went to their house, and I ate stew the likes of which I never tasted. Ben, there was happiness in the house. All the kids and his wife, nothing like I had ever seen before. After dinner, they showed me a small cot where I could sleep. But we didn't retire right away. There were stories of the sea to be told, especially of the pirate ship battle. When we finally did go to bed, I was ready to sleep. My scars were starting to itch as they healed, and sleeping on land felt a bit odd to me, but I did seem to drift off. The next morning, after a large breakfast, I thanked my hosts for their hospitality and left a gold coin on my pillow for reimbursement for all the kind help they were."

* * *

I made my way down through town back along the waterfront. Instead of looking for a boat to Greece, I was looking for a boat to Cuba. After all, my last orders were to get to Havana within one year. Just in case anyone survived, it would be my duty to meet them.

I happened to meet a first mate of a merchant ship that made runs to Cuba routinely. He said they could use a hand, not one for navigating but one for working. I assured him I had no problem with work. He told me to be at the docks and ready to sail in five days. He said the schooner's name was *West Wind*, and she moored at the south end of the piers. I told him I would be there. He also said they ran a tight ship, so I shouldn't be late. I again assured him I was seaworthy and understood a tight ship was a must. I walked away feeling pretty smart. I was only in town a short time and landed me a job right off. Five days went by slowly as I went down to the pier and saw my new home every day before I had to show up. She was a lot smaller than what I was used to, and she wasn't kept as tidy as the two other ships I was on. The lines were not in the best of shape, and the sheets were worn and rugged. I was there bright and early before anyone else had shown up. I didn't board her yet, for I had no permission to. Finally, a rough-looking white-haired gentleman in a dusty mariner's suit came sauntering up and asked what I needed. I told him the first mate had hired me and told me to be here this day.

The gruff old mariner looked me up and down, squinting one eye, and said, "Jesus, am I getting that old or are we hiring them younger?" I didn't quite know how to answer that, so I didn't say anything. He stepped closer. I could smell alcohol now and he asked, "What's the fella's name you was talking to, boy?"

I shook my head a little and answered, "Not sure, sir. He didn't give it to me."

He gave me a questionable look and asked, "What'd he look like?"

I was getting a little nervous now. I wasn't sure I had a job after all, but I answered, "A tall fella, sir, with brownish skin, wavy black hair. He dressed real nice and smelled like a whore."

The old sailor rolled his eyes back, leaned way back, and laughed a belly laugh so loud it echoed down the quiet empty streets then said, "You met Mr. Hernandez. That's him, all right." The man's face was permanently in a smile now, and he held out his hand as if to shake hands. "Welcome aboard, mate. I'm Captain Kelly, the proud owner operator of this here ship. And if Mr. Hernandez hired you, that's good enough for me. What's your name, son?"

I took his hand and shook it, answering, "Homer, sir. Homer Gre—" I stopped for a second not so you would notice. I was so fast at lying by now. I just blurted out, "Roach."

"Homer Roach, it's a pleasure to meet you, and welcome aboard."

I just shook his hand and said, "Thank you, sir."

He whirled around and started up the plank to board the ship. He turned and said, "You may come aboard, but wait for Mr. Hernandez to settle you in. I have work to do, and he won't be long."

I nodded and added a "Thank you, sir."

He then said, "Feel free to look around, see how she works. She's a fine ship."

I followed him up and dropped my bag at the rail and proceeded to look about the ship while he went to his cabin. He was right. It wasn't a long wait, and soon the crew started to show up. They all looked at me funny but kept to themselves.

Soon Mr. Hernandez arrived. As soon as he noticed me, he yelled, "Hey, kid, you made it." And he came over to greet me. "Well I'm glad you made it, um, what's your name again?"

I stood up straight and answered, "Homer, sir."

He smiled a big smile. "Homer, that's it. Hey, Johnson!" he yelled at a tall blond fella.

He stood up from the job he was doing. "Aye, sir," he replied.

"Do me a favor and show Homer his bunk area, would you please, and maybe a small tour of the ship."

The sailor dropped what he was doing and said, "Yes, sir." Then he smiled at me and said, "This way, boy."

And as we walked off, Mr. Hernandez added, "Then come see me, Homer, when you're done."

I turned and nodded an approval and waved. He took me below and showed me the bunks. He told me I could have Peter's old bunk. He wouldn't be back.

I asked, "What happened? Is he all right?"

The sailor laughed a bit and said, "Peter has a problem no one can help him with. We were in Tahiti, and he kind of spent some time with a chief's daughter on one of the small islands. Peter was given a choice of death or become a married man. Give up the sea and become part of their tribe." As we stepped into the crew's quarters, he added, "I think I'd rather be dead. Well, here's your new home."

He pointed at the lower bunk. It was nice that it was one of the lower bunks. I was too short to get in the others. It had a small hold for my belongings at the foot. I quickly stashed my bag in the locker and joined him to finish my tour of the ship.

The crew was a fun group of sailors. They were all polite to each other, something I wasn't used to. They asked each other to do things. On the ships I was on before, you were just ordered.

The ship ran well. Most of the men worked there because they loved the sea. They weren't getting rich, but to them they had all they needed. I was learning a lot. There was a military way to run a ship, then there was a private merchant ship way. It wasn't long before we reached Cuba. I was having so much fun, and I had a year before I had to meet in Havana. I asked the captain if I could stay on until March and then go to Havana. He was happy to let me stay and was pleased with my work. I went to many ports and learned to love the seas for all their mystery and adventure. They were all surprised at my navigation skills or that I could read and write at all. I have Captain Riggs to thank for that. So I, too, fell in love with the sea. I would get excited to pull into a new port, but after a couple of days, I would start to get an itch to get underway. The lessons learned about how a ship works and how to make her do things you didn't know were possible.

The captain was a very experienced man of the sea. He came from a long line of generations of seamen. I was having so much fun, I almost forgot about the treasure, and to be honest, I wish I had. But as the year rolled along and we neared the month of March, I knew I had to get off the next time we got to Cuba. The captain knew this also, and he was trying to get me there as timely as he could. I had told him I was meeting relatives there and then going to work for my uncle, and that's where I had learned all the mariner knowledge I had. I was becoming such a good liar by now, I almost expected to have family waiting for me when I arrived. When they got me as close to Cuba as they could and they dropped me off, it was hard to say goodbye. Those men were as close to family as I had ever had.

I had to see if anyone had made it through that battle. Captain Riggs was the first person that ever treated me with respect, and if he had not taught me what I had known today, I wouldn't be able to travel around and make a living as I did. He also saved my neck from a hanging. It was January 20 when they dropped me off. I had plenty of time to make my way to Havana. I had almost a year's wage with me, for I never went anywhere to spend it. All my shipmates would run to town and spend it on wine, women, and song. Every once in a while, I would go and spend some on a fancy meal, but most of the time I would stay aboard and make my own fare.

I found free passage on some local fishing boat. Communication with locals was a little difficult at first. My Spanish wasn't all that great. Going out to sea on those little fishing boats compared to what

I was used to was a little hair raising, if you know what I mean. I made it to the southern tip of Cuba and had to walk several miles to Havana. After walking through the primitive countryside, I was very surprised when I got to the city. It was big and busy. I could see why Captain Riggs decided to meet here. It would be easy to get lost here and hide among the many people. I made my way past some very wealthy homes and large hotels and soon stumbled across a very large open market. The smells were incredible, especially the food. I bought some roast pork rolled up in tortillas and some fresh fruit and found a quiet corner to watch all the people from.

I was insignificant to all that walked by, almost invisible. I saw every walk of life go by me that day, many different cultures. Beggars to royalty. Some of the rich had a slave carrying packages, and some were carried by four men while they rode in a covered chair between them. There were street dancers, food vendors, clothes merchants, and my favorite, a man with a dog and monkey. Both did tricks and were fun to watch. People gave out money to them for their trouble. I could have too, but I had plenty of money, more than a boy my age should have, and my street smarts told me to not give any out or show any of it. As I sat entertained by all that was going on down, in an alleyway right behind me, a serious commotion broke out. I turned to see a large man with a young man by the arm, pushing him along, shoving him out a side door. He gave an extra shove to the ground. He was yelling at him. My Spanish wasn't very good, but I understood something about stealing and being ungrateful. He was pointing down the road and yelling. The young man was crab walking, trying to get out from under this big man. He finally got out from underneath enough to get to his feet and started to run down the road. The large man reached down at his feet, picked up a rock, and threw it at the boy, just missing him as the boy rounded the corner out of sight. As I sat enjoying the show, the man threw his arms to his side in disgust and went back inside the door. Minutes later, he came out the front door of an inn and hung a sign out on the front porch that said Help Wanted.

As I finished my meal, I wondered what kind of help such an angry man would need. I grabbed my bag and went to ask the man.

After all, I had several weeks left and could use a place to stay. I walked in and approached the man. He was still very upset. He didn't hear me come in, and he was grumbling under his breath.

I said, "Excuse me, sir."

He jumped back a bit and looked up from his work and snapped at me. "What is it, boy? Can't you see I'm busy?" He didn't seem so large sitting down. He had dark black hair which matched his eyes and a light brown complexion. He had a mustache that was trimmed very neatly that went down to both sides of his chin. He had on a white shirt with a black string bow tie.

I answered his question. "The sign outside, sir. I'm new in town and—"

He interrupted me. "What sign!" he snapped. He had forgotten he hung it already.

I stayed calm even though I could tell he was still very upset. I approached the subject again. "The help wanted sign, sir. I was curious as to what help you needed?"

He sat looking distant for a minute, puzzled even as he looked past me toward the front. Then his eyebrows raised as he figured it out and asked, "The one I just hung?" He was looking confused again.

"Yes, sir, that would be the one," I answered.

He sat back in his chair and put his hands together like he was about to pray and tapped his bottom lip with his forefinger a couple of times, sizing me up. "Did angels send you to me?" he asked with a sly smile. He added, "I have never had the position filled so fast." He sat forward, leaning on his elbows, and asked, "Where did you come from really?"

I answered him, "Originally from Greece, but I have been sailing around the world on merchant ships for the past year."

He leaned in toward me a little closer and interlocked his hands, squinting an eye a bit. He said, "You've been sailing round the world, now today you feel like getting a job on land just like that?"

I knew in my heart if I would have said the truth, he would not hire me. My idea was not for any long-term commitment. Hopefully I would be off searching for treasure soon. So I did what seemed to come natural for me. I lied. "Well, sir, I decided to come ashore, find me a respectable job, learn a trade." It was hard to say all that when I didn't mean it, and I hoped he couldn't see through my deception. I felt like I had betrayed myself with that answer, for I loved the sea, the open waters, the adventure of it all. He interrupted my thoughts with a question. "Why Cuba?"

I looked him straight in the eye and said, "I have sailed through here several times and found it to be one of the most beautiful places I have ever seen."

He sat back a bit and smiled a large smile and said, "Yes, it is, my friend. Yes, it is." Then his face got serious. "Running an inn is a serious business," he said. "Many things to worry about and pay attention to. Our goal is to keep all of our guests happy. You will cook, clean, and be a servant to our guests to make their stay pleasurable." He then leaned back in his chair, crossing his arms. His shirt sleeves were rolled up a bit, exposing his large forearms. His face became serious and stern, and he said, "I'll give you a small room, two full meals a day, and your pay will be based on the amount of guests we have staying per day."

A sly smile grew across his face, and I got the feeling he was trying to pull a fast one on me, so I said, "I agree to those terms, but I want five dollars per month guaranteed regardless of guest registry."

He sat, looking at me quietly, then stood up and held out his hand to shake. "It's a deal, my young friend. And you, I think, will do well in this business. Your first job is to go get that sign out front and bring it to me."

I grabbed his hand and we shook, and I said, "Aye, aye, sir." I dropped my bag and went to get the sign. As I returned, he was standing out front of the large reception desk. He had my bag in his hand.

He said, "Rule number one, never leave anything in the main lobby. We will keep it clean and tidy at all times." He then snapped his fingers for me to hand him the sign. He took the sign from my hand and replaced it with my bag.

I said. "Aye, aye, sir."

He added, "From now on, you will call me Senor Ramirez. My full name is Jorge Martinez Ramirez. And who might you be, senor?"

"Homer Roach, sir," I answered without batting an eye.

"Well, Senor Homer, please follow me. We will put you to work right away, but first I will show you to your room and get you a formal uniform." With that, he turned and started walking, signaling me with his finger to follow. We walked down a long corridor, our shoes clip-clopping on the highly polished tiles.

We rounded a corner and dropped down two stairs to a large courtyard. It was beautiful, embellished with flowering bushes, and there was a large fountain in the middle. We walked past it to a small but heavily built door, rounded at the top, a small window cut in the stucco finish to the right. He opened the door which revealed a small room. Small in comparison to the rest of the building but huge to a boy who had spent a couple years aboard ships. It was about nine feet by seven feet and had a few cupboards and a closet. There was one small bed which was huge compared to what I had been sleeping on. A small wash basin sat on a small table. The window looking out onto the courtyard was the only window. The walls were heavy stucco painted bright white. He barked the order for me to put my bag in the closet and come with him quickly. We marched quickly back to the main lobby. He told me to go see Jesus two shops down on the right. He was a tailor, but he preferred to be called a textile merchant.

"You tell him you need two shirts, pants, tie, and a pair of shoes. I will deduct them from your pay slowly so you will have some payment to use," he said with a smile as if doing me a favor. "Now hurry," he said, slapping me on the shoulder. "I have a job for you when you get back."

I nodded an understanding nod and quickly ran out the door. I ran down the street. I found the shop he was speaking of. I bolted into the shop. Some bells hung on the door, making a racket and alerting the shopkeeper that a customer had arrived. The shop was long and narrow with extremely high ceilings. There were clothes lining the shop all over, shirts, coats, fancy dress, clothes, hats, and a wall of shoes like I had never seen before.

A voice hollered from the far end of the shop saying, "Un momento, senor." In just a few seconds, from the dark far corners of the shop, a small figure appeared. He was spouting in Spanish. "Buenos dias, senor."

I bowed a bit, saying in return, "Good day to you, sir."

He smiled a small smile, adding, "Oh, you speak English."

I answered politely with a "Yes, sir."

He quickly replied, "Then that is how we will, um, how you say, communicated."

I smiled and nodded, understanding what he meant. He was a small man, rounded at the shoulders. He shuffled when he walked. His clothes seemed too large for him as his pants were baggy and shirt hung loosely on his skinny frame of a body. He was bald except for a few dark black hairs that he combed across his vast baldness of his head.

"What can I do for you?" he asked, sizing me up already.

I answered him, "Mr. Martinez sent me to ask you for two pairs of pants, two shirts, a tie, and some shoes."

The old tailor just nodded and replied, "Si, senor, follow me porfavor." We walked toward the back of the store, and he was grabbing apparel as we went. He had already sized me up with his knowledgeable eye. He asked, "What happened to Alejandro?"

I answered, "I don't know what you're asking me?"

The tailor grunted and handed me the clothes. "Try these on," he said, walking away in disgust. I then figured out who he was talking about. Alejandro must have been the boy who was thrown out of the hotel. The tailor shook his head, saying, "I'll bet he was fired for stealing. Never did trust that boy."

I was amazed. Every piece of clothing he brought me fit perfectly. The shoes were a bit tight. They were shoes like I had never seen before, with soft shiny leather with a big brass buckle in the front. Like the royalty wore. I wasn't accustomed to wearing shoes. I was looking down at my feet and trying to decide whether or not I could stand them for very long when the man said, "Don't worry, barefoot boy. They feel tight for a couple of days, then you won't even know they're on."

I had to laugh a little. He was either a mind reader or he was just that good at his craft. I looked at him, and he nodded a comforting yes with his eyes closed, so I figured he was right about everything else. I would trust him on this. He showed me how to tie the tie. Once we were done, I had my uniform on, and looking rather good, I might say. I asked him how much all this was. He said Mr. Martinez would pay for it. I told him that I might just make it easier for both of them and let me pay for it now.

He raised an eyebrow and said, "It's quite a bit of money for a young man."

I said, "We don't know that until you tell me how much it is."

He agreed and told me it was one hundred dollars. I laughed out loud. "For two pairs of pants and two shirts and a pair of shoes?" I asked.

The old man didn't bat an eye and added, "There is a tie also."

I squinted an eye at him. "So it would have taken me almost a year to pay that debt off," I said. "Maybe I will get my uniform somewhere else."

The old tailor shot back at me, "Not for this quality, you won't."

I didn't want to make any enemies in this new town, so I decided not to argue any further. I looked at the material, rubbed it between my fingers, and agreed it would be hard to get that quality. I saw the old tailor relax just a bit. He still seemed a little put off when I said, "I'll still pay for it now."

He looked at me funny and mumbled something in Spanish that I didn't understand, and then added, "This is not how it's done."

I smiled and said, "But now you don't have to wait a year for your money, and it keeps us all honest."

He grinned a crooked grin and said, "You're wise beyond your years, my young friend."

I reached into the pouch I kept around my neck and fished out one of my gold coins that was worth twice what he was asking for.

He looked at me, a little surprised, checked it very close, and asked in a puzzled voice, "Where did a boy your age get an English gold coin?"

I shot back my answer in a cocky attitude. "I spent a year on a pirate ship."

He just nodded as if to understand, but he wasn't sure what to think. He hesitated then said, "I'll get you some change, senor."

I patted him on the shoulder and winked and said, "You just can't get quality like this. I don't need the change." I gathered up my clothes and said, "Mucho gusto, Senor Jesus."

He nodded and said, "If you need some clothes, Mr. Homer, you come see me. I remember I owe you."

I ran out the shop, down the road, and back to the hotel. I put my clothes in my room and made my way back to Mr. Ramirez. He looked up from his work and said excitedly, "Oh, you're back. Good." He spun around his chair facing me. He looked me up and down. He added, "You look good. Now I need you to go to the second-floor room 209. There is a guest there, a Mr. Hernandez. He needs his traveling bags brought down to the lobby. A carriage will be coming to pick him and his companion and the luggage up."

I said, "Aye, aye, sir."

He smiled and said, "You're not aboard a ship anymore, Mr. Roach. You address me with 'si, senor.'"

I bowed a bit and answered, "Si, senor." I ran off to find room 209. I knocked lightly on the door, and after a few seconds, the door opened, only to see a beautiful lady.

* * *

"Ben," the old man said, reaching over and putting a hand on Ben's shoulder. "That's the second time in my life I had fallen in love." He closed his eyes and slowly fell back against the headboard.

Ben rolled his eyes and shook his head at the old man. Ben could appreciate a pretty girl, but this old man sounded like he fell in love with every woman he met.

He continued, "She had black hair, olive brown skin, and the most intriguing deep brown large eyes. She was wearing a white dress, frilly at the top and cut so it dropped down to her breasts. Cut so low I thought they were going to fall right out any second." Ben kind of blushed at that part, and when the old captain asked, "You know what I mean, son?"

Ben could only nod with agreement, for he knew exactly what the man was talking about. He found himself staring at the women in the market in town, at those who wore those dresses.

* * *

Well, I just stood there like an idiot, looking her up and down. She must have been used to it, for she stood long enough for me to take it all in before she smiled a big smile with those white teeth and red lips. She then asked, "May I help you?"

It was then that I realized and snapped out of my trance. I stumbled to get the words out, but somehow I did. "I came to carry Mr. Hernandez down to the…" I realized what I had said and turned as red as a pepper, but she helped me.

She said, "I'm glad they sent a strong young man, but Mr. Hernandez can get himself downstairs. But do you know what would be an even bigger help to me? For my bags to get downstairs." As she said this, she opened the door wider to expose a mountain of bags and a sea trunk. She gestured for me to come in. I walked over to the luggage. She put her hand on my shoulder ever so gently and whispered closely in my ear, pointing to a trunk, "Please be careful with this one. It has my breakables in it." I'm sure it was to tease me a little. It was almost impossible not to stare at her as I grabbed a couple of bags to take down, and as I loaded my arms up with as many bags as I could carry, she said, "Thank you, boy." And she floated off like an angel.

I ran down the stairs, wanting to hurry. I made several trips running up the stairs and down, trying to get just one more look at that lady. After I got all the bags downstairs, Mr. Ramirez told me to wait by the luggage and wait for the carriage to arrive and help load it.

As I sat looking around, I started to marvel at the impressive woodwork of the massive polished pillars that took center stage. All had elaborate foliage carvings at the top and bottom. They stretched all the way to the third floor and supported the spiral staircase, and when looked at from the bottom, they would almost make you dizzy. My concentration was broken when I heard horse hooves out front. A driver yelled out a "Whoa!" and the horses stopped. I ran to the door. Two magnificent white horses were hitched to a carriage the likes I've never seen. It looked fit for a king. It was breathtakingly beautiful. A man jumped down from the driver's seat. He nodded a slight greeting to me as he started to walk by.

I asked in my best Spanish, "Are you here for Mr. Hernandez?"

He stopped and looked at me with a funny look. Then he looked past me into the hotel and asked, "Where's Alejandro?"

I simply answered, "I don't know." The truth was I did kind of know but wasn't sure enough to say so. I followed him around to the back of the carriage, and he pulled a line which rolled up a tarp. There was an area for packing all the gear.

"The heavy ones will go back here, and some of the others will go on top." I nodded and turned to go get some bags. He pushed my shoulder, spinning me around to face him again, and with a smile on his face, he said, "I will assist Mrs. Hernandez into the carriage, so stay out of the way and out of my view, if you know what I mean."

I surely did know what he meant. With that understood, we went in to grab some luggage and proceeded to load them. After we loaded everything, the driver patted me on the shoulder. "Tell them the carriage is here and ready to go, will you, boy?"

I ran up the stairs, and when I got to their door, I straightened my clothes, and my hair was pulled tight and tidy in a ponytail. I stood straight and knocked sharply. The door opened, and my smile disappeared. I'm sure my disappointment was obvious. But it was not a Spanish goddess that opened the door but a small little man in a white linen uniform, a slight heavyset build, gray to almost white hair and mustache.

I looked past him for my goddess, and my intentions were interrupted when he asked, "Yes, may I help you?"

I straightened up, regained my composure, and answered, "I'm here to tell Mr. and Mrs. Hernandez their carriage is here and ready, sir."

He just nodded and said, "We will be down shortly." And he closed the door.

I bowed from the waist an acknowledgment, a little embarrassed at my behavior but disappointed just the same. I bounded downstairs and met up with the driver and said, "Wow, he's an old man compared to her. Are you sure that's not his daughter?"

The driver laughed a little and said, "Very sure. He's just that rich."

It wasn't long before the couple came down the stairs, looking like a king and queen as they walked arm in arm down the spiral case. I stood at my position, hands crossed in front of me, trying not to be obvious as I watched her descend the stairs. As they passed me, the man reached out his hand to me, not really making eye contact. His hand was closed, and I wasn't sure what he was doing. He turned to me, a little puzzled, so he opened his hand, showing me two silver coins. And then he had to say, "Here, boy, this is for you." I held out my hand and accepted the coins.

She twisted her umbrella and gave me a shy and quaint smile. The driver had the door to the carriage open and standing at attention. He was much better at being inconspicuous than I was, and as Mrs. Hernandez reached the carriage, he held out his hand and she put hers in his, and he helped her up into the carriage. He did the same for Mr. Hernandez. Once both were loaded, he shut the door and turned and looked at me and moved his eyebrows up and down. It made me laugh a little, and I was jealous he got to hold her hand. He climbed up to his place and winked one eye at me, grabbed the reins, and gave them a simple slap. The horses who had stood so patiently went right to work. I watched as they drove off, then Mr. Ramirez called my name, so I went into the lobby.

He said, "You did a fine job, boy. But now make sure those horses didn't leave any undesirable surprises out by the front door. If they did, there is a shovel and broom in that cupboard over there. Then when you get done there, go to the kitchen and see Estella to see if she needs any help."

I turned to go do what I was told and stopped as I remembered something. I blurted out, "Oh, Mr. Ramirez, here." I was holding the coins out to hand to him. "Mr. Hernandez gave me these."

Mr. Ramirez chuckled a little, took my small hand into his large one, and using his other hand, he curled my fingers around the coins, saying, "No, my little friend. That is called paying for gratitude for services. Any monies given to you in that way is yours. You don't have to share with me. You keep it. But thank you for your honesty."

I just shrugged my shoulders and ran to check the front entrance. It was clean, so it was off to the kitchen to find Estella. Finding the kitchen wasn't hard. The smell of food was strong and not far from my room. As I rounded the corner to the kitchen, I found Estella, a very short and petite woman. Her hair was in a tight bun, wrapped tightly upon her head. She had a white apron on, soiled a bit from the day's work. She was an older woman and looked like she had worked around a kitchen her whole life. She looked up at me, a little startled, and started rambling things in Spanish. She was going so fast, I only caught a few words, and her hand gestures were pretty obvious. She wanted me out of the kitchen. I held up my hands and tried to calm her with the little Spanish I had learned on the merchant ship. She calmed a little and let me explain I was working there and came to see if she needed any help. She asked where Alejandro was. I just shrugged my shoulders, showing her I didn't know. Then I cupped my hand around my mouth and told her I thought he was thrown out for stealing.

She nodded her head in agreement and whispered back to me, "He was lazy too." I laughed a bit, and she laughed a little too.

I asked politely, "Is there anything I can do for you?"

She turned back to her work and said, "Can you catch a chicken?"

I answered with a little question in my voice, not sure if I heard her correctly. "Well, I have before."

She was kneading bread. She said, "Back in the courtyard. You go beat the bushes. You'll get chickens. Get two fat ones. Not roosters, hens!" She was shaking her finger at me. Then she went back to kneading the dough.

I nodded yes and started off to the courtyard, but I couldn't help but turn back and say, "Roosters, not hens."

At first she nodded in agreement, then she realized what I had said and she stopped kneading, looked up, and started to yell, "*No!*"

I had my hands up, correcting myself to her, saying, "Just kidding. Hens, not roosters. I got it."

She shook her head in disgust as she kneaded that bread even harder and mumbled something under her breath I'm sure wasn't nice. I went out to the courtyard. There wasn't a chicken in sight, but rather than beat the bushes I peeked into them. Sure enough, there were many chickens. So rather than beat the bushes and get them all riled up, I carefully reached in and grabbed two. I put them under my arms and took them to Estella.

She nodded an approval at my chickens. Then she said, "Go out back and butcher them and pluck them. I will cook them."

I looked at her and, with a question in my voice, said, "Out back?"

She rolled her eyes then explained how to get out back. I found the door leading to the back. The steep but short staircase led to a back street. There was a covered alcove where there was a machete a chopping block, and it didn't take me long to figure out what to do from there. As I finished and started back into the hotel, the road behind the hotel dropped off steeply, and you could see the tops of other buildings that all led down to the waterfront. In the shed, I found an apron which I was grateful for, a machete, and a few assorted knives and a butcher block. I went to the task of butchering and plucking the chickens, and when I was done, I took them to Estella. She thanked me and told me Mr. Ramirez wanted to see me, so I ran up to the front desk. As I got there, he handed me some linens and told me to take them up to the room the Hernandez's just checked out of. There was a girl named Amelia, and I was to see she got the linens. Then I'd assist her in any way to get the room ready for another guest. When I got there, the door was open, and Amelia was working away, expecting another old Hispanic woman. I was taken aback a bit by this exotic beauty. She had dark skin and ebony black hair that hung past her shoulders, and it was curly in tight ringlets. She was wearing a white cotton dress and an apron with lace. Her tall slender figure moved gracefully as she swept the floor, as if she was an angel dancing in heaven.

* * *

Ben interrupted the old man by saying, "Oh, please, I bet that was the third time you fell in love?"

The old captain's eyes went from a faraway dreamy look to instant anger and yelled, "Why do you keep interrupting my story? Do you want to hear it or not?"

Ben felt kind of bad for a second because it was a pretty good story. And Ben apologized, and the old captain continued.

* * *

Well, I addressed her by saying, "Ms. Amelia, excuse me. I have some linen for you."

It startled her a little. She spun around, put her hand on her chest, and said, "Oh, you scared me." I started to apologize. She stopped me, saying. "No, it's all right. What is it you wanted?" Her eyes were deep dark brown and her teeth pearl white. Her voice was soft. She was a bit shy at first, but that quickly changed. I tried to peek again, but I stood staring for a long time, just holding the linens out in my hand.

I started to say, "I, uh, just, uh, told to uh bring you." She stood looking at me like I was an idiot, so I took my eyes off her for a second and regained my composure. "Mr. Ramirez wanted me to bring this up to you." I got it out. Now I was feeling better.

She looked me up and down. "You are employed here?" she asked.

I answered, "Yes, I just started."

She looked past me out the door as if looking for something then asked, "Where's Alejandro?"

I knew that was coming, but once again, I just shook my head and said, "I don't know."

She reached over and took the linens from my hands and said politely, "Thank you."

"You're welcome," I replied. Then I added, "I'm supposed to help you."

She giggled a little and answered, "That won't be necessary. I'm almost finished." Then she asked, "What's your name?"

I snapped right up and answered, "Homer Roach, ma'am."

She looked up from making the bed and asked, "Where you from, Mr. Roach? Your accent is different to me."

I answered, "I'm originally from Greece."

She said, "My, my, aren't we a long way from home? What brings you here, Mr. Roach?"

I answered, "A boat."

She stopped making the bed and looked at me oddly. Then a slight smile came over her face, and she quickly repressed it, going back to making the bed. She said, "Oh, you're a funny boy."

I was a little embarrassed. I didn't mean to be so curt. I tried to correct myself, to redeem a little self-respect by saying, "I meant a merchant ship, but first I started out on a..." I almost said "pirate ship" but decided against it and lied again. "English warship."

She fluffed up the pillows, saying, "Well, funny boy Homer, there is only one way to Cuba, and that is by boat. Now I don't need any help from you, so you can go see what Mr. Ramirez might need from you."

I answered, "I suppose you're right." I turned to leave but stopped long enough to say, "It was a pleasure to meet you, Amelia."

She turned her back to me then said, "And you, funny boy Homer." I just wanted to die or disappear. I had somehow made a fool of myself.

Mr. Ramirez kept me very busy the rest of the night—cleaning, getting wood for the kitchen, helping with dinner, carrying luggage for new arrivals. It was a lot of work, but I kind of enjoyed this kind of work. Maybe because it was new to me. One thing I didn't mind at all was my bed, I didn't have to listen to fifty men snoring and changing shifts, and the bed itself was deep and soft. Time went by, and days turned to weeks. At times I would miss the sea, then I would catch a glimpse of Amelia, and all my thoughts of going to sea would leave.

I saved my tips, and when I got enough money, I went to Jesus to see about a proper suit. He was all excited, and as promised, he made me a real good deal. I put it on and went back to the hotel. Mr. Ramirez was quite impressed. I told him I wanted to court Amelia. He sat back in his chair and smiled.

"Well, my little friend, let me tell you the best way to do that. You first need to ask her father. I just happen to know him and could help you."

With my eyebrows raised, I said, "Oh, would you please, Mr. Ramirez?"

"For you, my boy, of course. I would help you," he answered, smiling from ear to ear. "But first you should ask her if she would be interested in spending time with you. Chaperoned, of course."

I nodded and answered, "Of course."

She accepted my request, and Mr. Ramirez helped me. We indeed did spend some time together. Chaperoned, of course. I would go to town each week and check for anyone looking like my old crew and would check the local taverns to see if anyone had appeared, but there was no sign of them, and my hopes of ever seeing my friend Reggie was getting smaller and smaller.

One day, a group of men checked into the hotel. They were sailors. I could tell right off they were English Navy. I could spot that a mile away. It surprised me they would stay in such a fancy hotel. They weren't in uniform, so maybe they were officers, but they didn't act like officers. Later that evening, they stayed up late drinking in the parlor. They were getting pretty drunk. I had gone to bed, but Mr. Ramirez stayed up to tend to the guests.

As the evening wore on, one of the sailors said, "Hey, I wonder if he knows anything." They waved him over, saying, "Hey, innkeeper, we have a problem. We're looking for a little pirate." They all laughed at the remark. Mr. Ramirez didn't know what the joke was, but he politely smiled and gave a courtesy laugh just the same.

And then another sailor said, "You see, my friend, we are here looking for a young boy who had sailed with some pirates, and when we captured their ship and we were hanging them. One said he had information that would be useful to getting the treasure back. We let him down. He said if we don't hang him, he would tell us how to find the treasures. He confessed that the young lad that was set free was indeed in with the pirates, and they carved the coordinates into his flesh. Then he was supposed to meet here somewhere in Havana with any survivors. Have you, sir, seen anything like that boy around here?"

Mr. Ramirez shook his head no and politely said, "No, senor." He started to remove some of the dishes that were on the table.

The drunken sailor grabbed Mr. Ramirez's arm and said, "After that fella gave us that information, we didn't hang him just like we said we wouldn't. We ran him through with a sword instead and threw him overboard."

They all laughed out loud except for Mr. Ramirez. He had served his share of drunks and heard a million stories just like this before. They went on into the early morning. The mess was still there when I got up, so I cleaned it up. Mr. Ramirez didn't get up at his usual hour, so I took care of the duties he usually would do. He finally made it up, grumbling about the drunken fools from the night before. And he earnestly thanked me for taking care of business. He then grabbed two cups of coffee and went to visit the old tailor's store.

They got to talking about the usual. They were sitting at the storefront. The old tailor asked him why he was so late this morning, and Mr. Ramirez told him about the drunken party at his parlor the night before. Then he started to tell him about the high sea stories that group had come up with, about the boy, and the map carved into his flesh. And as he was retelling the story, half laughing at the remake of the tale, the old tailor's face got serious.

He grabbed Mr. Ramirez by the arm and pulled him close as he whispered, "It's not a story. It's your boy."

Mr. Ramirez pulled his arm free and sat back, looking confused at the old tailor. "I don't have a boy," he remarked, looking a little confused at the tailor.

The tailor tried desperately to explain himself. "Homer. It's your boy, Homer."

Mr. Ramirez now just looked disgusted with the tailor. "Have you been drinking too?" he asked.

The tailor, trying to plead his case, said, "I saw him when he was changing. He took off his shirt and, well, I thought he had been badly burned or something. He is scarred all over his body." He jumped to his feet, proclaiming, "Then he paid me for his uniforms with a gold doubloon worth twice what the clothes cost. When I asked him where he got it, he told me he was a pirate for a year and winked his eye and left. I thought he was joking, but now, I'm not so sure."

Mr. Ramirez sat, looking at the evidence before him. He even asked himself, "I wonder how much the boy would be worth if I turned him in?" Then he shook his head as to physically shake that idea out. He turned to the tailor and grabbed his cup, saying, "This is just crazy talk, you old fool. You almost had me believing it. You better stick to making clothes. That boy is too nice to be a pirate and too honest."

The tailor grinned a bit and stood to go inside, saying almost to himself but as much as to Mr. Ramirez, "Yes, you are right." But even as he said it, he didn't believe it. He was sure in his heart that Homer was the man they were looking for. And he hoped his friend wasn't in any danger. "I'll see you tomorrow, and thanks for the coffee."

Mr. Ramirez turned, saying. "Buenos dias, amigo. Till mañana."

* * *

The old man sat forward and took another sip of rum, "It was a pirate's curse that was put upon me, Ben." He was looking at Ben through distant eyes. "When you have something like this carved into your body, it doesn't take long before someone figures you out. I found it no good to look for the treasure. Everyone was waiting for me to get it or lead them to it. Or skin me alive just to get the map." He took another swig of rum and let out an "Ahh." He wiped his lips and went on with the story.

* * *

Mr. Ramirez started thinking as he walked back to the hotel, *What if it's true? What if he was the boy they were looking for, and if he is, why doesn't he just go get the treasure and get rich?* That question answered it for him, because I was too honest. He would come back to meet anyone if he had promised he would. The thought of it gave him a chill up his spine. How many people know, and how many people will be coming to find him? Pirates coming to his hotel could be bad for business. He felt bad again being greedy. He shook his head again as if to shake that thought out.

Homer is an honest boy, and I should be honest with him, he thought. He walked back to the hotel slower today, thinking about how he would approach him and what he would say. As he entered the lobby, there I was polishing the front of the counter. The floors had all been scrubbed. None of these things he had asked me to do, and this made it even harder. I did these things because I was a hard worker and knew Mr. Ramirez liked it to look good. Mr. Ramirez didn't want to approach me. He liked my hard work ethic and my honesty, and I knew he was afraid of my answer. He knew that it had to be addressed, for this problem could be very dangerous for both of us.

He walked by, saying, "Homer, could I see you in the office?" Just with the tone in his voice, I knew something wasn't right. I followed him back to his office. He slumped into his chair, leaning heavily on his elbows with his hands clasped together. He didn't look me in the eye right off as he started to speak. "Homer, I, uh, don't know uh how to ask this, but I need to ask it, and I need an honest answer from you."

I was getting nervous. Had someone stole from him again? That was what I thought we were leading up to, and was he going to throw me out like Alejandro? I said, "Please ask me. I'll be honest with you."

"Homer, there's that group of sailors that are staying here. They are looking for a young boy that traveled with some pirates, and they say he has a map carved into his body and was to meet any pirates who survived here in Havana."

My face was filled with shock. That was not the question I was expecting at all. I had gotten pretty comfortable here with my little room. The people were nice. I almost forgot about all that business.

He looked me directly in the eye. "Well, Homer?"

I felt I had nothing to lose, so I said, "Yes, Mr. Ramirez, it would be me."

He was the one who looked shocked now. I don't think he expected that answer, nor did he want to hear it. He put his face in his hands and gave a big sigh. "You have a map carved into your skin?" he asked as he pulled his hands away from his face and folded them in front of him as if to pray. He then mumbled, "I had to let a boy go for dishonesty, and now it appears I have to let one go for honesty. Homer, I can't even begin to know how to help you." He talked with a heavy tone as it was breaking his heart. "You're a marked man, Homer. Those men talked as if they would skin you alive to get that map."

I had a whole bunch of emotions welling up in me too. I was welcome here, and people were nice to me and respected me. I ate good and lived good, and now it sounds as if he was going to ask me to leave. Tears welled up in my eyes as the thought of me having to leave was hurting me more than anything.

I was waiting for him to ask to see it or how much treasure there was, but he only asked, "How did you become involved with these men, Homer? You're so young."

I had nothing to lose, and for the first time in my life, I felt this man really cared about my well-being, not just how to exploit me, how to use me, so I told him the whole story. And for the first time in a long time, I didn't lie. Tears ran down my face as I recalled the past, not from the story itself and remembering it but for the ability to let it out without deception. He sat, purely shocked, at the story, amazed that I could even survive all that I did. As I finished, he had sat back, not wanting to believe, but he could tell I was telling the truth. That story could not be just made up.

He sat for a long minute in silence then finally spoke. "These men who were English sailors were Royal Navy but not officially here as such." He stopped again for a second. "So these men are no better than the pirates who took the treasure in the first place. If they find you and then find it, I doubt very much they would return it to England." He then saw the answer, and he said, "Homer, you need to go to England. Explain yourself to their government and help them recover their treasure, and then you would be free." I hadn't thought of that, but that sounded like a noble thing to do and the right thing to do. Of course, return the treasure and be forgiven. He then added, "Then come back here and I'll have your job waiting for you, if you would like to come back?"

I smiled a little at the thought that he would want me to come back. "Mr. Ramirez, you're right," I said. "That is a great idea, and yes, I would like to come back. I hope I haven't caused you any trouble."

He shook his head with a sad look on his face. "No, young man, you haven't caused me any trouble yet, but I am afraid if you stay, those men will cause you trouble. I will save your room, and here," he said, pulling open a drawer. He counted out some money and handed it to me.

I protested. "Mr. Ramirez, you don't owe me anything. You gave me a room to stay in, food, and taught me the hotel business, and all I have done is cause you trouble."

Mr. Ramirez interrupted me. "Homer, you are a hard worker, and these are your earned wages. I will not have you traveling around the world saying Mr. Ramirez is a cheap no-good liar who doesn't keep his word."

I thanked him for everything he had done for me and took the money he graciously offered. I tried to get him to tell Amelia, but he insisted I tell her myself, and he was right again. I also told him I would promote his hotel to all or any royal people I meet. He just laughed and said, "Be careful, amigo. Watch your back." We went to shake hands, and he pulled me in and gave me a big hug. At first I was uncomfortable, but it was so genuine, I couldn't help but hug him back.

I went to my room and packed my seabag. There was a small knock on my door, and when I opened it, there stood Estella. She handed me a wrapped cotton cloth filled with flour tortillas wrapped around chicken and beans, a flak of water, and some corn cakes. I thanked her, but she just waved a gesture for me to go away.

Amelia was harder. We had grown close. She was upset at me for not telling her the whole truth about my past and wondered how much I had lied about. Once she calmed down and I promised I would come back, she said, "Goodbye, funny boy Homer." She kissed me on the cheek, which turned red as her mother and father looked on. She said, "I'll miss you." I was so surprised again and taken off guard. I fumbled my words with her as I usually did.

I said, "I won't miss you." he bristled up, and I corrected myself. "No, I mean I won't forget you or that kiss."

She smiled a big smile and twirled in her cotton dress and waved as I made my way down the street.

It was really hard to leave now, but to stay would put them all in danger, and I couldn't live with myself if anything should happen to any of them. I made my way down to the waterfront, and after a few conversations with some sailors, I was able to find passage to England in return for work aboard ship. It was a passenger ship, something I wasn't accustomed to. There were very rich people called first class to folks like me with no class. My duties aboard ship were not what I was used to. It was cleaning up after the rich folks and getting anything their little hearts desired.

One day, while cleaning the upper decks, I overheard two men talking. Several times in their conversations, they talked about reporting to the king when they returned and giving a report to the admiral. I watched them closely every chance I could. Both were dressed in fine gentlemen's attire and well-groomed. One was younger man with a clean-shaven face, tall, and very fit. His hair was blond, pulled tight behind his head. The other was older, a little plumper, and sported a well-trimmed beard and mustache. I wanted to know who they were, and if I could speak with them, they might be able to help me if they truly knew the king. As I found out from my shipmates, the older man was a duke and the other a high-ranking officer from the Royal Navy. The next day, I tried hard to find a way to get to talk with them. I found myself staring a lot, waiting for a good opportunity so I could do what Mr. Ramirez told me to.

All of a sudden, I was grabbed on my shoulder and spun around. A very large man in a brown uniform stuck his face right in mine. With a growl in his voice, he said, "The duke don't like commoners staring at him, boy, so what are you lookin' at?" I could tell right away this was the bodyguard, and my constant interest in those two men had not gone unnoticed.

I tried to quickly cover and defuse the situation by saying, "I'm sorry, sir, but I had heard there was a duke aboard. I've never seen royalty up close, and I wasn't sure that was him."

The giant of a man squeezed my arm so hard it hurt. He said, "Now you have seen him. Get back to your duties and leave the duke alone."

The duke had shot a look our way indiscreetly as they moved away from the scene that was created. The bodyguard gave me a hard shove as he started to follow the two men. "Now how am I supposed to get close enough to the duke to ask for his help?" I asked myself. I just exhaled in disgust, saying, "Damn, it's always something."

I had spent a couple of days working on a plan, keeping a very low profile. I watched the duke's routines for the day and paid close attention to the bodyguard's movements. I noticed that he always ate alone a little ways away from the duke after the duke ate. I then had an idea, and I started to put it to work. I told the first mate I was having stomach problems. He sent me to the head chef, who many times acted as the doctor for the lower-class folks. I told him I was ailing and hadn't pooped in four days and needed some help. He agreed that that was too long, and he gave me a bottle of cascara oil made from a tree bark just for that reason.

The next morning, I waited for the two men to come for breakfast. The bodyguard came to retrieve the duke's food first and then tasted it to be sure no one had tampered with it. And as the chef prepared the bodyguard's food, I slipped around the corner and poured a dose of the oil in his coffee while no one was looking. I watched intensely as he ate. He finally took a swallow of his coffee and made a puckered face of disapproval and said out loud, "Oh, that's some bitter stuff this monin'." I was afraid he would not drink it, but he downed the whole thing. When he was finished, I ran out to take his dishes away. As I did, he complained about the coffee's taste. I apologized and said that seawater had gotten into the first-class beans and they had to use the third-class beans. He just growled, saying something like "I wonder how they drink that stuff." He snapped his fingers and said, "Get me another cup, but put some sugar in it."

I just smiled from ear to ear, saying, "Yes, sir."

I went to the kitchen and got another cup. I poured another dose into the cup with some sugar and delivered it, thinking this was going way too smooth. Then I went about my other chores and had to hurry because my officer wasn't aware where I was and what I was doing. I did my duties that were across the ship or on another level and then proceeded to do duties where I could keep an eye on the duke and the bodyguard. It took a couple of hours, but finally the bodyguard was holding his stomach. He leaned in to talk with the duke and scurried off as fast as he could. I knew this was my only chance.

I dropped what I was doing, ran up to the duke, dropped to one knee with head bowed, and said, "Please, sir, I need your help. It is an urgent matter which involves the king."

He was surprised, and he put his foot on my shoulder and pushed me to the floor, yelling, "Get away from me, peasant!"

I bounced back to my knees, saying, "Please, sir, you must hear my story. It involves treasure form Bloodthirsty Bob the pirate." He was just about to kick me again but stopped and looked shocked. "Please, sir, I must get word to the king."

He sat back with a curious look and said, "All right, you have thirty seconds to make your case and give me a reason to listen to you at all. And if I'm not impressed, I will have you thrown overboard, and perhaps you can swim to England and tell the king your story yourself."

I immediately said, "Then, sir, I will take these precious seconds to explain that if you throw me overboard, you will lose the only living soul that knows where the English treasures are hidden." I stopped for a second to let that sink in.

He said, "All right, continue. You have my curiosity going now." He leaned forward in his chair.

In my mind, Mr. Ramirez's words rang hard: *Watch your back.* He was right. I said, "When you get to England, ask the admiral about a boy that was held captive on the pirate ship and was brought back to England as a deckhand after they hung the crew of Captain Riggs. I know of this boy, and he has the maps to all the treasures' whereabouts. If you need to check the payment manifest records, they will show he was paid for half the journey."

The duke sat back, curiosity piqued at such a tale, saying, "Then what?"

"I will be at the same dock, we tie up to two weeks after we dock, to meet you. Hopefully that gives you enough time to get with the admiral and then to the king to get the Royal Empire's money back where they belong. Please, sir, for my safety and that of the crown, don't tell anyone of what we just spoke of until you speak with the admiral."

He sat looking at me in wonderment as he stroked his beard. He asked, "What if he has never heard of you?" He smelled of greed as his eyes squinted, and his voice and demeanor changed as he added, "Why don't you tell me where the treasure is, and I'll take it to the king myself."

I answered quickly, "With all due respect, sir, I have orders to tell the king only. National security and all, sir." I added that, feeling pretty smart.

He stood up in a bolt and yelled, "Whose orders?" His anger was growing at not being trusted.

"I was instructed not to say, sir," I answered quickly.

"Very well," he said, slamming his hand down on the table. "What's your name, peasant?" he ordered.

Humbly, I answered, "Homer, sir."

The duke pushed me over with his foot again and growled at me as he said, "Well, Homer, you insolent little shit, if he has not heard of your tale, I will hunt you down in two weeks and hang you for treason. Do you understand?"

As I started to get up, all of a sudden, I was hit in the head. It sent me crashing into a table. The bodyguard grabbed me by the arm and then crushed me in a bear hug to the point breathing wasn't an option.

"Shall I throw him overboard, Your Highness?" he asked, only too willing for a yes.

But the duke jumped up, held out his hand, and yelled, "No, no, don't, uh, put him down. I know this boy won't be bothering me anymore this trip, will you, boy?" I was shaking my head in agreement but couldn't even squeak out an answer. The duke said again, "Let him go."

The burly man threw me to the deck hard and kicked me away from their area. I limped away, trying to catch my breath. I couldn't help but turn around and yelled, "Hey, you big gorilla, what's a matter, your coffee giving you tummy problems?" Just then, the big guy figured it out and came rushing my way, bulldozing through chairs and tables. I quickly dove into the nearest companionway and down belowdecks, losing him easily. I spent the rest of my voyage mostly belowdecks and hiding form the duke and his big dog.

When we finally reached England, I had positioned myself in the crow's nest atop the main mast, watching the passengers disembark. I finally saw the duke go down the gangplank to the shore, where a carriage waited with several people to greet him. His bodyguard waited at the gangplank and did not get off the ship. The duke's carriage never left either. They watched all the passengers disembark. They were very intent on watching the crowd. I finally decided they were looking for me. They waited a long time. In fact, I was getting very hungry and tired. Bored would be more like it. I fell asleep for a while, and when I woke, it was dark. I looked out at the pier and could only make out what the few oil lamps placed along the pier would illuminate. I could make out two large men standing by the plank, and they weren't crew members, so I assumed they were looking for me for the duke. I climbed down the crow's nest and made my way below to grab my gear. I put it over my shoulder and walked, whistling a tune just like I owned England itself. They turned and stood at the ready and watched me come down.

I greeted them with a smile. "Evenin', gents," I said briskly.

And one tipped his head, but the other grabbed my arm, saying, "Hey, swab, we're lookin' for a young man about your age. Works on this tub. What's your name, boy?"

Without hesitation, I said, "Cecile Reginald Augustine Goodin, sir. What's yours?"

He spoke sternly, "We're lookin' for Homer."

I smiled. "Oh, Homer, yes, he works here. Are you relatives here to pick him up?"

They looked at each other, and the nice one said, "Yes, we're his cousins. We promised Auntie we would give him a lift home."

The other butted in, "So do you know where he is? We've been waiting quite a while."

I nodded and delivered a very convincing lie. "Yes, he will be coming along shortly. We just got done and were okay for leave. He shouldn't be long. He's packin' his gear right now. Well, you gentlemen have a nice night." And with that, I walked away. I didn't run, although my heart and legs wanted to, but I carelessly walked out of sight.

Now I knew where I stood with this duke. He was not a man of his word, and I wondered about his integrity. Would he be loyal to his king or loyal to his greed? I had two weeks, and I figured I would spend that time trying to find a way to see the king without him. I found a quiet little corner in a dark alley and curled up for the night. It had been a few years since I had to sleep in those conditions. I didn't realize how uncomfortable it was and how soft I had become. I did finally fall to sleep though. I was awakened abruptly by a business owner beating me with a broom, yelling for me to get away from his store and calling me a vagrant and other rude comments. I felt kind of bad at first and then saw several other folks being pushed out of their makeshift hotels also.

It was a typical cold drizzly day in England, especially compared to where I just came from. It wasn't my favorite place. I didn't spend much time there before, and I was hoping not to spend a lot of time here again. The people were very kind for the most part. I did find a small hostel and got a bed. I found my way to some water and proceeded to clean myself up in case I found someone to help me find a way to see the king. I tried asking around to some local people how to get an audience with the king. Most would look at me like I was crazy and then laugh out loud when they saw I was serious. One food vendor at the market, when I asked him, looked at me and, in a matter-of-fact kind of way, said, "You must murder a diplomat, and I bet you will get an audience from the king."

As he handed me my bread and cheese, an older man said, "I don't think that's wise advice, young man. First, you must go to the palace. I am headed that way, if you would like me to show you the way? If you are truly serious about the king and you're not some crazy assassin, I could possibly help you." I felt my burden lifted a little as I felt this man could help me.

I answered, "Yes, I would appreciate that very much."

"Then follow me," he said as he hobbled a bit.

I just obediently followed. I was asking him where I might find the admiral if the king wasn't available and how I should go about seeing the king, but he avoided my questions by trying to get answers from me, asking me where I was from and what my business was with the king. And neither one of us answered enough to get a decent answer. We wound around through cobblestone streets until we came to a very large castle. We walked along the outside walls then came to a small door just behind some bushes. The old crippled man, looking very suspiciously, pulled out some keys and fumbled with them until he found the right one. Then looking around again to check to see if anyone was watching, he unlocked the little door. He swung it open and signaled me to enter.

I was a little shocked and asked, "How did you come by this key?"

He laughed a quirky little laugh and said with a sly grin, "I'm the master groundskeeper."

Inside the door was a very long small tunnel. I could see a light at the end. I had to stoop a bit to get down. I figured that the old man was bent over so bad from walking this tunnel for so many years. As I stepped into the corridor, the man turned around and locked the door. It was very dark, but the light at the end gave a position to go by.

As we walked, he said, "I have a few things to attend to." And then he would show me a way to the king's area. As we entered into the light of the large courtyard inside the walls of the castle, the man held out his arm to me and said, "Wait right here please." I surveyed the area, large as it was. Guards were everywhere up on the wall, down around the wall, and all focused their stares on me. I was starting to feel a little uncomfortable. The man went up to one of the guards and pointed to me. As he was talking, the guard signaled another, and several started to walk toward me.

When they got to me, one guard said, "Mr. Goodin, you are under arrest by orders of the Duke of Cambridge, and you are to follow me."

I started to take two steps backward. As I did, they all drew their weapons. I threw up my hands in front, saying, "Wait a minute, you don't understand. I'm here to see the king of England about great important matters of the state."

I wanted to run down the tunnel, and the guard knew it because he said, "Please, there is nowhere to go. Just come with me."

I wanted to bolt so bad down that tunnel, but I forgot the one thing I was supposed to do was watch my back, and I let that old scallywag lock it behind me. That old scallywag sold me out. Why? And for what? How did he even know who I was? I was careful not to tell my name or where I was from. This made me kind of angry, and out of reaction, the guard reached for my arm. I bolted down on the off chance maybe the door wasn't really locked. But as luck would have, it was locked, and the guards didn't even bother to chase me.

The one who approached me first said, "Please, sir, there is no way out. Just come with us."

I came back out slowly, and as I emerged from the shadows, they seized me and dragged me to a dungeon. They tossed me in a cold and damp cell, and a small light shone through a small slit about twenty feet above my head. The floor was rock, the walls were rock, and there was nowhere to sit but on the floor. I started to feel a little sorry for myself. Having done nothing wrong, I have spent my share of time in jails. Time seemed like forever, and I only assumed that when the light disappeared from the slit in the wall that the sun had gone down. And when it appeared again, I assumed I had spent the night. Finally, after a long time of silence, I heard footsteps walking down the hall.

Then a voice said, "Stand away from the door."

So I did, then I heard the rustling of keys. And as the door creaked open, two guard rushed in and took me on each arm and, almost running, dragged me, my feet only touching once in a while as I tried to keep up. Upstairs and downstairs along long corridors, I couldn't have found my way back if I had to. We finally came to a large pillared doorway with two massive arched doors and two guards at attention at each door. They swung each one open as we approached. We entered a large room with an assembly of men all sitting in a line. They were all mumbling. About ten altogether were looking as regal as they could. They all started to quiet as I entered. Just to the right of the duke was my little scallywag friend, and to his left was my dear old friend the bodyguard. They marched me right up to the duke and threw me at his feet. My heart was pounding, and I kept bowed before him, keeping my eyes to the floor.

After a few seconds of silence, the duke finally spoke up. "Well, Homer, we meet again. A little sooner than the two weeks you wanted, but here just the same. Quit cowering and stand up and look at me!" he commanded. That sent a rush of anger through me because he was right. I was cowering, so I swallowed hard, took a breath, and remembered what Captain Riggs said; look a man in the eye and demand respect. He continued to talk. "That's better. I want you to know I talked with the admiral, and the king and instructed me to handle this matter myself. So I will need you to tell me what you know." I knew he was lying. I especially knew when he said, "Just tell us where the boy that has the map is." If he had talked with the admiral, he would have known that Homer was the boy with the map, and it would be carved on his hide, not carried around like some idiot with a piece of paper.

"I'm sorry, sir, but that boy was going to meet me at the docks in two weeks after I had spoken to the king."

His face started to turn red, and his words grew stronger. "Did you not hear me, boy? The king said I should handle this myself.

Now tell me the information or I'll have you flogged until you do." A panic ran through me for a second. He would first see my scars and figure it out, or he will mess the map up with a whipping.

I started to think how to get out of this, saying, "Sir, he told me he would only talk with the king. He knew something like this would happen, and if I don't go that day and show the right signal, he will leave and not return the treasure. That's what he said."

The duke, enraged now, yelled, "Something like this would happen? You little insolent pauper!" He threw his goblet of wine across the room. He marched down and pulled me to my feet and got right in my face, growling the words, "Maybe I'll just hang you today for treason."

I interjected through my gritted teeth from the pain, "If you do, you will be hanging the only way to get your treasure back."

The duke was going to work me now, asking, "Why doesn't this smart boy go get the treasure himself?"

"I don't know," I said. "Maybe he's loyal to the crown."

He shook me by my hair, saying, "What's in it for you, lad, huh?"

"I owed him my life. He saved me once at sea during a violent storm." That lie rolled off my tongue so smooth I believed it myself.

His fury was building so much he was starting to shake. He continued with the questions. "Why were you trying to see the king on your own instead of waiting for me in two weeks?" He bent my head back hard, looking me in the eyes. "Don't you trust me, boy?"

I didn't hesitate for a moment on that question. "No, sir, I don't!" The other men watching all gasped at my answer.

The duke felt the embarrassment of my answer and then back-handed me across the face, sending me to the floor. He then kicked me in the stomach, rolled me over, and yelled, "I am the eyes and ears to the king in this kingdom! I don't need a snot-nosed little peasant like yourself telling me where my loyalty lie. This is how it is going to happen, boy. I will keep you locked up until our rendezvous date. You will cooperate fully with me and me only. We will retrieve this treasure for the crown. If anything goes wrong, boy, I will have you tortured to the point of almost death, and then I will have a doctor

COCKROACHES IN THE BILGE

fix you up and do it again until I get bored with it." The men watching laughed a little, finding that amusing. "But if you are successful, I
will forgive you for your last comment and just hang you, make your
death fast and painless." The men around the room all agreed as they
nodded. I realized that I pushed a little too far this time. He stomped
back to his chair, yelling, "Take him away! I'm tired of looking at this
pathetic pauper!"

I was marched back to my cell, or should I say dragged with my
feet trying to catch up. And then they threw me in. I sat there, mind
racing. *How am I going to get out of this?* I laughed to myself a little
as I thought I didn't have to find a place to stay for a few nights. The
days dragged on, and my mind still raced. I started to feel the strain
of life, and death was nearing.

My thoughts were interrupted when at my cell door, a voice
yelled, "Back away from the door!"

I did, and two guards charged in, dragging me by my arms back
to the duke's chamber. This time, there were only three men with the
duke—the old scallywag that turned me in and two men that look
like soldiers. The duke waited for the guards to release me and then
left the room, closing the door.

Then the duke spoke. "Well, Homer, today is the day we go see
your secret friend. But I want to make you a deal. When you meet
with this traitor to the crown, I want you to give a signal to these two
men who will be watching you closely. If we are able to apprehend
this man, I will consider letting you go free, after we find the stolen
currency."

"What if he won't talk to me because he suspects something?" I
asked quietly, still bowed on the ground and on my knees.

"Once we have you both in custody, Homer, it will be easy to
get you both to talk. And if you are separated, it will be easy to see
who is lying also." He was so sure of himself, I was getting very nervous. The duke was a very clever guy, for my biggest problem was I
didn't have anyone to talk to, and if I just grabbed someone off the
street to pretend to talk to, they would be arrested also. It wouldn't
take long for the duke to figure out what I had done. "Now be off
with you," he ordered. "And remember, Homer, it's your life we're

talking about here." He laughed a little as he motioned for the guards to take me. They grabbed me and walked me through the castle and out that sneaky little door I came in through. They tossed me out on to the ground and shut it behind me. I found this very curios.

I looked around and found myself alone outside the castle walls, and I started walking in the direction of the piers. It wasn't long before the two undercover soldiers were within sight, one up ahead on horseback and one trailing far behind on foot. I had to admit, they were pretty good at it. I had a lot of time to think as I made my way down to the water front. It made me angry that I fell into such a stupid trap with that scallywag of a sneaky spy. And luck would have it that I would run into a duke, who wasn't loyal to his king. My mind was spinning with ideas, but none that looked feasible I was sure there were more than two soldiers watching me anyway. Now to come up with a fictitious friend without incriminating an innocent bystander. When we got to town, I figured I would get cleaned up a little, get some new clothes, and eat my last meal. And so I did. I told them all I was a special guest of the duke's and he sent me here for some clothes and a bath and some food. At first they questioned me, but I quickly pointed out the soldiers guarding my every move, and they all seemed to understand and allowed me the credit. So I ate like a king. The guards were getting anxious, but I still hadn't come up with a plan yet. When I finished eating, I made my way down to the waterfront and started to walk up and down. It was very busy with people from all walks of life. I was walking along, studying this one ship, when I passed a well-dressed lady and realized as I met her gaze how beautiful she was. And she in turn recognized me.

She stopped. "Why, Homer," she said. "My little assistant. What are you doing so far from home?"

I stopped dead in my tracks, shocked she remembered me at all. But it was Mrs. Hernandez from the hotel. A shock or panic ran through me. I couldn't talk to her, not now.

She reached out and stroked my coat, saying, "You look good."

I quickly said, "I'm sorry, madam, you must be mistaken."

She looked surprised and knew she was right, and she smiled that melting smile "Oh, Homer, you funny boy. Why are you here in England?"

I could see the soldiers closing in, taking a great interest in the meeting. I pleaded with her. "Please, Mrs. Hernandez, I'm not Homer today. I can't explain right now, but I need you to not talk to me or know me right now."

She said, "How did you know my name then, Mr. Stranger?" Then she giggled, pulling a handkerchief out of her sleeve.

I was saying, "You should leave me, Mrs. Hernandez. It was indeed a pleasure to see you though."

With that she dropped her handkerchief. And out of habit, I reached down and picked it up. The soldiers took that as a signal she was handing me something and pulled their swords and rushed us. Just as I thought, more soldiers came out of their hiding places. I noticed this as I handed it back to her.

She just started to thank me when the soldiers distracted her, yelling, "Stay where you are! Don't move!" She stared to realize we were being surrounded. I tried to explain she wasn't who they thought it was, but no one was listening to me.

I kept hollering, "She's not the one!" But they reached in and seized her by both arms, and a carriage a mobile cage for carrying prisoners came ripping around the corner. She was protesting their handling of her, and they had me by both arms as I was screaming also. Then they threw us in the back of the wagon and slammed and locked the door. Mrs. Hernandez was in shock as she sat on the floor of the carriage, for it was too short to stand. The wagon raced so fast, all we could do was hang on with both hands as it raced through town.

Mrs. Hernandez looked at me, and then her shock wore off. In an instant, anger overtook her face. She was still just as beautiful but a little scary. All she said was "What did you get me into, Homer? What...what have you done?" I tried to explain, but she was so in shock. None of what I was saying entered her mind. All she could do was hang on, scream a little on big bumps, and say, "Homer, what have you done?"

We rounded a sharp corner, and two large doors opened to the castle. The walls were high and heavily guarded. She continued to ask questions without waiting for answers, like "Why are we at the castle? We just had dinner with the duke last night. Why has he brought me here?" As they opened the doors to the carriage, she bolted out, yelling, "I want to see the duke this instant!" The duke's little scallywag snitch was there, looking very greedy, but his face changed immediately as Mrs. Hernandez stepped out. Her dress was a mess, and her hat was hanging awkwardly off of her hair that had fallen from the well-placed style she had it in earlier. I stayed curled up in the corner while brushing the dirt and straw from her dress as she ranted. He was over there apologizing, tripping over himself as he pushed the guards out of the way. He was groveling like the rodent he was.

"Countess Hernandez...I'm so sorry." Then he turned, spitting fire at the guards as he yelled at them, "Get back! What is the meaning of this? Who is responsible for this?" He grabbed Mrs. Hernandez by the hand. "Please let me get you to another location while I straighten this out."

She ripped her hand away and said, "Just get me to the duke at once!"

He turned and yelled, "I want everyone involved to be in the meeting chambers immediately!"

All the guards started to run around, almost in a confused state and knowing something was very wrong. They were sure they would all pay the price. I stayed very quiet in the corner of the wagon, and as the guard in charge started to get his men in control by ordering them around and get that wagon out of here, he yelled. So a guard jumped aboard, and we went for a stable area, the back door still unlocked and waving in the breeze. It pulled in, and the driver jumped out and unhooked the horses and removed all their tack. He threw it in a corner and ran off, I was assuming, to get to the meeting room. It was awfully quiet, so I stood up and started to look out the wagon, giving a faint "Hello."

"Hello," I said a little louder. There was no sound other than that of the horses. I eased myself out of the wagon and made my way to the door. I looked out cautiously. To my surprise, only one guard was in sight. The main gate sat open, and he was waiting as if for someone to come by. I sat with my conscience for a while. They obviously forgot about me. It won't be long before someone remembers.

* * *

The old man sat forward again. "Well, Ben, what would you do? Take this opportunity to leave or go try and help the most beautiful woman in the world explain herself?"

Ben laughed a little before he answered, "It sounds to me like she could take care of herself. I would leave."

The old man laughed out loud and took another swallow from the jug. "Excellent answer. That's exactly what I did." He bounced on the bed, slapping his knee. He laid back and went back to telling his tale.

* * *

I went in and turned the horses loose and shooed them out of the barn. And as they came charging out, the guard at the gate turned around, realized they were loose, and tried desperately to corral all of them. As he was busy, I slowly and calmly walked out the front gate. I traveled as far away as I could, as fast as I could. I was mindful to never let anyone see me with my shirt off or ever mention my stories of the pirate ship or treasure.

I traveled on merchant ships around the world. As time went on, I heard all sorts of sea stories about Bloodthirsty Bob and Mr. Riggs, about how they drew their treasure maps on the skins of children, and as the years went on, the stories got better and better. I finally saved up some money and decided to go in search of one of the treasures. The ship I was on at the time was heading to one of the areas, so I got off at a small island nearby and found a little skiff and went in search. It took me some time to try to read the map off my chest, but after a couple of days, I managed to locate it. I celebrated and took just enough to buy my own ship. Then I buried the rest back where I found it. I went back to England to find me a nice merchant ship. I wasn't worried about going to England due to the fact I was older, and Homer Gregoreouse no longer existed. Reginald Roach was there to purchase a ship. I found one, a three masted schooner. It was fast and had a large capacity for freight. I named her *Charee*, for the Countess Charee Hernandez. I chose my crew carefully and sailed with them for a couple of years to get to know them. When I had whittled down those that could be trusted and replaced those who couldn't, I let my crew in on my secret and told them if they were to be quiet about me, I would share the treasure. They all agreed, and I took a small band of men ashore one day and dug it back up. We had the time of our lives. Some quit the sea altogether and moved ashore, but we all lived well.

* * *

"But alas, I outlived most of them. Some never got to enjoy theirs. A young lad your age was swept overboard in a storm off the coast of Australia. Now there's a place, boy, very interesting. Would love to get back down there. As I sailed all over the world, I grew old, too old to run a ship. Someone said the new colonies of the Americas were the place to be, so here I came. *Charee* continued to work, and every once in a while, I would take a trip on her. But you know, lad, it's like riding your favorite horse. It's just not the same if you're the passenger while someone else has the reigns. Then one day, I realized that I was very old." His eyes rolled back in his head, and they had that look Ben had seen many times in this house. "I don't have much time left, Ben. Been here way too long as it is. Why, at the rate the population is growing around here, they push me off the edge before long anyway."

Ben didn't say anything. He used to sit and tell the old people that it would be all right, that they had a long time left, but he had learned that most of the time, they were very right and usually didn't last much longer. They were trying to tell you something in their vast age of wisdom, and all you could do was deny them the truth.

The old seaman took one more long sip on the jug and dropped it between his knees and said, "I want you to have the map, Ben."

Ben's eyes got huge as he sat back a bit from the news. Ben wasn't sure what he just heard, and he asked, "What...map...where?"

The old man looked shocked, shaking his head back and forth, saying, "Haven't you been listening to a damn thing I've said?" Ben felt a little silly because he was listening, and he started to realize what he had said. "I've been talking for six hours. It was important." His voice was getting louder.

Ben held out his hand to stop him from ranting, saying, "Yes... yes, I understand. I didn't realize there was more treasure."

The old sailor's eyes got big. "Ben, there's more treasure out there than you can even imagine. I only looked for two and lived happily ever after, as well as a crew of fifty men. It's out there, Ben, if you want. Do you want it?" The old man sat, staring at Ben with an intense stare.

Ben answered shyly, not really sure what he was agreeing to. The old man leaned in close to Ben and said in a rhythmic voice like a song:

> The way to English riches
> Are found throughout my stitches.
> Not on paper or tablet
> Or chiseled into stone
> But carved into me hide
> Deep down to the bone
> Each dot or dash or symbol that you see
> Helps you find the lost and hidden treasury
> The cuts and gouges are not just scars
> But the legend and directions according to the
> stars
> It takes you too many mysterious places then
> It gives you directions and how many paces.
> The paces are set at four feet six inches
> But don't get discouraged some paces were
> different.

I've only found a couple but many remain
So get yourself going to find riches and fame.

Then he whipped off his gown, exposing his whole body, and started to explain how the map read. He pointed out the two he had already found, and Ben could see where he had actually carved a line through them as not to forget. Ben started to see the deliberate pattern. It wasn't just random scarring at all.

He laughed a wheezy laugh and said, "I can see it in your eyes, boy. You're getting it, and you're thinking about it too. The treasure you can almost smell it." Ben didn't answer the old sailor, but this old man was sharp. He was right.

Ben was already picturing the treasure in his hands. His mind racing and wheeling about it, he only answered quietly, "Yes."

The old sailor said, "Well, then, boy go get some paper and a piece of coal." Ben was studying the map so hard, he didn't hear the old man. The old man slapped Ben upside the head. Ben jumped back, rubbing the side of his head. "Go, boy, we don't have much time."

"What?" Ben grimaced at the old man.

Talking slow as to a child, the sailor said again, "Paper and charcoal. Get it now." Ben started to jump up, and the old man said, "Here." He held up the jug. "Best put this back before you mom misses this. She will be up soon."

Ben looked out the small window in the room to outside. It was starting to get light. "Oh my." Ben sighed. "We've been talking all night."

The old man laughed a little, and as he coughed a chocking cough, he grunted out, "Well, I know for a fact that I have." He seemed to have a hard time getting his breath. Ben got concerned and sat him up, patting his back, but the old man pushed him off, saying between coughs, "Go! Go! Get the paper and coal. Hurry."

Ben ran out and down the hall. He quickly put the rum away then went about getting the paper and coal. Then he ran back to the old sailor's room. He looked pale now and a bit out of breath, but he managed to wave Ben into the room. He gestured for him to give him the paper and coal. Ben understood and handed it to him.

He choked out a few words. "Watch me." And he laid back, placing the paper on his body and lightly rubbing the paper with the coal. The map transferred itself onto the paper. "Do you understand?" the old man asked Ben. Ben nodded a yes, and the old man said, "Here." And he handed a letter to Ben. He removed a gold chain with a key on it from around his neck and handed it to Ben.

Ben looked confused at the gifts and started to ask, "What is this?"

The old man interrupted him. "Just do what the letter says and get this map copied right away. And, Ben." His eyes started to tear up a bit. "Thanks, boy. It was really nice to meet you." He coughed so hard and appeared he wouldn't get his breath again, but he managed to wheeze out, "Good luck in your adventures, boy." He grabbed Ben's hand with his, a weak grip compared to the vibrant and tough old sailor he encountered just a few hours before. The old man leaned back comfortably and then appeared to stop breathing altogether.

Ben sat bewildered for a minute, waiting for the next breath, but it didn't come. Ben then felt a bit anxious. "Hey, Captain," he said plainly. "You all right?" Then he felt a rush of panic. "Captain, Captain," he said, shaking him a little, but no response.

He was no stranger to death in this house, but he wasn't so used to them going so fast. It usually showed itself coming for days. This old man was showing all the signs of death. Ben reached up and pulled down on the old man's eyes, closing them completely. He then rolled him on his side a bit and sat back, staring at the old man whom he had sat for the last ten hours, listening to one of the most surprising stories he had ever heard. And in less than a second, the story and storyteller were gone. He was about to just go tell his mom that the old man had died. As he stood up, he saw the letter again and the key on the folded letter.

It said, "To my great-grandson Benjamin Summit." The handwriting was very legible and eloquent, not fitting of a dying, feeble old man. Then it dawned on Ben. When would he have written this? He didn't do it while he was there, and he didn't even have any paper.

Ben sat down again slowly and opened it. After all, it was addressed to him.

> I, Homer Gregoreouse, also known as Captain Reginald Roach, being of sound mind and body and soul, bequeath my worldly possessions to Mr. Benjamin Fredrick Summit, my great-grandson and only heir to my belongings.

There were two signatures at the end of this simple letter.

> Homer Gregoreouse
> Captain Reginald Roach.

Ben laughed. "That old coot," he said to himself. He had been living his whole life under an alias. Under the signature was a dark line. Under it was a note that read:

> Remove this note from this paper, Ben. Take the upper written part to Hieman and Harsgrove lawyers in town. They will tell you the rest of the story. But follow these instructions exactly as they're written. Call a mortician immediately upon my death and have my remains cremated *right away*! I hate to do this to you, boy, but you need to clean me up yourself and get me dressed. Tell them I want to be burned in the clothes I'm wearing and that you want to watch and be there to see your poor grandfather off. If no one sees the scars, it's just possible the curse will die with me. There are still people who believe the stories their grandfathers have told and know there is still treasure out there that hasn't been found. So quit wasting time, boy, reading all day. Get this bloody map copied and do what your told. Time is running out. That's an order, sailor.

Ben almost felt like the old man was still alive as he read this note. He could almost hear his voice barking the order. He quickly snapped to and started to copy the map as he had been shown. He realized that two pieces were not going to be enough. He went to the kitchen to grab some more. As he busted into the kitchen, he didn't notice his mom right off. He was in such a hurry. She was surprised as he busted into the kitchen with a start.

She was just tying her apron and let out a small "Oh," jumping a bit. This time of morning, no one was up but her, getting things ready for breakfast. Ben stopped in his tracks, looking as guilty as a condemned man could. She asked immediately, "What are you doing up so early, Ben?"

That's when she noticed Ben's studies were still on the table. Ben stood speechless as he tried to decide whether or not to involve his mom in this strange turn of events, especially when he wasn't sure what to make of it. But he answered her as honestly as he could without giving away too much. "I uh…uhm was studying and got very interested and lost track of time."

"My," she said. "What could possibly be that interesting?"

Ben's mind reeled for a second. "History," he blurted out. "History."

She could tell he wasn't telling the whole truth. She surveyed the area while he picked up his stuff, looking for a something that might give her more clues. She didn't see it, and Ben finished gathering up his stuff and quickly shuffled off papers and dropping them in his haste. He tried to pick them up fast so she wouldn't have an opportunity to ask another question. But he wasn't fast enough. She fired a point-blank question. "What was the history subject?"

"Piracy on the high seas," he shot back at her as he hurried out of the room. She felt that was an honest answer but not complete enough. Call it mother's intuition. Ben hollered out as he made his way down the hall, "Love you, Mom! I'm gonna try to sleep for a while then come help."

He melted her frustration and concern with that one little word, so she let it go…for now. She went about making breakfast for the twenty-five or so guests. Ben ducked into the captain's room and carefully went about transferring the maps off the old man's body. Ben's mom saw her next clue when she noticed the cabinet where the rum was stored was not closed tightly as usual. Then before she closed it, she looked inside. Everything on the shelf was pushed to one side, exposing the rum jug which is never visible without moving everything first. She reached in and pulled it from the shelf and gasped at how light it was and how much was missing. Pure anger boiled inside as she slammed the jug on the counter. She was talking to herself as she marched down the hall to confront him. All the lectures about drinking...he and that Jackie no doubt drinking till all hours. If he thought he was gonna sleep this one off, he had another thing coming.

"He'll work this off today," she was saying as she came to his room. She threw the door open and said, "Get your fanny out of bed, mister." She would have said more, but his room was empty. She stood puzzled as she surveyed the empty room. Still mad, she went looking for him, calling his name quietly but with a notable anger in her voice, looking in rooms as she went by.

The only sound she heard was the occasional cough or some old confused person yelling back, "What, what do you want?"

Not being Ben's voice, she paid them no mind. Almost all the guests room doors were either open or cracked a hair. She passed the old captain's room. The door was shut and quiet. She got to the end of the hall and returned to his door. She opened it slowly and quietly, only to gasp at the sight of Ben standing over the old man who looked very dead, and Ben with his piece of paper and rubbing charcoal over it. Several papers scattered on the bed. Ben was surprised also as his mother had entered the room with a gasp.

"Benjamin, what on God's earth are you doing!" she blurted out.

Ben jumped away from the bed, holding his hands up in front of him as if to stop a charging horse, saying, "Now, Mom, wait a minute! Please listen."

She cut him off as she stomped forward, snatching up one of the pieces of paper. "Listen to what, Benjamin? What are you doing?" Her forehead wrinkled in confused horror.

"Mom, please," he pleaded as he reached for her hand and took his map out before she could smear it. He turned her at the same time and reached up and shut the door. He was whispering now. "Here, read this and then let me explain." He handed her the letter the captain had written. She stood reading it, still a confused look on her face.

"His great-grandson? I don't understand. Where did you get this?" She was shaking the letter in her hand. "And leave you what?" she asked and then remembered the rum. "And what were you doing up all night drinking the rum?"

Ben could see her anger growing. He blurted out, "It wasn't me, Mom. It was him." He pointed to the captain.

"This frail old man, now dead old man, thanks to you, no doubt. And what are you doing to him now?"

Ben's voice raised a bit. "Mom, please stop and give me a chance to explain!"

She crossed her arms, squinted an eye, pursed her lips, and said, "Fine, Benjamin, explain yourself." Ben went into a condensed version of what the captain had told him, and he tried to explain that he couldn't tell it the same as the old man had last night. She was just as bewildered as before. She looked at the letter again as she had calmed a bit, and as Ben told his story, she realized she got money monthly from the law firm Hieman and Harsgrove. Now she was interested as he got into the story. Ben could see her shoulders relax a bit and could see in her face that she was calming down a little. He decided this was a good time to explain that the captain was so full of life, even jumping up and down on the bed. He had asked, no, ordered him to get the rum and how he couldn't believe how alive he was one minute and gone the next. The story was long, even by short standards. After about a twenty-minute speech, she could see in her heart that Ben believed everything the captain had told him. She could also see that he was excited and the idea of treasure and the high seas was in his eyes. This was a time she knew was coming. She could see her baby was growing up. And she couldn't count on him to be there forever. Ben rattled on about how the map worked and the scars telling the story, but all she could hear was his longing to go on an adventure. How could she blame a young man? Why would he want to stay here and play nursemaid to a bunch of old dying people? Chasing pirate treasure was much more intriguing.

Ben must have finished the story, for he stopped talking and asked, "Well, what should I do?"

She just looked into his sparkling eyes filled with excitement. "If that was the old man's last wish, Ben, then I think you should grant it." Her heart sank in her chest and felt heavy with burden.

Ben couldn't see that. He just said in an excited voice, "Oh, thank you, Mom. Thank you…and you know if the treasure is real and I do find it, someday you can quit working." She just turned to leave, and Ben whispered, "Hey, Mom, remember, don't tell a soul."

She turned back around, made a motion with her hand like buttoning a button on her lips, and went back to the kitchen, fighting tears back as she went. Ben continued to copy all the maps from the captain's frail body. His mind was racing from how to get there and what kind of house to buy his mom. In his haste, he realized that the charcoal prints smeared easily and that he would have to be careful until he redid them on other paper. When he had finished copying the maps, he dressed Captain Reginald Roach into some clothes he had on the shelf. It was a quality outfit that fit rather loosely. *He probably lost weight since he came here*, Ben thought. Once cleaned up and dressed, Ben thought he looked pretty good. He then covered him up with a sheet, patted his chest lightly, and thanked him quietly. Ben then made his way into town and got hold of a mortician. He explained that the captain's last wishes were to have his body cremated with his suit on. The mortician didn't see a problem with that at all, and he would come get the body today and would cremate it in the next three days.

Ben panicked at the sound of that and said, "But the captain was insistent that it be today. He said something about a curse he had carried with him for a long time and was worried if he stayed around for long, it would carry over to another living soul and haunt them till their dying day."

The stern-faced mortician looked at Ben with a curious look and asked, "What kind a curse you talking 'bout, boy?"

Ben squinted his eyes and made a hideous face as he explained, "It's a disease of the skin. Doctors don't know what it is. They can't cure it. Every time he's around any woman, he swells up, and his skin starts to fester like a bad blister. That's why he never married. No woman would have him." The man was making a face, mimicking Ben's as Ben said, "You come get him soon 'cause I don't want to be around him if it's catchy."

The man was looking at Ben for a short second then said, "Let's go get him and do it right away."

Ben said he would meet him at the home in a couple of hours. Then Ben made his way to the lawyer's office. He walked into the building and went up a few stairs. The door had the correct names on it, so he knocked a few hard raps.

A voice form inside said loudly but pleasantly, "Please come in."

Ben opened the door. There was a man sitting behind a large desk. Books lined the walls. He was a small man wearing a powdered wig, writing away with a quill pen. He was dressed in a finely tailored suit and ruffled shirt around the chest and cuffs. Ben quietly stepped in and closed the door quietly behind him. There was an unnerving quiet about the place except for the scratching of the pen on the paper. The fellow had small round glasses that sat on the end of his nose. He found a place to stop writing and looked up over the glasses at Ben and said, "Yes, how may I help you, lad?" He squeezed a slight smile onto his face as if it were practiced but not genuine.

Ben was a little nervous as he started to hand the man the paper from the captain and explained, "I was supposed to give this to Mr. Hieman and Harsgrove, sir." The man raised his head a little more and extended his hand to receive the document. "I'm sorry, sir, but I am to give it to Mr. Hieman or Mr. Harsgrove only, sir."

"Well, my sincere apologies, sir." He retrieved his hand and stood up, saying, "Mr. Harsgrove, attorney at law, at your service, sir. I hope you don't mind doing business with me because Mr. Heiman has been deceased for several years now."

Ben, a bit embarrassed, said, "No, that's fine." He handed Mr. Harsgrove the paper.

Mr. Harsgrove sat back down, adjusted his glasses a bit, and began to read. His face was sober. His eyebrows then raised then crinkled into the center. He turned the paper over to look at the back. He saw nothing then looked over his glasses at Ben. "Where did you get this?" he asked, very perplexed.

"He gave it to me last night, sir."

Mr. Harsgrove sat back, looking at Ben. "Huh, what am I supposed to do with this?" he asked Ben.

Ben was confused and replied, "I'm not sure, sir. He made it sound like you would know how to help me."

Mr. Harsgrove sat forward again. "And whom may I ask are you, sir?"

"Benjamin Summit, sir," Ben answered, feeling silly. He had even come into this place. Mr. Harsgrove's face softened, and he stood up.

"Well, Mr. Summit, it is indeed a pleasure to see meet you." He held out his hand to shake hands with Ben. Ben stood up right away and bent a little at the waist and shook hands with Mr. Harsgrove.

Ben returned the sentiment. "It's good to meet you, sir."

"Well, please sit down, Mr. Summit. We have a lot to talk about. I am aware of Captain Reginald Roach but was not aware that his name was also Homer Gregoreouse. Although that name is familiar to me also, but it seems to me that Captain Reginald Roach purchased the merchant ship *Charee* from Homer Gregoreouse."

"Yes, yes, that's correct," Ben interjected.

"Captain Roach is still at the home. At least that's where I send the money each month."

"That is correct, sir." Ben thought for a second then said, "Or did until last night."

Mr. Harsgrove looked up at Ben, asking, "What do you mean by that?"

Ben sounded very solemn as he said, "He died last night."

The lawyer sat back in his chair. "Well, I'm sorry to hear that, son. He was one of my first clients. And you say he gave you this last night?"

"Yes, sir," Ben answered.

"And then died last night?" He was asking questions now like a lawyer would.

Ben answered again, "That is correct, sir," as if he were under oath.

"So we might say he was of sound mind but not of body, as it is stated in this document. Would you agree, Mr. Summit?" He was staring at Ben over the top of his glasses.

Ben gave thought to what this man just asked and replied, "Yes, I guess you could say that."

The lawyer sat back with his hand on his chin and let out a noise like hum. Then he said, "I need a little time to look into this matter. Do you mind waiting?"

Ben quickly answered, "Actually, sir, I need to meet the mortician back at the home. Can I come back at another time? Tomorrow, perhaps?"

Mr. Harsgrove stood up from his chair. "Why, of course, lad. Tomorrow would be fine, any time, and I will have looked into this matter by then."

Ben bowed at the waist a bit as he started to exit and said, "Thank you, sir. I appreciate your help."

Mr. Harsgrove smiled. Ben thought it was as good as he could muster. "Good day, lad."

Ben left reluctantly. He really wanted to stay and find out what that old sailor had left him, and he wasn't comfortable leaving his only paper that the old captain had given him with that lawyer. He was surprised at how Mr. Harsgrove was taken aback by the fact that Captain Reginald Roach was also Homer Gregoreouse and how the lawyer was hesitant at first to help until he realized that Ben was the beneficiary to the estate. On the way home, he laughed to himself. *The curse is already making you crazy.* When Ben got back home, he had about an hour until the mortician was to arrive, so he went to doing his usual chores around the home. It wasn't long before the mortician arrived in his black carriage and unloaded a pine box. Ben helped him carry it in. They both hoisted the captain into the box, then they both carried it to the carriage.

The mortician said, "It's nice when they're old and small. Makes 'em lighter and easy to carry."

Ben nodded an agreement, feeling a little creeped out. That would be part of his job's daily conversation. The man himself was kind of creepy, very tall and skinny, with extremely pale skin. He wore an all-black suit and a top hat. His eyes were sunken beneath his brows, and there were darkened circles around each socket. His hat cast a shadow over his eyes so it looked almost like he didn't have any eyes at all, and then add the fact the man worked with dead people all day long. It didn't help his image any. Ben had helped him load many bodies from this house, but Ben would just wave goodbye. This time, he has to ride along to see the captain was burned with his clothes on and the man doesn't see his scarred body. Ben rode in the front seat with the driver, and they made small talk on the way.

He would say things like, "I like my job, boy. You know why?"

Ben would hesitate, smile, and say, "No, why, sir?"

"Because my customers never complain." Then he would laugh.

Ben would smile and give a slight courtesy laugh, but Ben's mind was in another place. First, he had been up since the night before, and the lack of sleep was starting to catch up to him. He about fell asleep on the ride out of town even with his partner rambling on. They made their way through town and then to the outskirts. They wound their way to a large barn. Ben couldn't help but notice the large amount of nameless headstones waiting for someone. The area where the pine boxes were constructed was littered with shavings and unfinished caskets. The carriage pulled up to the large double doors, and the master of death, as Ben decided to call him, dismounted and swung the doors open. Then without even getting back on the carriage, he gave a slight whistle, and the team of horses walked into the barn and stopped at their destination without any direction from the master of death. Ben was thinking of getting down when the horses took off by themselves, which almost sent him falling out of the seat. The master of death wasted no time running around, getting everything ready. Ben looked around the barn. It had pulleys and chains running everywhere. The furnace made of crude blocks was long and had a chimney that went higher than the barn. He started the wood that was already stacked in the burn box. The draw from the long skinny box area to the extremely tall chimney made for an intense draw, and you could hear it grow as the fire burned hotter.

"Come and give me a hand, boy," the mortician said, and Ben ran over to assist. They unloaded the captain from the carriage. That's when Ben realized that a lot of the chains there were to help move things like the caskets. The roar of the fire was building to the point they had to talk a lot louder to hear each other. The man told Ben, "We better hurry. If that fire gets too hot, we won't be able to get him in there." They slid the casket up to the mouth of the door, and he attached two chains to preplaced holes in the bottom of the box. He then went to a system of chains and started to pull, and the casket slowly slipped in. The heat was unbearable. The furnace roared like some prehistoric creature as the captain's box and body were consumed by the fire. The mortician seemed to settle down a bit after that, and the mortician started to speak again. "Well, let's go. This will take a while."

Ben was amazed at the way the machine and burner worked. He asked him, "This is quite an amazing workshop you have here. Did you build it?"

He laughed a little. "Nope, can't take credit for that. It's been here for years. It was built by the colonies when they first arrived. As the colonists started dying of unknown diseases, they built this to burn the bodies." His face came to life as he talked about the story. "Back then, they were dying of malaria or Indians or dysentery or by killing each other. Back in those days, it was my grandfather who was running this baby." He patted the furnace. "My dad and I, we just kept it up. It takes a different person to work with the deceased, but after growing up with them, it doesn't bother me a bit." Ben could agree with that. He had seen his share of the elderly die. The mortician went about his business, putting the horses away, cleaning up, and putting the harness away.

Ben found a nearby chair and sat down. The mortician patted Ben lightly on the shoulder. Ben awoke with a start, not sure where he was exactly. He was sitting up in the chair, looking around, then realized where he was. He rubbed his eyes and apologized for falling asleep.

"It's quite all right, lad. You slept hard. You must have needed it," he said, smiling at Ben.

Ben looked around. "How long did I sleep?" Ben asked sleepily, slightly embarrassed.

"Good couple hours, I reckon," the mortician answered.

"Really?" Ben said, surprised.

"Here you go, lad." The mortician handed Ben an urn. It looked like a fancy vase to Ben. t had a cork in it and was sealed with wax.

"What's this?" Ben asked, confused.

The mortician laughed. "Why, it's the reason you came, lad. That there is your precious captain."

Ben felt a little uneasy holding it, all of a sudden saying, "Oh… well…thank you."

"I'll hook up the team and give you a ride back."

Ben declined, thanking him, but he thought he would just walk back, wake him up a bit, and give him time to think.

The mortician understood and added, "Now I did like the old man, so there ain't no chance of me getting that there curse, right?"

Ben answered in his most convincing voice, "Oh, most assuredly, sir. You will not be cursed."

Ben stepped outside to the fresh air. It was a nice day, and his mind needed a little clarifying. He needed a little time by himself. A lot had happened in the last twelve hours. Ben reached town, and as he walked down the street, people who knew him would holler or wave. If he heard them at all, he would politely smile, but he was in no mood for a conversation. His mind was somewhere else, whirling with thoughts of what to do next. How to go about finding any treasure if he had any for real. The captain could have been delusional, what with as much rum as he choked down in the short time they talked. And if he did find it, would it still be the property of England if he recovered it? Should he consider returning it? In the midst of his wandering mind, a hard slap on his shoulder brought him to his senses immediately, and he jerked his head around to see what it was.

A voice rang in his ear. "Wow, I haven't seen you think that hard since you were trying to decide to ask Mary Oltmier to dance or not. And do you remember what happened, huh? You hurt yourself. I remember well. You fell flat on your face."

Ben didn't have to even look to know who it was. He knew as soon as he started talking it was Jackson Huntington, his best friend since he could even remember. His dad owned the local butcher shop and delivered out to the home. Jackie would ride with his dad on deliveries. He and Ben would play ever since they could walk. They also went to school together. Jackie's parents were like his second family, and Jackie was like another son to his mom.

"For one, Mr. Smarty Pants, I did not hurt myself, and I wouldn't have fallen if some certain wise guy didn't tie my laces together under the bench before I stood up to go ask a girl to dance."

Jackie laughed under his breath and said, "Oh yeah. Oh, we're not going to start that fight again, are we? I thought we had settled that by now?" He gave Ben a push on the shoulder.

Ben, a little annoyed by his friend, asked, "Why aren't you working?"

Jackie crinkled his eyebrows, saying, "It's lunchtime, my little friend." He grabbed him by the back of the neck and shook Ben's head around a little. Ben hated it when Jackie called him that. But Jackie knew that, and that's why he would call him that. Jackie got away with a lot of things like that because of his size. He was six feet three inches tall and weighed two hundred and twenty pounds, all muscle. He lugged meat all day when he wasn't in school so he was just as strong as he was big.

"So what's got you so concentrated, Mr. Summit? You thinking about Mary Oltmier again?" Jackie always gave Ben a hard time about her, but Ben knew he only did in the confidence of both of them. Ben still blushed a little because he did like her a lot. Jackie sensed Ben was getting irritated with him, and he grabbed him by both shoulders as they walked along and shook him a little, apologizing for giving him such a hard time. Ben almost dropped the urn. He juggled it a little but kept hold of it. That was the first time Jackie had noticed the urn Ben was carrying.

"What you got there, my friend?" Jackie asked, pointing to the urn.

Ben rolled his eyes. "Remember that old captain guy at the home? The one that was always yelling about cockroaches?"

"Ohhhh, yeah," Jackie answered after he thought for a second.

"Well, you're lookin' at him," Ben said, holding the jug up so Jackie could see.

"What do you mean? He's in there?" Jackie asked, a little confused.

"These are his ashes. We cremated him this morning." Ben hadn't slowed his stride the whole time they were walking and talking, and Jackie was getting far from his lunch.

He could also tell Ben was preoccupied by his business today, so he stopped walking and said, "You ever get tired of hanging out with dead guys in a jar, come by and see me. It's been a while."

Ben waved back to his friend and now yelling because of his distance, "Soon!" Jackie waved at his friend and watched as his troubled friend kept a fast pace headed for home.

Ben reached the home and went and found his mother. He asked what she might need for help, and she took one look at his tired eyes and put her hand on his cheek.

"There is some stew on the stove and bread in the oven. Why don't you eat and get some rest? You can catch up on your chores later."

Ben felt a wave of relief as he was starting to feel tired now. He started to turn then asked, "What should I do with this?" He held up the urn.

She smiled a shy smile. "Just leave it in the kitchen. I'll put it in the pantry in a safe place."

He thanked her and was off to eat. With his belly full and late afternoon turning into early evening, Ben fell hard asleep. He awoke with a jolt from a horrible nightmare. His heart was beating, sweat was dripping down his face, and he was breathing hard. When he had lain down it was light and now it was pitch black. He had a hard time focusing as to where he was. Once he figured it out, he settled back down, amused with himself, and muttered, "Just a dream." And he drifted back to sleep, He awoke early the next day, ready and refreshed. Ben rushed around, finishing the work he usually did and catching up on what he hadn't done the day before. He had a renewed excitement about any treasure or nontreasure. He was just going to see what Mr. Harsgrove had to say this day and go from there. He was loading the wood box by the woodstove when his mom got up and came to the kitchen.

He greeted her with a brisk, "Good morning, Mother."

She answered a polite, "Good morning, son. Did you sleep well?"

"A bit restless but well."

"You look rested," she answered back.

Ben shot a question at her right away, knowing she would give him an okay, but he asked to be polite. "By the way, Mom, I have an appointment to see Mr. Harsgrove today at nine o'clock, if that's all right?"

"What did you find out yesterday?" she asked, not having talked with him after he returned the day before.

"Oh, he needed a day to look into the matter and would see me today about it." Ben was waiting for the "don't get your hopes up" speech. He might have relatives already living or he really owed more than he had. But she didn't say any of that. He just nodded an understanding as she put her apron on and tied it behind her back. He thought he might just get away without any speech as he started to leave the room. It came.

"Ben," she said quietly. "Would you do me one favor? Read everything carefully, and don't agree to anything until you and I discuss it. Would that be all right with you?"

He rolled his eyes a little, thinking to himself how she made it sound like his decision to let her in on the final decision. But he was grateful she was letting him go through with any of this treasure business, so he graced her with a formal agreement, saying, "But of course, Mother." Ben rushed around, getting his work completed, and when he did, he ran to find his mother and told her he was going to the lawyers now and would be back soon.

She hollered as he was leaving, "Remember what I said!"

"I will, Mom. Love you." He was in such a rush running out the door. She said she loved him too, but he never heard it. He was already out of hearing distance.

Ben reached the lawyer's office. He knocked with the elaborate knocker on the door. He heard a voice yell, "Please come in!" Ben entered to see Mr. Harsgrove peering over his spectacles. He perked up immediately. "Oh, Mr. Summit, please do come in and have a seat." He stood as he talked, pointing to a large leather chair just opposite his desk. Ben worked his way to the chair, and Mr. Harsgrove continued. "Give me one second, sir, and we will get into your business." He sat back down, scribbled on a piece of paper, and seemed to finish quickly. He set it aside and said, "Excuse me for one minute, sir. I will be right back." He left the room for a minute and then returned. When he did, he was carrying a small chest with a large lock on it. Mr. Harsgrove set the chest down. It had a rounded top and was covered in dust. It was decorated with ornate metalwork. He then fumbled around with some papers then cleared his throat and began to speak in a serious matter-of-fact voice. "Mr. Summit, you are the sole heir to Captain Reginald Roach's assets and properties and are responsible for debts or loans outstanding. Besides the annual income from the shared profits of the merchant ship *Charee*—"

Ben interrupted, "What income?"

Mr. Harsgrove looked over his glasses at Ben. "Please, Mr. Summit, you may ask any questions after I have read this first." Ben nodded an understanding and sat forward, trying to hear all the details. Mr. Harsgrove adjusted his glasses and continued to read silently to find his spot. "That's it," he said as he found where he left off. "Income from the merchant ship *Charee*. Also this chest that was being held in trust for one Homer Gregoreouse. To whom the rightful heir to the estate of Captain Reginald Roach will have the key to open said chest." At that point, Mr. Harsgrove stopped speaking and looked over his reading glasses. "Well, sir, do you have a key?"

Ben was taken aback then realized the old man did give him a key. He had put a leather lace through it and hung it from his neck. He scrambled to pull the key from under his shirt. "Uh…yes I have the key, or rather a key," he stammered." He pulled it out, dangling from his hand. Mr. Harsgrove reached across, and Ben handed it to him. "He didn't tell me what it was for. He just told me to hang on to it."

Mr. Harsgrove was still looking over his glasses at Ben. As he clenched the key in his hand, he asked, "How much do you know about your great-grandfather?"

Ben wasn't expecting that question. But then again, he wasn't surprised anybody acquiring any sort of monetary amount for claiming to be someone's relative should be questioned. "To be honest, Mr. Harsgrove, I know very little about him. He wasn't close at all."

Mr. Harsgrove expected as much and wasn't surprised by the answer. He just nodded and stood up. He walked around the desk to the front door, opened it, and peeked out. Then he shut it hard and locked it. "Okay," he said. "Let's look inside." He came back around and put the chest on the desk so they could both see. He placed the key in the hole and turned it just as if the lock were new. It turned with ease, and the box lid was free. Mr. Harsgrove hesitated, looking at Ben. He said while rubbing the lid, "Ben, this chest has been in my family for a long time. My grandfather was a sailor. He sailed with a man by the name of Homer Gregoreouse. He then sold the merchant ship *Charee* to Captain Reginald Roach. My grandfather sailed with Captain Roach for some thirty years. My father told me stories of how they anchored off an uncharted island in search for any tradable goods. What they found was a lost treasure of riches beyond belief. Captain Roach shared his fortune with all the men aboard, making them all very rich. My family owes Captain Roach a great debt and a sincere appreciation. I was able to go to law school and become successful. My father told me of the stories, for he, too, worked on the ship. He said that Captain Roach didn't just happen upon the treasure but knew where it was and probably knew where more was, but he never went after it. That is why I was surprised at the fact that Homer Gregoreouse was also Reginald Roach. I spent all night trying to figure out why Mr. Gregoreouse would sell himself his own ship and change his name unless it was to hide from something. But that's all speculation, son, and I won't bore you with my tall tales. I will tell you, though, that this chest has been in the family for a long time. My grandfather was asked to keep it for Captain Roach, and he gave it to my father and was told to hold it, that someone would come to pick it up. Well, true to his word, here you are." Ben's head was swirling with all this information. He understood more than Mr. Harsgrove of the details, though, but was just as confused on others. "When I graduated, I met Captain Roach one time. At that point, the chest was given to me to hold, and we also set up a business deal that my firm would handle all the finances for the merchant ship *Charee* in return for an annual fee." Ben wasn't sure why he was going into this detailed story. He just wanted to open the chest. He just wanted to take what was his and go home. Mr. Harsgrove continued to talk. "This is an exciting day, Mr. Summit, for you and me. It does surprise me that you lived here all that time and he never discussed this with you or came in with you before now."

He then opened the chest. He looked somewhat bewildered. There was nothing in the chest but a small notebook and owner-ship papers for the merchant ship *Charee*. Mr. Harsgrove fumbled through the notebook, scanning the pages fast for something. Ben didn't know what. He then looked more carefully over the ownership papers. He set them down and looked into the empty chest, knock-ing on the side and bottom and poking at the interior. He had such a troubled look on his face.

Ben had to ask, "Is there something wrong?"

"No, son, just wanted to make sure I didn't miss anything."

"Like what?"

Ben's question reeked of honesty. An old lawyer like Mr. Harsgrove realized he hadn't a clue what Mr. Harsgrove was looking for. Mr. Harsgrove remembered the stories from his grandfather of Homer Gregoreouse. How he was aboard the ship that sailed with Bloodthirsty Bob, how he knew where the treasures were hidden. He expected a map of sorts or charts, not some nonsense journal of fam-ily history. He expected the ownership papers for the *Charee*. After all these years, nothing, nothing at all. This was a big disappointment after waiting all those years. His grandfather never knew that Homer carried the map with him at all times, and even more surprising was the fact that Captain Roach was Homer. He truly expected to open that chest and find some gold pieces and a treasure map. But nothing in there looked like a treasure map, and he knew in his heart that they did not happen upon that treasure by accident. He always believed, as his grandfather and his father both were convinced, that Captain Roach knew where it was and that there had to be more! Ben was sitting patiently as he watched Mr. Harsgrove, waiting for him to finish explaining the details of the old captain's estate.

Mr. Harsgrove composed himself, realizing he was wrong, and the disappointment showed all over his face. He began, "Well, Ben, here this chest, and belongings are yours now. And we should change the ownership of the *Charee* into your name. I would hope that our business relationship could remain intact and you would consider continued use of our services as well as our partnership in the shipping business?"

Ben was slowly reaching for the chest but slowed almost to a stop as Mr. Harsgrove spoke. Ben leaned forward in his chair a little bit and asked with a confused look on his face, "What partnership? And do you mean the *Charee* is still a working vessel?"

Mr. Harsgrove laughed a little out loud. "Why, yes, son. You really didn't know anything about the ship?" Ben just sat there in awe, shaking his head no. "Well, let me enlighten you about several things. My grandfather and your great-grandfather were business partners. They would purchase goods to be shipped and resold. Each would cover fifty percent of the cost of the goods. The *Charee* would transfer the cargo, and the business would pay for the shipping, thus covering the cost of the sailor's wages and upkeep of the *Charee*." Ben sat, nodding. He understood. It all made sense. These two men had a business together, but *Charee* was not part of the business. Captain Roach owned the ship, a separate business, so he was making money off both sides. "I have books of all her transactions, her sailing schedules, list of crew members, and wages paid. All these are available for you to look at. In fact, she's due to Homeport next week, so you could see her and meet the captain if you would like." Ben was in a bit of shock. The old lawyer was loving it. It reminded him of the few times his clients thought they were off the hook for some dreadful crime and he had pulled out a witness to crush the defendant's innocent claims. That was the look on Ben's face, so the next part he was about to really enjoy. "Your great-grandfather also left you with a sum of money held in the local bank, a total of eight thousand two hundred forty-three dollars and sixty-five cents." Ben's eyes got as big as dinner plates, and his mouth hung open. He was unaware that he was sitting there like that. Mr. Harsgrove was aware. He could tell Ben had no knowledge of any of this. "I also was power of attorney and handled all the financial matters for a small fee annually."

Ben picked up as he said small fee. Then had to ask, "What is a small fee?"

Mr. Harsgrove answered, "That's a fair question." And he reached behind him for a large book and placed it in front of him. Thumbing through the pages, he came up with a figure. "It averages about five hundred dollars a year."

That surprised Ben. That was a lot of money. Ben made one hundred dollars one year he worked all winter supplying wood for a particular cold winter. It was a lot of work, and Ben felt he had earned every penny. Ben was a little uneasy about spending money, and now he was what he would call filthy rich.

"So how much do I owe you for today?" Ben asked shyly.

"Not a thing, young man. You see, that's part of the annual fee." Ben relaxed a bit, and Mr. Harsgrove could tell. "That is the deal with your grandfather, but it will be up to you if you want to continue our relationship."

Ben nodded and then corrected Mr. Harsgrove, "That was my great-grandfather."

Mr. Harsgrove cleared his voice and admitted, "Yes, of course, your great-grandfather."

Ben just sat back in his chair and asked, "So I'm the owner of a merchant ship still working, half of its cargo, a bank account of some eight thousand dollars, and an old chest with a notebook?" Ben held up the notebook.

"That is absolutely correct, Mr. Summit. And if you would sign here and here." Then he turned a page. "And here. I can transfer the money into your name, and this second page says that you and I will continue business as usual. Our families will continue as we have for years as prosperous business partners." He pushed the papers toward Ben and handed him a quill.

Ben was just about to do as he was told but then remembered what his mom had said. He started to hand the quill back to Mr. Harsgrove, saying, "Sorry, Mr. Harsgrove, but I promised my mother I would show her anything I was signing first so she could see it first. So with all due respect, sir, I don't have a problem with you and I doing business together as usual, but I should honor my mother's wishes."

Mr. Harsgrove's face lost his smile only for a second, but he regained composure. "Of course, young man, I think that would be the best. I totally understand." He carefully put everything back into the chest. He included the papers form the manifest from *Charee*, adding, "I will need these back, of course."

Ben nodded and agreed. "Of course. I will take care of them."

He handed it over to Ben, asking, "Can you handle that chest, son?"

"I will manage fine, sir. Can I talk with you tomorrow?"

"That would be just fine, Mr. Summit. I will look forward to seeing you." Ben turned and thanked Mr. Harsgrove again as he hoisted the chest onto his right shoulder. "Shall I get the door for you?" Mr. Harsgrove started to rise out of his chair.

Ben answered confidently, "No, sir, I've got it." Ben let himself out and felt a large weight lifted as he got fresh air and out of that stuffy office. His mind was whirling with thousands of thoughts. He laughed out loud, saying to himself, "I have eight thousand dollars." The thoughts were fear, jubilation, and downright giddiness. "And a ship!" he yelled out loud. "I own a ship!" His pace was fast getting home. When he got home, he found a secure spot for his chest and went to find his mother. When he found her, he was talking so fast she could hardly understand anything he was saying.

She finally grabbed him by his arms. "Please," she said. "Ben, I am very happy for your newfound fortune, but I have many guests who need me right now, and I must attend to their needs. We will talk later, and you can explain it all to me then. But right now, I have to attend to these souls."

Ben hated it when she was right and always so reliable. He thought how most these people have no idea how lucky they were to have his mother watching out for them. Ben agreed they would talk later and went about his chores at the home. He was telling himself at times, "I have enough money to hire someone to do this."

Back at Mr. Harsgrove's office, he was frustrated and disappointed. He could tell that boy was telling the truth about most of the situation but felt he was holding something back. He chuckled a little, thinking of all those years his family had held that chest. He had wanted to open it just to see what's inside, especially knowing now that Homer Gregoereouse and Captain Reginald Roach were the same person. He had even stronger feelings that there was more to this story than before, and he was sure that there was more treasure out there somewhere, but did Ben know about it? Then he cursed himself for not looking closer at the leather-bound notebook. It didn't make sense why he would know about the treasure but not the merchant ship or the money.

Back at the home, Mrs. Summit was starting to get a little excited to hear what Ben was rattling on about if, it was even true. She found herself being happy for Ben one minute if it was true and very angry the second at the old man for putting ideas into her son's head and hurting him if it wasn't.

Ben was doing the same thing, imagining himself owning a large sailing ship, having his mom quit working like she did. Then he would feel angry at the old man for messing with his life like that. His life was pretty easy. He knew what he was doing, where it all was going. Now it was all messed up. He didn't know anything about the shipping business, and how was he supposed to trust Mr. Harsgrove? "I don't even know how to sail a boat," he thought out loud at one point.

Finally, his mom came to him and said, "We have time now, Ben, if you would meet me in the kitchen."

Ben ran down to his room and retrieved the box and ran back to the kitchen. Ben laid everything out, showing her which one was the ledger and pointing out Mr. Harsgrove's recorded services and payments. Ben was rattling on about the eight thousand dollars. Mrs. Summit was shocked, asking, "Are you sure that's what he said, Ben? Eight thousand dollars?" Ben assured her that's what Mr. Harsgrove said. Her mind was reeling with all this information as she looked through the books. After examining the books a while, she stood up to grab some hot water for her tea. As she stood up, she got a look in the chest for the first time, and something grabbed her attention. She stopped, and her forehead wrinkled a bit as she saw the leather folder, asking, "What's this?" She reached in to take a better look.

Ben just waved it off. "Oh, that's just some notebook that the old man wrote in. Mr. Harsgrove looked though it pretty thoroughly." As she pulled it out, her whole demeanor changed. Ben had seen his mom upset before, but it had been a long time since he had witnessed her cry. Tears welled up in her eyes as she turned the book over a couple of times. Ben asked, "What's a matter, Mom?"

She answered, choking back the flood of emotions that were coming over her, "I know this book. I have seen it before."

Ben was confused, asking, "Where?"

"In my father's desk when I was very little." She opened it carefully, and she looked in the first page that said Homer Gregarious Journal, and she pushed the journal to the table with both hands as her knees felt weak. There on the page was a small childlike scribble when she was only about five years old. Ben stood up, thinking he was going to have to catch her, but she caught herself. "This is why I remember so well. This book, Ben, I scribbled on this page and got in a lot of trouble. Then I never saw it again. Until now! What is this doing in an old chest?"

Ben was watching in shock at the transformation of his mother's expressions. She picked it back up and started to thumb through it. A few pages in, she came to a page that read *To my family* in bold letters. Her mind tried to put it all together and why this book would be in her father's possession. As she read on, it became very clear.

I am writing this to all of you who may have survived the curse. In reading this, it means I have passed on. I have traveled the world and seen many things, and you would think I would have been satisfied with that. Out of all my travels, there was one thing so beautiful and demanded my attention as powerful as any drug I have encountered. It literally demanded my attention, and I do believe it would have been all I needed to live a long and fulfilled life. But due to the greed of many, not to mention my own, the curse got in the way, or we all could have lived happily ever after. In my travels to Cuba when I was a young man, I fell in love with a young lady, Amelia Cantu. After several years at sea, I found a lost treasure of the English Navy and found myself very rich, so I purchased the ship *Charee* and went back and married Amelia. She and I had a daughter. We named her Carmen. The British Navy never stopped looking for me. Thinking I knew where the treasures were hidden, they were relentless and soon found my home. They tortured my wife, who knew nothing, to death.

Ben's mom let out a gasp as she read that part.

She had luckily had a friend watching our daughter while she went to market where the soldiers grabbed her. When I returned to find out the bad news, they agreed to watch Carmen for me while I was at sea. She was raised under the name of Carmen Cantu Hoitron.

Ben's mom gasped out loud, putting her hand over her mouth. Under her breath, she mumbled, "That was my mother's maiden name." Ben sat watching his mother as her face showed all kinds of reactions, her eyes watering as she read on. Then her face went hard, like she was mad. He recognized that face. Because what she was reading now was very upsetting to her. He was explaining in the note that he had always kept track of his daughter through all her growing up. He stayed hidden from everyone until he found out she was about to be married. He couldn't stand it, and he had to see her. He figured that after sixteen years, the legend of roach boy had been forgotten. She was very receptive, and things went well after he explained why he had to stay hidden and it should be their secret. But she must have told her husband. They were married about five years and had a little girl. Alas, the curse ran its course, for her husband, a kind man, was talking a bit too much while having some drinks in a pub. The legend of Homer Gregoreouse came up, and he bragged and told all the knowledge he had heard over the years. About a week later, he was seized by some rough-looking English sailors. He never returned home.

> My daughter went into hiding and raised her daughter by herself. I also went back into hiding and sold my ship to a man by the name of Captain Reginald Roach. Captain Homer Gregoreouse was never heard from again either. Her daughter grew up and got married. She soon had a son by the name of Benjamin Franklin Summit. As I write this, I plan to speak to him tomorrow. The funds in the bank and the *Charee* could be worth enough to help he and his mother in life comfortably. Knowing full well that a couple of drinks of rum will be my demise, I hope the curse will die with me. God bless you all, and I wish you a happy and prosperous life.

With that, she slammed the binder shut and threw it across the room, yelling, "Damn him! Why...why didn't he say anything?" She was crying real tears now, and Ben was a little too afraid to ask.

He squeaked out a question. "What's wrong, Mother?"

Ben's mom looked down at him and tried to regain her composure. She put her face between her hands and wiped the tears from her cheeks. Then she wiped them on her apron, putting a hand on Ben's shoulder. She was choking back another crying spell. "The captain was your great-grandfather, Ben, and he was my grandfather. I thought this thing would throw a few dollars your way. I saw no harm in it, but now you are the true heir to Homer Gregoreouse's estate, and best to my knowledge heir to a damn curse of treasure that has claimed the life of over half of my family."

Ben wasn't sure what she was talking about, so he tried again. "I don't understand, Mom."

She tried to calm a bit as she tried to explain, "Ben, he was your true great-grandfather. His wife was murdered for the treasure. My father was murdered for the treasure. Don't you see, Ben? That's why he calls it a curse. He had to change his name and hide from his own family because of that treasure, and now he has involved you!" Her eyes started to tear up as she spoke.

Ben was starting to understand now why this was so upsetting to her. Ben asked, "Did you know all along who he was?"

His mom just shook her head no and forced out a muffled, "No, I just discovered it now through that notebook." Ben hadn't even bothered to read it in all his excitement. His mother's eyes got big, and a rush of fear came over her face. "You haven't told anyone about this, have you?"

"No, Mother" was his answer, and it was honest, and she could tell.

"You didn't say anything to Mr. Harsgrove?"

"No, no, I didn't. But he looked like he was looking for something in that chest. He went over it pretty intently and asked me questions like what I knew about my great-grandfather." Ben just put it all together as he was talking. He, too, was surprised to find out that Homer Gregoreouse and Captain Reginald Roach were one and the same. Then Ben went on to explain Mr. Harsgrove's family involvement with their family.

She finally reached over and took his hand in hers. "Ben, this is a big decision. If you decide to let this ship go and not get involved, that would be one way. But if you decide to keep the ship, you must never speak of the treasure or look for it to anyone. Do you understand?" She was more or less pleading with him with her eyes and heart, but she knew if she made him give it up, he would blame her for the rest of his life if things didn't turn out the way he thought they should. "Mr. Harsgrove appears to have good business sense and ethics. You could learn from him if you choose to continue to do business with him." Ben could see it was breaking his mother's heart, but he had his mind made up to run the ship. She turned to leave the room and said, "I'll support any decision you make." And she walked out of the room. He thought hard all the rest of the day and all night. He didn't feel like he had slept at all.

When Ben got up, he still felt a heavy load on his mind. He knew in his heart his mom didn't want him to be a part of the ship, but he knew she truly would support him if he did. The trip to Mr. Harsgrove's office was a long one. The papers were all signed, all except for one, and Ben had a question he needed answered first.

He knocked heavily on the door, and the voice of Mr. Harsgrove bellowed, "Come in!" Mr. Harsgrove was peering over his glasses as the door opened. "Come in, Mr. Summit. His voice cheery. "Please, come in." Ben put the books on the large desk. "Please have a seat." He was pointing to the only chair in the room with his quill. "Well, how did your consultation with your mother go?"

Ben hesitated as he gave him his answer. "Oh, all right, I guess." Ben was interrupted.

"She didn't see a problem with my books, did she?"

Ben quickly said, "No, no, nothing like that. In fact, Mr. Harsgrove, she felt you were an honorable man and thought if I were to do business with you, you could teach me a lot. So we decided to honor my grandfather's wishes and stay in the shipping business. And if your offer still stands to remain partners in merchandise end of the business, we would like to honor that also."

Mr. Harsgrove jumped to his feet and reached across the desk to shake Ben's hand. And as he did, he could see there was something on his mind. He said, "You know, for a lad who has just been made a very rich businessman, you don't seem very happy. What's eating at you, son?"

"My mother is afraid for me, and I don't think she wants me to leave."

Mr. Harsgrove laughed a little and said, "Who's leaving? You don't have to go anywhere. You can stay right here and let the business run itself."

"That is a problem, Mr. Harsgrove. I would like to be part of the ship. Actually work on it."

Mr. Harsgrove dropped a look over the top of his glasses, and a surprised look came over his face. He shook his head no as he said, "Oh, Mr. Summit, I, uh, I don't know. That's hard labor and very dangerous even as a passenger."

Ben interrupted, "I don't want to be a passenger, Mr. Harsgrove. I want to go as a sailor and learn from the bottom up."

"As a common sailor? Mr. Summit, you are a wealthy gentleman now. You don't have—"

Ben interrupted again. "Mr. Harsgrove, I am a businessman of something I know nothing about. I believe I would make better decisions if I knew what my business was doing. I also think I would prefer to have no one know who I am as far as them knowing I own the ship, and that way there won't be anyone treating me any different than anyone else."

"Preferential treatment is what you are talking about," Mr. Harsgrove interjected.

"Yes, that's what I mean."

Mr. Harsgrove had a thought run through his head just before he told Ben he really didn't think he should go aboard. Why did he want to get on that ship so bad? Maybe he did know about more treasure. Maybe he would be worth watching on the ship. He might be a personal compass to the treasure.

"Why not," Mr. Harsgrove blurted out.

Ben's eyes went wide. "Are you serious?" he asked, almost hopping out of the chair and thanking Mr. Harsgrove. They finished filling out the paperwork and the details of how the business was run. Mr. Harsgrove gave Ben a list of things he would need to pick up for his newfound occupation as a deckhand. As he started to leave, Ben turned to Mr. Harsgrove. "No one should know who I am."

Mr. Harsgrove agreed he would keep it a secret. But as Ben disappeared, Mr. Harsgrove made a decision to find the *Charee* and get to her before she made it to Homeport so he could talk to the captain so he understood the whole story. And that way, he could pay attention to Ben to see if he wanted to go to a port that was not on the trade routes. That way, they might be able to tell that he was treasure hunting. He would keep the secret from all but the captain.

Mr. Harsgrove quickly packed some belongings, took some money, and ordered a carriage in town to pick him up and take him to the closest port the *Charee* would visit.

Ben had gathered a few things on his list, and as he wandered through town, he ended up near the Huntington Butcher Shop. So he dropped into visit with Jackie. Mr. Huntington was cutting on some sort of carcass. He looked up as the little bell on the door rang, introducing a customer had entered. A big smile came across his face as he said, "Well, Mr. Summit, what a pleasure to see you." He was wiping his hands on his apron and reaching out to shake Ben's hand.

Ben met his grip and returned, "Pleasure's all mine, sir."

"Where you been, boy? Ain't seen you for a while," Mr. Huntington asked.

Ben answered like he was bored, "Oh, you know, working around the home."

Mr. Huntington went back to cutting the meat but asked, "And your mom?"

Ben smiled a little. "She's good." But what he really wanted to talk about was his new fortune. Ben asked how Mrs. Huntington was to be polite.

Mr. Huntington wrinkled his nose and squinted his eyes as he answered, "Oh, I'm glad you asked. She is as mean as an old broken mule, ornery like a rattler in a burlap sack. She's normal, I guess, so she must be well."

Ben had to laugh at that. Mr. Huntington and Jackie were always making jokes. Ben loved the way they always made jokes and got along. They seemed like the happiest family in town. Ben admired the relationship Jackie had with his dad. Truth be told, Ben would have been a little jealous, but the Huntingtons treated him like family, and Ben looked at Mr. Huntington like a father.

Just then, Jackie came bursting through the back door, yelling, "Pa! Pa!"

Mr. Huntington yelled back, "What, boy?"

"Mr. Barker wants to butcher his sow next week! Wants to know if we could pick it up!"

Mr. Huntington yelled back, "I could pick it up myself, but a little fella like you would probably need some help!" He winked at Ben. Ben smiled at the joke, knowing Jackie would have some comeback.

He rounded the corner, wrapped his arms around his dad, and lifted him off the ground. "I ain't having any trouble getting this hog off the ground." As he swung him around, they both laughed.

And as he set his dad's feet on the ground, Mr. Huntington said, "There's a strong one there to help you." He was pointing at Ben standing by the door. Ben blushed a little at the comment.

Jackie looked over to see it was Ben. "Hey, little friend. It's about time you came by to tell me the story."

Mr. Huntington perked up. "You got a story, Ben?" he asked with surprise in his voice.

Ben was so excited to tell them, and now that Jackie was there, he blurted out the story. He went on about the few nights before with the old captains story and him finding out he was his real great-grandfather. How he left him the ship, how he was going to go learn the shipping trade. The two men sat, spellbound by the story being told. True to his great-grandfather's ways, though, Ben left out the part about the map, the treasure, and the curse altogether. As he did, he had a shiver run through him. He thought, *It must be greed. Makes a man lie to his best friends. That must be the worst part of the curse.* His two most trusted friends felt it as he hesitated at parts of the story to avoid the truth.

Mr. Huntington finally asked, "What's a matter, boy? Something about this bothering you?"

Ben quickly recovered by saying, "I'll just miss all you folks, traveling like that."

Mr. Huntington said, "You know, son, if this ship's homeport is Homeport, then you will be back to visit quite often." He patted him on the shoulder as he stood up and added as he went back to his worktable, "Sounds like a wonderful adventure, Ben, and I'm glad for your newfound fortune."

Jackie sat a bit stunned as it was sinking in. He might never see Ben again. He just assumed things would never change. They had known each other since they could first walk. He felt as close to Ben as a brother would to a real sibling. But he did what Jackie did best and made light of the whole thing.

"Don't you worry, Ben. While you're away, I'll take real good care of Mary Gene for you." Ben had a crush on Mary Gene for the last year or so.

Jackie was sitting on the edge of a butcher block, and as his dad passed him, he mumbled, "You're lucky that man calls you a friend." And he pushed Jackie over backward onto the sawdust-covered floor. Jackie was still laughing as he hit the ground. His dad turned around and said to Ben, "Don't you worry, Ben. I'll take care of Mary Gene for you while you're away."

Jackie jumped to his feet. "What! You crazy old man, you can't take care of the one you're married to now!"

Jackie was brushing the sawdust off, his dad paying no attention to Jackie's comments. Looking at Ben, he said, "Stop by and say goodbye before you ship out, will ya, son?"

Ben assured him he would. Ben marveled at those two sometimes. It hurt Ben inside. He wished he had a father that he could joke with and call a friend. Ben explained he had to leave and would see them both before he left. Jackie extended his hand to Ben, and Ben took it earnestly. Jackie pulled him in hard, put him in a headlock, and ruffled his hair with his other hand.

Ben struggled and pushed free, shoving him hard in the chest to get clear, yelling, "Damn, you never stop, do ya?" They were both grinning as he reorganized himself.

Jackie, smiling from ear to ear, said, "You'll miss me, Mr. Summit."

Ben straightened his hair as best he could, leaving with a wave to Mr. Huntington and saying, "I doubt it." Ben was feeling melancholy. He was only about half a block away when he heard footsteps running fast behind him. He turned and realized it was Jackie, running fast and directly at him. He spun in defense, for he never knew what Jackie was up to.

Jackie eased up, put his hands on both Ben's shoulders, and said, "Take me with you, Ben."

Ben was shocked, not sure of the intent of the request. "Do what?"

Jackie's face was serious, a look Ben wasn't used to. "Take me with you…please."

Ben, still unsure of what he was being asked, said, "On the boat?"

Jackie shook his head, wrinkled his brow, and said sarcastically, "No, for a ride on your shoulders back to your house. *Yes, the boat.*"

Ben looked back at the butcher shop. "What about your family? What about the business?"

Jackie had the most serious look on his face Ben had ever seen on him as he answered, "Ben, I love my mother and father more than anything else on this earth, and I don't mind cutting meat either, but I sit on that dock three times a week, watching ships come and go. I know in my heart there's a whole new world out there, and I want to see it."

Ben wasn't sure what to say. He knew exactly how Jackie felt. He did it all the time himself. And seeing Jackie so serious with no joke or smart or sarcastic remark, Ben said, "I will talk with Mr. Harsgrove, see what I can do."

Jackie let out a huge burst of air as if he was holding it, waiting for Ben's answer. Then he jumped in the air and rubbed the top of Ben's hair, messing it up and yelling, "Thanks, Ben! You're a good friend."

Ben just sat there, watching his big old friend practically skip down the street and back to the shop, thinking, *Well, that mature moment didn't last long.* Ben figured as long as he was in town, he better go ask Mr. Harsgrove about the possibility of getting Jackie aboard. He got to Mr. Harsgrove's office and knocked and waited for Mr. Harsgrove to yell "Come in," but it didn't happen. He knocked again, but nothing. A little disappointed, he started to leave when the door cracked open a hair. An old black slave woman stood at the door. She had a hard face, not making eye contact.

She volunteered, "Massa not heah. Be back next week." She started to close the door.

Ben stopped it. "Where did he go?" he asked, confused.

She answered, a bit annoyed at his actions, "Massa went to the big ship. He be comin' home on it."

Ben just bowed a bit and said, "Thank you, ma'am. You've been very helpful." He started to turn and leave.

She said, "Mr. Summit." He stopped, surprised she knew his name. "Mr. Harsgrove can be a fine man till money get involved. I know your mom. She a fine lady, and I's sure you is too. Be wary, son." With that said, she closed the door. Ben wasn't sure what to think of that but spent a lot of thought on it as he walked home. He thought of Mr. Harsgrove's quick departure to catch the *Charee* and ride her home. *Maybe he does that all the time*, he thought.

* * *

Mr. Harsgrove caught up to the ship as the crew had just finished loading some tobacco and was just about to untie from the dock. Mr. Harsgrove jumped from the carriage almost before it had stopped, yelling, "Hold those lines! Hold those lines!" He was quite a sight, running down the pier with long overcoat flapping like big bat wings, his skinny legs on the fat body struggling to hurry down the pier as his large buckled shoes made a loud clip-clopping noise. His long thin white hair was flowing behind.

The deckhands looked at each other as their captain's orders were to cast off, but this man seemed determined to stop the ship. The first mate noticed the commotion and realized it was Mr. Harsgrove. He quickly informed the captain, who looked at the situation. Once a ship that large starts to move, you just don't stop it. He quickly ordered the crew to throw a large net over the port bow and ordered to turn the stern hard to starboard. The big ship started to swing.

The captain then yelled over the side, "Grab the net, Mr. Harsgrove!"

He reluctantly did as he was instructed. He desperately had to make this ship to put his plan into place. Mr. Harsgrove managed to get a hold and swung his legs up. He managed one leg to slip through the net and hung on with both hands. He was just about to heave a sigh of relief when he heard the carriage driver yell, "Your bag, sir!"

Mr. Harsgrove looked around and saw the driver trying to reach the bag out to him. He reached out as best he could, got a hold of the bag, and lost his grip on the net. If it weren't for the one leg caught in the net, he would have ended up in the water. So there he was, hanging upside down by one leg and too fat to reach up and grab a new hold on the net.

The captain, seeing that things were under somewhat control again, ordered his first mate to pull the man up and then ordered the helmsman to straighten her out and said he was pleased with his work and he did a fine job. Then he turned back to the first mate and said, "Would be a shame if he were to hit the water once or twice before he made it to decks, don't you think?" He winked once and turned to go to his cabin.

The first mate, with a question in his voice, asked, "Is that an order, sir?"

The captain turned, almost walking backward, saying, "No, sir, more like a conscience decision."

The first mate smiled real big, saying, "I've a pretty clear conscience, sir." And he gave a thumbs down to his crew, which then lowered the net.

Mr. Harsgrove was already yelling to be pulled up, and now he was really making it clear to go up, not down. Hanging upside down, he tried in vain to raise himself up the net, but to no avail. He went in headfirst.

The first mate gave the order to bring him up. "Once was enough," he said. "Can't be too healthy for the marine life to keep dipping a lawyer in the water." They all had a laugh at that. As he reached the top, they pulled him over the gunnels then lowered him to the deck. Some were still laughing, but most of them near him tried to hold back their laughter.

Mr. Harsgrove knew he was the instrument of a joke. At first he was very angry, not even able to speak civilly. "Get your hands off me, you vagrant swine!" he yelled, shaking their hands off him. As he tried to stand, two others reached down to help him. He swung his bag, knocking their hands away. "*Leave me be!*" And as the momentum carried it around, it hit a man square in the chest. It was a man the crew called Goliath. He was a giant of a man. He towered over Mr. Harsgrove, and he leaned down, putting his face right in Mr. Harsgrove's. It surprised Mr. Harsgrove.

Goliath said in a thundering voice, "Maybe we should put this rude bottom fish back where he came from, boys."

Mr. Harsgrove changed his tone right away. Patting Goliath on the shoulder, he forced a smile on his face and a phony laugh to go along with it. "Not necessary, my good man. Just having a little fun myself with you boys as well. Uh, if you will excuse me, I must see the captain." He sidestepped Goliath, squeezing his way through the crowd. He made his way to the captain's quarters.

The captain greeted Mr. Harsgrove as he entered the cabin. "Good afternoon, Mr. Harsgrove. Such a pleasure to see you."

Mr. Harsgrove was still a little snippy as he made the comment, "Don't give me that shit, Joseph. That wasn't funny, what you did out there."

"I suppose not, Arthur, especially if you were the one upside down."

Mr. Harsgrove interrupted him. "I could have drowned!"

The captain let out a laugh, saying, "No, Arthur, you would have to be human to drown, and everyone knows lawyers aren't human. But really, Arthur, what brings you here on such a perilous journey?" He stood up and grabbed two glasses and poured some rum into each one.

Mr. Harsgrove was removing his wet clothes and purposely shaking them onto Captain Nelson's desk. "I needed to talk to you before you landed in Homeport."

The captain said while handing him the glass, "Why? Is there a problem at the port?"

Mr. Harsgrove thanked him as he took the glass and left the suspense hang for a minute as he took a sip.

The captain said, "It's not like you to risk life and limb to see me, Arthur. What could be so special?"

Mr. Harsgrove was waiting for the perfect time, for he knew the reaction was going to be good. And as the captain took a sip of his rum, just as he was about to swallow, Mr. Harsgrove, in a matter-of-fact attitude, said, "Homer Gregoureouse just died."

The captain coughed as the drink he just took went the wrong way down his throat. Coughing and talking at the same time, he managed to get out the questions, "Where…how…how do you know this?"

Mr. Harsgrove now had a smug look on his face. "Oh, it gets better."

The captain, composing himself a bit, sat on a corner of the chart table. "Better?" he asked.

"Oh, yes, much better," Mr. Harsgrove continued. "When our fathers sailed together and Homer Gregoreouse found the treasure, our families became very rich."

Captain Nelson threw his hands in the air and yelled, "Arthur, this is not news! It's history! You traveled all this way to give me a history lesson."

Mr. Harsgrove was loving this moment and was giddy with laughter while his old acquaintance rambled on. He was about to keep rambling, but then he realized his friend's smug look. "Sometimes history is only as accurate as those who tell the story. So allow me to tell you mine. A young man by the name of Benjamin Summit came to me with the last will and testament for Captain Reginald Roach."

Captain Nelson was just about to say something to interrupt this already known story when he realized, "You mean to tell me Captain Roach is dead also?"

Mr. Harsgrove held a finger up to silence Captain Nelson. "I mean to tell you that Captain Roach and Homer Gregoreouse died on the same day at the same time in the same place."

Captain Nelson still looked confused as to why that would mean anything to him. "Homer Gregoreouse sold the *Charee* to himself as Captain Reginald Roach, and then Homer disappeared off the face of the earth." He had his friend thinking now. "Our grandfathers kept that secret pretty well, don't you think?"

Captain Nelson was pacing a bit, a concerned look to his face, and stopped. "Who is this Benjamin Summit?" he asked sternly.

"The great-grandson of Homer Gregoreouse, thus the great-grandson of Captain Reginald Roach," Mr. Harsgrove answered smugly.

Captain Nelson shot another question at him. "Does he know about the treasure?"

"That's a fair question, my friend. It appeared to me that the boy didn't even know his great-grandfather, nor did he know anything about the ship and the money. And he certainly never mentioned any knowledge of the treasure."

"I'm surprised you mentioned the money at all."

Mr. Harsgrove took offence to that remark and defended himself directly. "Joseph, I have been forthright and honest with that family for many years. After all, we both still owe that family a large debt. Even after we opened the box."

Captain Nelson jumped back to his feet. "The chest...you still have the chest?"

Mr. Harsgrove said, "Yes, of course."

"Oh, you're a better man than I, Arthur. I would have smashed that thing open years ago. So what was in it?"

"The boy had the key, which was a surprise. But nothing was in it."

"Nothing!" Captain Nelson interrupted again.

"Well," Mr. Harsgrove continued, "there was a booklet or notebook with their family history, and it helped to prove that Ben was the rightful heir."

The captain was shocked. "No hidden compartment or something where a map could hide?"

Mr. Harsgrove took another sip of his drink, shaking his head. "I looked. Nothing. But that doesn't mean he doesn't know anything about the treasure. That's what brings me here." The captain was interested now. He was sitting back down and leaning forward. "He came to me the next day, asking to crew on the ship."

The captain sat up with a puzzled look on his face and spouted, "On this ship?"

Mr. Harsgrove held up his finger to quiet Captain Nelson. "Yes, on this ship. But hear me out. I think the boy is holding out. I think he knows something more. So I figured we put him on as a deck-hand and watch him. We see if there is any place he gets particularly curious about or wants to get dropped off. That kind of thing." The captain started to see the lawyer's logic now. "He told me he wanted to be just a deckhand. No special treatment, and no one should know he is the owner."

The captain rolled his eyes and rubbed his forehead. "That's all I need, to play wet nurse to some rich little land lover."

Mr. Harsgrove was taking a little pleasure in watching his old friend feel a little pressure from this news. "Just remember, my friend, he is the sole owner of this vessel."

Captain Nelson stopped rubbing his forehead and dragged his hand down his face but stopped as he heard that comment. He peeked through his spread fingers at Mr. Harsgrove. "I do wonder about your loyalty to our friendship, Arthur," he said sarcastically.

Mr. Harsgrove put his coat sleeve on the cabin floor, saying, "So do I, Joseph. So do I."

Captain Nelson stood up and went to the cabin door, opened it, and yelled, "Get me Mr. Hawkins in here please!"

There was a faint "Aye, aye, sir."

It wasn't but a few seconds later that a young man came, neatly dressed, strong build, clean-shaven face, auburn hair tied tightly behind his head. He had a ruggedly handsome face with a strong square chin. He entered, snapping to attention, saying, "Yes, sir, you called?"

Captain Nelson stood up to respond, "Yes, Mr. Hawkins. Mr. Harsgrove will be joining us back to Homeport. Would you be so kind as to see to some accommodations for him?"

Without hesitation, Mr. Hawkins said, "He may have my quarters, sir."

Mr. Harsgrove started to say, "No, I don't want to put you out of your quarters—"

But Mr. Hawkins interrupted him, "Not at all, sir. I can assure you it is one of the better rooms on board. Besides, when I sleep among the men once in a while, I learn a lot about the ship and its inhabitance, if you know what I mean, sir? If you will allow me about twenty minutes to get the ship underway, I will ready my cabin for you, sir."

Mr. Harsgrove bowed his head, saying, "Thank you, Mr. Hawkins. You're a good man, and it is a pleasure to see you again."

Mr. Hawkins bowed from the waist and added, "Thank you, sir. The pleasure is all mine."

* * *

Back at the home, Ben waited anxiously, deep in thought. He was caught between scared to death and anxious to get started. He saw Jackie several times and had to assure him he would ask as soon as Mr. Harsgrove returned. Ben usually went to town about once a week, but in the last week, he went every day and stopped at the pier. It was about the ninth day. Ben was busy at the home doing his chores when he thought he heard a faint cry.

"Ben!" it said as it got closer to the house. Then the front door flew open with a boom. It scared Ben half to death. It was Jackie. He yelled, "Ben, she's here!"

As their eyes met, they stood looking at each other with very sober looks on their faces. Then as if someone turned a switch on with both of them, they both started to smile. Ben started to nod, and his eyes got bigger, and he said almost in a whisper, "She's here." Simultaneously, they hugged each other, then together they locked arms and started dancing around in a circle, yelling, "She's here!"

Mrs. Summit came running to see what the commotion was about. But as she rounded the corner and saw the two boys dancing for joy about their new adventure. She teared up. She started to get teary-eyed and backed up around the corner. She composed herself and wiped her eyes.

Ben noticed her dress by the corner. He stopped dancing and yelled, "Hey, Mom, the ship is here!"

She patted her eyes and forced a smile on her face, saying with a cracked voice, "Yes, I gathered that from the ruckus being made out here." She tried to look excited for the boys, and in a way, she was. But in her heart, she also knew the ocean was unforgiving, and many men went out and never returned. But that notion didn't cross the mind of a young man. She gathered some strength and patted his face softly and said, "You better go look at your ship."

Ben's face lit up. "Yes, I should. May I go now?"

His mom forced a smile. "I think that would be best."

Jackie waved a slight hello with his hand, saying, "Good morning, Mrs. Summit."

She smiled at him and returned his greeting. "Good morning, Jackie. How's the family?"

He showed his bashful side to her as he answered, "Oh, they're fine, thanks."

"Well, tell your mother hello for me when you see her, will you, son?"

Jackie bowed his head, saying, "Yes, ma'am, I will."

She waved them off as if shooing away some dogs out of the yard. "Get going. That ship might leave again before you two get a look at her."

Jackie turned and was out the door in a second. Ben felt the uneasy feeling and turned, asking, "You all right, Mom?"

She kissed his cheek and said, "Go before I change my mind."

Ben gave her a big hug and whispered, "I love you, Mom."

She hugged him back. "I love you too. Now get going."

As he ran out the door, she stood with her hand on her cheek where he kissed her, as if his essence would stay there as long as she didn't move her hand.

Ben and Jackie ran down the road as if they were in a footrace. About a quarter mile down the road, they both slowed, breathing hard. They walked at a fast pace down the road until they got to the top slope that gave a view of the bay. They could see her. They both stopped, admiring her from that vantage point. They both agreed she was the finest looking vessel in the bay. The truth was, she wasn't all that special. Just a cargo ship. She had been in that bay a million times, but the boys never really paid her any mind till now.

Ben and Jackie ran down the road that led to the piers. They reached the piers and walked in awe of her as they approached her. There was a gangplank from the main deck to the dock, and men were bustling around, doing all kinds of busy jobs. They stood by the plank, deciding whether or not to go aboard, when a sailor came walking down the plank with a seabag on his shoulder, just like the one Ben had purchased for this job.

As the sailor reached the bottom, Ben politely asked, "Excuse me, sir, but would it be possible to see the captain?"

The sailor looked them both up and down and replied in a very rich accent, "Sees the captain, eh? Depends on what ye wants to sees 'im about."

Ben stood taller and said, "We've come to be deckhands."

The sailor's eyes crinkled up, then he let out a loud hearty laugh, throwing his head back and grabbing a line so he didn't fall backward with the weight of his bag. Ben and Jackie looked at each other, not getting the joke at all. The sailor looked back at them and, giggling a little in his voice, said, "Why don't you two land lubbers march right up to Mr. Awkins and tells 'em what you just told me, and if he don't laugh in your face like me, maybe you could see the captain." He stepped off the plank, bowed, and made a gesture with his hand, indicating they could proceed up the plank.

Ben thanked him as he stepped up the plank. Jackie bowed a bit to the sailor. They both were not feeling as excited as before. They set foot on the deck. Men were hustling about, yelling orders as they went bumping into them as they stood in the way on decks. Ben asked a sailor finally as he brushed by them, "Excuse me, sir, but could you direct me to Mr. Awkins?"

The sailor stopped in his tracks. "You mean Mr. Hawkins, swab? And by the way, I ain't no sir. You'll find him up at the wheel, mate."

They looked up to where the sailor was pointing. A lot of men were working that area, but the man they needed to see was very obvious and was staring right at the two of them. He didn't miss much on his ship, and he used his index finger and pointed right at them. He then motioned for them to come up to where he was.

Jackie was really nervous now, and without taking his eyes off Mr. Hawkins, he said, "I bet that's him."

Ben could only answer quietly, "I bet you're right."

They carefully wound their way around the cargo and lines and men as they made their way to the stairs leading up to the wheel area. As they reached Mr. Hawkins, he greeted them immediately. "Good day, gentlemen. I am the first mate. How I may help you?" He stood straight, hands behind his back. His appearance was very impressive, neat, and proper. He sized the two young men up as he waited for his answer.

Ben was just about to answer when a voice from the main deck called out, "Mr. Hawkins, we could use two swabs below to move some cargo, sir."

Without taking his steel blue eyes off the two boys, he answered the sailor, "Take Carlos and Henry off cleanup."

"Thank you, sir," the sailor ended, and off he went.

He was still staring at the boys whose attention was on the sailor leaving, and he added, "Well, gentleman, I'm a busy man. What was it you needed?"

Ben straightened up, trying not to look afraid, and asked, "I would like to see the captain, sir, if it is possible."

Mr. Hawkins stared at Ben without answering him, making Ben a little nervous as he waited for his answer. Then he turned to Jackie and snapped at him, "And you, sir?"

Jackie showed his nervousness more as he answered, "Uhm… if we could, sir."

Mr. Hawkins could see this young man as big as he was, was scared to death, so he played it a little more. "Could what, sir?" he asked sternly.

Jackie stammered as he spoke, "Well…uh…see the, um, captain, sir…if it's possible…sir." Then he forced a smile on his face.

Mr. Hawkins stared at the two of them, intimidating them with his silence. Then he sharply said, "The captain won't be seeing anybody today." And he turned and started to walk away.

Ben stared at Mr. Hawkins, stunned for a second. Jackie was looking at Ben. Ben not only felt a rush of courage, but it was touched with anger. He stepped toward him, saying, "Mr. Hawkins." Jackie grabbed his arm as he started to speak. Jackie didn't want him to make Mr. Hawkins angry, and he had seen Ben when he got uppity. "Mr. Hawkins stopped in his tracks and turned. Ben pulled his arm from Jackie. "I was sent here by Mr. Harsgrove to speak to Captain Nelson when he would be available."

He stared at Ben for a second. He appreciated a man with courage, and this boy was not as afraid as he thought. "And who shall I say would like to see him?" he asked, putting his hands back behind his back.

Ben stepped a few steps forward. "Benjamin Summit," Ben answered.

Mr. Hawkins nodded, and as he turned, he said, "Wait here. I will see if he is available."

Just as Mr. Hawkins got out of sight, Jackie punched Ben in the arm. "That was great!" he said. "I can't believe you did that."

Ben felt a little flushed after that. He finally took a reasonable breath. He had never been so scared in his life. It felt like hours before he returned, but it was only twenty minutes. While they waited, they looked about the ship and dreamed of all the adventures they would have.

Mr. Hawkins returned and said, "The captain will see you now. Please follow me." They followed right on Mr. Hawkins's heels, matching his brisk pace. When he stopped at the captain's cabin, the two boys almost ran into him. He knocked two sharp knocks on the cabin door.

A voice inside called out, "Yes."

Mr. Hawkins opened the door just enough to announce, "Mr. Summit is here to see you, sir."

"Show him in" was the answer that came next.

Mr. Hawkins opened the door wide and gestured to Ben to enter. Jackie started to follow, and Mr. Hawkins stopped him by putting his hand on his chest. Jackie looked at him with a little of his temper showing. Mr. Hawkins admired that, and he could see this boy could have a temper as big as he was. He was impressed with the change in attitude. To Mr. Hawkins, there was no room on his ship for a man who was afraid to speak how he felt and do what he's told.

Mr. Hawkins told Jackie, "The captain needs to speak with Mr. Summit alone for a minute. He is aware you are here and will talk with you next." Jackie felt a rush of relief and thanked him for letting him see the captain. Mr. Hawkins said, "I assure you he will see you. Just wait out here. Now if you excuse me, I have duties to attend to." He then stepped into the cabin, closing the door.

Mr. Harsgrove was sitting in a chair, smoking a cigar with a drink in hand. The captain was also smoking a cigar. Ben had a hard time getting a breath at first. The smoke was so thick. Ben wasn't surprised to see Mr. Harsgrove aboard, given the information from the housekeeper. Ben acknowledged Mr. Harsgrove, greeting him properly and bowing at the waist. Then he addressed the captain. "Captain Nelson, my name is—"

The captain interrupted, "Benjamin Franklin Summit. Mr. Harsgrove was telling me all about you, son. So you want to be a sailor, eh? Sail the seas."

Ben was nodding as he answered, "Yes, it's been a dream of mine for years."

Captain Nelson raised an eyebrow, took a sip of his rum, and puffed a big puff on his cigar, blowing it at Ben. "Your whole long life you have dreamed of this? And how long has this lifelong dream of yours been in existence?"

Ben was confused at the question. "I'm not sure what that question means, sir."

The captain leaned forward on his elbows and onto his desk. "How old are you, son?" His voice stern, and his eyes were squinted.

Ben was taken back a bit but tried not to show it as he looked the captain in the eye, not backing down at all. "Sixteen years, sir."

The captain smiled a little, sat back in his chair, and took a sip of his drink. Looking smug after a second of silence, he asked, "You ever been to sea, boy?"

Ben shot a puzzled look at Mr. Harsgrove as he thought, *Didn't he tell him anything?* He answered, "No, sir, I haven't."

The captain's face got serious again. "Well, it's not for sissies."

That comment made Ben angry, enough for him to remind the captain that he owned the ship now and he could hire his own captain. That was exactly what Captain Nelson wanted, to push Ben enough to see if he would play that card. To push him to order the captain around. That was what he didn't want aboard ship, some land lover that wanted to run his ship for him. But if this kid could take a beating and still hold his tongue, it might work out.

Ben looked the captain straight in the eye and said, "Sir, this is a chance of a lifetime for me. If I don't go, I will stay here for the rest of my life, working in a convalescent center. I might as well call myself a dying old man, but if you give my friend and I a chance and we don't work out, you can leave us at any port you choose." His speech, brief as it was, reached Captain Nelson. Mr. Harsgrove was a bit stunned as well.

Captain Nelson shot a glance at Mr. Harsgrove and then back to Ben. "All right, I'll take you, but I don't know anything about your friend. Who are we talking about?"

Ben felt a rush of relief and answered, "Oh, I'm sorry. Jackie Huntington. He's been a friend of mine since childhood."

The captain puffed on his cigar. "Mr. Harsgrove never mentioned Mr. Huntington."

Ben found this to be a good time to let Mr. Harsgrove in on the fact he knew he had gone to meet with the *Charee*. "No, sir, I didn't have a chance to speak with him about it. He left town so suddenly to meet up with the *Charee*."

Mr. Harsgrove interrupted, "Oh, it wasn't so sudden. I often go meet with the ship and ride her home."

Mr. Hawkins looked at Mr. Harsgrove with a questioning look. He had crewed as first mate for five years and was a crew member before that, and he never remembered him coming aboard, not even when in port.

Captain Nelson saw the confused look on Mr. Hawkins's face and regained control of the conversation. "So, Mr. Harsgrove, what do you know about this Jackie Huntington?"

Mr. Harsgrove thought for a second. "I believe he's the son of a local butcher, a good boy, and hard worker."

Captain Nelson looked at Mr. Hawkins. "Is that the boy waiting outside?"

Mr. Hawkins snapped to attention with a "Yes, sir."

Captain Nelson threw his arm in the air. "Show him in."

Mr. Hawkins opened the cabin door and stepped one foot out. "The captain will see you now."

Jackie stepped past him and thanked him as he passed. Jackie took a quick look around the room. He recognized Mr. Harsgrove from town. He had delivered meat to his house before. He then peered through the cigar haze and saw Captain Nelson sitting at his desk, cigar in one hand and a drink in the other. He didn't appear as well-kept as Mr. Hawkins. His shirt was unbuttoned to about mid-chest, and he had a very hairy chest. He had the stubble of a few days' growth on his face, and his hair hung down loosely to his shoulders. He had hints of gray also. His face was wrinkled enough to show he was as old as Mr. Harsgrove, but in much better shape.

The captain was surprised at the size of Jackie. "So you little boys want to be sailors, eh?" large smile came over Jackie's face, and the captain was quick to say in an extremely condescending tone, "Something funny, boy?"

Jackie's face became serious again, but he answered, "Sorry, sir, but I haven't been called little since I was twelve years old." Mr. Hawkins cracked a smile and had to repress a laugh out loud.

The captain held his intimidating composure, "Well, big man, I haven't a lot of room for a man your size on this ship. They don't fit in many places. The only thing they are good for is moving heavy objects once in a while. I have a man for that job right now."

Jackie was starting to wish he hadn't put himself in this position. He was starting to think that a meat cutter might not be a bad profession to be in. The captain was trying to push Ben to the breaking point and demand he was the owner and he would do things his way. He couldn't run a ship with that situation hanging over his head. But if Ben could mind his tongue, let the captain do what he did best, he wouldn't mind teaching this land lover or his friend the ways of the sea. Ben held his tongue, but he was a little surprised at the rudeness of the captain. The captain, on the other hand, could see Ben's frustration and was impressed that he kept his thoughts to himself.

Mr. Hawkins was very confused about a lot of this, of Mr. Harsgrove's blatant lie, the captain's rude attitude toward a couple of young men obviously ready to go to work. Something was going on that he wasn't aware of, but he was certain it had something to do with Mr. Harsgrove. So he kept out of it. It wasn't his business.

The captain could see he had pushed this thing far enough. He relaxed back into his chair, saying, "I'll tell you what." He puffed his cigar and drank what was left in his glass as everyone sat breathlessly, waiting for his thought. "The man I spoke of earlier, the large man in my employment, the one that can lift large amounts of weight." The two boys nodded as to assure him they remembered his mention of him. "If you beat him in a wrestling match, I'll give you the job."

Ben and Jackie looked at each other then back at the captain. Mr. Hawkins raised an eyebrow, for this was definitely not the normal routine. The captain sat back, feeling quite smug at the prospect of his idea. If Ben could keep his mouth shut while his friend got beat around, then he could hire them both and not worry.

Ben couldn't help but worry a little, so he asked, "If Jackie wrestles, or rather outwrestles your man, he comes aboard?"

The captain laughed a little. "Precisely" was his answer.

"This isn't like to the death or anything, is it?" Ben asked out of concern.

The captain was getting tired of waiting. He looked at Jackie. "Well, you up for it, boy?"

Ben started to say, "Jackie, I don't know."

Jackie had looked around at the other men. Ben was the only one who seemed at all worried. The rest looked like all they wanted was the entertainment. Jackie interrupted Ben before he could finish his warning. "Of course I'm up for it." Jackie, although very big and very strong, had not been in a great deal of fights. He was always bigger than most, so no one ever bothered to challenge him. He wanted this more than anything in his life. He looked back at Captain Nelson, met him eye to eye, and said, "Yes…I'll wrestle your man."

The captain was surprised at this answer. He really thought this kid would run from the idea. But without blinking an eye or showing surprise, he said sternly, "Mr. Hawkins!"

Mr. Hawkins snapped to attention. "Yes, sir," he said as he readied himself for an order.

The captain continued, "Find Goliath and call all hands on deck to midships. We have some entertainment this afternoon."

He turned on his heels. "Aye, aye, sir." He was out the cabin door as he finished.

Ben grabbed a hold of Jackie's arm. "Are you sure you want to do this?" he asked quietly.

He put a hand on Ben's shoulder. Loud enough for everyone to hear, he said, "I have nothing to lose, Ben. If I win, we sail the seas together and see the world. If I lose, I go back to cutting meat and listen to your stories when you come home." Jackie then leaned across the captain's desk, holding out his hand said. "Thank you, sir."

The captain, out of respect for this young lad's courage, stood up and took his hand, adding, "Good luck, young man." Then turned to Ben and held out his hand to him. "Welcome aboard, son," he said earnestly.

Ben shook his hand, saying, "You won't be disappointed, sir."

The captain stepped around the desk, saying, "Come with me, boy. I'll show you where to get ready." As they all headed for the door, he hesitated and looked at Mr. Harsgrove, who was contently smoking his cigar and nursing his drink. "Are you coming, Mr. Harsgrove?" the captain asked.

Mr. Harsgrove sat up, downing his drink. "Why, yes, of course. Wouldn't miss it." He had no idea what was going on, but he didn't want to appear ignorant in front of all the men. The little band of men dutifully followed the captain around the ship to what he called amidships to a large open deck space where men were already assembling. He grabbed two buckets, turned one upside down, and ordered a sailor standing by to fill the other with seawater. When he returned, he told Ben and Jackie to wait by the bucket, and Mr. Hawkins would come assist them.

Both Ben and Jackie were getting a little nervous as things started to unfold. The captain and Mr. Harsgrove took a place front row. Two men came running into the area. Spectators had started to form a large circle. They were carrying a large hawser line and placed it on the deck in a circle, just smaller than the group that was watching.

Jackie quietly whispered to Ben, "He never did mention whether it was to the death or not." Ben just watched carefully as the scene unfolded.

Mr. Hawkins appeared from nowhere. "You gentlemen ready?" They both jumped, startled by the voice behind them. They both just nodded, not really ready, but they didn't want to say anything. He continued talking. "The rules are simple. No weapons of any kind allowed in the ring. Punching, kicking, wrestling, and shoving all well. Absolutely no biting. The first man to put his man out of the circle of line is the winner. If both of you go out of the circle, you start over. You stop when I say stop, and you start again when I say start, not before. You will get one warning. After that, you will be disqualified. Do you two understand?" he asked. They both just nodded a yes. After a second of silence, he turned and started to leave.

Ben asked, "Anything else that might help, sir?"

Mr. Hawkins stopped in his tracks and spun around. "Yes. Take off all your clothes except your pants. Gives your opponent less to hold on to as he tries to put you out of the ring. Also, you should wet yourself with the water before you start. Makes you slippery and hard to hang on to. The rest is up to you, son." Jackie thanked him. He just smiled and said, "If you win, you get the job. Thank me later if you get it and still like me after we've been to sea together for a while."

As he stepped away, the crowd that had gathered erupted with a roar as Goliath entered the area. He was about six feet seven inches, weighed about three hundred pounds, not much fat included. He was a monster of a man. Both Ben and Jackie were surprised as they surveyed the man. He had a long braid of hair which went to the middle of his back, and his face was shaven clean, all except a thick mustache that ran from under his nose and down his cheeks to his chin, where they stopped. His arms and chest were huge. He had a large scar across his chest, which was very visible as he started to stretch out to get ready for the encounter. Jackie started to mimic his stretching moves.

Ben turned to his friend and said, "You must want this pretty bad." He patted his shoulder.

Jackie didn't even act like he heard Ben. With a low, calm voice, he asked Ben, "How much do you think he weighs?"

It was so quiet and calm, Ben wasn't sure what he said. "How... much what?" Ben stammered.

Jackie calmly asked again, "How much do you think he weighs?"

"I don't know. A little over two hundred."

Jackie laughed a little. "I'm two hundred and twenty. I'll bet he's close to three hundred." Ben nodded in agreement. Jackie started to stretch a little more vigorously. "Can't be any harder than putting an angry boar back in its pen."

Ben was surprised at his friend's confidence and added, "Yes, I suppose it wouldn't be." He chuckled to himself as he patted his friend's shoulder. Then they both started to laugh at loud. Maybe it was to release the stress of the situation, or maybe it was one of those crazy times you found yourself in with a friend. Ben and Jackie had found their way into many of those.

The ship started to get quiet as they realized Jackie was laughing out loud. Then one sailor yelled out, "Hey, Goliath, this boy's laughing at you!"

Ben and Jackie stopped as they noticed everyone was staring at them. As their eyes surveyed the crowd, they both met each other's eyes again and at the same time said, "Goliath." And they started to laugh again.

Even some of the crew members were starting to laugh, but that ended quickly as Captain Nelson's voice rang over the crowd. "Mr. Hawkins, let's get this started!"

The crowd got eerily quiet as Mr. Hawkins stepped into the ring. Then he waved for each man to step into the ring while saying, "Gentlemen, to the center, please." They stood face-to-face, Goliath sizing Jackie up and down and growling. Jackie was sizing Goliath also, but he was trying to figure how he was going to transport three hundred pounds of meat out of the circle. Mr. Hawkins asked, "Do either of you have a weapon of any kind?" They both shook their heads no, never taking their eyes off each other. "Do you both understand the rules?" They both nodded yes. "Well then, start!"

He jumped out of the ring just as Goliath took a left swing at Jackie, but Jackie expected as much. He ducked the punch, and Goliath threw himself off-balance. As his body turned, Jackie gave him a hard push on the rear with his foot. Goliath took three large steps, trying not to fall down, and found himself at the edge of the ring. Goliath then used his arms, and like a bird flapping his wings, he managed to stay in the ring. The crowd was yelling loudly. Moneys were changing hands as they gambled on who would win. Jackie saw his opportunity and figured one more shove as he tried to regain balance. Jackie charged at him with his shoulder lowered. Just as he reached Goliath, he had regained his balance, still on the edge of the circle. But he had been doing this a long time, and his instincts knew Jackie was coming. He dropped down to his knees, and Jackie flew over the top of him. As he did, Goliath grabbed his arm and pulled him into the ring, or he would have been out for sure. It all happened so fast, Jackie wasn't sure what happened. All he knew was Goliath was in his face.

With a scowling face and a deep throated growl, he said, "That would be too easy, laughing boy." Then while sitting on top of him, his hand wrapped around Jackie's throat and readied his fist with his right hand. His face twisted as he reared back, ready to plant one in Jackie's face. Jackie, realizing his fate, quickly moved his head forward as he tried to sit up. Goliath, rather than smashing Jackie's soft nose, hit him directly on top of his head. Goliath let out a cry of pain as his grip came loose. Jackie let out a word his mother would wash his mouth out with soap for saying and pushed Goliath off and got to his feet, still rubbing the top of his head. Goliath, holding his wrist, let out a bloodcurdling scream and charged at Jackie with his shoulder down. He drove it into Jackie's stomach. Jackie let out a burst of air with an *ooof*. He then grabbed Goliath around the waist as they both flew out of the ring and into the circle of sailors. The crowd stopped the momentum of these two giants. Goliath got off Jackie immediately and jumped back into the ring. Jackie started to get off his back and then seemed to fly to his feet as the crowd picked him up and threw him in to the ring. His momentum had him running to keep his balance right at Goliath, who had his right hand cocked to plant on Jackie as he approached uncontrollably. But he quickly ducked the punch and wrapped his arms up around the giant's legs. He then, just like lifting a carcass with his strong legs, hoisted Goliath straight in the air.

Goliath rarely found himself in this position. Jackie performed this feat so fast he tried to gain balance but fell back at a fast rate and landed on his head. He lay stunned for a second, and Jackie jumped on him, trying to push him out of the ring. Goliath regained focus, and Jackie felt a sharp blow to his head, which loosened his grip. Goliath had hit him with his elbow and rolled into the ring, which now made Jackie closer to the edge, off balance. So he instinctively rolled into the ring. He was lying now on top of Goliath. With his back on Goliath's stomach, he swung his legs around and put Goliath's head in a scissor hold and rolled out of the ring.

Ben was yelling, jumping up and down, trying with everything he had to help his friend. He was twisting and turning, cringing at the right times. Jackie sprang to his feet and jumped back to the ring. Goliath wasn't so spry this time. That knock on the head still had him a little stunned, and he was surprised at this kid's abilities. The crowd helped him up, spun him around in the right direction, and shoved him to the ring as they did with Jackie. This time, Jackie was ready, and as the wavering giant came at him, Jackie grabbed the back of his head. Goliath charged hard, intending to push this little youngin' out of the circle. Jackie dropped hard to his back, planted his feet into

Goliath's belly and, with all his might, launched that piece of meat up in the air in a somersault. And he landed clearly outside the ring. The crowd went crazy with yelling as money changed hands.

Ben ran into the ring, helped Jackie up, and asked him, "You okay? That was fantastic." He was smiling ear to ear as his friend gripped his hand to help him up. As soon as he was standing, they both were being mobbed by people patting him on the back.

Even Captain Nelson reached over and shook his hand. "Welcome aboard, mate," he said, patting him on the back.

It took Jackie a second or two to realize he had just beaten Goliath. He turned to see Goliath being helped up, and as soon as the big guy was on his feet, he marched straight over to Jackie. At first Jackie thought this wasn't over. Goliath stopped short and held out his hand. Jackie met his hand. and as soon as he did, Goliath pulled him in close, threw his left hand around Jackie's back, and pulled him in close. Jackie's instincts were to resist, but the giant's strength just sucked him close.

He said in a raspy, deep-throated voice, "Nice job, kid. Welcome aboard." He then released Jackie as the crew cheered again.

Jackie just stood, stunned for a second as people walking by patted him on the shoulder and congratulated him. He and Ben stared at each other, and finally Jackie started to jump up and down with excitement. He was pounding on Ben's shoulders, saying, "We're going to sea."

Then a sailor came up to them both, saying, "Excuse me, gents, I hate to interrupt your little celebration, but Mr. Hawkins would like to see you right away." He pointed up at the wheel where Mr. Hawkins was standing.

They looked to where the man was pointing. Mr. Hawkins was standing, hands behind his back, surveying the ship as it bustled back to normal. He then looked at Ben and Jackie, motioning with his index finger to come to him.

Ben said, "Thank you, sir."

The man laughed and said, "I'm no sir, boy. I'm just a mate. Me name's Martin."

"Well, thanks, Martin," Ben and Jackie said. They took off to join Mr. Hawkins.

When they reached him, he reached into a nook next to the wheel and handed Ben a piece of paper. He said, "Get the items on this list. You will need them out at sea. This Tuesday, report back here at o six hundred hours ready to work." He saw the blank look in their eyes, and so he said, "That's six o'clock in the morning." They both looked a little more relieved. He then added, "That will be all, gentlemen."

Ben reached out his hand to Mr. Hawkins, and he met his gesture. Ben thanked him for the opportunity. Mr. Hawkins just nodded and said, "Welcome aboard, gentlemen."

They left the ship laughing and pushing each other as they went down the gangplank, feeling on top of the world.

Mr. Hawkins watched the two leaving the ship and was glad these two were joining the crew. They seemed like nice kids. They were always short a few crew members, and there was a huge plus side to these two. They were educated, a rare trait among deckhands. Something was unsettling to Mr. Hawkins about the whole situation. Mr. Harsgrove lying about coming aboard all the time and the way the captain treated these boys for applying for a job. None of this was normal, and he knew something different was taking place, but it was none of his business. And if the captain wanted him to know, he would tell him. His job was to mind the ship.

Mr. Harsgrove and the captain were in the captain's cabin discussing business and wondering if allowing that Jackie kid on board would mess with any plans about finding any treasure. Then the subject turned to if maybe his friend knew something, it might make it easier.

Captain Nelson laughed. "I didn't think that kid would win that fight, and then we wouldn't have had to worry about it."

Mr. Harsgrove snapped at him, "You should have told him no right from the start! You didn't need anybody."

Captain Nelson just grinned at the lawyer scolding him, so he interrupted, "Mr. Harsgrove, how would that have looked to my new

COCKROACHES IN THE BILGE

employee, huh? Me saying I have no place for his friend and the next day hiring someone?"

Mr. Harsgrove shrugged his shoulders and nodded an agreement. But he added, "I know there is treasure still out there."

"I'm sure there is too, and I promise you when or if we find it, you will get your grubby little fingers on some. Now get the hell off my ship and let me get some work done, you greedy buzzard."

Mr. Harsgrove huffed at the remark and grabbed a few cigars out of the captain's box. "Very well. I shall leave you to your work. I, too, have matters I must attend to. Don't forget my manifest." As he started for the door, he reached for the rum bottle to pour himself one.

Captain Nelson slapped his hand, saying, "I think you mooched enough booze and cigars off me for one week, and your manifest will be at your office tomorrow by courier as usual. Now go." With that, the captain slapped him on the shoulder and took the glass out of his hand. Mr. Harsgrove huffed again and waved at him in disgust as he stormed out.

* * *

Ben and Jackie were running around town, gathering their suggested gear. At the first store they went to, the shopkeeper asked the boys what they were up to. Ben and Jackie told the exciting story of the wrestling match to get aboard. The shopkeeper was all ears to hear such a tale. He was good friends with the Huntingtons, and when they were finished, he asked Jackie, "What's your folks think about this adventure?" The fun and excitement seemed to drift right out of Jackie's sails. He looked at Ben with saddened eyes.

Ben knew right then what was wrong. "You haven't told them, have you?" Jackie just shook his head no.

The shopkeeper butted in, "You better tell them, boy."

Jackie just nodded to him too and asked, "Please don't say anything, Mr. Wilson. I will go right now."

Mr. Wilson nodded agreement and said, "Yes, you should do it right away."

185

He looked at Ben again. "I better go now before they hear it from someone else."

Ben agreed, and they headed off for the butcher shop. Jackie wasn't even sure what to say at this point and was starting to get very nervous as they neared the front door.

Jackie turned to him. "I think I better do this alone."

Ben just nodded an understanding nod and said, "I'll see you soon then."

Jackie turned back to the shop door and opened it slowly. He noticed the shop for the first time, little things he had always taken for granted, like the smell of the wood shavings on the floor. Memories unfolded as he made his way to the office area where his dad did his paperwork. He heard the door open, but he could tell it was Jackie. He also could tell that something wasn't right. He recognized the shuffle of his feet, but today they didn't have his usual bounding energetic steps.

As Jackie came into view, he asked without even looking up, "Where you been all day, son? Lookin' for a suitable wife?" As usual, the Huntington way of life was to make light of it as much as possible.

Jackie laughed, answering, "No, Pa...I...uh...need to tell you, um, something." Sensing the seriousness in his son's voice, he stopped working and looked up. As he did, he could see in Jackie's face something was very wrong. Jackie stammered as he tried to get it into words. "I, uh, well, you see, Pa, um, you know Ben uh..."

His dad reached over and gently touched his arm. "Just tell me, son."

Jackie took a deep breath and, speaking very fast, said, "I've got a job as a deckhand on the merchant ship *Charee*, and I start tomorrow." He said it so fast, his dad sat forward in his chair, squinting at the lad.

He asked, "What did you say?"

Jackie said it again but slower. "Dad, I took a job on the merchant ship *Charee* as a deckhand." Then he sat when he realized his dad understood that by his raised eyebrow. He added, "I start tomorrow." As Jackie watched, his dad started to get that look on his face when he was in trouble as a young boy, when he would get caught stealing cookies. Then his dad looked away at the floor and chuckled a little and shook his head.

"When we came to the colonies, my grandfather and dad started this. It was a very hard place to live, and after, as you know both men died of malaria, when I was young, I started cutting meat for extra money to survive. After the town started to grow, I saw an opportunity to build this shop. It has served me well, and I won't lie to you, I always thought you would take it over." He was still looking at the floor, laughed a little again, and cupped his hands as he looked Jackie in the eye and continued, "Truth be told, son, I would walk those docks of the waterfront many times wishing sometimes I could hop on one of those ships and see what's out there." He reached up and took Jackie by the forearm. "I knew this day might come. You're smart, strong, and hardworking. You know you can always come back to this if it doesn't work out."

Jackie patted his dad's hand and said, "I know, Dad. I know." Mr. Huntington stood up and hugged his boy like he hadn't for years. Jackie hugged him back just as hard. "Thanks, Dad," Jackie said quietly.

As they separated, his dad slapped his shoulder as he fought back tears swelling in his eyes. "You better keep your wits about you." But in the tradition, he did the Huntington way to lighten the serious moment, saying, "I do feel sorry for you though."

Jackie looked confused at his dad. "Sorry for me? I'm about to see the world and go on an incredible adventure."

His dad stroked his chin. "Yes, that's all true, but you still have to tell your mother."

The weight that just lifted off Jackie's shoulders just dropped back on. Jackie stood silent for a moment as his dad started to sit back down to his work.

Jackie said, "Maybe you could tell her for me?"

His dad laughed a sarcastic laugh. "Me? I'm not telling her, huh. I have to sleep with her, remember?" He decided he would get the rest of his supplies and maybe someone else would tell her before he got home.

* * *

Ben had just reached the home and found his mom working away. He startled her a bit as he approached for her mind was far away. running through memories of her little boy and the life they shared. He noticed she hadn't noticed him walking in. He said quietly, trying not to scare her, "Mom."

She let out an "Oh," spinning around and grabbing a hold of his arm, holding her chest with the other hand. "You startled me." She grabbed hold of both his hands and forced a smile on her face and asked. "Well, how was she? Is it something you think you want to try?"

Ben answered her, but not with the answer he knew she wanted to hear. He answered her with the truth. "She's magnificent, Mom. The captain is a little on the rough side but appears to be good-hearted. The first mate is extremely observant and orderly. I'm sure I will learn a lot from him. The crew seems nice and accepted us."

His mom interrupted, "Us? Jackie gets to go also?"

Ben pulled her down to sit on the bed and started the tale of the wrestling match and how Jackie beat the giant and how he was now part of the crew. She didn't listen to much more of what he said. She was a little relieved about the fact that Jackie was going along also.

The next few days dragged by for Ben and Jackie as they waited for Thursday morning. Jackie did finally tell his mom, and after a couple of yelling matches and Jackie's dad intervening, they reached an understanding. She gave him her blessing. Wednesday night, Ben and Jackie were surprised by a party their parents put together. A large meal was prepared, and friends and relatives came to wish the boys off on their journey. It helped take their minds off the next day's excitement.

Thursday morning, they were up early. There was no way they were going to be late, as Mr. Hawkins had warned them. When they arrived, Mr. Hawkins was at the wheel and gestured for them to come to him. They made their way up to where he was standing, the excitement making their hearts pound. The ship was eerily quiet as most of the men were still sleeping. There were a few men stirring, and they were most likely the night watch. Ben was starting to wonder if Mr. Hawkins ever left the wheel area.

Mr. Hawkins greeted them with a crisp, "Good morning, gentlemen."

They both answered in unison, "Good morning, sir."

He got a big grin on his face and said, "My, my, don't you two look like a couple of little sailors with your seabags on your shoulders." Jackie and Ben glanced at each other and smiled, thinking to themselves that they did. Mr. Hawkins then explained where they were to stow their gear and which bunks would be theirs but cautioned them not to go below until after o six hundred. "That's when the day crew is scheduled to get up, and you don't want to wake them before their time. It's dangerous." He then informed them to wait until the men were up then go below and stow their gear. "In the meantime, since you're so prompt and early, take a walk around the ship and get your bearings. After you store your gear, get to the galley and get some breakfast. Then get back up here. I promised you two work, and I have plenty for you. We have a lot of goods to unload and a lot of goods to reload."

Ben said, "Sir, do you mind if we set our gear down somewhere while we look about? That is, until the men get up?"

Mr. Hawkins smiled a sly smile and answered, "Not at all, sailor. Just don't touch anything around the ship unless told to."

The boys chimed an "Aye, aye, sir" in unison dropped their gear and ran off to tour the ship. Next thing they knew, Mr. Hawkins was guiding them, pointing out parts of the ship and giving nautical terms for parts, pieces, and places. Then at o six hundred, he excused himself and sent a sailor below to wake the men. Ben and Jackie waited till a large number of men had come above decks. Then they followed Mr. Hawkins's orders, found their way to their bunks, and secured their gear. Then they made their way to the galley. As they entered the room, the cook gave them an evil eye. His hair was long, white, and bushy. It met with a beard of the same color, and neither one was well-kept. His aged face had a scar that ran from his upper forehead down his face on the left side, skipping a small section where his eye socket indented, but you could tell it affected that eye some. It finished its jagged journey down his cheek and stopped at his chin. As Ben and Jackie neared the food line, he came around the serving table favoring that left side as his leg seemed to not bend well at the knee, and his left arm was shorter than his right and a bit deformed. He jumped right in front of Ben and stuck his face right into Ben's, not leaving much room between their noses.

He growled at Ben as he spoke. "Watve we ere, a couple of stowaways for a free breakfast?"

Ben was bending over backward trying to get his face away from the old man's, but the line behind him wouldn't budge. The old man barely had any teeth, and his breath was a pretty good indicator that personal hygiene was not a priority.

Goliath tapped the old man on the shoulder and said calmly in his deep, hollow voice, "It's okay, Chef. They're crew members. Just started today." He then turned the old man around out of Ben's face and put his arm around him, walking him back to his place behind the counter.

The old man yelled, "What's this world coming to, feeding a man before he does any work? They better work all day to pay for that breakfast they're about to eat!"

Goliath just patted the old man on the shoulder and assured him he would see to it that they did. Once he was satisfied that the old man was back where he needed to be, he walked back over to Ben and Jackie with a big smile on his face and winked his eye. He pointed his finger at them and, sounding menacingly, said, "You two better put in a full day or Chef and me, we'll feed you to the sharks for dinner."

As they reached the old man again, he grunted as he slopped the gruel onto their tray. "*All day.*" They found a seat and sat quietly like the rest. They were all eating. Not much conversation was going on.

A small scrawny sailor sitting across from them said, "Mornin', maties. Sorry about Ole Chef. He's an old one, he is. Not too good with manners. He's been on this tub since a fellow by the name of

Homer Gregoreouse owned it. Then he sold it to Captain Reginald Roach, purchased it, and acquired Ole Chef in the process." Ben about choked on his biscuit. The sailor kept talking, and Ben had to look back at the old man who knew his great-grandfather. "That ole dog's getting into his nineties and still cooks three times a day. Ees fun to listen to though. E tells stories about the old days about Homer Gregoreouse being a pirate and all. Coming on to some treasure is how he bought this tub and shared it with the crew." He laughed and added, "Like that would likely happen. He also talks about Homer Gregoreouse and Captain Roach bein' the same guy."

Ben sat in shock, trying not to show it. Jackie, though, was not surprised. He had heard most of this story. He hadn't heard much about any treasure, but the rest of the story was true to his understanding.

Then Jackie interrupted the sailor and said, "Well, Ben here is Homer's—" He never got to finish the sentence as Ben knocked his glass of water into Jackie's lap, stopping him from talking.

"Oh, I'm sorry, Jackie," Ben said as he started to help him clean up then got right in Jackie's face, making his eyes wide and looking straight into Jackie's eyes. "What were you saying?"

Jackie then remembered his code of silence about Ben's involvement with the ship and any relationship to Captain Reginald Roach or Homer Gregoreouse. The sailor paid no mind to the disturbance and kept on talking. "Ole Chef there will tell you. He got a share of that treasure. Spent it all on wine, woman, and song, and all he's got left is a song." He let out a squeaky laugh, grabbed his plate, and stood up to leave. "Me name's Arnold Freewater. The men call me Squeaky." Then he looked puzzled and laughed a squeaky little laugh and left.

As he got out of sight, Ben slugged Jackie in the arm hard. "You have to be careful what you say," Ben snapped at Jackie.

"I'm sorry. I will. I thought it was just a story, but when two old guys tell the same story, it's got to be true."

"It is true, Jackie, but I need you to keep it to yourself." Ben was dead serious, and Jackie knew it.

"I'm sorry, Ben. I will honor your request. I promise." Ben felt Jackie's sincerity and sat back in his seat. Jackie then leaned in close and, in a quite whisper, asked, "Do you think the part about the treasure is true?"

Ben felt a twinge of guilt. Here it was, that curse again. Ben almost told him about that part but was afraid it would put him in danger also. Ben's plan was to sail around on the *Charee* for a year and keep a journal of every port they visited. Then he would compare them to the maps and see if they came anywhere close to any places the treasure would be. So Ben lied to his most trusted friend. "He never mentioned that to me."

They finished eating and took their plates and utensils to the area where everyone else had laid theirs. The old man was standing at the spot, glaring at them. Ben forced a smile on his face, and the old man scowled harder and growled like an animal at him. Ben dropped his utensils and turned to get out of there fast.

Jackie was his usual nice self and said, "Thank you. That was good."

The old man's nose wrinkled up like a cornered dog and barked, "Get to work, you lazy scallywag."

Jackie jumped back, and all the sailors in the galley started to laugh. Jackie stepped out into the passageway. Ben was laughing, covering his mouth. Jackie couldn't hold it back. He snorted before he just let out a laugh, and they laughed all the way to the top decks. Jackie said, "He reminds me of Mrs. Olson's dog." Ben laughed even harder. Jackie's eyes were tearing up. He was laughing so hard, he could barely get out, "You remember?" He slapped Ben on the back.

Mrs. Olson's dog was a shorthaired mongrel. When you walked by her place and made eye contact with it, it would start to growl. If you stood long enough, his hair on his back would raise up, and he would start to bark then launch off the porch like he was going to rip your throat out. But he would only come so far then stop as if he had an invisible rope around his neck, walking back to the porch with hair raised and growling. Jackie and Ben, when they were smaller, would tease the dog if they passed Mrs. Olson's house. Their favorite game was to have one of them walk by going one direction and the other come from the other direction, both staring at the dog. The dog would get so frustrated he would just sit shaking and whining.

As they appeared on deck, Mr. Hawkins was there to greet them. "You two go with Squeaky and Virgil. They will put you to work."

Virgil was a younger man in his early twenties, short and stout with a round face and ocean-blue eyes. His hair was a sandy blond tied tightly and hung to the middle of his back. He had a mustache that went down to his chin. His chin and cheeks were shaved. Ben thought this was odd. Jackie found it intriguing. Squeaky thanked Mr. Hawkins and promised to work the two to death the first part of the day. He winked at Mr. Hawkins, who smiled a small smile as he turned to walk away and left them with a "Carry on, gentleman."

Virgil spun on his heels and said, "Come along, gentleman." As he passed Squeaky, he said, "I didn't promise anything."

He looked back at Ben and Jackie and said, "No, you sure didn't" and laughed again.

They wound their way down several steep companionways and into the ship's inner belly. The air became damp and musky, smelling of bilge water. Ben had a smile come over his face as he thought, *Cockroaches in the bilge*. Another smell permeated the air as they came to cases of tea.

The men stopped and, pointing to the cases, explained, "These cases of tea need to be brought to the center of the ship where you will stack them on a cargo net. Come this way. I'll show you." He waved his hand to follow, and they made their way forward until they came to an area about ten feet square with a net already spread out on the deck, taking the whole area. Heavy lines attached to the corners ran up through a gaping hole in the amidships' upper deck. The sun shone down through the hole, lighting the square area below and making everyone squint as they came into the lighted area.

Squeaky explained, "The cases are loaded from the center out, making a large circle." He walked around, showing the perimeter and boundaries of the net. "How much you can put in here will depend on what we haul. The tea, for instance, can go to here, and don't stack it any higher than this." He put his hand up to Ben's shoulder. "Too much weight and we will work too hard to raise it and too little we're wasting valuable time and energy getting this crap loaded and unloaded. When you are loaded—"

Virgil interrupted, "You pull this line hard once." There was a small line that led to the upper decks also, and he reached for it and pulled it. You could hear a bell ring up above. The lines got taut, and Virgil stepped into the net.

Squeaky yelled, "Not yet!" But the lines closed up the net around Virgil, and he smiled and said, "See you above decks, mates."

The net closed around him and he floated out of the area up into the sunlight. Squeaky shook his head in disgust, and the two boys laughed under their breath.

Virgil yelled down, "Never stand in the middle of the net!" Ben flashed back to the story again of how Homer was loaded aboard the pirate ship way back when he was just a boy. He then yelled, "They will drop it back down!"

Squeaky took over again. "When it comes down, spread it out. Make sure the lines are not tangled and load the tea as fast as you can. Ring the bell when you're ready. It's not a hard job, gents. Work hard and fast. Do you boys understand?" They both nodded an understanding. "Good. Do the tea first. When it's done, we will line you out on the next commodity. Once we empty this barge, we'll fill err back up again." The net came down with a thud, and Squeaky showed them how to unfold it quickly. And with that, he said, "Well, go to work." He left to go topside to help supervise the unloading process.

Ben and Jackie went to work. Just as they were told lugging cases of tea, arranging it just so and a tug on the line, the bell would ring, the net would close around the crates, and off it would go. As the day wore on, Mr. Hawkins would appear every once in a while and see the two boys sweating as they bustled around, nodding his approval. That would spur their enthusiasm on. After a long morning of unloading, they were fed a meager lunch of bread, apple, and water. Then back to work. While they came up for lunch, they were able to see the unloading process, how they came up out of the hold under Squeaky's supervision, raised up and swung across the deck and lowered carefully on to the pier. There it was inspected by prospective buyers then loaded on to carts to be redistributed to local merchants. Among the many goods they unloaded that day were kegs of rum, seeds form Britain fruit trees, and some personal items someone had shipped to the colonies for certain people. They even unloaded a piano. It was crated up, but they could tell as they moved it, it would ring an off-key cord. They started to figure out that weight had every-thing to do with where it was placed in the cargo area. The heaviest went to the center, lighter went to the bow or stern. Right side was called starboard, and the left was port. Things were evenly stacked on both sides as to keep the ship balanced. If it hadn't been for the hard work the boys put in that day, sleeping would have been difficult, what with 80 percent of the crew snoring. It seemed like there was someone getting up and moving about all night, then the coughers and mumblers. It was surprising to the boys that anyone could sleep.

Ben was sore all over his body. He wasn't as used to labor as much as Jackie. The next morning, they had finished emptying the ship, and now it was time to fill it. Chef was his typical grumpy self. It was all Ben could do to keep from asking questions about his great-grandfather. As Ben's muscles started to warm up, the tasks became easier. They loaded tobacco, dried corn, and cotton. Lots of cotton. They were heavy bales, about a hundred pounds or so. Squeaky told the boys the hard part was keeping the products dry so they would be in good shape when they got to the next port. Otherwise, they would mold and become unusable. Ben was paying particular attention. After all, this was his business now, and these were the things he should be aware of. It took a couple days to get things loaded and secured for a long journey.

Mr. Hawkins informed them that they were to sail to England the next day, and if the boys chose to, they could stay at their homes for the evening and get a final farewell to their parents. "I'll need you two back here at o five hundred." He knew these two wouldn't miss that time as if their lives depended on it. They both went home and had a good evening, but morning came fast. The boys met on the road that led to the piers. They couldn't stop talking the whole way there. Mr. Hawkins saw the boys coming and could see the excite-ment in their attitudes. It reminded him of his first time at sea. He was much younger, all of about seven. His father was an English officer for the British Navy. Mr. Hawkins's mother died when he was seven, and his father decided to have him aboard ship as the captain's steward. Mr. Hawkins had known nothing else but a life at sea. He was raised by sailors and educated by captains and his father. He knew of no other way than the navy life. His father died of an illness he contracted from some foreign port. They lost several men to the disease. Mr. Hawkins was only fifteen at the time. He served in the Royal Navy until he was twenty years old. He ran into Captain Nelson one night in a pub. He fell in love with the idealism of the new colonies and the states, as they were starting to call them. He joined Captain Nelson as the first mate on *Charee*. Captain Nelson doubled his wages, and first mate was a large promotion for him. He had sailed on the *Charee* ever since. He could go on to be a captain of his own ship, but he enjoyed the *Charee* and the crew. The lifestyle was relaxing. The Royal Navy could tend to be very stressful and unrewarding at times. The move to the new Americas was one he learned to enjoy, and he admired the freedoms the states provided. He had adhered to their ways and values and started to question the motives of the British. As long as Mr. Hawkins was at sea, he was happy. And he knew his crew was happy also. So he watched with admiration as the two young men boarded his ship with unbridled excitement, the desire in their hearts and dreams yet to be discovered, he wondered commitment at sea means risking your lives to save others. Mr. Hawkins would never question this, but would they? They walked up the gangway and right up to Mr. Hawkins. He smiled. 'Early as usual. I like that. I see your mommies haven't talked you out of this crazy idea."

Jackie spoke up. "Oh, don't think she didn't try. She even made my favorite food to make me think twice."

Mr. Hawkins laughed. "I bet she did. Breakfast was early this morning, gentlemen. I hope you ate already. We have to catch the outgoing tide, so you two have ten minutes to get yourselves readied. Then report back up here and you can watch how we will get this big lady out of this tight spot she's in."

They chimed in unison, "Aye, aye, sir." And off they went. As they passed the galley, Jackie couldn't resist teasing the old dog Chef. He stuck his head in the galley. The old man was there washing dishes and securing things.

Jackie yelled, "Hey, any chance of getting some breakfast? We just came aboard."

The old man spun around quick as a cat and started yelling as he hobbled toward Jackie, "You missed it, you lazy scallywag? Next time get up on time, momma's boy! It's not my job to babysit you!" He was swinging a frying pan as he came at Jackie. Jackie took off running, bouncing off other sailors as they were going the other way. They complained.

He was saying, "Sorry. I'm sorry. Ooops, sorry." They soon realized why Jackie was running. When the crazed old man wielding a fry pan came into the passageway, they dropped down, protecting their heads. Then the old man, realizing he wasn't going to catch this smarty pants, let fly the pan. It hit the bulkhead just above Jackie's head. Jackie was pushing Ben trying to get out of range.

Ben was laughing as he tried to hurry and asked, "What did you do that for?"

Jackie was laughing even harder as he answered, "You know, Ben, Mrs. Olson's dog loved it when we came by. When we got older and quit, he seemed to get depressed and never left the porch. He died soon after that. Trust me, Ben, I just saved that old man's life."

Ben shook his head, saying, "Jackie, you sure do look at life in a different way. But remember this, old friend. Mrs. Olson's dog never bit us. I'm not so sure this old dog won't."

They stowed their gear and met Mr. Hawkins at the wheel, watching sailors bustle about. It looked like at first glance nobody had a clue what they were doing, but as things took shape, everyone had a job to do and knew exactly what to do. Some men were what they called standing by, waiting for specific jobs that would need to be done immediately and couldn't wait for someone to make their way to the job that Mr. Hawkins would command. The sun had not completely come up yet, so it was slightly dark. Captain Nelson appeared quite suddenly by Mr. Hawkins's side.

"Everything on schedule, Mr. Hawkins?" he asked in a calm voice.

Mr. Hawkins answered him in a confident voice, "Everything's on schedule, sir."

The captain looked around, adding, "As usual, Mr. Hawkins." Then he looked at Ben and Jackie standing quietly behind them. "What are these two doing on the bridge?"

Mr. Hawkins turned and straightened to attention. "I thought they would be in the way on decks, being their first day, sir, and thought if they were to watch the procedure once first, they may have a better idea on how it would be when they were involved, sir."

The captain nodded. "Very well, Mr. Hawkins. They are your crew and a fine job you do. I trust your judgment with these two." He looked at Jackie and Ben once more, and as he walked away, he said, "Carry on." The captain headed back to his cabin as Mr. Hawkins went back to barking orders, and the big ship made a large sweeping turn. Sheets went up. She started to head out to sea. It was magical the way such a large object could float with such precision and grace. As she picked up speed, the two boys kept looking back at their hometown disappearing into the distance. It was a weird feeling for both as they quickly started to get farther out than either had gone before.

A deep throated voice from behind them made them jump as it said, "I hate to ruin the moment for you, boys, but yous got work to do." They turned to see that it was Goliath. "Come with me. I'll show what needs to be done." They followed, and they were put to work doing small jobs, polishing and scrubbing. As the day wore on, Jackie started to feel a little queasy, and as the rolling waves got bigger, he felt worse.

Ben finally noticed he didn't look right. He asked, "Hey, Jackie, you okay?"

He turned looked at Ben with a truly green and flushed look on his face. He shook his head no and threw his body against the gun rail, hanging half over the rail and throwing up again then again. The sailors who started to witness this started to whoop and holler.

This did not help Jackie at all. In fact, the antics of the sailors and his embarrassment made it seem even worse.

After about an hour of suffering, Squeaky came up and pulled Jackie off the rail and said, "You need to see Chef. He can fix you."

Jackie shook his head no in confusion, saying, "You got to be kidding me, right?"

Squeaky just laughed and answered, "Nope, he's the doctor here. Bet you wished you were nicer to that old man now, eh?"

Jackie struggled up a smile. Between retches, he managed to say, "You don't understand. I saved the old man's life." Then went back to bending over the side .

Ben was getting concerned for his friend but kept working. He stopped only to ask Squeaky, "He'll be all right, won't he?"

Squeaky smiled at Ben as he guided Jackie by the arm. "He's chumin' for mermaids, is all."

Ben was caught off guard. "He's what? Mermaids?"

"Throwin' bait overboard for mermaids. They love land lovers."

Jackie tried to defend himself. "I'm no land loooover," he got out as he wretched again.

"Come on, boy. We had better get you below. This condition is contagious."

"Contagious?" Ben asked, surprised.

"Oh, yes. Sometimes even us old salts sees a man chumming for mermaids, we start to feelin' it too." Ben understood now. He did start to feel it every time Jackie retched over the side. He, too, had to swallow back a little. "Give us a hand, mate," Squeaky said to Ben.

He jumped up and grabbed Jackie's other arm. Squeaky snagged up a bucket as they passed it. The other sailors were all whooping and hollering as they went by. They got him to the galley and got him sat down. With his face buried in the bucket, heaving as he sat, Squeaky went to get Chef.

It only took a second when he heard, "Well, well, well, what have we here. A stowaway land lover, deadbeat scallywag." He was crouched down inches away from Jackie's face. "You're willing to eat my food but not at the price of working for it."

Jackie would rather die than get help from this old guy. Squeaky tried to help a bit by saying, "Please, Chef, just help the boy. We got enough work to do, and he's slowing us down."

Chef turned his eyes toward Squeaky. "Ah, right, just for you, Squeaky. But if he gets one drop of puke on my floor." He looked up at Squeaky then and finished, "I gets im in the galley to help me clean for three days."

Squeaky rolled his eyes. "Okay, but I pick the days. I didn't bring him on to play nursemaid to you."

Chef grinned, showing his decaying teeth. "Don't forget who cooks your food for yas, Mr. Squeaky, and what you might just happen to be in your gruel in the morning."

Ben wrinkled his nose at the thought, and Jackie hugged the bucket a little closer. Squeaky just gave a defeated wave and spun to leave, saying, "Just fix im, Chef, will ya, please?"

Chef just wheezed a laugh and turned to hobble over to get something he keeps just for this problem. He returned with a bottle of some ugly looking yellow liquid. Jackie looked up from the bucket as the old man shoved it at him.

"Take it," he said. "And drink it down fast. Keep it down. No matter what, make it stay down." The old man grabbed hold of the cork with his teeth and pulled it out. Jackie could smell the vile stuff right away and wasn't sure he could even get it to his lips without retching. He took hold of it and downed it as fast as he could. It tasted like unsalted hog fat. He felt it wanting to come back up. He retched a couple of times but held his mouth with his hand and controlled it. The old man grabbed the bottle from his hands, held it up, and looked at it. "Wait a minute, that's the grease from the breakfast this morning. That's not the cure at all." Jackie lost it. He tried to make it in the bucket but missed. Old Chef let out a wheezy laugh, "Oh, would you look at that. It's me lucky day. I get a galley bitch for three days."

Jackie, now holding the bucket with his knees at the bottom and the top secure with his hands, mumbled with drool dripping from his lips. "I've just been bitten by Mrs. Olson's dog." The old man looked at him curiously. Jackie asked, "Am I gonna live?"

The old man patted his shoulder, nodding and saying, "Oh, yes, you're gonna live." And he hobbled over to the cupboard again, pulled down a jug, and poured some liquid in a cup and hobbled back over to Jackie. "This is the real thing," he said, holding it out. Jackie hesitated as he reached for it. "Go on, boy. I got you for three days, and you ain't no good to me in this shape. I'm an old man and ain't got time nor patience to play nursemaid to you. Do like I told you before. Drink it straight down and don't let it back up. It will take a minute, but you'll feel better." The taste wasn't much better than the last bit he was given. Chef stood there, encouraging him. "Keep it down, boy." Jackie had to swallow hard, but after a minute or two, he started to feel better. Chef could see it in his face as the color came back. Jackie rubbed his sore stomach muscles and let out a relief breath. The old sailor put his hands on his hips. "Well, now, you lazy little scallywag. It's time for you to earn your keep, and you can start by cleaning the mess you made on my floor." With that, he threw a mop on the floor at his feet.

Jackie said earnestly, "Thank you, sir."

Chef squinted one eye and said, "I ain't no sir, boy, and you can thank me by getting off your lazy ass and get my galley clean. Everyone topside who had heard the story thought it would have been easier to throw up for three days rather than be Chef's slave for three days.

Ben was put to work on all kinds of different jobs. Jackie spent his time scrubbing and cleaning. Chef was impressed. He was a hard worker and never complained. They didn't speak much. The crews up on decks were all nice to Ben, showing him ways to jobs. Dinnertime rolled around, and groups were sent below to eat. Ben got down to the serving area. Jackie was there to serve, putting up with everyone's comments from "nice galley bitch" to "you would make someone a good wife."

Ben couldn't help but laugh a little when the guy in front of him said, "Hey, Rrrralph, what's for dinner? Stew?"

Jackie saw Ben laugh a little. so when he came up with his plate, Jackie served it a little hard, splashing it a bit onto Ben. After the third day, Ben happened to be walking by the galley and caught a glimpse of Jackie sitting in the galley, talking and laughing with Chef, and they appeared to have a fine conversation. Ben shook his head and kept walking, thinking, *Maybe that old dog did die from loneliness.* Jackie had a way with people, always did. It didn't surprise Ben he had won the old man's favor.

They sailed on what everyone called a nice run for several weeks. Mr. Hawkins kept a running log of daily reports of the ship's progress, weather, dead reckoning, and anything of interest on board. But once a week, Mr. Hawkins and Captain Nelson would get together and go over everything together about the condition of the merchandise below to an intense survey of the condition of the ship. They would discuss crew supplies and crew morale. At one point during one of their meetings, Captain Nelson started to ask Mr. Hawkins how the two boys were doing. He answered him that they were doing famously. "Hardworking intelligent lads. Ben especially was one for detail. He was asking me about learning navigation and piloting skills."

The captain interrupted his speaking and asked, "Why, is there someplace in particular he wants to go?"

Mr. Hawkins was taken back a bit and hesitated as he gave thought to the question. "Not that I'm aware of, sir. He just seems very interested in the ship as a whole. He took time on his own to learn the wheel and how the rudder works. He even climbed into the bilge and stayed in there for quite a while."

The captain's eyes got bigger and then squinted in thought. He mumbled, "He's looking for something."

Mr. Hawkins heard something, but the words were not audible. So he asked, "I'm sorry, sir, what did you say?"

Captain Nelson realized he had said it out loud. Trying to be clever, he said, "Oh, I'm sorry, just thinking out loud. You see, Mr. Harsgrove and I made a little wager. We both felt that the boy, Ben, wasn't going to last the trip and would jump ship sooner or later, so we are both trying to guess where and when. So keep me abreast if you hear anything like any places he might inquire about. Would you please?"

Mr. Hawkins shrugged and answered, "Of course, Captain."

Ben never really gave thought to the treasure for most of the time, only when he would write down the ports of call they would stop at. He was so engulfed in the open seas, amazing sunsets, and wild storms. Just learning how the ship works and reacts. The shipping trade itself was a fascination. Both Ben and Jackie were well accepted by the crew. Goliath was training Jackie in the art of fighting. Ben was privileged to be in on a few lessons himself. Mr. Hawkins occupied most of Ben's free time, teaching him maritime ways. Mr. Hawkins would tell Ben, "As long as you know how to shoot a pistol, Ben, there's no reason to know how to wrestle." They had been at sea for about eight months and were both getting pretty salty. They were heading for home, and both Ben and Jackie were excited to tell of their adventures on the high seas. Ben found himself standing at the bow a lot, looking at the water being cut by the bow and looking back toward the stern in awe. This glorious ship actually belonged to him. He grew fonder of her. With each day, he learned something new, like how she reacted to certain conditions and what some of her shortcomings were. Jackie was always trying to get him to let the secret out that he owned the *Charee*. Ben reassured him he would when the time was right. Jackie was just confused as to why his friend would be so secretive, but he also trusted him enough to leave him alone about it. Jackie was having the time of his life, so why worry?

As they approached Homeport, they both thought it was as odd to come in seeing it from the water as it was watching it when they left. But this time, they were coming in from the water on a tall gorgeous ship. As they got in closer, it appeared to not be much different than any other ports they had come into. People were hustling around, loading and unloading goods. Vendors were trying to sell their goods to prospective buyers. And like every port they had been to, they had plenty to do to get the ship docked and put away so they could start unloading their goods.

The boys were busy doing their jobs when Mr. Hawkins came to them. "The captain would like to speak with you, Mr. Summit," he said pretty much in passing.

Ben jumped to attention. "Aye, aye, sir," he snapped, and off he ran to the captain's quarters.

He knocked a couple of raps on the door and heard a faint but distinct, "Come in." Ben entered the cabin, and the captain was shrouded in a fog of cigar smoke, standing and looking at charts with his back to Ben. He turned to see who it was. "Oh, Ben," he said, turning around. "Have a seat, boy." He pointed to one of the chairs that decorated his cabin. Ben obeyed and sat immediately in the chair as instructed. "Shot of rum?" the captain asked, holding up a glass.

Ben answered, "No, thank you, sir…haven't quite got a taste for it yet, sir."

The captain laughed. "You spend enough time at sea, son, you'll acquire a taste. We had some pretty calm seas this go around, but I can guarantee you do this long enough and you'll get into some seas where you're begging forgiveness from God and reaching for a rum bottle between sentences." He stepped over close to Ben and sat on the edge of the desk. "Mr. Hawkins has been telling me good things about you and your friend."

Ben interrupted, "Thank you, sir. We think a lot of him and the crew, sir."

The captain nodded agreement. "Well, good. We would all like you to be happy. But I was thinking you seem to be more on the ball of the workings of the ship, and Mr. Hawkins and myself would like to see you learn more about the workings of the ship navigation and such. After all, there aren't too many people that would go voluntarily and sit in a bilge for a long period of time and crawl around in it just to understand the workings of a ship and to see how it sounds.

Ben was surprised. He didn't realize anybody even knew he had done that. It just showed him that this ship was big but small enough where everyone knew what was going on all the time and he had better watch his step.

The captain kept talking. "I was hoping that you would stay on with us. Move you up through the ranks as an apprentice to Mr. Hawkins. Get you some more hands-on learning about navigation, piloting, and the such."

Ben's eyes got big. "Do you mean it, sir?" Ben asked enthusiastically, hoping that he wasn't just making a joke of the whole thing.

"Absolutely." The captain nodded with assurance. "I've already spoken with Mr. Hawkins, and he is very willing to work with you. In fact, it really was his suggestion. Besides, kid, it's your ship. If you want to learn more about her, I applaud you for it."

Ben was so excited he didn't even care if he got paid for this job. He thanked the captain over and over until the captain excused him and told him to report to Mr. Hawkins, to see if he needed anything today. He thanked the captain again as he bounced out of his chair and out the door to find Mr. Hawkins. As he approached, Mr. Hawkins could tell that the captain had talked with him about his new opportunity by his gait and the huge smile that stretched across his face. Mr. Hawkins put his hands behind his back, and without acknowledging Ben, he surveyed the decks with his gaze.

Ben approached, stood at attention, and said, "Captain sent me to see you, sir."

"Mr. Summit," Mr. Hawkins started. "I need you to help unload this vessel. When we are done, you will take two days off, as this is your homeport. Then be back to clean and reload Ms. *Charee*."

"Aye, aye, sir," he said. Ben was about to run off to do what he was ordered.

Mr. Hawkins added, "Mr. Summit, how was your talk with the captain?"

Ben turned back to Mr. Hawkins, feeling a little better. He was a little disappointed that he wasn't going to talk about it. "Very well, sir." And he smiled at Mr. Hawkins.

Mr. Hawkins finally made eye contact with Ben and asked sternly, "Are you willing to work extra hard and learn as much as possible but still do your normal duties?"

Ben removed the smile from his face and stood straight and gave a resounding, "Yes, sir!"

Mr. Hawkins smiled at Ben and then said, "Carry on, Mr. Summit."

Ben's grin returned. He bounded away, yelling, "Yes, sir, Mr. Hawkins."

Ben and Jackie worked extra hard and fast that day to get done what they needed so they could get home to their friends and family for a couple of days. To most of the other deckhands, this was just another stop along the way. And the boys were pushing them to go faster. Before they were done, Jackie's dad showed up at the pier. He had heard that the *Charee* had come in. He inquired to a sailor coming off as to where he might find Jackie, and he guided him to the gangplank. As usual, Mr. Hawkins was aware of the man standing at the gangplank. He looked confused, so he sent a man to see what he needed. When he found out it was Jackie's dad, he told him to bring him up to the observation deck. Mr. Hawkins met his dad there and introduced himself to Mr. Huntington and offered him a tour of the ship. Mr. Hawkins praised Jackie's work ethics and abilities. He was feeling pretty proud but not surprised. They even ran into Chef, who praised Jackie and told his father that he was very lucky to have such a wonderful son. Mr. Hawkins was very surprised. He knew Jackie and Chef were growing close, but Chef always referred to him as the pile of dung or the lazy land lover and on and on. As they finished the tour, they went below to see Jackie as he worked. When Jackie spotted his dad, he dropped everything and ran over and gave him a big hug. They both started talking at the same time. Jackie was asking about home, and his dad was asking about sailing. They both just started laughing.

Jackie grabbed his dad by the shoulders and spun him around, saying, "Go home, old man. I'll be home soon, and then we will catch up."

His dad nodded agreement and added, "You better get to work. Your boss was just telling me how lazy you were and wondered if I would take you back."

Jackie just laughed and waved him out. Mr. Hawkins and Ben watched these two with a bit of jealousy and admiration, just from a longing for the relationship they both missed from their own fathers. Mr. Hawkins said he would show Mr. Huntington out. Mr. Huntington reached over and grabbed Ben and pulled him in for a hug and Ben returned it.

"You better come see me too, boy," he added. Ben couldn't help but feel compassion for Jackie's dad and felt special for including him.

"I was planning on it, sir," Ben added.

"Good. Love you, boys!" he yelled as he followed Mr. Hawkins out of the hold.

Jackie and Ben stood watching as he disappeared into the dark of the ship. They looked at each other with a new sense of urgency and went back to work with a revived enthusiasm. They finished that day at about eighteen hundred hours. Mr. Hawkins excused the boys, and off they ran.

Ben was glad to be home and see his mom, but she couldn't seem to stop crying. She said it was tears of joy, but Ben knew different. She just missed him and realized he liked what he was doing and would leave again. By the next day, she was better. He helped her with some chores that she had a hard time doing herself. That evening, Ben and his mother went to visit the Huntingtons, and they heard all the boys' tales of the sea. The next day, Ben had to return to the ship. His mom tried hard not to cry, but her emotions took over, and although Ben felt sorry for her, he made his way to meet with Jackie, and they made their way to the ship together. They weren't wet behind the ears. Now they were seasoned, and they approached the ship with a different swagger this time.

They no more than hit the deck and Squeaky was in Ben's face without even a hello. "Mr. Hawkins wants to see you, Ben. Right away."

Ben smiled. "And hello to you and thanks."

He smiled back at Ben and slapped him on the back. "Welcome back, son." He turned to Jackie and looked him up and down. "Didn't get enough of the old sea, eh?"

Jackie threw his arm around Squeaky. "I only came back because I was worried about you." Jackie picked him up in a bear hug.

Squeaky was kicking and wiggling, trying to get free, and yelling, "Put me down, you overgrown cow!"

Jackie dropped him to his feet. Squeaky pushed himself away from Jackie, grumbling, "What are you worried about me for?"

Jackie lowered his head, shaking it in a shameful look. "Squeaky, I have seen you work. You would never get this ship loaded or unloaded without us youngins' to help." Squeaky took offence to that and started to defend himself, yelling about all the years he had been doing it before Jackie was born. Jackie patted him on the shoulder as he walked away. "Believe me, Squeaky, I never said I could do your job, my friend. No one can organize or handle this cargo better than you, Squeaky. That's what I came back for, is to learn your ways."

Squeaky, still mad a bit, settled down a little. "Damn right, you overgrown baboon. I'm not sure I will teach you anything now."

Jackie dropped to his knees and put his hands together as in prayer, saying, "Oh, please, Squeaky, teach me how to make that pissy whiny face you make." Squeaky waved his hand in disgust and stormed off. Jackie was crawling on his knees, yelling, "Yes, that one, that's it!" He was reaching out like a legless beggar. All the sailors who could hear the whole ordeal were laughing to tears.

Ben had reached Mr. Hawkins, who was watching the show that Jackie was creating with Squeaky. As Ben arrived at his side, without looking away, he said, "Your friend is quite a character. I see why you like him."

Ben smiled to himself but asked, "You wanted to see me, sir?"

"I was told you need to see Mr. Harsgrove in town." Ben got a puzzled look on his face and asked, "Do you know what about, sir?"

"Haven't a clue, son. Just relaying Captain's orders, so get going and get your butt back here. We have a lot of goods to load to stay on schedule." He stayed at his usual attentive stance as he spoke.

Ben asked, "Permission to stow my gear below first, sir?"

Mr. Hawkins had a slight grin on his face. He was pleased how fast Ben was picking up the ways of a mariner—never assume you do anything without permission first. "Permission granted, but don't dillydally."

"Aye, aye, sir," he snapped, and off he ran to take care of business. He reached Mr. Harsgrove's office and knocked then heard a faint "Come in." Ben entered but was surprised to see Captain Nelson there also. Ben first thought he was in trouble, but he couldn't think of anything he had done wrong. He just asked, "Good morning, Captain Nelson, Mr. Harsgrove." He nodded to both of them. "Is there a problem?"

Captain Nelson piped up first. "Heavens no, boy. Come in and sit down." He jumped up and positioned a chair.

Ben felt a little uneasy with these two. He was not sure why. They were both smiling and friendly. Mr. Harsgrove started talking as soon as Ben started to sit.

"Ben, I was going over the ship's manifest, the figures from this year's voyages. We had a pretty good year with a twelve percent increase from the year before. Ben, Captain Nelson and I were talking, and we could see a twenty to twenty-five percent increase in business if we make some changes."

Ben was good at math, and he knew 25 percent was a large difference, so he inquired, "What would those be?"

Mr. Harsgrove sat back and shrugged his shoulders. "Just a few adjustments to the holding area. You got to spend a little to make a little," he said smugly. "Isn't that right, Captain Nelson?"

Captain Nelson was looking at Mr. Harsgrove with a concerned look as he raised his glass, answering, "Absolutely, Mr. Harsgrove. Absolutely." Then he shifted his look back at Ben.

"I still don't understand what is wrong with the hold as it is?"

Mr. Harsgrove was clearing his throat as he prepared to ease into the subject, and Captain Nelson knew he was about to try and sugarcoat some explanation, so he took it upon himself to just say it. "Slave trade, boy."

Ben's eyes got a little bigger. "You mean as in from Africa?"

Mr. Harsgrove could see that Ben was caught a little off guard, and he thought he should step in to try and calm the situation a little. "Yes, Ben, slave trade from Africa. There's big money in it. Oh, we would have to remodel the hold a bit to accommodate the cargo, but it's all doable. Captain Nelson has looked into many ships that have made the changes and studied how to pack them and all."

Captain Nelson watched Ben intensely for his reaction. Ben was still silent and caught a little off guard as he knew what slave trade was. He was not ignorant to it. It was a way of life all over the South. He never saw himself in the middle of it before. He also knew he was with two very intelligent men. He scanned their faces as he was thinking. His mother never agreed with slavery. He had witnessed auctions in town before, and to watch those people's faces, he didn't feel right about it either. Ben's mom was offered several times some to help out on the place by the state. But she gratefully refused. He remembered once, they came to the home with one lady. They insisted she was state property and his mom had to take her. Ben's mom was very upset and tried to get them to hire a free girl and pay her wages. She even told them that if they let that girl stay, the first thing she would do was set her free. Ben remembered the look in the girl's eyes when his mom said that, the longing look as she stared at my mom with her hands on her hips. I know in my heart she wanted that man to say, "I don't care what you do with her. The state bought her. You can do what you want with her." But he didn't. I remembered tears in her eyes when he said, "Mrs. Summit, you ain't nothing but a nigger lover, and I ain't fixen' to see you waste the state's money. I'll just put her to work at the prison." And he pushed her toward the wagon, tied her, chained hands to the buggy, and made her walk behind as he went down the drive. I know Mom wished she had kept that poor girl and kept her thoughts to herself and turned her loose. The state never did give her another chance to try her new theory. As a matter of fact, they hardly ever gave her anything at all. As he looked at the two men, he saw something his great-grandfather had warned him about just before he died—greed. Greed at any cost.

The air grew with tension as he hesitated for an answer. Ben answered with a question. "Slavery has been around for a long time. Why hasn't the *Charee* been outfitted before and involved in the trade?"

Both men took a quick glance at each other, wondering which one would answer. Mr. Harsgrove jumped in. "Well, you see, uh, we, uh, just never really thought about it much before." He was feeling pretty comfortable in his lie as he rambled on. Captain Nelson was nodding in agreement with everything he was saying. "You see, son, I was at a dinner where some very affluent people in the shipping industry were talking and were discussing the large opportunity that the slave trade offers. So I talked it over with Captain Nelson, who approved the possibility of making *Charee* worthy of such trade, and now we are asking your opinion on the matter." Mr. Harsgrove kept on talking, but Ben wasn't hearing much. He knew he was being lied to and attempted to be manipulated.

Mr. Harsgrove was starting to get more animated with his story, and Ben interrupted him midsentence. "Excuse me, sir."

Mr. Harsgrove almost tripped on his words as he was rattling on. "Uh…yes, what is it, son?"

"Do you gentlemen need my answer right now, or can I think on it for a day or two?"

Captain Nelson stood up. "Of course, take your time. We can't work on the *Charee* until our contracts we have now are fulfilled. But the sooner we know, the sooner we can start to gather orders for the slave trade. You understand, don't you?"

Ben nodded and added a quiet, "Yes, sir." With that, Ben stood up. "Well, gentlemen, with that settled, may I have permission to return to the ship, Captain, and unload her?"

Captain Nelson waved his hand in the air. "By all means, you are dismissed."

"I will give you an answer in a couple of days." Ben stopped. "Mr. Harsgrove, could you please make a copy of the manifest and profit and loss statements? I would like to see where we are at, and give a copy to my mother. And see that she gets some income if possible."

Mr. Harsgrove was at a loss for words but stammered out, "Of course, Mr. Summit, I will, uh, have it for you in a couple of days when we get together again."

"Thank you, gentlemen. I will see you back at the ship, Captain."

He looked disgusted and waved his hand as if brushing off a fly. "Yes, yes." As he closed the door, he could hear the men still talking.

A voice from around the corner took him by surprise. "Watch your back, boy. You're messing with their money."

Ben could see it was the cleaning slave that warned him before. Ben nodded in understanding and quietly said, "Thank you." And he headed back to the ship.

As he headed back to the ship, the slave woman's voice kept running through his head. It bothered him why those two men would lie to him. Why hasn't the *Charee* carried slaves before? As he approached the piers and could see the *Charee* being loaded, he looked around the docks, and for the first time in his life, he actually noticed the slaves. They were working away, unloading the goods to be loaded aboard with the cargo net. He saw some being treated fairly well and others being treated horribly. The one thing that was consistent was that not any of them appeared happy. As he approached the crew loading the net, he greeted them, and they returned the greeting, which made him feel accepted.

As he climbed the gangplank to the main deck, Squeaky yelled out to him, "It's about time you showed up! Get below and help motivate that Jackie kid. He's been slower than molasses all morning."

Ben nodded and added an "Aye, aye, sir." And he ran below.

When he reached the hold, Jackie was working away, sweat running down his face, and snapped at Ben. "Where the hell have you been? That Squeaky took it kinda personal this morning, and now I think he's trying to kill me."

Ben patted his shoulder. "I was with the captain and Mr. Harsgrove. Come on, friend, we'll get caught up. Then we'll make Squeaky sweat."

Jackie wrinkled his forehead. "What did they want?"

Ben just shook his head. "I'll tell you later. Besides, I need your opinion on something."

Jackie had seen that look before on Ben's face and figured he would talk with him later, so he just went about their work. By the end of the day, Jackie realized they hadn't said barely a word to each other. Jackie finally asked shyly, "You all right, Ben?"

He still looked troubled as he answered Jackie, "I have to make a decision about a question put before me by Captain Nelson and Mr. Harsgrove. They want to remodel the *Charee* to ship slaves from Africa."

Jackie's eyes got big, and he let out a laugh. "How would you stack 'em?"

Ben punched him in the shoulder and said, "Could you get serious for once in your life?"

Jackie composed himself and said, "Sorry, little friend." He put his arm around him. "So what's troubling you?"

Ben went into a long story about the day and explained it bothered him that his great-grandfather never hauled slaves before.

Jackie stood up off the crate and said, "Come on."

Ben asked, "Where are we going?"

Jackie just smiled and said, "Just come with me." Ben just shook his head and followed. He followed him up to the galley. Jackie yelled, "Chef, you old goat! Where are you?"

The old man hollered back, "What do you want, you whiny little land lover?"

Ben was confused as to what Jackie was up to. "I've got someone who wants to meet you."

The old man hobbled around the corner, mumbling, "I ain't got time to entertain. I'm a busy man. 'Sides, I can't stand people, so what the hell you bothering me for?" As he came into sight, Chef looked around. "Who are you talking about, kid?" Jackie pointed to Ben. Ben looked as confused as Chef. Chef started to bellow, "Well, I know this derelict."

Jackie jumped between Chef and Ben. "You just think you do." He had hold of both the old man's shoulders. "Ben here has something to tell you, and then he has something to ask you."

Jackie turned and smiled at Ben. Ben said, "I'm not sure what you mean. What am I supposed to, uh, tell him?"

Jackie just grinned bigger. "No one knows Homer Gregoreouse better than this man right here." He had turned, standing at Chef's side. He still had one arm around Chef's shoulders. Chef was just as confused, looking from one boy to the other. "And I think it's time to tell someone. Besides, who would believe this crazy old coot anyway?"

Chef piped up, "Well, somebody better start telling me somethin' or I'm gonna start swingin' pans to clear this here galley." Then he tried to push away from Jackie's grip. "And who you callin' old?" Jackie kept a tight grip on the old man's shoulders as Ben was starting to comprehend what Jackie was talking about. Chef spoke up again. "Spit it out, boy. I ain't got all day." He pushed Jackie's arm off, turned, and waved his hand at Ben in disgust. "I ain't got time for this foolishness." And he turned to walk away.

Ben wasn't sure where to start or what to ask. As the old man turned to leave, Ben blurted out, "How well did you know my great-grandfather Reginald Roach?"

The old man stopped in his tracks. Slowly, Chef turned around. "Of course, I should have seen it before." A big smile came across his face. "I knew him as well as any man on the *Charee*, but not well enough to know he had family."

Ben interrupted him to say, "Too many people still believe in the English treasure, and he was afraid for us, so he never let anyone know he had family. Seems as though they had killed most of us to find it. In fact, we didn't even know he was family until a little while ago."

Old Chef shook his head. "Damn treasure is more a curse than a blessing." He pulled a chair close and pointed to one. "Sit, boy. Let's talk." They sat and talked for almost an hour. Ben told him the whole story, except of course the part about the treasure. Every once in a while, the old man would say something like "Well, that old sea dog." And at one point, he said, "I think I was the only one who knew that Reginald Roach was Homer Gregoreouse. At least the only one still alive." He also was surprised that he had died. He thought he had died years ago. He hadn't seen him for so long. When Ben was finished, they sat quietly for a second. Then Chef said, "You had a question to ask of me?"

Ben looked shyly at Chef and said, "Yes, I have been asked to use the *Charee* to haul slaves."

Chef held his hand up to stop Ben from talking. "Captain Nelson and that weasel of a human being Harsgrove, am I right?"

Ben looked at the floor with shame and said, "Yes."

Chef sat up with the expression that he knew he had hit the nail on the head. "What's your question, Ben?"

Ben met the old man's eyes and asked, "Slavery has been around a long time." Chef nodded in agreement. "Why didn't the *Charee* get involved with this before?"

Chef sat back in his chair, sighed big, and said, "Captain Reginald Roach always asked the crew's opinion on what to haul and where we went, not that it would make a difference sometimes, but

214

sometimes it would. This subject, he brought before us. I remember he explained he once was a slave on a pirate ship, and no one should be treated that way and all men should be free. He also said, 'Besides, if everyone else is shipping slaves because the money is good, then that means more ships will be needed to haul other goods, ones that don't involve my conscience.'"

Ben sat there and tried to digest this theory. He broke the silence by saying, "What do you think I should do?"

Chef sat forward, his voice solemn and sharp. "I go where the ship goes, Ben. Been through too much to let what we haul bother me any. I'll just say I feel in my heart you are as good a man as your great-grandfather. I will sail with you anywhere. This is your ship now, sir, and how your heart goes and feels will be your answer. It would mean more money, bigger profits, so we would all profit, right?" Chef chuckled a bit. "Us as in the crew?"

Ben nodded and said, "Yes."

Chef sat up straight again. "My boy, the only ones who profit anymore is Mr. Harsgrove and Captain Nelson. We haven't been treated with respect since the day we were told Captain Reginald Roach was ailin' and Captain Nelson would take charge of *Charee*. You know, I was a crew member when he found that treasure. I was very handsome and very young. He shared it with the whole crew. Most of the crew was smart with their shares, and most all quit sailing and remained very rich. I was very stupid with mine and lost it all. I blame no one for my foolishness. Wine, women, and song. All I've got left is a song."

They sat quietly for a minute and Ben asked, "What should I do?"

Chef got up, hobbled away, and said, "It's your ship and your decision. Just listen to your heart. Unfortunately, there is only yourself to blame if it's the wrong one. Can't help ya there, son."

Ben was confused all day as he tried to make up his mind. He felt better after talking with Chef even though he left the decision up to him. That night, he could hardly sleep. He tossed and turned until he finally dozed off, only to be awakened by someone yelling, "*All hands on deck!*" Ben ran with the others to the main deck. Mr.

Hawkins was at the wheel, hollering for Ben to come up to him. The wind was fierce and the waves huge. He tried his hardest, but it was almost impossible to get there. He finally made it, and Mr. Hawkins told him, "Go below and secure the cargo."

Ben made his way to the lower hold and found the cargo falling all over the place. He started to chain it down and lash it with lines to secure it. Then a voice came from the cargo. "How's your heart, boy?"

Ben squinted. It was dark and hard to see, but the face became very vivid. It was his great-grandfather tied to the cargo. Ben stepped back. How was this possible? He said, "Let me untie you."

His great-grandfather said, "No, don't. We belong here!"

Ben then looked. Lightning flashed. Ben could see now he had tied and chained the hold full of black people. He closed his eyes and shook his head. They were cotton bales, he was sure.

Captain Nelson stood behind him and said, "Now beat them!" He was holding out a whip. Ben refused. Captain Nelson said, "Then I will." He cracked the whip across his great-grandfather's face.

Ben jumped to stop him and missed, and as he hit the floor, he jumped in his bunk, still yelling, "*No!*" He opened his eyes. He was in his bunk, sweat dripping from his forehead, breathing hard.

Someone said, "Shut up, Ben. No one asked you."

Ben lay as still as could be, just breathing and listening to his heartbeat. He must have dozed off again, for the boatswain's whistle woke him. He felt relieved as he bounced out of bed. He knew in his heart what his decision was. He got dressed and headed for breakfast. Jackie saw immediately that Ben was feeling better, which made Jackie feel better also. Ben reached old Chef. He slopped Ben's food onto his plate, saying, "Sleep well, Your Highness?"

Ben thought the old man knew exactly what happened in his dream as their eyes met. Ben shot back at him, "Yes, yes, I did, and thank you. And if you don't mind, maybe we could talk again some time?"

Chef winked at him, saying, "Keep the line movin', girlie sailor. You want a wet nurse, you shouldn't have left home." Jackie was laughing at the two just in front of him. Chef slapped his food down extra hard and snapped, "What are you laughin' at, you overgrown cow? I'm surprised we don't have to change your diapers daily." Jackie dropped his tray on the counter and grabbed Chef by his beard and planted a big kiss on his lips. The old man's eyes got as big as dinner plates as he struggled to push away from Jackie. The line behind him let out a collective "Ohhh!" They all backed up, many wrinkling their noses or turning their heads. Jackie let go, picked up his tray, and ran. Chef was still in shock for a second, composed himself as he loaded up a spoonful of gruel, and slung it at Jackie. He was well out of range. Everyone started to laugh. Both Jackie and Chef were spitting and wiping their mouths.

One sailor yelled out, "How was it, boy?"

Jackie answered, "Like kissing a mud shark, or maybe a cow's ass. Not sure though. I've only done one."

"Which one?" another sailor asked.

Jackie shook his head. "Oh, I don't kiss and tell."

Another yelled out, "Hell, I wouldn't either. For the likes of things you kiss, why would you brag?" Even ole Chef had to laugh a little at some at what was being said. The line started to move, and things got quiet and went to normal.

Squeaky came by and pointed to Ben and Jackie and said, "You two are to see Mr. Hawkins down below."

Ben barely looked up and answered, "Aye, aye, sir." They finished eating and went below. Mr. Hawkins was there.

"Mr. Huntington, you and Mr. Summit will finish loading the cargo. Then you will lose him as a partner and he will work with me. You will then be free to learn how to whine like Squeaky, for that will be who you will work with."

They both nodded and in unison said, "Aye, aye, sir."

The day went by fast as Ben and Jackie loaded cargo. Then when they were finished, Ben reported to Mr. Hawkins. Mr. Hawkins loved to teach, and Ben was fun to teach. The day went by, and it was time for bed. Ben had forgotten all about his decision he had to report on the next day. It wasn't until the next morning after they were shaken from their bunks and at breakfast when Squeaky came bounding in, out of breath and excited.

He stopped in front of Ben and Jackie, pointed at Ben, and said, "You're to see the captain as soon as you are able."

A wave of fear rushed over Ben as he remembered he had to face those men again and deliver his answer. Ben just mumbled, "Aye, aye, sir." He stirred his gruel a little then dropped his spoon in it and stood to leave.

Jackie asked, "Not going to eat breakfast?"

Ben looked at him and sighed. "Kinda lost my appetite."

Jackie nodded. He remembered also. "Good luck in there."

Ben looked back at his friend with eyes burdened with responsibility and nodded. As he put his dishes away, he saw Chef looking at him. As they made eye contact, Ben said, "My heart and conscience are clear."

Chef laughed a loud chuckle and said, "I think I just saw a hair sprout on your chest. Maybe the boy's becoming a man!"

Ben needed that. He felt for the first time he wasn't just a boy anymore. He was the owner of this vessel. His decision, right or wrong, was his to make and theirs to follow. He lifted his chin and walked a little straighter just like his great-grandfather told him to do when you wanted someone to respect you and take you serious.

Mr. Hawkins watched as Ben headed in the direction of the captain's cabin. He wondered what the secretive business of Mr. Harsgrove and the captain and Ben had in common. He wasn't accustomed to having secrets aboard ship, but he was also an obedient servant to the ship and the captain. And if the captain felt it was none of his business and it didn't affect the ship or crew, he was fine with that.

Ben reached the captain's door and knocked twice loudly. A muffled voice said, "Enter." Ben stepped in. The captain was sitting behind his desk, going over some papers. He looked up. "Oh, Ben, please come in. Sit down." He was motioning to a chair in front of the desk. Ben took the seat, awaiting the captain's anticipated question. He finished what he was writing and sat forward, putting his hands together as if praying, his elbows resting on the desk. Tapping his index finger to his lips, he eyed Ben. He was making him feel uncomfortable. Finally, he said, "Well, boy, you have had some time to think about this. Are we going to start making some real money here? Or just keep plugging along hauling tobacco and cotton around the world?"

Ben adjusted himself straight in his chair and looked the captain straight in the eye. "My decision, sir, is to keep plugging away. It was my great-grandfather's wishes, and I plan to honor that."

The captain slammed his right hand down on the table, making a loud bang. Ben blinked, and he jumped, not expecting that reaction. But he held his composure. The captain yelled at the same time, "Boy, you don't know what you're doing or saying! You haven't thought this out very clearly!"

Ben could feel his anger rise as his face got hot. He tried not to show it as he calmly said, "On the contrary, Captain, I gave it considerable thought and consulted some very knowledgeable people on the subject, and I feel—" "*Just get out and do your duties!*" the captain interrupted. Ben felt his anger growing again. "You don't understand, boy. It's not just about the money. It's about politics and a way of life. Oh, what's the use in trying to explain it? Just get out, you rich little bastard."

Ben was mad, but that last comment made him stifle a laugh. He had never been called that before. A rich little bastard was what he was now. The captain's brow furrowed, and Ben, with a restrained smile, stood and forced out an "Aye, aye, sir." He stood to leave. He was just stepping out of the cabin.

The captain had turned his back to Ben and muttered under his breath, "You probably know where the treasure is too."

Ben hadn't quite closed the door behind him, but he heard it just the same. His heart jumped a beat, and a knot hit his stomach. He stopped for a second, reopened the door, and asked, "Did you say something, sir?"

The captain spun around, pointed at Ben, and yelled, "*Get out!*"

Ben shut the door fast and was confused by the captain's attitude. Then again, he wasn't. It was greed driving this man. Ben realized right then and there that no matter how much a human being wants, he will always want more. He shook his head and said to himself, "Greed." He went off to find Mr. Hawkins.

Mr. Hawkins's curiosity was piqued. The captain usually never talked with the deckhands. That was his job. So Ben's increased attention with Mr. Harsgrove and now this had him really wondering. When Ben returned, Mr. Hawkins tried to be sly and asked, "How did your talk with the captain go?"

Ben let out a big sigh. "Not so well."

Mr. Hawkins really was expecting a little more information than that. So he asked, "Is Mr. Harsgrove a relation to you?"

This question took Ben by surprise. "Well, no. Why do you ask?"

Mr. Hawkins knew he went too far. "He and the captain are pretty close friends, so I just assumed."

Ben interrupted, "Oh, that. I had a relative die, and Mr. Harsgrove was helping me out because he was in charge of the estate." It wasn't a complete lie, but enough that he knew Mr. Hawkins wasn't fooled. He kept on though. "Mr. Harsgrove was a friend of the family, and he was instrumental in getting me a job on the *Charee* because I had a keen interest in sailing, and he thought it might be a good education for me."

Mr. Hawkins could feel Ben's uneasiness about lying and decided to let the boy off the hook. He interrupted, "Well, that explains a lot. I didn't mean to pry."

Ben's face showed relief as he answered him, "Oh, I don't mind."

Mr. Hawkins thought, *Yes, but would you mind telling me the truth?* This ate at him a bit. Sure, it wasn't his business, but the ship was his business, and he wasn't used to having secrets kept from him. Oh, there were always those like who stole the rum from the cabinet, those petty lies that don't ever get answered, but this…this was a little deeper, and it bothered him. This deceit was with the captain and a few crew members. He didn't like that feeling, but he wasn't going to push the issue yet.

The next day, the ship was ready for sail at eleven thirty. Ben had avoided seeing the captain and went home for the evening and spent one more night before they left. While at home, he compiled the maps and hid them in a hollowed-out book to conceal them. He made it back to the ship after a sad goodbye to his mother and stowed his gear. *Charee* departed right on time. The winds were fair, and she quickly maneuvered out of sight. The next week was business as usual. Ben did his usual duties, and when he was free, he would catch up to Mr. Hawkins, who would give him nautical lessons in navigation. Each night, Ben would go over his maps to see if *Charee* was anywhere near the expected treasure areas. He did find a match near the Virgin Islands. Depending on how long they stayed in the port, Ben could find a small boat and take it to the treasure area, which was on an isolated and unpopulated area forty miles from where the *Charee* would be docked. Ben decided he would make a final decision based on how long they would be in port.

Ben only saw the captain a few times while they were under way. He wasn't his friendly self. Mr. Hawkins noticed it also. Three weeks into their journey, they ran into some nasty weather. As the wind kicked up, so did the waves. The crew was ordered to be ready. Anyone not on watch was ordered to the topside, ready to batten down the hatches. Ben had always heard that phrase, but now he was truly about to do it. Ben and Jackie were told to secure anything loose. It was soon decided that there would be no dinner that night, that it was too rough and dangerous to cook. Sail area was ordered taken down. The weather grew worse with each passing hour. Waves were starting to come over the bow. The decks were awash with seawater.

Goliath picked Ben up as he was washed off his feet and yelled to the boys so he could be heard over the roar of the wind, "Keep a hand hold, boys! Your about to sail through your first hurricane!" With that, he laughed out loud.

The daylight turned to night as the sea grew angrier. The clouds smothered them, taking away the horizon. Orders had to be passed from one sailor to the next to be heard over the roar of the wind. A voice would only carry a short distance. Ben and Jackie started to get a little nervous, but the rest of the crew seemed at ease with all that was going on. They had all been through this before, and they tried to assure Ben and Jackie that *Charee* knew what she was doing, and she didn't want to go to the bottom of the ocean either. Mr. Hawkins stood at the wheel, staring the storm in the eye. After a bit, there was some yelling and pointing. Mr. Hawkins looked up to see that a top spar and sail had broken free. It was swinging on a halyard and smashing against the mast and entangling lines. Then in the few seconds that this was discovered, the sail it was tied to started to open. Mr. Hawkins yelled for Stephan, his most experienced ratline climber and rigging expert, to hurry up the mast and cut that thing loose. It went through several men and finally reached Stephan, who was watching the ordeal and was basically waiting the order to do so. He looked back at Mr. Hawkins and waved an acknowledgment.

The captain appeared at Mr. Hawkins's side. He was shaking his head no. Captain Nelson waved his arms in a fashion to let Stephan know he was not to do as told. He understood that part. What he didn't understand was why. He stood by at the ready with a confused look. By then, Mr. Hawkins was starting to realize he was being contradicted and turned to see the captain behind him. As he did, the captain yelled, "Send Ben and Jackie up to cut it loose!"

Mr. Hawkins turned, not second-guessing the captain but second-guessing what he just heard. "Did you say Ben and Jackie, sir?"

The captain's face was red with anger. "*Give the order! You heard me right!*"

Mr. Hawkins knew time was of the essence, but he wanted to be sure the captain knew these two hadn't had much experience on the rigging yet. "But, sir, those two boys haven't been in the rigging much and—"

He never got to finish. The captain's face grew even more twisted with anger. "Those two want to be sailors so damn bad, let's see what they're made of. *Give the damn order!*"

Mr. Hawkins turned and reluctantly passed the order to a sailor standing by, who looked confused but passed it to the next, who looked back at Mr. Hawkins with a question on his face. Mr. Hawkins nodded his approval, and so the word was passed. Each one was looking back at Mr. Hawkins with a surprised look. It finally made it to Ben and Jackie, who were quite content hanging on for dear life. Even though Mr. Hawkins watched as each sailor looked back for conformation and he approved the message, when it got to Ben and Jackie, they didn't look back. He knew they wouldn't. They looked up to where the trouble was, and both hopped up to go take care of the order given to them with no question or fear. Mr. Hawkins was relieved they didn't look back. If they had, he would have felt like he was delivering a death sentence. He turned back at the helmsman. "Whatever it takes, keep her as close to the wind as you can while they're up there."

The helmsman knew what he needed to do, and with all he could do to keep his feet under him, he barked, "Aye, aye, sir."

Several sailors were getting lines ready to throw just in case they went overboard. Ben and Jackie were scared to death and trying not to show it. Stephan was at the point on the ratlines that they were to climb and explained the best way for them to climb and complete the task ahead. They started to climb. The lower part was hardest, for not only was the ship pitching hard front to back side to side, a wave would hit them and they would hang on as hundreds of gallons of water would engulf their whole bodies. The sailors would stand at the ready to see if they were still on the lines after each wave. And they were laughing out loud although no one below could hear them. They would howl with excitement and hang on tight. The ship swayed more as they got higher, but the waves couldn't hit them anymore. Jackie and Ben whooped and hollered encouragement at each other. They finally came to the loose spar, and the sail that was whipping in the breeze would crack like thunder as it angrily beat in the wind. The spar which was a good twenty-five feet long and about ten inches round came swinging at them while they tried to get above it on the lines.

Ben was above Jackie, and it narrowly missed his head. Then the sail came slapping against his body. As it pulled and it went by, Ben yelled to Jackie, "Keep your eye on that thing! I'm sure it's coming back!"

Jackie yelled back, "We gotta time this thing!"

Ben could see he was right. "Stay below me and wait till I get above it, then you go!"

Jackie yelled back, "Yes, that will work!"

Ben waited for a second. As he felt the sheet start to come back around him, he scurried up the lines as fast as he could to get above the swinging spar. He got just above it as it came whistling at him.

He hung on, waiting to have it swing by under him, but as it swung, his left foot was caught in the sail. And as it flew by, it tightened around his ankle. It reached the point where it pulled Ben's foot. It was like a team of horses had pulled his leg, ripping his grip loose from the rigging. Jackie looked on in horror as he watched Ben swing out across the decks and out over the water. Ben felt himself pulled from the rigging, expecting to fall and hit the water or the deck. He instinctively grabbed the sheet as he fell backward and caught a glimpse of the ocean as he swung over it. He heard Jackie yelling to him to hang on, but Ben was pretty sure it was hanging on to him. He felt the tight grip of the sail to his foot. The ship started to tilt to the other side. The spar, the sail, and Ben all started to swing back the other way. As he flew like a bird toward Jackie, he kept his wits about him.

He yelled, "Get ready!" He swung past Jackie's head. Jackie wasn't sure what he meant by that, watching his friend fly by for a ride of his life. Ben used the momentum to swing harder, shifting his weight. He swung toward a stay and reached his arm around it, locking his elbow and holding with his other arm to keep that arm. Once he knew he had a grip, he yelled, "*Climb, Jackie, go!*"

Jackie now understood what he was doing as he held the spar from swinging back. Ben held the life-threatening battering ram steady while Jackie climbed safely above the danger. Ben was holding tight as the ship started to shift again. The pressure started to build. He could hear yelling down below. He saw Mr. Hawkins and the crew cheering him on, which helped him hold tight as he felt the pressure of the weight of the spar and sail. He quickly added a leg wrap and held on as Jackie scrambled above the danger. Jackie was ready in case Ben couldn't hold it. He climbed fast and did make it above the spar. Ben held himself with all his might against the pull of that big log and sheet, the wind tugging hard. His arms and legs burned as he held, tense to the rigging. The pull from his ankle was so extreme that it felt as though his hip might get dislocated. Jackie worked fast and diligently. He made it up onto a spreader and retrieved the line which kept the sail furled to the spreader, working fast. He pulled the slack in keeping the sail from getting any bigger.

He then took a loose line and fashioned a noose. He dropped it down using the wind to guide it and lowered it to Ben. Ben's eyes were shut, concentrating on hanging on until he heard Jackie yelling. He looked up as best he could and saw the noose coming.

Jackie yelled, "When the pressure goes slack, put your other foot in the noose and hang on!" Ben wasn't real sure what Jackie was up to, but it beat anything he was doing right now. The ship tilted to the other side, and Ben reached up and snagged the line Jackie was offering him. He released his grip on the stay as the spar and sail started to shift to the other side. He quickly put his free foot in the noose, and at the same time Jackie yelled, "Let go! I got you!"

Ben was still unsure of what Jackie was up to, but he had to trust his friend. Ben's right foot was still tangled in the sail as he let go now. And now he at least had some control over being upright so he could see what was going on. As he swung across the ship, he could see the crew's eyes wide open as well as their mouths as they watched in shock at the show before them. Then out over the water he went. The stormy seas didn't look so menacing when he was suspended above them like that. Jackie had gotten into position. Using the spreader as his fulcrum, he pulled with his legs, quickly taking the slack with his arms and resetting himself to pull again with his legs. Slowly, Ben felt himself start to rise. He looked up as the spreader and sail all started another trip across the ship. He saw Jackie pulling him and the spar up. He was getting close to the spreader that Jackie was working. Once more over the water as he came, swinging back this time, not quite so dramatic. He was able to reach up and put an arm on the spreader and started to help Jackie pull this monster in. Sitting and straddling the spreader, they secured the spar and the sail. Ben untangled his foot, and they could hear the crew cheering as they started to take a breath. Their eyes met, and they both started to laugh.

Ben said, "That was fun. You should try it some time."

Jackie just laughed harder. "Just remember, it's my turn next time." They found their way down the mast to the crew, who were slapping them on the back and congratulating them on living through that.

Even Stephan came over and said, "That's not quite how I would have done it, but good job."

Mr. Hawkins was smiling and shaking his head at the spectacle he just witnessed, and he turned to see the captain storming off to his cabin. Mr. Hawkins let out a sigh of relief that those two boys made that fix without getting killed, but now he took a big breath again. He had a storm to get through. The bad weather lasted two days. Most ships would experience an angry crew, edgy about any small things. Mr. Hawkins knew how to run a crew. He could tell when a man needed to be spelled for a break and when a man could last a little longer. He made sure that the men ate. Maybe not a hot meal but food just the same. By the second day, as the winds started to die down, the sun shone through the remaining clouds. The crew went about their normal duties like nothing had happened. There was some cleaning to do. The bilge needed to be pumped again. That night they had their first hot meal. Everyone was excited about that. Ben and Jackie finally got a turn to eat.

They entered the galley and heard old Chef yell, "Well, well, if it isn't Lazy and his partner Good-for-Nothing." He shoved a large spoon at Jackie and said, "Here, Lazy, feed this mob. Good-for-Nothing, come with me." Ben and Jackie looked at each other, a bit confused and hungry. The old man started again, "Come on, gorilla boy, get your ass back here and get to work."

Jackie laughed as he said, "Don't make me kiss you again, you old goat." He stepped around the corner.

Chef mumbled as he motioned Ben too follow him, "Do that again, boy, and I'll gut you like a sea bass."

Ben followed the mumbling old sailor as he hobbled into a storage area. He could hear Jackie yelling like a street vendor, "Come and get while it's hot! It's not tasty or recognizable, but it is hot."

Ben smiled, knowing it was making Chef cringe. Just out of sight of the crew, Chef spun around, grabbed Ben by the collar, and spun him into a corner. It surprised Ben, not only for doing what he did but the strength he had when he did it. The old man's face was dead serious as he squinted one eye as he spoke.

"Listen up, boy, and listen good. Why do you suppose the captain chose you two to climb the riggin' the other day? Huh?"

Ben just shook his head as he tried to speak. "I, uh, I don't know."

Chef gave him a little shake as he asked him another question. "Had much time in the riggin'?" Ben was going to say no, but Chef beat him to it. "Of course you ain't. You made an enemy, son, a big one, and you had better start to think about how he might benefit if you were dead. Got relatives? Who gets the *Charee* if you die? Maybe your little lawyer friend has some ideas for you." Ben was getting uncomfortable. He kept asking questions but wouldn't let him go or answer any. "These are some questions you need to ask yourself, boy, and watch your back. I don't think this is over yet." Chef could tell by the look in Ben's eyes he was starting to understand.

Ben reached up and patted his shoulder, saying, "Thanks, Chef, I appreciate that, and I will watch my back. Funny, you're the second person to tell me that. I wish I knew how."

Chef let go of his collar and said, "I will try my best to help if I can."

Ben looked him straight in the eye. "You already have Chef more than you know." Chef pushed him out of the storage area, yelling, "Now get back to work, you girlie sailor! You don't deserve to eat, neither one of yas!" He reached where Jackie was. He pushed him and took the spoon out of his hand. "To the end of the line for you two beggars." Then he slapped Jackie hard on the butt.

Jackie jumped forward with an "Ouch!"

"That's for your comments on my cookin'."

Jackie turned and puckered his lips and made a kissing sound in the air as he got back in line.

Ben was quiet for the rest of the day. He was in deep thought, sometimes working himself up to a real mad. He wanted to march right down to the captain's cabin and fire him on the spot. Then at times he wasn't sure if Chef was seeing things clear. What happened in the rigging the other day was his own clumsy fault. By the end of the day, he decided to let it go and watch his back just the same. Things went along as normal. Mr. Hawkins never said a word about the incident other than he and Jackie having done a fine job up there and not killing themselves was an accomplished feat. Ben felt a change in his and the captain's relationship. He never spoke directly to him anymore. He would tell Mr. Hawkins to tell him even if they were in the same room.

Mr. Hawkins knew something was up but didn't bother to ask Ben or the captain. He figured those two needed to work it out. He secretly hoped they would do it soon for fear Ben might get set up again to die, and Mr. Hawkins liked the boy too much to let that happen again. While training, Mr. Hawkins would occasionally say things like "You know, Ben, when you're running a crew, the best thing to have is honesty between you and your crew." This would tear at Ben's conscience. Many times he wanted to blurt out the truth and tell the whole story. Mr. Hawkins sensed this and would prepare himself for Ben's confession, but it never came.

As they neared the Virgin Islands, Ben started to get excited, and his thoughts were on looking for the treasure. Ben's training in the navigation and charts made more sense of the treasure maps. Ben was still a little concerned about the captain's comments about treasure. He was going to share it with the crew as his great-grandfather did, but he didn't want to get any hopes up until he knew for sure there might be real treasure out there. If there wasn't any, he would be satisfied just running a merchant ship and let the curse go away and be forgotten.

The *Charee* made her way to Saint Thomas Island, and they found their way to Charlotte Amalie, a bustling port. Mr. Hawkins had explained to Ben that Saint Thomas Harbor was and still is a favorite place for pirates. "So keep your wits about you when you go ashore and don't discuss *Charee's* contents or destination."

Ben asked in a roundabout way, "How long will we be in port?"

He pondered the question for a second and said, "It appears a week or so. The sugar plantations are a little behind because of the storm."

Ben was excited. He couldn't wait to get back to his bunk and look at the map of this area and try to pinpoint where the treasure might be. He asked another question, trying not to show his enthusiasm. "So are the men allowed some leave while in port?"

Mr. Hawkins was going over some paperwork and mumbled, "Yes, of course." Then he looked up and asked, "Why do you ask?"

Ben's face flushed red. He didn't expect that question. He tried to cover himself by quickly answering, "No reason, really. Just seemed like a nice area. Thought Jackie and I could go see some of the island while we're here."

Mr. Hawkins just nodded, went back to what he was doing, and mumbled, "Yes, they are remarkable." He knew in his own mind Ben was lying to him again.

The next day, they docked in St. Thomas Harbor. The ship was secured, and with their duties done, Ben was released to leave the ship. He had a very hard time convincing Jackie he had business he had to take care of alone. His first order of business was to find a small boat to rent, borrow whatever he could, but it had to be seaworthy to get around the islands. It was roughly thirty two miles from the harbor to a small island, unnamed and not on the charts. Ben had taken the coordinates from his great-grandfather's map and found no island on the charts. There were many islands out there that were not on the charts, so Ben wanted to go to the area. If no island existed then, there was a good chance there was no treasure either. Ben had resolved the fact that if there was no treasure, he could be happy just running the *Charee* for the rest of his life. Ben found a thirty-five-foot gaff rigged ketch. A skinny old man owned it and ran it. He ran passengers and goods around the islands. Ben tried to talk the man into leasing him the boat by himself, but the old man would not consider this. It was his home. Ben tried to find something else, but unless he was to buy a boat, the old man was his only way to get around. So he decided to let the old man chauffer him around. Ben went back to the ship and grabbed some gear. He stopped by a mercantile store and bought a shovel. As he came out of the store, he ran right into Jackie. He was surprised and looked as guilty as a dog in the henhouse.

Jackie was a little surprised, too, then noticed the shovel. Jackie could tell Ben was feeling guilty about something, so he didn't cut him any slack. "What the hell are you up to, Mr. Summit? You have been acting pretty strange."

Ben stammered to come up with an answer. "I, uh, um, uh." Ben was tired of lying to his best friend. He finally decided to add another person to suffer the knowledge and curse of the treasure. Ben squinted his eyes at Jackie and said, "You really want to know? Then go get yourself a shovel and meet me at the north end of the pier in the harbor." Jackie nodded as a big grin came across his face. Ben added, "Don't say anything to anyone. And whatever you do, don't bring anyone with you. Can you do that, Jackie?"

Jackie nodded again. He was getting that feeling Ben was going to do something unexpected. Like the time he and Ben at the county fair got Susan Chambers for being a high and mighty and always putting Ben and Jackie down. Susan Chambers was a self-proclaimed singer, and every year she would put on a show. She would sing and dance, and everyone in town would clap appropriately because her dad was one of the wealthiest men in town. Ben had the idea to sneak into her room where her costume was, and he carefully put ground corn into the bottom hem. Not too much or she could tell just enough. Then Ben and Jackie went over and borrowed four large sows, ran them through a mudhole, then herded them over to Susan's makeshift stage area. As Susan started her show, Ben and Jackie helped the sows find their way onto stage. They had to give Susan a little credit. She kept on going even though the sows were rooting around the stage area. The audience got a laugh out of it, but one of the sows got a whiff of the corn in her dress. Now she could fend off one, but four pretty much knocked her down and removed her dress. It was pretty humiliating for her. No one ever really knew who did it, and there were enough kids in town who didn't like her, so it was hard to decide. Ben and Jackie felt they had received a little justice. Ben was acting like that now, and Jackie couldn't wait to see what he was up to.

Jackie purchased his shovel and went to the pier to join Ben. When he got there, Ben was at the end of the pier, waving at Jackie in a "hurry up and come here" way. As he neared the end, Ben stepped over the edge and started to descend. That's when Jackie noticed a small mast bobbing from below the pier. As he got to the edge, he looked over to see a small sailing ship. Jackie was a little curious now. He climbed down and boarded the vessel. Ben, smiling from ear to ear, introduced Jackie to the old man at the tiller.

"Jackie, meet Miguel. He will be our captain." Jackie smiled and nodded a hello.

Miguel nodded back and immediately barked an order, "Senor Jackie, hold us steady against the pilings while I untie the stern. Ben, you untie the bow." Both boys went to work, following orders. The old man was impressed. He started thinking this trip would be fun, having crew members that were seasoned sailors. Once the boys had done what they were told, Miguel yelled to Jackie to push off hard. Jackie shoved with all his might. Miguel told Ben to raise the jib. Ben went to work pulling on the halyard to raise the sail/ It went up fast and tight. The wind was at their backs as the sail filled. The boat started to move. They went out only so far, and Miguel ordered the boys to get on the main sail and ready to haul her up. The boys got into place. Miguel swung the boat around, heading into the wind. The *genoa* fluttered as they lost the wind. Miguel hollered, "Pull 'er up now, Ben!" And Jackie pulled fast and together, and it went right up. Ben was a little worried they were heading right for shore. Miguel came about filling the sails, and she came alive as the sheets fluttered and then with a bang filled with power as they headed back out to sea. Ben and Jackie both were surprised at how easily this boat maneuvered, how fun it was to feel it under their feet.

Ben started to raise the mizzen. It only went so far before the pressure of the wind made it almost impossible. Jackie saw the dilemma and jumped in, grabbed hold of the line, and together they yelled, "Pull!" And when they did, they would pull together. They inched the mizzen up three times altogether, and it was up and taut. They were heeled over on a broad reach and quickly pulled out of the bay. They both looked back to see what Miguel might need next. He waved them back to the cockpit area. They both carefully made their way to the cockpit.

The old sailor put his hand on Ben's shoulder. "You boys did great," he said. "Now take this." And he guided Ben's arm to the tiller. Ben took it, but wasn't too sure of the intentions. Miguel smiled. "Just keep us on this heading." And then he walked around the boat, making adjustments as he went, coiling lines, and changing the position of a block or two so she was running to her best potential.

Every once in a while, he would point to Ben to go more into the wind or fall off the wind. Ben was having a time of it with the tiller. It worked opposite of the wheel on the big ship, so it was easy for him to stray from his course. As the old sailor made adjustments to the boat, it started to pick up speed and heel over more. Ben and Jackie were used to the ship heeling some, but this was dramatic. The rail was in the water. They felt a little uneasy, but the old man looked very comfortable and pleased with his direction they were heading. Ben and Jackie were enjoying the ride, and Jackie kept laughing at Ben, who would steer the boat so that it didn't lean so bad, but the old man kept telling him to fall back off and keep the heading. He finally came back to the tiller and explained how the ship worked. He then put Jackie on the tiller and taught him to feather the tiller, moving it slowly little bits at a time, keeping the boat steady and making some time.

To Ben and Jackie, it was fun and exhilarating to be on the sea. Once Jackie started to get comfortable with it, Miguel went below. He came back up with a jug in his hand. He popped the cork with his teeth then took a swallow. He handed it to Ben, who shook his head and refused it. Jackie, on the other hand, shrugged his shoulders and took the jug and sniffed it.

"I think it's rum," he blurted out.

The old man nodded and said, "Si, finest in the land. My brother makes it."

Jackie took a swallow, made a small face, but said, "Mmm, that's good." Jackie elbowed his friend. Ben looked up, lost in his own thoughts. Jackie pushed the jug at him. He had such a large grin on his face Ben couldn't say no, so he decided why not. He took the jug and took a large swig. He coughed a few times and shook his head with a shiver and handed the jug back to Miguel. He was pleased. He was always uneasy if his passengers wouldn't partake in a taste of rum.

Ben was feeling a little more relaxed now. He was able to take in the beauty of the ocean, wind, the blue sky, and the laughter of his close friend. They had sailed about an hour when Jackie told Ben, "You never did tell me what this is all about. But if this is all we do for a couple days, it's okay by me."

Ben's face became serious, for that hour he didn't think about the treasure at all. Ben called to Miguel, who was down below, and asked him if he could take the tiller for a minute. Then he took Jackie to the bow, out of hearing distance from the skipper. Miguel watched the two boys as they talked and saw Jackie's face get more and more intense.

Then Jackie let out a yell. "We're gonna be rich!"

Ben punched him in the chest hard, saying, "Keep it down." Ben looked back at the skipper and saw he was watching them, but he looked away as if not paying any attention. Ben looked back at Jackie. "That's exactly why I didn't tell you before," he said sternly. "A lot of people have died because of the knowledge of this treasure. Keeping it a secret is of the most importance. Do you understand, Jackie?" Ben's voice reeked of sincerity. "Besides, I don't even know if there is any treasure. That old man could have made the whole thing up."

Jackie laughed a little, saying, "That old man didn't make the *Charee* up."

Ben's face lit up, and he grabbed Jackie by both shoulders and said with intensely bridled excitement quietly, "We're gonna be rich."

Jackie and Ben sat laughing, and Jackie turned to the old skipper. "How about another taste of that rum?"

The old man smiled a large smile and reached over to where he kept it in its own little holder built into the rigging. He held it up and waved for the two young men to come back and join him. The skipper had a feeling he knew what these two were up to. He had seen it a million times. Someone sold a fake map to the treasure of Bloodthirsty Bob. He has sailed many out to the uncharted islands, only to see their disappointed faces. It hasn't happened for a long time. The boys sat down, and the skipper took a swig then handed it around. Jackie took a couple of swallows and passed it to Ben.

The old skipper looked at Jackie and said, "Here, amigo." He pointed to the tiller. Jackie jumped up and took the tiller. The skipper went below and in minutes came back up with a platter full of tortillas wrapped around some meat and beans, bananas, mangos, and pineapple. He pointed to the food. "Eat." Then he moved into position to take back the tiller.

Ben asked, "What about you? Wouldn't you like to eat first?"

The old man smiled at Ben. "Young man, I am an old man. I don't need much food. All I need is a girlfriend." He wiggled his eyebrows up and down as he said the last line. Jackie laughed so hard and fast he almost blew his mouthful of food. The skipper decided that these two youngins' should save their money and he would help them out. He asked, "How much did you pay for the map?"

Ben thought he was talking about the chart that he had borrowed from the *Charee* that helped him try and pinpoint around the area of which there was no island charted. But the old man knew where Ben was talking about. There were a lot of islands that were not on the charts of the merchant ships. Ben answered, "Oh, I borrowed that from the *Charee*, the ship I was on."

The old skipper shook his head no as he added, "The treasure map you two have."

Ben and Jackie stopped eating, frozen in place. Their eyes were locked in place at each other. Ben tried to collect himself and said with a question in his voice, "Treasure map?"

The skipper looked blankly out over the horizon. An awkward silence fell over them for a second. The skipper broke the silence. "Look, boys, I'm just trying to help you out. I really don't care how much you paid for the map. I just thought I could save you some money. If you didn't have to pay me for three days, we could just have a nice sail for the day and go home." He kept talking as Ben and Jackie tried to wipe the look of shock off their faces. "I am surprised. I haven't seen this done for years, selling maps to Bloodthirsty Bob's treasure. I have taken many men out to find this treasure, but no one has ever come up with it. I had my suspicions as soon as you two boarded with shovels in hand."

Ben decided to give in a little and asked, "You know about Bloodthirsty Bob's treasure?"

"Of course I know about him. Many pirates sailed these areas. He was the most notorious of them all. Beat the British up pretty bad and hid it somewhere on these islands...but which one?"

Ben was getting a little uncomfortable with this conversation. Maybe his great-grandfather was playing a trick on him, but then again, the scars were a pretty elaborate hoax. Ben went to see how much the skipper might know. "You ever hear of Homer Gregoreouse?"

The old skipper shook his head no as he looked out over the water, appearing to ponder the name.

"How about Captain Reginald Roach?"

The skipper sat with that look on his face and then answered, "No, senor, him either."

Ben rested a little easier with the fact that this wasn't local knowledge. Jackie was eating quietly, trying not to get involved in this conversation at all so he wouldn't make a mistake and say something he shouldn't.

The skipper pointed to the bowl of food and said, "Senor Ben, would you hold this please? We're going to tack. And you, Senor Jackie, take the helm, porfavor."

Jackie jumped up, taking the tiller. They were on a starboard tack, and he wanted to change his heading to a port tack. He explained what was about to happen on his command. He gave the command, and the boat swung to the right. Ben quickly put the bowl on the low side. The skipper and Ben quickly let lines loose and hauled in the sheets to the other side. The main swung across with a loud jar to the sheets that held it in place. The small ship was on a different tack and right up to speed. Ben and Jackie were both surprised at how fast the ship reacted and how easily two or even one man could sail this vessel. The skipper went around, making small adjustments to get the maximum speed out of her.

As he was out of sight, Ben turned to Jackie. "If there is any treasure and we find it, we have to buy a couple of these." Jackie just sat grinning from ear to ear and nodding with agreement. The old skipper made his way back to the cockpit and relieved Jackie from the helm. As soon as he did, he went right back to the conversation they were on before.

"So tell me, why are two young muchachos like yourselves chasing dreams of treasure instead of chasing senoritas?"

Jackie piped up, "Oh, don't worry, skipper. I get my share of the ladies. It's Ben here I worry about. He has eyes for only one girl."

Ben's face went red from embarrassment. He made a fist and shook it at Jackie, and he made a face that was threatening.

"So this young lady, you thinking of marrying her?" the skipper asked.

Ben was about to answer, but his old friend interrupted, saying, "Well, that's possible, Miguel, but she first has to know that he is alive."

Now Ben was too embarrassed to say what he was going to say. The old skipper smiled, saying, "This girl you admire from afar, she doesn't know you?"

Ben shyly answered, "She knows me…she…she just doesn't see me the way I see her."

Miguel shifted himself on the tiller and leaned closer to Ben, saying in a quiet and sympathetic voice, "My young friend, woman, even young ones, they see things and think things, feel things that they only tell their closest friends or even to the family dog. Sometimes they don't tell anyone. You have to bring it up let her know how you feel. Ask her straight out if you have to before someone else does." He patted Ben on the shoulder, nodding. "Then if she tells you to leave her alone, then you jump back into the water. There are many fish in the sea." They all laughed at that then settled into their own thoughts for a while. A few islands came into sight. The skipper finally broke the silence. "There, that's your island." He pointed ahead.

Ben stood up, trying to get a better look. Jackie had dozed off and was startled awake by the skipper's announcement. Ben looked back at the old man. "Are you sure?"

The skipper got a big smile on his face. "Young man, I have been sailing these islands since before I could walk. I knew which island you were talking about as soon as you gave me it's position."

Excitement was building in the boys as they looked at the island, as they approached their future, if Ben's great-grandfather was right and this wasn't some scam. The old skipper tried to warn them there may not be any treasure. He could only smile at these two. They were nice boys, and they seemed so full of hope and promise of a bright future. He envied their youth. He had forgotten how to dream of treasure. He wasn't sorry for his life. He had lived well, but to watch these two reminded him of his youth. Miguel piloted into a protective cove and dropped anchor. The two boys readied the small rowboat lashed to the roof of the cabin. Once lowered into the water, the two loaded their gear and shoved off and waved goodbye to the skipper. He just bid them good luck and went about small mainte-nance on the ship.

As they reached the shore, they pulled the dingy up far enough out of the water onto shore, where they knew the tides couldn't take it away. They learned that the hard way when sent to shore once for an errand by Mr. Hawkins. They pulled it slightly out of the water, and when they came back with their goods, they found the dingy floating out to sea. Lucky for them, a fisherman had witnessed the whole thing and returned it to the boys. Then they returned to the *Charee*. Mr. Hawkins had witnessed the whole thing also, so they all sat down for a talk about not taking the sea for granted, how drop-ping your guard around her can cost your life or limb. Ever since then, Ben and Jackie pulled their boats up on shore to the nearest vegetation and tied them for good measure.

They unloaded their shovels and gear, and Ben brought a hand-held compass, and the two were off to find treasure. The sun was starting to set, and Ben knew they would have to start in the morn-ing. They had a restless night's sleep on the beach. But when they awoke at first light, they got up and started hunting. Ben was get-ting very excited as the pieces of the map were falling into place. Landmarks mentioned in the map were in their respective places. He followed the legend so many paces north to the pile of rocks with a single palm tree sticking out, so many degrees from the palm tree north by northwest, so many paces to the large rock shaped like a sleeping elephant. The two palm trees at the trunk dig directly in between them. It was still early afternoon, and they started digging with a lot of enthusiasm. They would normally be hungry by now, but they were being fed on greed now. There was nothing more important now than finding the treasure. Dirt was flying out of the hole. Each took turns digging while one rested. The only thing that wasn't in the code was how deep the hole needed to be.

Ben kept saying with each turn, hopping into the hole, "That sure would have been a nice thing to know."

Jackie was starting to get a little annoyed. The hole was now about five feet round and a little deeper than Jackie. He was tall, so they knew they were deeper than six feet. The boys were dripping in sweat and covered in dirt, and the promise of treasure started to look unrealistic. They both realized they were hungry, thirsty, and tired of digging. They used the signal to switch by dropping the shovel and yelling, "*Switch!*" Then the one would reach his hand out to the other one to pull him out of the hole. Jackie, out of frustration, threw the shovel hard to the ground nose first into the dirt. The handle hit the wall of the hole, knocking a large chunk of earth away from the side and into the hole, burying Jackie up to his knees.

He stood looking at the hole, shocked, then said, "Dammit, Ben, this game isn't fun anymore." He grabbed the shovel and threw it out of the hole. Ben reached out and helped him out. Ben sat down, dangled his feet to drop into the hole, and slid off the edge. Something ripped his pants and scratched him good too. Ben was getting frustrated and turned around and slapped the earthen wall to protest and for payback for some of the pain. The shovel made a loud resounding *tink* sound and bounced back at him. It was at that point he saw what ripped his trousers. He could make out a corner of a chest. He stood in disbelief for a second then started to dig at it with his hands. Jackie had not seen any of this discovery yet. He had plopped himself down and took a large drink of water. He was just about to tell Ben that they should stop this nonsense and go back to the ship.

Just as he was about to speak, Ben's voice came out of the hole, quietly at first, then building as he dug. "It's here. It's here! *It's here!*"

Jackie dropped the water jug and threw himself over the edge on his belly on the dirt mound to see what he thought his friend meant.

Peeking in the hole, he realized and mentioned to Ben, "We dug right past it."

Ben was digging like a madman. Jackie launched in the hole to help his friend dig. They were both digging away at the sandy soil. Neither one was speaking as they worked at the chest. It was bigger than each one imagined. Once the chest was uncovered, both stood back and marveled, still in silence as they stared at it in disbelief. After a second or two of silence, they looked each other in the eye and locked arms and danced whooped and hollered in the hole.

Ben stopped. "What are we going to do with it?" he asked, looking at Jackie.

Jackie replied, "The first thing I'm gonna do is buy me one of those little boats…then maybe a big one like yours. And if I got any money left over…" He hesitated "I'll buy my dad's butcher shop and then fire him just to see the look on his face."

Ben looked puzzled at his friend's comments, saying, "No, no, how do we get it out of this hole, for one thing, and then back to the ship without anyone seeing it?"

Jackie started to see Ben's point. Then he said, "You know, Ben, you always have to see things rationally, don't you? I tell you, it kinda takes the fun out of life."

Ben rocked back on his heels a little and looked surprised by that comment. With his feelings a little hurt, he mumbled, "I don't always, do I?"

Jackie could see he took that way too seriously. He patted him on both his shoulders. "It's a good thing, little friend. Besides, if it were always up to me, we would probably end up doing things like swinging from our ankles in the rigging during a hurricane. That's why we need someone with a steady and focused mind on this crew."

Ben couldn't help but laugh at that and gave Jackie a shove back, saying, "Come on, let's get this thing out of here."

Jackie said, "Fine, but remember, it's my turn next time. You always get the fun stuff."

Ben nodded and added, "We have to look inside and see if there is anything in this."

Jackie laughed. "There you go again." He shook his head as he pulled on the big trunk. It slid out of its hole onto the soft dirt. Jackie could tell it was heavy as it hit the ground. "It may be just the body of Bloodthirsty Bob in there and no treasure at all," Jackie said jokingly.

Ben looked at him. "Now you sound like me."

Jackie quickly sassed him back. "I wouldn't mind that at all, Ben. You have a very pretty voice for a man."

Ben ignored him, shook his head, and took his shovel and beat on the lock that held the trunk closed. It didn't appear to be doing anything. Jackie reached over and grabbed a big rock and tried to pound at it. It didn't seem to do anything.

Jackie was getting frustrated. "What the hell was the point of locking it?" he said between swings. "If you gonna bury it."

Ben chuckled under his breath as he watched Jackie chisel away at it. He added, "I don't know, but it appears to be working."

It was starting to get dark in the trees, and Ben figured they didn't have much time left before it would get dark. Jackie wandered around as Ben whacked at it with his shovel. He found a bigger rock. He returned to the hole and took three hard swings with it. The lock broke open. Ben was scouting for a better tool to use when he heard, "It's open." Ben came racing back, and the two just stared at it for a minute. It was about four feet long, three feet deep, and not much wider than two feet. The top was arched. It was handsomely ordained with artistic brass straps and corners. It had a large round gold plate formed to the top that had an official looking symbol, and if the boys could read Latin, they would have realized it said *Property of the British Treasury*. They both took hold of a corner of the chest lid and slowly, against the protest of the hinges, pushed it open. They were immediately exposed to a bounty of coins, jewels, and gold. It glowed in their faces. They stood for a moment with grins on their faces. Jackie finally reached out and carefully ran his hand through it.

Jackie finally broke the silence. "It's real, Ben. The old man was telling the truth. Now you can worry about how to get it back to the ship."

They managed to wrestle the chest out of the hole. It wasn't easy, so they knew carrying it back to the boat would be hard. Jackie had an idea and ran around. He gathered up some log pieces about four feet in length. He laid them out in front of the chest. The forest was starting to get dark as the sun was dropping to the horizon. It was going to get dark fast now. Ben looked at him with a curios smirk.

Jackie said, "Remember in history the Egyptians moved those huge blocks by rolling them on logs?"

Ben suddenly realized what Jackie was up to. They wrestled the chest onto three logs and laid three more in front. They started to push the chest. It rolled easily across the logs. They got excited now, and at first progress was a little slow, but after a short time, they got a rhythm going. As one would push, the other would pull. Then Jackie would pick up the free log from behind as it appeared. He would toss it to Ben, who was pulling. He grabbed the logs and placed them in front of the chest. They started to walk right along through the jungle and toward the dingy. They worked for hours, even past dark. When they reached the shore, the night was clear. The stars shined brightly, looking like they went on forever. The schooner sat anchored out in the bay. The two boys, worn out from their day's work, sat up against the trunk. The sand was still warm from the day's baking sun. They talked, looking out over the bay with the stars and the lapping water on the shore about their wants and needs and how to split it up among the crew on the *Charee*. Then almost simultaneously, they both dropped off to sleep.

A screeching seagull jolted Ben awake. The sun was high in the sky. Ben looked over to Jackie, who was sound asleep. Ben shook him to wake him. Jackie stirred a little and wiped his eyes. Then he sat up quickly, whirling around to look at the chest. He hugged it, saying, "It wasn't a dream." Ben smiled. "No, it wasn't, and neither is how we are going to get it aboard the *Charee* without being seen."

"Didn't we settle that last night?" Jackie had a confused look on his face.

Ben, too, looked a little bewildered. "Yeah, I guess we did." Ben added, "We better get moving. Besides, I'm starving."

They took the dingy down to the water then wrestled the trunk slowly down to the dingy. They almost tipped the dingy over as they tried to lift it into it. Jackie shoved them off as Ben took to the oars and started to paddle toward the ship.

Jackie laughed as he said, "As much labor is involved with this chest, I think we're underpaid."

Ben smiled a little, but he was still bothered by how this was going to work out. The skipper had been watching them all morning with a spyglass but couldn't truly make out what they had, but in his own mind he knew they were either trying to bring a big square rock back or they had found something on that island. He was very curious as the dingy approached the ship. As they came close enough to see the skipper, he went below to make some lunch as he didn't want to get caught spying on them. Ben had already made up his mind to let the old skipper know about the treasure and buy his silence. The skipper heard the dingy bump the side of the ship.

Jackie's voice broke the silence. "Ahoy there, skipper!" He yelled once then again, "Hey, skipper, you home?"

The skipper popped his head out of the companionway, answering, "Si, senor. Que pasa, amigo?"

Jackie hollered out to him, "Miguel, can you give us a hand?"

The old skipper, ready to satisfy his curiosity, bounded out of the cabin to look over the side. He saw two young men smiling as big as the ocean, pointing at one big dirty chest. The old skipper, when he finally exhaled, said under his breath, "God be with you boys. You found it."

Ben answered him even though it was not a question by saying, "Yes, we found it, and we need a hand getting it aboard with your permission, sir."

The skipper came to his senses by shaking his head and said loudly, "You found it."

Jackie couldn't help it. He jumped up on the deck, took hold of the old skipper's arms, and said as he jumped up and down, "We found it. We found it." The old man started to jump up and down with him, and Jackie stopped him. "Let's get it on board." He grabbed the bowline from the dingy that Jackie was holding and swiftly tied it off. He took a spare line lying about and tossed it to Ben. He tied off the stern and ordered Ben to fasten the line to a cleat on the dingy.

The skipper tied his end off to the ship. As he did, he looked Ben in the eye. "Did you open it?"

Ben's smile grew wider. "Yes, we opened it." He dropped down to his knees "Is it full?"

Jackie dropped down to his level right by his ear and said, "Stuffed to the gills."

He reached over to another coil of line and threw it to Ben. "Here, tie this around it."

Both boys, out of habit, yelled, "Aye, aye, sir!" Jackie jumped down to help him. They both secured the line around the trunk. While they did that, the skipper went to the mast and took the main halyard off the sail and dropped it to the boys. They tied it off, and the skipper hauled the slack out then gave a tug, and his feet came off the ground and the chest didn't budge.

"Ay, caramba!"

Jackie jumped back up on to the ship, grabbed hold of the line, and gave a pull. He got it to raise. By then, Ben could get on board and assisted. As it rose up the side of the ship, the old skipper held it off the sides with a gaff hook while the two young ones lifted it up to the deck and let it down easy. As it settled to the deck, the skipper rubbed the top as if caressing a family dog. Then he undid the knot that was holding the halyard in place and swung it to Ben, who secured the line with Jackie. Then they all stood by the chest as Ben opened it again. They weren't as surprised this time by the bounty which laid inside but were spellbound again by its glowing beauty.

The skipper stood in awe and mumbled some words that Ben nor Jackie understood. Then he crossed his chest to his head and, looking up to the sky, and quietly said a few other words. Then he focused back to the boys and said in English, "I certainly hope it's not cursed." Ben and Jackie looked at each other and then held back a laugh. The skipper looked puzzled. "Who sold you the map?"

Ben answered, "We didn't buy it. We inherited it." The skipper looked a little confused. Ben patted his shoulder. "Skipper, that treasure has been a curse for a long time, and if you could get us some food, we will stow the dingy and get underway. We have to get back to the *Charee* before tomorrow. And I will tell you all about it on the way back." The skipper just nodded agreement and went below to put some food together. They ate and secured the dingy, pulled up anchor, and got underway. Ben asked the skipper, "About what time will we reach the *Charee?*"

The skipper looked forward and up the mast. "If the winds stay with us, we could be there as early as one o'clock in the morning."

"That's perfect," Ben blurted out, and he explained to the skipper that his intentions were to smuggle the treasure aboard the *Charee* and figure a way to share it with the crew. They talked for hours as Ben told the story of his great-grandfather and how they ended up in this place. He did, however, leave out the part about many other treasures that were out there. After a while, they had talked and decided a plan to get the treasure aboard the *Charee*.

They had reached the port about one thirty in the morning, just like the skipper said they would. They sailed in to port and close by the *Charee*. They went right past her, and Ben and Jackie made a constant visual to see how many people were on watch and where they were located. As they expected, there was one man at the gangway and one at the bridge keeping watch while about three others were doing maintenance on the vessel. That would be their job later on in the evening, for they were due back this day at nine o'clock. The skipper docked at his usual spot at the end of the pier. The skipper left the boys on the boat and ran into the dark streets. He seemed like he was gone for a long time, but it only really took him about ten minutes. When he returned, he was carrying a half dozen canvas bags. While he was gone, Ben and Jackie had off-loaded the dingy and had it ready. They then emptied the treasure trunk into the bags at a manageable weight. They dropped them into the dingy. Ben pushed Jackie and the skipper off as he stayed on pier. Jackie rowed them out to the quiet blackness of the port. Ben took his seabag over his shoulder and headed for *Charee* to board her as normal as he could without creating any suspicion. He came up the plank and greeted the sailor on duty. The man at the wheel waved as he recognized it was Ben. Ben made his way toward the crew's entrance, and as he reached, he looked back to see the sentries were not watching. He went around the house to the starboard side of the ship that was facing the bay. Jackie had quietly made his way along the starboard side of *Charee* just close enough that anyone on duty would have to lean over the rail to see them. He made sure to lift the oars quietly and drop them in ever so softly as not to make a splash that would alert anyone to look over the side. Ben pulled a line out of his bag and dropped it down to the dingy. Jackie quickly tied a bag of treasure to it and gave two tugs to say it was ready. Ben hauled away as fast as he could and put it against the house. He was standing in a spot that could not be seen from the wheel area, but that didn't mean someone wouldn't walk around once in a while just to stay awake on his shift. So Ben and Jackie and the skipper worked as fast as possible to bring the treasure to the decks. Ben stacked them in a line, hoping the shadows would hide it if someone was to look down that way. They were running out of darkness. It would be light in a few hours, so they hurried as fast as they could. Jackie tied the last one on and signaled to Ben, and Ben waved an understanding wave to Jackie, and he pushed off and silently rowed away. He then took one bag at a time and made his way to the open cargo hold.

As quietly as he could, he lowered the bags down into the darkness. Each bag was tied shut with a line, and a loop was left in the top. Ben threaded his line through it and lowered it double, then he could let go one end and retrieve his line, leaving the bag below without having to run down to untie each one. On the second to the last bag, the line tying it close slipped off and it poured out, making a clang and a bang. Ben couldn't see down the hole. Ben closed his eyes, wishing he could disappear as the noise rang out in the silent evening. He threw the line down in the hole and grabbed the last bag. He scurried to the edge of the entrance as he watched from the shadows the two on watch were looking at the direction the noise came from. Then one made a gesture that he would go look into it, and the other waved at him to let him know he understood. Ben was in a panic. If the one guard kept watching his partner and his partner was heading his way, he couldn't slip undetected to the cargo area and pick up his treasure. He sat, frantically trying to decide what to do. Then he heard a familiar sound.

Jackie, coming up the gangway, yelled to Laurence up at the wheel. "What, no one here to watch the gangway? Where's your partner? Sleeping?" They both turned to see Jackie coming aboard. And as they turned, Ben took the opportunity to jump down the entrance to the hold without being seen.

The crewman at the wheel yelled back to him, "Quiet down, boy, or you'll wake the only crew aboard!"

Jackie saw that Ben had made it without being seen. He waved to the crew at the wheel, and the other sailor shook his head and went to look in the direction of where the noise came from, where he was going to investigate before Jackie came aboard. Jackie walked calmly below. Once out of sight, he ran down to the cargo area to meet with Ben. Ben was already gathering the bags and putting them out of sight in case anyone would happen to look into the cargo area or walk in by accident.

Jackie approached him quietly and whispered with a smile across his face, "We did it."

Ben whispered back, "Almost didn't make it. You came right at the right time."

They both gathered a couple of bags and made their way to the entrance to the bilge. Ben jumped into the opening, and Jackie handed him the bags. Ben crawled in far enough so even if someone pointed a light inside to take a look, they wouldn't see the bags. Jackie ran back for some more bags and would hand them to Ben. Once they were done and the last bag was stored, Ben started to feel better. The treasure was aboard, and no one knew it was there. The boys made their way to the bunks. They were pretty empty with the crew all ashore, spending their wages. The only ones who stayed behind, like Ben and Jackie, will have duties tomorrow, or they are married men who save their moneys for when they get home. Ben and Jackie fell asleep right away. They were exhausted. They were awakened by the crew coming off duties. Jackie couldn't wait to have some real breakfast because Chef would make special meals for the small crews left on duty.

They got in line and reached Chef, who was dishing people up. He looked at the two boys and growled some words while squinting at them. "Where have you two been? It's not like you two freeloaders to disappear in port, let alone miss a meal."

Ben started to say something, but Chef slapped his food down on his tray hard and said, "Never mind your excuses, boy!" Then he leaned in close and whispered, "Beware, boy. Mr. Hawkins had told the captain you two had rented a boat to go see the islands." He hesitated and looked around to make sure no one was listening. "He got very upset, I hear, and especially at you, lad." Just then, a sailor rambled up with his tray. Ole Chef stood up straight with a grimace. "That ain't a hair, and if it was, it's a nose hair. Now get back to work, you loafers."

The other sailor asked, "Why are you so hard on them boys, Chef? They work hard."

Chef growled and said, "Cos I don't want them growin' up like a girlie sailor like yourself."

The sailor just laughed at him. Ben and Jackie had to smile too. Ben was hungry enough, but his appetite was diminishing fast. Just as he started eating, Squeaky came running in, yelling, "Mr. Summit, Mr. Hawkins wants to see you immediately!" Then he ran out. Ben swallowed his bite of food hard, and any hunger he had was gone from worry. His face showed worry, and Jackie so badly wanted to ask, "Do you think they know?" But there were too many sailors sitting around to even mention anything about the treasure.

Ben tried to think positive and said to himself and out loud, "He probably just wants to discuss our leaving time."

Jackie just nodded, and everyone else ignored his comment. It didn't pertain to them, and it wasn't uncommon for a sailor to be summoned to Mr. Hawkins for some reason or another. But Ben's conscience was eating at him. As Ben got up, his friend met his eyes with an understanding gaze, and he nodded as if he knew Ben's feelings and to wish him good luck. Ben nodded back to let him know he appreciated it. Ben made his way out of the galley and up to Mr. Hawkins's cabin.

He knocked twice and heard a voice yell, "Enter!" Ben swung the door open, and Mr. Hawkins looked up from what he was working on. His face became as stern as his request. "Mr. Summit, come in and sit down." He pointed to a chair. Ben came in and sat. And as he sat, Mr. Hawkins stood up and assumed his usual attentive stance with his hands behind his back. He started to pace slowly, and Ben kept eye contact with him in silence. Mr. Hawkins circled around him till he would have to turn in his chair, so he stared blindly at the wall as Mr. Hawkins circled. The silence made Ben uneasy and added to the suspense that Mr. Hawkins was evaluating him. He squirmed in the chair.

As he came around to his other side, he started to speak. "Mr. Summit, you are a likable fellow." As he spoke, he continued to circle Ben. "You're a hard worker, very attentive to your position, and a good student." As he rounded to the front, their eyes met again. Mr. Hawkins locked a stare. He leaned on the corner of the desk, crossing his arms in front of him. "But you're not always honest with me. You're holding things back." Ben felt as though he hadn't breathed since he entered the cabin, and he could feel sweat beading up on his forehead. "So, Mr. Summit, I will ask you some questions, and you will answer me in a way that pleases me and I feel you have answered me honestly. Or you will sit here and I will keep asking questions until I get an answer I like. Or you could, if you prefer, get off my ship right now and you won't have to answer any." Ben's mind was racing, and he wanted to tell him everything. No more lies. He admired Mr. Hawkins and wanted to show him the respect he was due. Mr. Hawkins continued, "I don't usually get involved with a crew member and the captain. Usually when the captain and a crew member have a problem, he usually has me sack them, or they walk the plank in the middle of the ocean, or they work it out between themselves. But this problem is starting to affect the ship and the safety of the crew. So why Ben, is his dislike for you so strong? Why are you still aboard this ship? What makes you so special?

Ben sat lower in his seat, feeling like he was at school and being yelled at by the headmaster. Breaking eye contact, Ben corrected his posture and sat up straight. "I, uh, I'm, uh, not sure."

Mr. Hawkins was thoroughly frustrated. He crossed his arms across his chest, narrowed his eyebrows, and added, "I'm pretty sure you do, Ben. You see, Ben, the captain won't talk to me about it either, and he outranks me. But, Ben, I outrank you." He leaned in with his hands on his knees, putting his face inches from Ben's. "I expect an answer today. *No...no,* I demand the truth today!"

Ben was staring into Mr. Hawkins's eyes, and he felt his starting to well up with tears. He could tell Mr. Hawkins would only accept the truth. Ben had a million lies running through his head. He decided to set this man straight. A rush of relief rushed over him. He blurted out, "I'm the great-grandson of Homer Gregoreouse."

Mr. Hawkins face went from mad to confused. He shook his head as if trying to make sense of what Ben just said. "What is being related to an ancient pirate got to do with this?"

Ben corrected himself. "Homer Gregoreouse was Captain Reginald Roach."

Mr. Hawkins went from confused to shock, and he slowly fell back against his desk, looking at Ben with a huge question mark on his face. His brow wrinkled a bit as he tried to comprehend what he had just heard. He eased himself to a sitting position at the edge of his desk, saying, "Homer Gregoreouse is Captain Reginald Roach." He said this mostly to himself as he worked this out in his mind.

Ben answered, "Yes" very quietly.

Mr. Hawkins again mumbled, "And you're his great-grandson."

Ben sat up straighter and, with a bit more confidence, answered, "That is correct, sir."

Mr. Hawkins eyes roamed around the room as he again spoke as if he were alone in the room. "So that explains your relationship to Mr. Harsgrove." Then he looked at Ben again with a wrinkled brow. "Why so much secrecy?"

Ben sort of shrugged his shoulders and replied, "After my great-grandfather died, Captain Nelson and Mr. Harsgrove decided to let me come aboard to learn the trade, but it was my request that I remain anonymous as to not be treated different from the rest of the crew."

Mr. Hawkins eyebrows raised, and he pointed at Ben, saying, "You're the owner of the *Charee*?"

Ben nodded, saying, "Yes, sir, I am."

Mr. Hawkins laughed and reared back his head. "Oh, no, you don't sir me. I should sir you."

Ben jumped up out of his seat. "That's exactly what I didn't want. I wanted to prove myself as a sailor, a mariner of men. I want the crew to respect me like they did my great-grandfather."

Mr. Hawkins put his hands on Ben's shoulders. "Okay, okay, just sit back down. We're not done yet." Ben sat back down. Mr. Hawkins leaned back against his desk. "Believe me, son, when I tell you, you have the respect of this crew. And you have mine, or we wouldn't be talking right now. With that all said, why is the captain so angry with you?"

Ben sighed a heavy sigh and answered, "He wanted the *Charee* to haul slaves, but I didn't want to mostly because my great-grandfather didn't want to, and I don't feel right about it either."

Mr. Hawkins nodded in understanding, saying, "As owner of the vessel, I would stand behind your decision. So why would he get so mad if you were to sail around the islands?" Ben shrugged his shoulders. He truly didn't know why the captain would get so upset, but he did have an idea. In his silence, Mr. Hawkins folded his arms across his chest and said, "Ahh...we were doing so well. Then you had to lie to me again."

Ben defended himself. "It's not a total lie. I'm just not sure of what I think is the reason or not."

Mr. Hawkins sarcastically said, "Oh, do tell, Mr. Summit. What's your theory? Do tell."

Ben squirmed a little in his chair. Telling the truth about the treasure was always difficult, but he let it out. "There is a question about treasure."

Mr. Hawkins raised his eyebrows, saying with a question in his voice, "Treasure?"

Ben kept going, nodding in agreement. "The treasure of Homer Gregoreouse. You see, you called him a famous pirate, but he was actually a slave aboard the ship. He was the only living soul left from that ship, and he knew where Bloodthirsty Bob's treasure was hidden."

Mr. Hawkins laughed out loud. "I remember my grandfather telling tales of Homer Gregoreouse." Then Ben noticed Mr. Hawkins had a revelation. "That's why he wanted me to keep track of any areas you might be curious about or wanted to go," he said out loud but mostly to himself as a thought. Then his expression change again. "*He lied to me also!*" he blurted out. "He told me he had a bet on you and Jackie that you wouldn't make it on the ship, and he wanted to be aware so he could hedge his bet with Mr. Harsgrove. Well, it's been a year, and this is the only time you have ever shown an interest in any area." Then he laughed a little. "So what were you and Jackie doing these last two days? Treasure hunting?"

The weight of all the lies that Ben was carrying was lifting, and he felt better for it, so he said a resounding "Yes, sir, we were."

Mr. Hawkins was still laughing a little as he asked, "Well, did you find the elusive bounty of Bloodthirsty Bob's plunder?" Mr. Hawkins was laughing harder now. Ben didn't recall ever hearing him so jovial before.

He let out a quiet, "Yes…uh…yes, we did."

Mr. Hawkins's laugh dwindled fast as he looked at Ben for the truth and could see in Ben's eyes he had, for the lad had a smirk on his face. He watched Mr. Hawkins's face turn to surprise. All he could say was "You did?"

Ben only nodded and added, "It was right where my great-grandfather told me it would be."

Mr. Hawkins stood up and paced a bit, stroking his chin. "None of this explanation is going anywhere near what I thought it would," he mumbled, eyeing Ben as he paced. "I thought you were a relative of Mr. Harsgrove, or better yet, an offspring of Captain Nelson's he had just discovered, but this tale you tell now, I don't think you could even make this up. So Homer Gregoreouse was a pirate after all, and the tale of the lost treasure is true, and Captain Reginald Roach was Homer Gregoreouse. And I was working for him the whole time. I even sat and had dinner with him on several occasions." Mr. Hawkins was still shaking his head and trying to fathom all he had heard.

Ben interrupted his thoughts. "Sir, when my great-grandfather found the first treasure—"

Mr. Hawkins's eyes got wide and interrupted Ben. "The first treasure!" he blurted out.

Ben continued, "Yes, the first treasure. He shared it with the crew. I would like to do the same, if I may, sir."

Mr. Hawkins wrinkled his brow, saying, "You want my permission to share your found fortune with your crew?"

Ben nodded. "Yes, sir."

Mr. Hawkins patted Ben's shoulder. "That's a noble act, Mr. Summit, and I am sure your crew would appreciate it. That does explain what you were bringing aboard last night. It is here on the ship, isn't it?"

Ben was surprised then. He did know that Mr. Hawkins knew most everything that went on aboard his ship. Mr. Hawkins leaned back and rubbed his chin. "You know, Ben, that treasure truly belongs to Britain."

Ben sat straight up in his chair, looking Mr. Hawkins in the eye. "That's what my great-grandfather thought also, and he went to England to return it. but everyone he tried to get him to help tried to steal it for themselves. It also caused the death of eighty percent of my family. Mr. Hawkins, sir, with all due respect, I call it restitution for crimes committed against my family."

Mr. Hawkins was taken aback. He smiled big. "Well, son, you missed your calling. You should study law and become a lawyer, not a sailor."

Ben sat back in his seat, having made his point. Ben was shaking his head no. "It's greed, Mr. Hawkins. Something about this treasure, it breeds it. It takes over anyone who comes in contact with it. It's a curse, not a blessing. Here's a perfect example. I should be happy just to own this beautiful ship, but no, I had to chase the treasure also, just to see if it was there."

Mr. Hawkins made his way to his seat, and silence filled the room as they both contemplated what had just transpired here. Finally, Mr. Hawkins spoke. "What are your plans now, son?"

Ben's gaze went to Mr. Hawkins. "Well, sir, I would appreciate you not telling the captain right now about you knowing about my ownership of the *Charee*. And I would like to keep learning from you like before, if that would still work for you?"

"Your wish is my command, sir, but I will not directly tell the captain any of our conversation. But if he were to ask me, I will be obligated to tell the truth, just as I would for you, sir."

They sat for a silent second, and Ben asked, "May I go about my duties, sir?"

Mr. Hawkins smiled and said, "Yes, permission granted." As Ben stood to leave, Mr. Hawkins held out his hand. "Thank you for your honesty, and it is a pleasure to work for you, sir."

Ben took hold of his hand and shook it. "The pleasure is all mine, Mr. Hawkins. And please don't call me sir anymore."

Mr. Hawkins winked at him. "Get back to work, you scurvy dog. Quit wasting my time. I'm a busy man, you know. I work for a man who expects a lot out of his employees."

Ben met back up with Jackie, and they went about their business of duties. They only talked about the treasure once, and that was to get together tonight and talk about how to divide it up.

That same day, Skipper Miguel was in town at his favorite pub, eating well and buying drinks around for all his friends and some who weren't. Ben and Jackie had given him a substantial tip for his help and to buy his silence about the treasure until the *Charee* left port. But the rum was flowing, and Miguel started to talk more and more. People wanted to know what he was celebrating and how he came by all his money. Soon he was getting drunk enough, and he started to forget what lies he told. Finally, he took two of his closest friends aside and made them promise on their mothers' grave not to tell a soul about the treasure. And as day turned to night, many people were making the same promises to their friends. Until one person was telling another friend quietly in secret that the owner of the ship *Charee* came here in search of Bloodthirsty Bob's treasure. And after days of searching, he found it.

Captain Nelson was sitting about two chairs away and, hearing the name *Charee*, became curious as to what the old man was saying and listened intently. He then positioned himself to watch the old man, who continued to eat and drink. After a couple of hours, the old gent left the pub. He was walking down the cobblestone streets, or staggering was more like it, singing an old song as he went messing up the words to the second chorus and starting over with the first. He was heading to his home. All of a sudden, without warning, he was being pushed fast from behind. He was picking up his pace to an almost run. He tried to look behind, but whoever it was had a hold of his collar, and he couldn't turn his head.

He got out a "Hey, what are you...stop..." And he was forced around a corner into a dark alley. An extra push from his shoulders sent him flying headfirst into the darkness of the alley. He was able to turn his head just enough to make out a large dark figure, and he heard the recognizable sound of metal being pulled from a sheath. He then saw a flash of light on the large knife the assailant held in his hand. The figure reached down and grabbed a handful of his hair. The old man was speechless with fright as the stranger put the knife to his throat.

The stranger quietly but menacingly whispered, "Tell me all you know about the treasure found by the owner of the *Charee*."

The old man was scared out of his wits. His mind fumbled to think, and it was hard to breathe with the way the stranger sat on his back, his head pulled up tight. He managed to speak between gasps for air. "It was Miguel. He owns the *Opal*. He took the owner to an island, and he found it."

The assailant pulled back harder and put the knife against his throat harder. "Where can I find this Miguel?"

The old man, not wanting to betray his friend, winced with pain. He managed to say, "I...I...don't know." He felt the knife now starting to cut into his skin.

"He's your friend. If you want to live, you had better tell me."

The old man, to save his own life, gave in. "His ship sits at the end of the piers on the north end." The old man's head slammed hard into the stones on the ground, and a foot kicked him hard in the ribs and took his breath away. He lay still for a while until he made sure he didn't hear the footsteps of his assailant anymore.

Captain Nelson made his way back down to the piers. He went to the north end. There were several cutter rigs tied up. He walked up and down the pier until he found the *Opal*. He went aboard and looked around but didn't find anyone, so he went to the upper docks to wait. He hid in the shadows. After an hour had gone by, he started to get anxious and decided he would come back later. Just as he was about to step out of the shadows, a figure appeared, staggering and talking to himself. He made his way to the ladder leading to the raft of boats lined up on the lower piers. He then watched as this little man made his way down to the *Opal* and climbed aboard. Captain Nelson's heart started to race as he made his way to the ladder. The skipper, even as drunk as he was, could tell someone had just set foot on his ship.

The old man stood motionless for a minute in quiet then yelled, "Hola!" Then he tried English. "Who is there?" But no one answered, and the skipper knew something wasn't right. He reached into a cabinet and pulled out an old pistol he had kept for years. He used it only to shoot any large fish he might catch, but even that was far and few between once or twice in the last ten years. He yelled again, sounding more intense, "Who's there?" But no one answered. His heart was pounding as he made his way to the companionway. He stepped carefully and quietly up the few stairs leading out of the hatch. Captain Nelson was poised on the hatch lid, ready like a cat waiting for a mouse to come out of his hole. He grabbed the skipper's hand that held the gun first then wrapped his whole arm around Miguel's neck. It took him by surprise. It happened so fast. Captain Nelson lifted him from the hatch, his feet kicking, looking for ground. He couldn't yell as the breath of life was being choked out of him. Panic ran through him like a lightning bolt. He was too stunned to even think of pulling the trigger on the gun. His hand was slammed against the boom. He felt the sharp pain but did not let go of the pistol. A second slam sent the pistol bouncing across the decks. He then reached up with his other arm to try and get some pressure off his neck. And as he did, his attacker dropped him back into the hatch. He fell hard to the floorboards, and he tried to gather his wits and get to his feet, but his attacker was already on top of him. He put his foot hard into the skipper's back, forcing him hard back down to the floor. He jumped onto the old man's back, pinning his arms with his legs and pulling his hair, raising his head back hard until he heard him groan with discomfort. Then Miguel felt a sharp blade of at his throat.

A voice filled with hate whispered in his ear, "Well, skipper, you seem like a smart fella. Let's play a game. I ask you a question, you tell me an answer. If I like your answer, you live. If I don't"—he pushed the knife harder into his throat—"I open your throat from ear to ear. Do you understand the rules?"

Miguel could hardly breathe with the weight of this man on his back. And with his head pulled so tightly backward, he could hardly breathe. He wheezed out a "Si."

His assailant said, "Good...good. First question. You took someone out for a treasure hunt. Is that true?"

Miguel wheezed out another "Si."

"Now let me guess. Two young lads, one small to average size, dark hair, one very large and strong with dark hair?"

He sucked a breath in and another restrained "Si."

Captain Nelson forced a laugh out. "See, I knew you were smart. You play this game well, amigo. Now one last question and you win your life. Where did they put the treasure?" He eased the pressure on the old man's neck so he could speak.

He coughed and gagged as he drew in life-saving air. He felt guilty betraying the boys. He was asked not to say anything, and he had betrayed that silence. If he saved his own life, he would jeopardize the boys, if he hadn't already. The young man was right. It was a curse. His life was a fine one before. Now his choice of words, no matter what, he would have to live with forever. If he lied, this madman would kill him, or he turned this brutal killer on to the boys. He told as much truth as he could and hoped he still left out enough to make it work. He strained out the words, "They put it into canvass sacks and carried it away."

His assailant whispered in his ear with a maniacal voice, "Oh, we were doing so well." Then he slammed the skipper's head against the floor hard and pulled his head back up. He yelled, "Where! Where did they take it?"

The old man winced with pain as he felt blood start to trickle down his face. He said, "I...I...don't know. They didn't say."

His head was dropped back to the floor with a heavy thud, and his assailant sprang off his back. He heard him hurry away. Miguel tried to get up fast and redeem himself for letting the boys down, but he had taken quite a beating, and even though he tried to scramble out of the cabin and retrieve the pistol, that scallywag was already long gone. He worried for the boys. He hoped he had not sentenced them to death. He could only hope they were smart enough to be weary and ready for such a man as this.

Captain Nelson was not a coldblooded killer, but he wouldn't hesitate to get what he felt was rightfully his family's inheritance. And now he had enough information to confront Ben.

* * *

Ben and Jackie spent most of the night in the bilge, dividing up the treasure as fairly as they could with a list that Mr. Hawkins supplied them with. The coins were easy, but the jewels and gold trinkets were not so easily divided. They were both feeling good about this, and how fun it was to give back to the men who had helped them so much to be mariners. They didn't finish before they both felt they needed some sleep. So they figured they would finish the next night. They both hit their bunks and were out in minutes.

Ben was awakened sharply with a hand firmly over his mouth and the captain's face by his ear, whispering, "Get up quietly and meet me in my cabin."

Ben's heart was racing as the captain removed his hand and disappeared into the darkness. Ben sat in shock for a minute while his mind raced. He then slid out of his bunk. He crouched down by Jackie's bunk and woke him up.

Jackie groaned a little, squinting his eyes open. "What time is it?"

Ben shushed him. "Shh…I don't know, but the captain was just here and told me to meet him in his cabin."

Jackie sat straight up, looking at Ben. He asked, "Now?"

Ben answered, "Yes, and he reeks of rum. He seemed angry, the way he was acting. I'm a little worried."

Jackie started to get up. "I'm coming with you."

Ben put his hand on his chest. "You wait here. He wants to see only me. But if I don't come back in an hour, you—"

He didn't get the rest out. Jackie interrupted him, pushing his hand out of the way. "I ain't waiting no hour. Don't worry. I will watch your back, but you ain't going alone."

Ben rolled his eyes. "Okay, but stay out of sight."

Ben took off, and Jackie got dressed. He then went straight to Chef's quarters and knocked, whispering, "Chef…Chef, wake up."

The door swung open fast. The crippled old man stood ruffling his hair, standing in his nightshirt and squinting to see. "What the hell do you want? Can't you see I need my beauty sleep?"

Jackie chuckled under his breath at that one. "Chef, there ain't enough time left in the universe to fix what you look like."

Chef got his growly face on. "You woke me up to insult me?"

Jackie put his hand on the old man's shoulder. "No, sir…no, sir, we have trouble, and I might need your help."

The old man looked confused, asking, "My help?"

Jackie said, "Yes. Let me in and I will explain." Jackie told him all about the story, from the treasure to the captain wanting to see Ben.

Chef's eyes got big when he came to that part. He jumped up and threw on his pants. He said, "I've heard enough. Let's go." He hesitated and pulled a pistol from a drawer and stuck it in the belt. The top of his pants held it in place by his belt.

Jackie's eyes went large. "Do you think that will be necessary?"

Chef shoved him toward the door. "I sure hope not, but it can't hurt."

Jackie was pretty concerned about a man his age packing a gun around. He was also concerned that it looked as old as Chef. He tried to say, "I don't think we need the gun, Chef."

Chef pushed him again, putting his finger to his lips and shushing Jackie. Jackie nodded in understanding. As they neared the captain's cabin, Chef motioned to an open porthole window on the portside. They crept below it to listen.

Ben had already answered most of the captain's questions. He had told him honestly about the treasure, that he and Jackie were planning on sharing it with the crew. That was where Chef and Jackie came onto the conversation.

The captain spoke. "Well, Ben, that would be a noble gesture, and I appreciate your honesty. I am a little surprised by it. Now, Ben, I would like you to give some thought to what I am about to say next. Back in the States, there is talk of a civil war between North and the South." He hesitated. "You were aware of that, weren't you?"

Ben nodded in agreement, saying "I had heard that things might go that way."

The captain started to pace as he talked. "They're trying to take our lifestyles away."

Ben interrupted, "You mean slavery?"

The captain hesitated for a moment. "It's not just slavery, son. It's that they want to tell us how to live, what we can or cannot do. They go against everything the constitution was based on." His voice got louder as he went on. "Look, Ben, our whole society will change. The way we think, feel, and behave will be the way they want us to, not each individual state to make its own laws. *Where are our freedoms, Ben?*"

Ben was a little surprised when he yelled that part, but Ben remained calm. "What of the freedoms of the black man?" Ben asked quietly.

Captain Nelson stood staring at Ben, and Ben could feel his anger grow. The captain marched over to Ben. "Why you little nigger lover. I knew you were a sympathizer from day one." And he reached down and grabbed hold of Ben's shirt, on both sides of his collar. Ben had already shifted as far back into his chair as he could. He held on to Captain Nelson's arms, trying to break his grip. The captain pulled him from the chair and slammed him against the wall. With his teeth clenched and a growl in his voice, he said, "Let me make something very clear, boy. I am going to take that treasure back to the Confederate cause to help in the fight for the Southern rights of the Southern man. You got that, mister?"

Ben was shocked and at first felt a rush of fear as the captain tossed him against the wall. Now his anger was starting to swell. Still holding the captain's arms, he squeezed a little tighter and said, "Captain Nelson, you are hereby relieved of your duties as captain of the *Charee*."

The captain's face turned red, and Ben thought he was going to explode. Veins bulged around his neck. He reached down quick. "As you please." And before Ben could move, he had produced a knife and put it to Ben's throat. "I wondered when you would play that card, you little peckerwood." He growled as he pushed the knife harder. Ben could feel the knife cutting into his skin. "You tell me where the treasure is right now or I will kill you where you stand, and then I will go get your little friend Jackie, and I promise you he will tell me over time."

Ben tried his hardest to remain calm and not show fear. He squeaked out from the pressure of the knife against his throat, "Captain Nelson, take the knife away from my throat and let me go, or I will press charges."

When Jackie heard that, he said out loud, "Knife!" Chef looked at him wide-eyed.

The captain heard it too. "Well, what do you know?" He loosened his grip on Ben and yelled, "Get in here, boy, and join the party!" Jackie was sitting back against the wall with his hand over his mouth, wide-eyed and looking at Chef. Chef motioned with his head to go into the cabin then put his finger to his lips to make sure he stayed quiet. Jackie slowly got up and made his way to the cabin door. The captain yelled again, "Hurry up, boy! I don't want to butcher your friend up for shark bait!"

Jackie stepped in, holding his hands out and talking to the Captain. "Easy, Captain. I'm right here."

The captain spun Ben around, bending his left arm behind his back and putting the knife to Ben's throat again. "So how much did you hear, Mr. Huntington?"

Jackie kept eye contact with Captain Nelson the whole time. "Oh, I heard it all, sir. You want to steal Ben's treasure to fund the war back home. More importantly, I heard him relieve you of your duties, and I also heard you threaten his life. How I am doing, sir? Did I miss anything?"

"Where do you stand on the North and South issue, boy?"

"To be honest, sir, I am not sure. I don't know all the particulars of politics. I do know that my family has issues. Some agree and some don't agree with the slave trade, but I do believe in the constitution, sir, and I do know that murder is against the law." Jackie tried to remain in a calm demeanor as his friend looked at him with fear in his eyes.

"Well, aren't you two just the little smarty pants." He dragged Ben around to the back of his desk, keeping the knife tight against his throat. He released his arm from behind his back, and Captain Nelson reached quickly in a drawer and pulled a pistol. Jackie started to get closer as the captain pulled Ben toward the desk and lunged toward the two. The captain let go of Ben's arm but stopped his charge when the captain pulled the pistol out and pointed it point-blank at Jackie's head. "Whoa, big fella." He removed the knife from Ben's throat and pushed him forward. Then he planted his foot into Ben's back, sending him to the floor hard. "Now why don't you two make your way over to that wall?" He was waving the pistol end in the direction he wanted them to go. Jackie reached down and helped Ben up, not taking his eyes off the captain. They both moved to the wall the captain was pointing at.

Jackie said loud enough for Chef to hear, "You know, Ben, that gun only has one shot in it, If we both jump him, he can only shoot one of us." He was hoping Chef would go get help.

The captain raised the pistol, aiming at Jackie's head. "Yes, Ben, make a move and I will blow a hole in your brainless friend's head, seeing how he just volunteered to go first. Now, boys, you're making this harder than it has to be." He reached over to close the cabin door, not taking his eyes off the boys.

He then felt cold steel against his head and a familiar voice say, "I only have one shot, too, Cap'n. The only difference is, I only need one, so why don't you put yours down?"

He could feel the old man's hand shaking a bit and hear fear in his voice. The captain didn't move. He didn't show fear, and he didn't even look over to him as he answered, "Chef, why would you want to get involved with these two scallywags? Just put the gun down, old man."

Chef only replied, "No, sir, I think you should put yours down."

The captain laughed a sinister laugh. "Chef, you don't understand. These boys have something of mine and—"

Chef interrupted him. "Sir, the only solution to this problem I can see is we both drop our guns."

The captain said, "Very well. Let's put our guns down together."

Chef said, "That's okay by me."

The captain held his gun straight up so Chef could see and let it dangle from his trigger finger. The boys felt a rush of relief as the gun wasn't pointed at them anymore. "I'll just put mine on the floor." He was stooping as he talked. Chef kept his pistol pointed at him as he started to crouch to put his gun down. He spun fast, grabbing Chef's pistol hand. As he did, Chef startled and pulled the trigger, but it wasn't pointed at the captain anymore. The shot was deafening in that little room. The stray bullet struck Jackie in the left arm. Jackie flew backward as the impact hit him and he let out a grunt. Ben realized he had been shot and tried to stabilize his falling. Jackie was looking at the captain as Chef struggled for control of the two pistols. The captain struck Chef with the pistol in his hand across the face.

Jackie yelled, "Get the captain!" to Ben.

The captain heard that, and as Chef struggled to hang on to the captain, he struck Chef again. He looked back at Ben as Chef hit the floor. Ben grabbed a book off the desk and hurled it at the captain, who was trying to get a shot at Ben. The book hit him directly in the head, and he had to protect his head and didn't get a shot. Ben made a leap to the captain, pushing his hand up as the gun went off hitting the roof of the cabin. The captain took hold of Ben's hair and slammed his face into his knee, sending Ben head over heels. The captain then pulled his knife from its scabbard. Ben was holding his nose which was bleeding profusely, but he knew the fight wasn't over, so as he scrambled to get to his feet, the captain then kicked Ben in the chest. He was on top of him in a flash and raised to stab Ben.

As Ben was about to try and stop the captain from plunging a knife into him, they heard, "*Stop right there!*" They all recognized the voice, and everyone stopped to see Mr. Hawkins in the doorway with a pistol of his own in hand and a very angry look on his face. "What the hell is going on, Captain?" he asked, knowing in his own mind what it was.

The captain, a little distraught, realized how all this looked. He took a breath and regained his composure. He slammed Ben's head hard against the floor and jumped to his feet. "Thank God you're here, Mr. Hawkins. These mutinous dogs were trying to take over this ship." Mr. Hawkins surveyed the chaotic mess before him. One man bleeding in pain, and two men were unconscious on the floor. The captain adjusted his appearance. "I want these men put in irons."

Jackie interrupted, "He's lying, sir! He was going to kill Ben if he didn't tell him where the treasure is."

The Captain interrupted him. "Shut up, you little peckerwood! You're under arrest." Then he started at him with his knife in hand. Mr. Hawkins reached over and spun the captain around with the knife hand. The captain swung at Mr. Hawkins with his free hand. Mr. Hawkins moved fast enough so the captain missed his aim and threw himself off-balance. The captain screamed, "You don't know what you're doing! Let go of me, damnit! That's an order!"

Mr. Hawkins said as calmly as he could, "I will obey that order, sir, if you were to drop the knife and calm down."

Ben was starting to come to his senses. He looked up to see Mr. Hawkins bear-hugging Captain Nelson. Captain Nelson released his grip on the knife, and it fell to the floor. Ben quickly retrieved it after seeing the treachery he was capable of.

"You don't understand," the captain explained again.

Mr. Hawkins pushed him toward the open cabin door hard and released him, putting some space between them in case he was to attack again. He said, "Fine. Explain yourself."

Ben had made his way over to Jackie, who was holding his very bloody arm and appeared to be in a lot of pain. Through gritted teeth, he said, "I'm fine. Go look at Chef." Ben nodded in approval.

The captain started to plead his case. "They broke into my cabin, waving a pistol in my face and demanding I turn my ship over to them to hunt treasure, of all things. This is a blatant case of mutiny!"

Ben was checking on Chef. He was breathing but very unconscious.

Mr. Hawkins said, "I have sailed with you for many years, and I have never seen you this upset, but I am confused as to what you're trying to say. It doesn't make sense."

"Are you calling me a liar?" The captain was very agitated.

"No, sir, it just doesn't make sense. The boy already owns the ship. He wouldn't have to take it by force. Besides, they already went treasure hunting and told me they found it."

The captain's eyes went big. "You've seen it?" he asked, his face almost mesmerized.

Mr. Hawkins's brow wrinkled as he looked at a man he thought he knew. But now he was not sure he recognized him at all. Mr. Hawkins answered, "No, I haven't seen it."

The captain thrust a finger at him. "How the hell do you know there is any? And what makes you so sure that what this boy is telling you is the truth? The owner of this tub? Mr. Hawkins, I thought you were sharper than that."

Mr. Hawkins stood for a minute, looking at both parties. The captain made a valid point, but Mr. Hawkins's gut feeling was to believe the boys. "So you're telling me these two boys came aboard this ship and sailed her for a year so that they could come here one day with the help of an ancient man and steal her for themselves."

The captain got excited. "Yes, that's what I'm saying."

"That, sir, is a hard one to swallow. Mostly because ole Chef here is as loyal to this ship as they come. I say we get Jackie and Chef to a doctor. We put them on standby arrest until Chef can clear this up for me. And, Captain, I will ask you to step down from your duties until a decision is made. I'm sorry, sir, but if these boys are telling the truth, you, sir, have committed some serious crimes here."

He never got another word out. The captain turned and ran out the door. Mr. Hawkins stood in disbelief. He turned to Ben. He had just gotten Jackie's shirt off and exposed the fresh wound. Mr. Hawkins tore a piece of Jackie's shirt and wadded it up tight, put it against the open sore, and told Jackie to keep pressure on it. He told Ben to go to town. At the south end, there was an inn, Casa something.

"Do you know which one I mean?" Ben nodded. He understood. "Find the proprietor. Tell him who you are and that Mr. Hawkins needs a doctor aboard the *Charee* right away. Got it?"

Ben said, "Aye, aye, sir" and took off running.

Mr. Hawkins looked at Jackie's arm. "You know, son, it doesn't look too bad, but I bet it hurts plenty." Jackie nodded agreement as he winced in pain. Mr. Hawkins moved it around to get a better look. "Keep that compress tight until the doctor gets here." He then dropped down to see Chef. His breathing was slow and steady. He still had good color to his face. He tried to rouse him, shaking him and yelling his name, but he got no response. He was an extremely old man, and Mr. Hawkins was afraid that a punch in the face might be more than the old guy could handle. It was only when he took a coat down out of the locker to prop his head up a bit did he realize that there was a lump on the back of his head the size of his fist. He realized he must have hit it hard when he went down.

Ben made it to town, worried Captain Nelson would catch him somewhere in the dark before he could get to the inn. He located the doctor. He was very accommodating, took hold of a black satchel, and told Ben to lead the way.

Any sailor who was on that night was pretty aware of what happened that night. Many were shocked and bewildered by the captain's actions and why Chef of all people he would hurt. Mr. Hawkins told just enough information to keep them satisfied so as not to lose control of the crew and ship. The week they had planned to stay was almost up, and most of the crew would be returning in the next couple of days, so he would wait and tell them all when the crew was assembled. The crew that was there had ole Chef laid up really comfy with a soft bedroll and extra pillows, waiting on him hand and foot and arguing outside the door that he was too hot or was too cold. They tried giving him water and rum to see if it would bring him around.

The doctor arrived and was taken to Jackie first. He looked at the arm and told a couple of sailors standing by to get some water boiling and some clean rags and to bring them in. He patted Jackie on the shoulder, saying, "We'll get back to you in a minute." Jackie understood. Besides, he was worried about the old man.

When the doctor arrived at Chef's cabin, he had to ask the whole group of sailors to make way so he could see him. Then a booming voice was heard behind the doctor, making him jump. "All right, you swabs, get the hell out the way and let the doc get to the man!" Everyone got quiet and turned to see Goliath pulling seamen out of the way, helping the doctor make his way through the narrow passage. As the doctor made it into the cabin, Goliath's voice boomed again. "Get back to work, you lazy scallywags!" And he let the doctor tend to his duties.

The doctor politely thanked everyone as they filed by Goliath and the door. He turned and said, "Thank you, sir" to Goliath and patted his arm. Goliath just nodded as he closed the door behind him and stepped out. The doctor went to Chef's bedside. He was breathing normal. He then checked his wrist for a pulse. It was strong and normal. He then opened his shirt and was about to listen to his chest.

As he put his head down to Chef's chest, Chef said, "Hey, Doc." The doctor sat straight up, seeing the old man with one eye open and the other closed. He continued to talk. "What's the chances of you telling them this old salty dog needs a few days in bed with a jug of rum and his meals brought to him?"

"I think we could arrange that. But first let me take a look at that head." The old man rolled over and winced a little as the doctor took a look, poking at it. "Well, it's a sizable knot. You're a little more lucky than that poor lad who was shot."

Chef flipped around, looking at the doctor. "*Shot?*" he said. "Which one?"

"He's a tall and big kid."

Chef's eyes glazed over as he looked away from the doctor. "Jackie," he said quietly under his breath.

"Yes, I do believe that was his name."

Chef grabbed hold of the doctor's coat. "Was? Is he…"

The doctor patted his arm. "Oh, no, he's fine. Just a flesh wound in the arm. I don't know the whole extent of his injuries but—"

Chef interrupted him. "Why the hell not?"

The doctor said, "Matter of fact, he was worried about you."

Chef pushed him off the side of the bed. "What the hell you wastin' time on an old barnacle like me for? Get up there and tend to that boy."

The doctor just laughed to himself and said, "Yes, sir." And he turned, thinking he had never treated a man as old or as spry as this gentleman.

As he reached for the door, Chef yelled out, "And don't forget the rum!"

The doctor smiled. "I won't forget the rum."

As he started to open the cabin door, the old man lay back down and assumed his death position and groaned a little.

Just as he opened it, Goliath said, "I thought I heard the old man speak?"

The doctor looked back. Chef was squinting and peeking out of one eye. The doctor replied, "Yes…yes, you did. I had to examine the injury, and it was a reaction to the pain. He needs his quiet and rest." He looked back again to see a wry smile appear on the old man's face as he settled down in the bed.

As Goliath closed the door quietly, he asked, "Will he be okay by dinner?"

The smile dropped off Chef's face as the cabin door clicked shut. As the doctor made his way down the passageway, he was asked the same question, and he assured them all he would be fine. He started to wish a little that he should be cared about by his peers when he was that old. He made it back to where Jackie was. He took another look. The bleeding had slowed. The bone looked like it hadn't suffered any trauma. He noticed Jackie was a little shocked from the experience. His forehead was sweaty, and his skin a bit pale. He pulled a small bottle from his bag. He poured out a small amount into a cup and handed it to Jackie. Jackie took the cup with his good arm. As he did, the doctor said, "Drink it fast. It tastes horrible, but it will help with the pain."

Jackie took a breath and drank the elixir in one fast swallow. He coughed and sputtered as his face contorted, and his whole body gave one big shiver. "Whoa, god, that's awful. That's worse than my uncle's attempt at making whiskey." Ben laughed a little. He remembered that stuff too. If he remembered right, Jackie's dad would use it to start fires instead of drinking it. The doctor, after a few minutes, looked at the arm again. This time, Jackie didn't flinch. He raised it up to get a better look. "Whew, this stuff works pretty fast."

The doctor just smiled. "How did this happen?" he asked quietly.

Jackie's head started to swoon as he was feeling no pain at all now. "The captain wanted us to give him the treasure, but we were stingy and said no…so he shot me."

The doctor looked up at Ben and Mr. Hawkins for more clarification, but they looked on in agreement. His brow wrinkled a bit, he asked, "You mean Captain Nelson shot you?"

Jackie laughed out loud, very much under the influence of the medication now. He said, "Yep. Thanks to ole Ben there. He was gonna shoot Ben in the head, but Ben, quick as a cat, pointed the gun at me, *Boom*!"

The doctor turned and looked at Mr. Hawkins. He had known Captain Nelson for years. He was having a hard time believing he was capable of such a crime. He was looking at Mr. Hawkins for reassurance of what he just heard. Mr. Hawkins nodded to assure that the tale this medicated lad was telling was true.

The doctor worked diligently on the wound, and just to keep the conversation going, he asked, "What treasure was he asking for?"

Once again, Jackie, under his happy influence, blurted out, "Ben's great-grandfather's. He was a pirate."

The doctor turned and looked at Ben. "Your great-grandfather had a treasure?"

Ben didn't like the way this conversation was going. Jackie wasn't good at keeping secrets sober, but under the influence of this drug, it was impossible to shut him up. Ben was looking at Mr. Hawkins for a little help, but Mr. Hawkins believed the truth would set you free. The doctor was just digging in for the ball round embedded in Jackie's arm.

He was sitting there with a grin on his face from ear to ear and let out a yell, "Ow, Doc, you ain't digging a well here!"

The doctor was concentrating on getting any fragments he could find and lost track of his question, and Ben let it go also. Ben asked Jackie, "You doing okay?"

Jackie smiled even bigger. "Ben, I couldn't get any better." Then his face became very serious. "Ben, you're a great friend. I love you, Ben. You're like a brother to me, Ben." And he reached up to try and pat Ben.

The doctor put his hand on Jackie's chest, saying, "Please, son, sit still just a little longer."

Then Jackie turned his head toward the doctor, panning his vision slowly around the room and centered on the doctor's face. "Doc! You still here?" He was grinning huge. Ben and Mr. Hawkins broke into a little laugh at his antics. "Hey, Doc, ole Chef gonna be all right, isn't he?"

The doctor, not taking his eyes away from his work, said, "He will be just fine. A few days' rest and a little rum and he will be just like new, up and kicking."

Jackie, with a serious conviction, said, "Doc, you got to understand. He's a very cantankerous old mule. You can't fix him to kick. Someone will get hurt." Ben and Mr. Hawkins broke into a loud laugh.

The doctor shook his head with a smile. Jackie looked on, bewildered by the humor in what he said. He was serious. As the doctor finished up, he wrapped it tight and told Mr. Hawkins he shouldn't use it for about two weeks. "And it will be sore in the morning and maybe a few days, but after two weeks, he should start to use it carefully. He will start to get his range of motion back." Mr. Hawkins thanked the doctor and made sure he was compensated for his efforts. Just before he stepped off the ship, he turned to Mr. Hawkins and asked, "Where is Captain Nelson now? Do you know?"

Mr. Hawkins's answer reeked of despair. "I don't know, to be honest, Doc. He left after the incident."

The doctor shook his head, adding, "You two have been together a long time. What do you think happened?"

Mr. Hawkins looked past the doctor. "Well, sir, I think the boy, Ben, said it best. Greed…greed is what happened to the captain."

The doctor just politely nodded in agreement but was still truly confused about the problem. "Well, Mr. Hawkins, those men of yours will be fine. Just make sure that Jackie boy exercises that arm in two weeks, and change the dressing every day until that wound quits weeping." Mr. Hawkins understood fully, shook the doctor's hand, and bid him a goodbye.

It was getting on to later morning, and there was a list of things that needed tending to. He got with Squeaky on the bridge and had him make sure the cargo was getting the attention it needed. And to get the tasks for departure secured, he left him with the fact he would be in his cabin most of the day if needed. He first stopped back at the captain's quarters. He entered to find Jackie sound asleep and Ben nodding off with him. He touched Ben's shoulder, which awoke him with a start.

Mr. Hawkins asked, "How's he doing?"

Ben shrugged his shoulders as if to say, "I don't know" but answered quietly, "He just fell asleep."

Mr. Hawkins nodded. "He'll be all right. Why don't you come with me for now?"

They went over to Mr. Hawkins's cabin, and he said, "Sit down, Mr. Summit. We have a lot to discuss."

Ben sat down, thinking he was going to get a tongue-lashing for the night before. He wasn't quite sure what he was in trouble for, but he felt like a kid about to be spanked by the schoolmaster. Mr. Hawkins began as he reached for a big leather binder off a shelf by his desk. "You do have a way of making life interesting, Mr. Summit." He laid the binder down with a thud and sat in his chair, pulling himself closer as he opened it, thumbing through many pages. He then dipped the ink quill in a well and started to write. Ben sat in an uncomfortable silence as he listened to the scratching on the paper.

Ben finally broke the silence. "Sir, did you need me for anything, or may I go about my duties?"

A sly smile appeared across Mr. Hawkins's face, which broke the stern look he was holding. "Yes, Mr. Summit, I still need you. We are writing in the ship's log."

Ben looked confused. "The ship's log? I thought it was a captain's log?"

"Oh, Mr. Summit, there is a captain's log, but there is a ship's log also. Both should seem about the same. The account of any events should be close to the same accuracy. I have a feeling this time it might vary a bit. Anything I deem pertinent will be recorded, and I think we have certainly had some pertinent events around here lately to write about. And you're here because I am not sure how it will end." Ben's eyebrows wrinkled a bit as he tried to understand. Mr. Hawkins went back to writing. It seemed like an eternity but was really only about ten minutes. "Well, Mr. Summit," he blurted.

Ben jumped a little and interrupted, "Why do you keep calling me Mr. Summit?"

Mr. Hawkins sat straight-faced and said, "You are the owner of the ship *Charee*, are you not?"

Ben sat up straight. "Well, yes, I guess I am."

Mr. Hawkins's face became hard as he looked into Ben's eyes then asked, "You guess you are or you are? Which is it? Look, Mr. Summit, I am documenting what I saw last night, an account of events. You told me you are the owner of the *Charee*, but I have no way of knowing this for sure, and what the captain says may be true. Maybe you and Jackie have planned this all along. My instincts tell me I should believe you. The captain's behavior is another indicator that I should believe you. So I am asking you now to document in the log. Are you or are you not the owner of this vessel?"

Ben could feel the gravity of the situation. There was a huge legal issue at hand. "Yes, sir, I am the legal owner of the merchant ship *Charee*."

Mr. Hawkins nodded as he scribbled away at the paper. He stopped and again looked up. "Do you recall the time in which you relieved Captain Nelson from his duties as captain of the merchant ship *Charee*?"

Ben paused as he tried to remember what time it might have been. "I would not say I would know the exact time, sir, but I would guess…" He hesitated as he saw Mr. Hawkins raise an eyebrow. "I'm sorry. I would say it was approximately, oh hell, Mr. Hawkins, I don't even know what time it is now."

Mr. Hawkins closed his eyes and shook his head. "Right now, Mr. Summit, it is thirteen hundred and twenty minutes. If I may say, sir, I heard gunshots at zero five hundred hours. Would you say you relieved him of his duties before or after that?"

Ben's eyes focused on the floor as he tried to reenact the event. Ben could tell that Mr. Hawkins was acting like a judge in court, and that made Ben even more nervous.

"Well, Mr. Summit?"

Ben rubbed his forehead. "I…I'm really not sure. I…"

Mr. Hawkins used a calmer voice as he could see Ben getting frustrated. "Ben, this is nothing if you were to get dragged into court for this. You are in a very important position now. Your decision affects the lives of all the men aboard. Which also affects lives off the ship as well." Ben could see what he was saying and took a deep breath. He nodded in understanding. He still felt a pit in his stomach. "You have somehow come aboard this ship and changed a man I have known and sailed with and trusted for many years in one night and changed our relationship." Ben started to say he was sorry, but Mr. Hawkins stopped him. "Don't be sorry, Ben. It is not your fault directly, but you placed yourself in command of this ship by relieving him of his duties. He in turn has accused you of mutiny. And I hope for your sake you can truly prove you are the owner, or when we return, you and Jackie will be hung. This is why I need to document what happened in detail."

Ben nodded again, composed himself, and said directly, "It was before the shooting started. He had me up against the wall with a knife, and you say you heard the shots around five twenty, then I would put my time at just before five, four fifty."

"Very good," he said as he scribbled in the book. He scribbled for a second then asked, "Who will be his successor?"

Ben looked confused. "I guess I don't understand the question."

Mr. Hawkins explained, "Was there someone you wanted to take his place as captain? It would be your duty to appoint or have someone appoint a captain or assume the role yourself."

Ben looked at the floor again. "I um…I guess…"

Mr. Hawkins slapped the desk hard with his palm. Ben jumped in his seat. "Be decisive. I don't mind if you take a minute to think, but stop ho humming while you do it! Or tell me you haven't decided yet but do not guess."

Ben stared at him for a minute as he thought about the question. He spoke up. "You. You could be captain."

Mr. Hawkins then asked, "Are you ordering me or asking me?"

Ben shrugged his shoulders. "I'm asking you, I guess." Mr. Hawkins closed his eyes and slapped the desk again. Ben realized his mistake. "My apologies, sir. I am asking you, Mr. Hawkins, if you would consider being captain of the *Charee* during Captain Nelson's absence?"

Mr. Hawkins smiled a bit and winked his eye. "You're catching on, son. I would be honored to fill the position of captain of the merchant ship *Charee* while a captain is absent. And that is how I will write it in the log."

Ben nodded in agreement. Ben and Mr. Hawkins worked on the logbook for about another hour. When they were finished, Mr. Hawkins asked if he could appoint Squeaky to the position of first mate. Ben agreed to that request. He was smart about the ship and had great respect from the crew. He explained that he would appoint Ben but felt Squeaky had a lot more knowledge about the ship and crew and would be more of an asset while underway. Ben understood completely and agreed with Mr. Hawkins and respected his choice. Mr. Hawkins stood and went to the cabin door. "I'll send for him to tell him."

Ben nodded agreement and stood to stretch himself. He truly felt a weight lifted as he now understood his position as owner of the vessel and his obligations to the ship and the crew. Before he was just told he was the owner, but now he was acting the role, and he knew he would have to be confident in his decisions.

Squeaky showed up with a concerned look on his face. "You called for me, sir?"

Mr. Hawkins was seated. "Yes, Mr. Freewater. Please have a seat." He pointed to a chair. This made Squeaky even more nervous as he called him by his surname. He panned the room back and forth from Ben to Mr. Hawkins, trying to read their faces.

Finally, he asked as he sat, "Is there a problem, sir?"

Mr. Hawkins could tell he was uncomfortable, so he played along. "Only if you answer the question wrong." Squeaky's face became very concerned. Mr. Hawkins stood and stepped to the front of his desk, leaned back, and rested his palms as to ponder the question. "Would you, Mr. Arnold Freewater, consider taking the role of first mate of the merchant ship *Charee*?"

That was not the question Squeaky was prepared for. He sat, stunned for a second, as the question sunk in. Then squirming in his chair, he answered, "I…I wouldn't mind it a bit, sir. But what about you, sir?"

Mr. Hawkins stood and walked back to his seat. "We've had a bit of a problem aboard ship, Mr. Freewater." He sat in his chair and leaned back. "Captain Nelson was relieved from his duties."

Before he could say any more, Squeaky interrupted, defending the captain. "With all due respect, sir, the ways I hears it, he was defending his ship." He stood and pointed at Ben. "He and butcher boy conspired with Ole Chef to overtake the ship and go treasure hunting." His voice started to rise, and his face started to flush red. "And you, sir. I'm surprised, Mr. Hawkins, that you stood by these scallywags and are now working with these mutinous dogs to have their way."

Mr. Hawkins had crossed his arms, and his forehead wrinkled. He had never seen Squeaky so riled up. He then interrupted Squeaky, holding his hand out to him to quiet him. "Mr. Freewater, before you go much further, I would like you to meet Mr. Benjamin Summit, the owner of the merchant ship *Charee*."

Squeaky was still red and worked up from his little tantrum, and his gaze rolled from Ben to Mr. Hawkins as he started to become aware of what Mr. Hawkins had just said. As he stood in shock and was bewildered, Ben couldn't help but let out a little giggle. He hadn't seen Mr. Hawkins play with someone like that before.

Mr. Hawkins said, "Please, Mr. Freewater, have a seat and allow me to start from the beginning so you have some facts to work with." They talked for a long time, with Squeaky apologizing to Ben several times as the story unfolded. He was also surprised at the captain's attitude change and was very interested in the share of treasure he would receive. They finalized the story with the treasure being in a safe place and to keep it a complete secret. The whole crew would be back in the next day, and at seven hundred hours, Mr. Hawkins would address the crew and explain everything. Squeaky needed to get someone on cooking duty as long as Chef was laid up. They left with a sturdy handshake and congratulations for the promotion.

Squeaky stopped short at the door. "Thanks again for your confidence, gentlemen. I will try not to let you down."

Ben stood up and reached for his hand, saying, "No, sir, thank you. and I know you won't let us or your crew down. That's why we picked you." They both shook hands with sincerity. As Squeaky stepped out, Ben turned to Mr. Hawkins and asked, "Are we through yet?"

Mr. Hawkins smiled a bit. "Yes, Ben, we are done for now."

"May I go check on Chef and Jackie then resume my duties?"

"By all means, Mr. Summit, please carry on." As he reached the door, Mr. Hawkins said, "It's nice to work for someone who cares."

As Ben turned to leave, he said, "Let's hope it's a long relationship."

* * *

Ben looked in. Jackie was still sleeping soundly, so he made his way to look in on Chef. He got to the cabin door and was greeted by Goliath. Ben nodded and asked, "Chef in here?"

Goliath nodded a yes, but when Ben went to open the door, he found Goliath's large hand on his chest. "Doctor says no one is to see Chef for three days."

Ben looked puzzled. "Is he all right?"

Goliath answered, "He's got food, water, and rum. He needs anything, he is gonna blow the boatswain's whistle."

Ben just smiled. "Well, I see he's in good hands." He patted Goliath on the arm. Ben made his way to the galley. He figured with Chef down, any help would be necessary. After they got a meal out, Ben went back to see how Jackie was doing, and this time he was awake. He complained that it hurt, but after a minute or two, he dropped back off to sleep. Ben made himself comfortable in the captain's cabin in case Jackie woke up and needed anything during the night. Ben was awakened by a hard knock on the door, and Squeaky's head looked in cautiously.

"Damn, boy...I...I mean, sir, I have been looking for you everywhere. Mr. Hawkins wants to see you right away."

They both jumped as someone yelled, "Shit!" Jackie was waking up. "Damn, that hurts."

Ben turned to Squeaky. "Tell Captain Hawkins I will be right there."

Squeaky snapped to. "Aye, aye, sir."

Ben went to Jackie's side and helped him to sit up. His head was spinning, and it took him a second to get upright. "Damn, Ben, this really hurts."

Ben patted his friend on his good shoulder. "Doc says it will be for a couple of days, then it will—"

Jackie interrupted, "How's Chef?"

"Last I checked, Goliath was his nurse, and the patient was doing fine."

Jackie relaxed a bit and let out a sigh. "That makes me feel better. That old goat had me worried."

Ben was hustling around, getting ready, and as he was ready, he looked at Jackie. "You okay if I go?"

Jackie made a crying face. "No, Ben, don't go! I love you, Ben. Why do you always leave me when I need you most? Kiss it. Make it better, Ben."

Ben rolled his eyes as he exited the cabin, mumbling, "Well, it's good to see you are back to normal."

Last thing he heard as he shut the door was Jackie yelling, "*I love you, Ben! What about the children?*"

Ben made his way to the wheel, passing many crew members. They all looked at him with a suspicion. They had all gathered as ordered, and rumors were flying around. Ben was surprised they didn't try to lynch him right there for some of the things that were being said. Mr. Hawkins was standing as usual. He was surveying the crew, hands behind his back, listening also to what was being said but not showing any emotion. As the crew realized he was there, the crowd started to get quiet. They turned their attention to Mr. Hawkins.

As they did, Mr. Hawkins started, "Welcome back, gentlemen. I trust your leave was an enjoyable one." There was some underlying laughter and a few muffled comments. "You're all accounted for, so we won't have to go to town and bail anyone out of jail this time, eh, Mr. Jenson?" The crew laughed louder this time, and all turned to see a red-faced sailor trying to fade as they all looked his way. Mr. Hawkins held up his hand to silence the crowd. "As most of you know, there has been some changes while we have been docked here. Many rumors and fabricated stories, but I will set you straight today. I will start by introducing Mr. Benjamin Summit, proud owner of the *Charee*." The crowd had an underlying rumble as the crew was caught off guard. "Captain Reginald Roach has died, and this is his only heir. He came aboard as a deckhand to learn the trade from the bottom up. He didn't want anyone to know because he didn't want to be treated any different. He didn't want to be pampered. In light of the circumstances before us now, his identity is known to us. He would like to stay on as crew member and continue to learn from your vast nautical knowledge. He hopes that you would not treat him any different than you have been."

A sailor yelled out, "I've some dandy jobs he can do down in the head!" The crowd burst into laughter. Ben recognized the sailor and made eye contact with him and laughed along. He knew it was only in jest.

Mr. Hawkins raised his hand again to quiet the crew. As they did, he continued, "Now, gentlemen, there are other rumors that need to be straightened out. Captain Nelson is no longer captain of this vessel." A few low murmurs were heard through the crowd, but nothing audible. "He was relieved of his duties by Mr. Summit who, by the way, had just cause and is his right as owner. He has placed me as acting captain at this time until further notice. I know some of you have sailed with Captain Nelson for many years, and this is a big change. Mr. Summit and I have talked, and we feel we have an exceptional crew and would like to see all of you stay on. We will understand that if anyone is uncomfortable with me as captain or Mr. Summit as owner and you would like not to be part of the crew, you may talk with us about where you would like to get off as we travel back to Homeport. We also discussed that we would give a large bonus to anyone who does stay and helps us get back to Homeport." Excited voices started to grow through the crowd. Ben looked at Mr. Hawkins, a little surprised they hadn't talked about that at all. Mr. Hawkins looked back at Ben and winked to let him know he had surprised him. He held up his hand again till the crew quieted. "Also, Mr. Freewater will act as first mate, and you should show him the same respect you have all shown to me. On a good note, Chef, who was injured, is doing well, and the little mate Jackie won't be playing any pranks on anyone for a while. And if he does, you can just punch him in the right arm." The crew broke into a loud laugh. He held up his hand and waited again. And as they went quiet, he started, "That's all I have, gentlemen. Any questions you may have for me or Mr. Summit, or if you have decided to not stay on, please see me in my cabin. Thank you for your time. And please go about your duties. I will now turn this ship over to Mr. Freewater."

The crew became loud immediately as Mr. Hawkins signaled to Ben to follow him. Ben was more than happy to follow him to get an explanation of what just developed. As they entered his cabin, Mr. Hawkins launched right into the answer Ben was about to ask. "Ben, I know you are wondering why I said to the crew about a bonus, but let me explain. These men as are very suspicious of changes. Why, some are downright superstitious. Any small change and you could lose half your crew. So I ran an idea through my head. As I started, I was going to mention the treasure, but I think it would serve you better if you would sell that stuff for cash. It would make it easier to divide among the crew. And it is something they could use right away easily. Now with this carrot on a stick, you can easily get your cargo back to Homeport, so I hope that was all right with you. But we really didn't have time to discuss it. And no one is sitting around trying to figure out where the treasure is hiding on the ship."

Ben sat for a second, taking in what Mr. Hawkins was saying. Then he said, "No, that's fine…I, uh, think it's a good idea. But how do I turn it into real money?"

Mr. Hawkins put his hand on Ben's shoulder. "I think you and I need to go town and see if we can figure that out. But first, let's make another check on our wounded."

They checked on Jackie and found him fast asleep. They both backed out quietly. Ben looked at Mr. Hawkins and said, "I would have thought hunger would have him awake by now."

Mr. Hawkins grinned. "You're right. We better find a cook before he wakes up again."

They headed for Chef's quarters. Goliath had left his post for other duties, but the crew was well aware they were not to bother the old boy or risk the wrath of the giant man. Just as Mr. Hawkins reached for the handle, he stopped. There was someone singing an old sea chantey: "What do give to a sailor, darling? What do you give to a sailor, darling? What do you give to a sailor, darling, early in the morning?"

Ben looked confused at Mr. Hawkins, and he wrinkled his brow. "Is someone singing to him?"

Mr. Hawkins shrugged his shoulders and opened the door quietly. And to their surprise, stood Chef in a nightshirt with a brown jug in one hand and a cigar in the other, dancing around the room and singing. His back was turned to them, and as he danced around, he finally saw Ben staring with his mouth wide open and Mr. Hawkins looking at him with an inquisitive look on his face. Chef stopped in his tracks. Then he fell off balance, struggling to catch himself in his bare feet. "Oh my" slipped from his mouth.

Mr. Hawkins smiled. "I'd say the patient is looking pretty good, wouldn't you, Mr. Summit?"

Chef bowed at the waist. "Why thank you, Mr. Hawkins." He slurred then staggered a bit. "I am feeling much better, but I am still a little dizzy."

Mr. Hawkins's brow wrinkled, and he fought back a laugh. "I do believe I know a cure for that, Chef, but it will take two more days, and I will expect you back at your post."

Chef tried to bow again but stopped and said, "Aye, aye, sir."

He started to leave but turned to chef and said, "Oh, by the way, Chef."

Chef snapped to attention. "Yes, Mr. Hawkins."

"It's Captain Hawkins from now on."

Chef rocked back on his heels. "Beggin' pardon, Captain… must have missed that chapter."

Captain Hawkins just smiled. "Two days, Chef. Enjoy it." And he stepped out. He pushed Ben out of the door, laughing at the expense of the old man. Mr. Hawkins shook his head, saying, "I don't know what keeps that old man alive."

Mr. Hawkins and Ben went to town to find someone willing to buy him out but did not find anyone with enough collateral. Mr. Hawkins helped Ben decide to give the gold coins evenly to the men and to sell his jewels and other gold material for himself. Given they didn't have any other choice. That's what they planned to do. When they returned to the ship, it was bustling. Mr. Freewater had everyone doing their duties, and everything seemed to be in order. Captain Hawkins made sure to tell Mr. Freewater what a good job he was doing and that's why we chose him. But as Mr. Freewater turned to go back to his duties, Captain Hawkins asked "Who's doing meals?"

Mr. Freewater had a flash of panic cross his face. He was stammering for words. He managed to say, "I'll get right on that. I mean, I'll get someone on that."

Ben spoke up. "Mr. Freewater, sir, I would be happy to see the crew gets fed, if it's all right with you, sir?"

Squeaky looked a little shocked then looked back at the captain. "That would work for me, if Captain Hawkins doesn't mind?"

Captain Hawkins was taken back a bit this time. He wasn't used to being called that yet. He put a hand on both their shoulders and added, "Gentlemen, whatever it takes to get this ship ready to go by six thirty tomorrow morning. I trust any decisions you two will come up with."

At six thirty, Mr. Hawkins surveyed his crew. They were all working hard. He was pleased no one had approached him to leave the ship. Mr. Freewater was well in control. Even Jackie was up this day, making his way around decks and helping where he could with one arm. The winds were favorable, and it looked like departure would be easy. It set them on a good run for Homeport. Ben was doing a fine job of getting the crew fed thanks to his experience at making large amounts of food at the home with his mother. A few days out and Chef joined him in the kitchen. Ben noticed right away something was different with Chef. Others noticed after a couple of days. He wasn't his ornery old self. It was starting to bother Jackie. He cornered him in the galley one day and tried to get him to talk, but he would have no part and told him to get the hell out of his kitchen. Jackie put his head back through the door and told him if he needed to talk about something, he better let him know. He would listen.

He started to close the door and he heard, "Ain't nothing been the same since you two came aboard."

Jackie stopped short of closing the door and opened it slowly. "Were you speaking to me?" he asked.

The old man growled, "You heard me."

Jackie asked quietly with sincerity, "Did we do something wrong?"

His eyes jumped up to meet Jackie's stare. "No...no." He shaking his head. "It's just the changing times. You two reminded me of that, the way you two are living for the adventure and seeing the beauty of the ocean. Laughing at the storms or watching the stars on a clear night. Most of all, you two remind me that I never took time to have a close family, no grandchildren, no woman to call my own." His face was facing down as if too embarrassed to be spilling his guts out to Jackie, but he kept on. "Then when I got hurt, you guys and the crew. you guys all cared. It made me feel all gushy inside. Then Ben stepped in and showed me I'm replaceable. He's a pretty good cook, if you didn't notice."

Jackie sat down beside him and threw his arm around the old man. He felt like the old guy was a little more frail today. He whispered, not directly at the old man, "You know, Chef, Ben and I, in fact, the whole crew thinks of you as family. And you're right, Ben is a pretty good cook for a couple of days, but with each day he gets more and more tired of it, and the quality goes right downhill. Or hadn't you noticed? He's only doing that to keep the crew happy. Besides, he used to help his mom fix meals at a large home for aged, and that's how he knows his way around the galley. He couldn't wait for you to get back."

Chef looked up at Jacki. "Aye, mate, are you sure?"

Jackie squeezed him with his good arm tight. "Sure. I'm sure, mate. We loves ya. Why, I didn't kiss you 'cause you're pretty."

Chef came alive on that note and aggressively shoved Jackie away. "Ain't you got work to do?"

Jackie was grinning ear to ear and stood to leave. "I'm sure I can find something to do." Jackie left laughing to himself, and Chef went back to his old self.

The *Charee* was making good time. The winds were strong and steady. They figured they would make Homeport in a couple of days. Captain Hawkins estimated their arrival just an hour before sunset. As usual, Captain Hawkins was correct. As *Charee* eased her way into port and the hawser lines were drawn into dock by a large team of mules, a large group of men in gray uniforms started to assemble on the dock. They all were armed with long guns with bayonets on the end. Captain Hawkins was observing this and started to get a bit uncomfortable at the sight. His suspicions were confirmed when he saw Captain Nelson on horseback in gray uniform, talking with another man on horseback. Captain Nelson was pointing to Captain Hawkins and then at Ben, who was working on deck.

Captain Hawkins yelled out, "Mr. Summit, to the bridge please!"

By now, the crew had started to notice the large group of soldiers gathering on the dock. Mr. Freewater noticed Captain Nelson and yelled out, "There's the cap'n!"

Captain Nelson yelled out, "Mr. Freewater, to the bridge please!"

Ben and Squeaky went to the bridge and met with Captain Hawkins. Ben arrived first but hadn't really noticed the men on the dock yet. Squeaky came right behind him. "Hey, did you see Captain Nelson down there? He beat us home. Wonder how he did that."

Ben turned and then noticed the soldiers and Captain Nelson were pointing right at him.

Captain Hawkins only answered, "Yes, I see him, but I don't like the looks of this, gentlemen." Ben got a cold shiver up his spine. This did not look good to him either. Captain Hawkins said, "Squeaky, I need you to get your men ready to cut the lines that hold *Charee* to dock and have them ready to back wind out of here on my command. Do you understand?"

Squeaky started to say, "But, sir, we have to unload first." He then took another look at the mob of soldiers and said, "Aye, aye, Captain. We'll be ready sir." And off he ran.

Captain Nelson saw the men reacting to what Mr. Hawkins had told Squeaky and knew what he was preparing to do. He yelled, "Mr. Hawkins, I need to speak to you!"

Captain Hawkins said to Ben, "Wait right here. Don't move." Captain Hawkins made his way down to the rail, and as he did, he yelled a response back to Captain Nelson. "Captain Nelson, it's good to see you, sir! You disappeared so suddenly, I wasn't sure what to make of the situation you left behind, sir!"

Captain Nelson yelled back, "Mr. Hawkins, I—"

Captain Hawkins interrupted him. "Excuse me, sir, but I would prefer you address me as Captain Hawkins, for the record, sir."

Captain Nelson laughed a little and shook his head. "That's what I love about you, Captain Hawkins. You're a stickler for details. All is proper. We wish to have Mr. Summit come with us for questioning and come aboard to inspect the cargo."

The crew was intensely watching this conversation. In fact, the whole dock was at a standstill as these two talked. "You may not take Mr. Summit into custody at this time, but you may ask his permission to join you. And may I remind you, Captain, if you are to set foot on this ship, I will have you arrested to stand trial for attempted murder and assault."

Captain Nelson's face changed form a smug grin to instant anger. "Tell Mr. Summit to come to the rail. I wish to speak with him." Ben could already hear the conversation from where he was.

Captain Hawkins asked, "What issues are involving the merchant ship *Charee* and her crew, as captain I have a right to know."

The man sitting on horseback next to Captain Nelson spoke with a very thick Southern accent. "It has come to our attention, sir, that the merchant ship *Charee* is involved in a treasonous act, consisting of if not limited to supplying our enemies to the North with moneys and weapons and supplies."

Captain Hawkins sat confused for a second. He had suspicions but still had to ask, "What enemy would that be, sir?"

Now the officer had a confused look then answered politely, "It appears, sir, you have been gone a while. I am sure you have heard there have been tensions between the states. While you were gone, our neighboring states have succeeded to form the Union, and they have declared war against us." Captain Hawkins rocked back on his heels a bit, thinking they actually did it. He continued, "So you see, sir, if you would allow us to come aboard and search the vessel, sir, and we find nothing, then we will be on our way. If we find contraband, we will want to take Mr. Summit into custody for trial."

"Allow me, sir, to discuss it with the owner!" he yelled out to the officer. He bowed in understanding and agreement. The crew was all abuzz about a civil war and the effect it would have on them and their livelihood.

As he turned to talk with Ben and the crew, he heard Captain Nelson yell out, "Quit stalling, Mr. Hawkins! You're wasting everyone's time here!" The officer looked at Captain Nelson with a look of displeasure.

Mr. Hawkins ignored Captain Nelson's remark and said, "Mr. Summit, may I have a word with you?"

Ben answered, "Aye, aye, sir." And he bounded down to where he was standing.

Captain Hawkins stood at attention as Ben approached and quietly mentioned, "Do not aye, aye me, sir. Right now, you are the owner of the *Charee*, and I work for you, do you understand?"

Ben answered, "Yes, sir."

"Good. Let's discuss this situation we are in."

As they talked, the officer below looked on with curiosity then turned to Captain Nelson. "That young lad he is talking to is the owner?"

Captain Nelson was sitting, looking very agitated, and answered, "Yes, he is. And, sir, if I know the captain of that ship right now, he is prepared to cut the lines loose and run. You should train your guns on that crew and be ready, sir."

As they talked and prepared, Captain Hawkins explained to Ben, "You have been set up, Benjamin. I am sure what Captain Nelson has accused you of, they will find it aboard. If the states are at war, you will become a casualty."

Ben's mind was swimming. "They started a civil war?"

"That's how it appears, Benjamin, so you have a very weighted decision here. Your crew is ready to run if you desire. You are the owner of this vessel. We have not tied up to this land or have we set foot on it. They don't have any proof yet that you have done anything wrong, but if you run, they could consider you a threat and open fire. If they come aboard and decide you are aiding and abetting the enemy, you could be hung or shot. Hell, the whole crew could be if they see it that way."

Ben stood thinking for a second then nodded his understanding. He turned and yelled, "Mr. Freewater, may I see you here please!"

He heard an "Aye, aye, sir." And he made his way to the rail where Ben and Captain Hawkins were standing. Mr. Freewater stood looking eye to eye with Mr. Summit. "Yes, sir," he snapped.

Ben, not wavering, locked eyes with him. "I need to know what the men and yourself are thinking about and what we should do."

Mr. Freewater didn't hesitate to answer. "Well, sir, the men who live here are concerned and would like to stay. The rest of us don't care either way, and the dark men like Goliath never get off the boat here anyway. It's not safe for them. But I would tell you this, Mr. Summit. We are all ready to cut and run if that is your decision."

Captain Hawkins put his hand on Ben's shoulder. "That says a lot for you, Mr. Summit."

Ben turned and nodded to Captain Hawkins, then turned his attention to Squeaky. "Thank you for your input. It helps a lot with my decision. You're a good man, Mr. Freewater. Keep your men at the ready, sir, and get with Jackie. Pull the gold out and get each man his share."

Squeaky's eyes got big. "Gold, sir?"

"Yes, gold. A couple of thousand dollars' worth to each man."

Squeaky turned on his heels with an "Aye, aye, sir. And thank you, sir."

Ben added, "Let me know when it's been distributed. And tell the men to conceal it on themselves. Do not leave any lying around. You got all that?"

Squeaky snapped again "Aye, aye, sir."

Ben turned to Captain Hawkins and nodded, saying, "Those men are nothing more than pirates in uniform."

Mr. Hawkins smiled a bit, saying, "I agree, sir."

When Ben looked back out at the pier, Captain Nelson was no longer with the officer. He was on horseback with about fifty armed soldiers. Ben yelled out to the group, "My name is Benjamin Summit! I am the owner of the merchant ship *Charee*. To whom am I addressing?"

The officer sat straighter in his saddle. "I am Colonel Belcher of the Confederated states, sir!"

Ben returned, "Well, Colonel Belcher, why are you holding my ship hostage, and what are the charges against me, sir?" Captain Hawkins was standing by, surprised at the way Ben was handling this in a professional manner.

The colonel sat straighter in his saddle. "Well, sir, we have information from a reliable source that your vessel is supplying the Union Army with money and arms. Aiding the Union Army is a treasonous act of war and is punishable by article fifteen, sir. It would be nice if you were to cooperate, sir. We would certainly appreciate it."

Ben was angry at first. Then he felt every eye was on him and could feel the pressure mount with each second of silence that ticked by. "Colonel Belcher, sir, I have nothing to hide, and although I do not support the southern states' decision, I do not support the North's either. I am merely a merchant marine delivering goods. I will let you come aboard, sir, for your inspection for my logs and records will show my innocence. But before I do, I have council that lives here in town and would like him present as you inspect my ship. His name is Mr. Harsgrove, and he resides in town on Fisher Avenue. If you were to send word for him, I am sure he can help us resolve this issue."

Colonel Belcher yelled back, "I know of this Mr. Harsgrove, and this could be arranged!" He turned and yelled to one of the soldiers, "Corporal Kenson!"

A soldier came forward with a snappy "Yes, sir."

"Would you please go to town and see if Mr. Harsgrove is and see if he is available to come back with you?"

He snapped another, "Yes, sir," and ran off.

Captain Hawkins almost clapped at the performance he just witnessed, the transformation from boy to man right before his eyes.

Ben then added, "I give you my word, sir, that no one will come or go from this vessel until Mr. Harsgrove arrives. But we will continue to work aboard as we have many duties to perform for moorage."

Colonel Belcher bowed his head in agreement and said, "That would be acceptable." Then he turned and ordered, "At ease, men." Most dropped down to one knee.

Ben then turned and quietly asked Mr. Hawkins, "What do you think is really happening here?"

Mr. Hawkins looked at Ben with an unsure look and added, "I don't know, Ben, but Mr. Harsgrove and Captain Nelson are old friends, so be very careful how you play this."

Jackie came up to meet them and blurted out, "What the hell is going on?"

Ben turned to his friend. "It appears that the civil war was started when we were gone."

"That's what I heard. Is it true?"

Mr. Hawkins interrupted, "We aren't one hundred percent sure, but those men in uniforms and guns make a pretty convincing argument."

Jackie shook his head. "What's that have to do with us?"

Ben answered him, "It appears that Captain Nelson told the Confederate Army that we were supplying the North with supplies."

Jackie shook his head. "That Captain Nelson is starting to get me pretty angry." They both nodded agreement. Jackie asked, "What are we going to do?"

Ben didn't' answer but did ask, "Did you and Squeaky get the treasure out and distributed?"

"Yes, I dug it out, leaving all but the coins. And he has the manifest and is dividing it up right now. In fact, that's why I am here, to give Captain Hawkins his share." He handed a bag of gold coins to Captain Hawkins.

Ben sighed. "That's good. Thank you." And with despair in his voice, he added, "Let's hope we get a chance to use it. As soon as everyone has his share, would you see to it that the crew assemble topside, please, Mr. Huntington?"

Jackie respectfully answered, "Aye, aye, sir." And he ran off to follow orders.

Captain Hawkins bounced his gold in his hands a few times, making it jingle. Ben turned around at the noise. Captain Hawkins was grinning. "Thank you, sir. This is very generous of you. That's about five years' worth of wages here." Ben just nodded agreement. "You know, this is what they will be looking for, Ben, and there is no manifest to explain all this gold."

Ben nodded again, deep in thought. "Where do you suppose Captain Nelson went to?"

"I've been wondering the same thing." He tossed his bag of coins in the air again and caught them. "I'll say it again. It has been very interesting meeting you, Mr. Summit. Very interesting indeed." Ben went below to make sure the rest of his treasure was hidden deep in the bilge where a man would have to crawl, smashing himself tight to get at it.

Evening was coming fast, and as Ben made his way to the upper decks, he was met with much noise and commotion. He came to the main upper deck. almost all of his crew was rounded up and being held at gunpoint by soldiers. They were being corralled into a circle. And as Ben tried to object, yelling for Colonel Belcher, he was met by Captain Nelson with a pistol pointed at his forehead.

"I should put a bullet in your brain right now."

Ben was very angry and said, "Not like you haven't tried that before, Captain. Only this time, the whole crew is a witness."

Captain Nelson slapped Ben hard with his free hand. Ben turned back to him, rage running through him. He doubled his fist, and Captain Nelson pushed the pistol under his chin and forcibly pushed his head backward, looking up the masts.

Ben squeezed out, "Where is Mr. Harsgrove?"

Captain Nelson growled in his face. "He won't be here in time to save your ass, boy." Then he shoved him hard into the group of sailors. The men caught him as he stumbled toward them. They were all stunned by the captain's anger and attitude. He yelled out, "All secure, Colonel!"

Two soldiers dropped a gangplank into place, and the group on the dock came charging aboard. Ben was surveying his options. He saw Captain Hawkins doing the same, and he made his way over to him. "How did they get aboard?"

Mr. Hawkins's face showed disgust as he answered, "They came by boat off the stern, sir. Scaled the ship and took us by surprise. I'm sorry, sir."

Ben patted his shoulder. "Captain Hawkins, there is nothing for you to be sorry for, sir. None of this is your fault. Maybe if I had been honest with you earlier, we wouldn't be in this predicament."

Colonel Belcher came aboard and announced loudly, "You are all under arrest for treason!"

The men erupted in protest, and all the soldiers pointed their muskets at the crowd. Then one shot rang out, and the crowd became silent. They all turned to where the shot came from. Captain Nelson was standing with his pistol pointed in the air, smoke rolling from the barrel.

He yelled, "*Sit down, you swabs, right where you are!*" Two soldiers cocked their guns, ready to fire. And as most started to sit, a deep growl and yell rang across the ship. Everyone's attention turned to it just in time to see Goliath. He charged the two soldiers and grabbed one in each arm and took them over the rail with him. Captain Nelson yelled, "No, Goliath!" But it was too late. It all happened so fast. Both soldier's guns went off on impact. One hit another soldier, and the other went straight up. Then chaos erupted. Guns boomed and men jumped overboard.

Captain Nelson pulled Ben backward by his collar and put his pistol to Ben's head. "You aren't going anywhere." He dragged him away to a secure spot. The colonel was trying desperately to gain control. By the time he had, more than half the crew had escaped, and some were dead and some were wounded. As they did get control, he ordered some men to find lanterns and torches to help secure the area. Captain Hawkins was being held by two soldiers holding guns to his back, and his hands were bound behind his back.

Mr. Hawkins saw Ben and Captain Nelson, and he smugly yelled out, "Captain Nelson, you are hereby under arrest for attempted murder, assault, and—"

He never finished what he was saying. Some soldier said, "Shut up, Yankee. He hit him with his rifle butt, knocking him to the ground.

Ben lurched forward, yelling, "*Hey!*"

Captain Nelson whacked him hard on the back of the head with his pistol butt. Captain Nelson said to a couple of soldiers, "Let's get these two to the stockade so we can start rounding up the rest of the crew."

Ben was hurt but not unconscious, and he started to struggle as they tried to drag him. Mr. Hawkins was out, and they easily dragged him by his arms. They got Ben's hands tethered and then dragged him off as well. They had turned him to face Captain Nelson as they bound his hands.

Ben looked him in the eyes, saying, "Why…why are you doing this? You had a share of the treasure coming to you. You could do anything you wanted with it."

Captain Nelson laughed out loud then backhanded Ben across his face. "Get this treasonous bastard out of my face, and get me five men to start searching this tub."

Ben and his crew were herded down the pier and into town to what was called the jailhouse. They were tossed into cells, cramming as many as they could into each one. The men were all yelling. The scene was out of control on their part but very controlled on the soldier's part. Ben quickly got his cell to calm down and get quiet. And then he told the cell next to him to get their men quiet and worked their way down until the jailhouse was quiet.

Ben said, "Listen, men, we need everyone to calm down for a minute and let's get a roll call see who is here one at a time."

The men could see where Ben was going with this. From the farthest cell, a man yelled, "Stevenson!"

Another yelled right after him, "Heffler!"

"Smith!"

"Kameron!"

"Huntington!"

That was what Ben wanted to hear. The names kept coming. When the farthest cell was done, the next cell started. When they got to Ben's cell, he noticed there was no Freewater or Captain Hawkins, and as they finished, he asked, "Did anyone see Captain Hawkins?"

The third cell down answered, "Yes, he's here."

"Is he all right?"

"Yeah, he'll be all right. He's got a nasty bump on his noggin' though, but he'll come around."

"Keep an eye on him please."

A voice yelled back, "Aye, aye, sir!"

Then questions started round: Why are we here? What have we done? What are they going to do to us? Ben didn't know any of these answers. He was just starting to tell them what he did know when a group of soldiers marched through the door. They stood at attention as another dressed more proper came in. He was some sort of officer, and everyone got quiet.

The officer yelled, "I am looking for Benjamin Summit! Please speak up!"

Ben yelled, "Here, I am here!"

The officer turned that direction. A second of silence was shattered as another voice called from another cell, "Over here, I'm Benjamin Summit!" Ben started to correct the officer, thinking that the sailor misunderstood what the man asked.

Then another voice yelled, "I'm the real Benjamin Summit!" Before Ben knew it, the place erupted with voices yelling, "I'm Benjamin Summit!"

The officer, looking extremely frustrated and red-faced, yelled above them all, "*Y'all hang for treason then!*" He turned on his heel and stomped out. And when he did, the jailhouse erupted in cheers.

One sailor was heard saying, "That was worth hanging for."

Ben worked at quieting them down. When he did, he hollered to all the cells, "Why did you men do that? They may have just wanted to talk, and I could have cleared this whole thing up."

A voice from the crowd said, "With all due respect, sir, we didn't see a whole lot of justice coming from that group. What we seen was a lynchin' mob."

Ben pleaded with them to let him talk to the soldiers and to get a hold of Mr. Harsgrove to get at the truth. They all agreed to be quiet the next time and let Ben talk. Hours ticked by, and no one came. Everyone was quiet for now, waiting. Light started to bleed into the cells from the small windows with bars on the north side of the corridor. *Must be morning*, Ben thought as the sun was just on the rise. The silence of men sleeping was shattered by a loud commotion outside the hall door, then some shooting then an explosion sent the doors to the hallway flying with debris and dust. A group of familiar faces appeared, Goliath being one of them. They ran down the hall, unlocking the cells and handing out guns and swords to everyone. They were arming as many as they could.

Goliath was hollering, "Get to the ship!"

Captain Hawkins came to a little bit with the explosion, but two men started to help him to his feet. Goliath burst into the cell, threw him over his shoulder, and took off running. Ben and Jackie never thought they would see such a sight in their town, a band of armed sailors running wild through the downtown. And Ben never thought he would see the day he would see a ninety-year-old man riding his friend down the streets of his town yelling, "Faster, you lazy scallywag!" and spanking him as he ran. They only encountered the soldiers at the jail, but when they turned the corner of the pier and the ship was in sight, a small handful of soldiers guarded the *Charee*.

When the first two sailors rounded the corner, two of them dropped to one knee, took aim, and hollered, "Halt or we'll shoot!" The other soldiers realized the intrusion and started to ready their guns. Then the screaming mass of fifty men all armed rounded the corner. The soldiers realized they were not going to hold this group off. All it took was one to yell, "Retreat!" They abandoned the pier, and the crew of the *Charee* stormed aboard their ship. Mr. Freewater started to give orders, and every man knew his job so the *Charee* was ready to sail in no time.

Goliath set Captain Hawkins down lightly, and he mumbled something about "getting hit on the head didn't hurt half as bad as riding the back of Goliath."

Ben laughed a little but was too focused on getting the ship underway. Captain Hawkins grabbed hold of Ben's arm and told him to check the wheel and gears. Captain Nelson would have anticipated such a move and would have disabled it below. Ben could see he was coming around, and he was glad. He would need his experience to get *Charee* out of the harbor. He went below and found the cargo hold in a shambles and the men's barracks torn to pieces as they searched for the treasure. Ben wanted to go check his stash, but there wasn't time. He found the wheel had been disengaged from the tiller and was thankful Captain Hawkins had sailed with Captain Nelson for so long to think like him. For they wouldn't have gotten very far if he hadn't thought ahead. He quickly put it back together and made his way to topside. He saw Captain Hawkins leaning on a banister, and Mr. Freewater was getting ready to raise the first sail. As it started to unfurl, shots rang from the dock and wood splintered off the gun rail and decks. Men ducked, but every man kept working. They saw a large regiment of soldiers starting to come out to the pier with Captain Nelson at the lead. Squeaky ordered them to return fire, and that made the soldiers look for cover, buying them only seconds but enough to get a few more sheets into the wind. The wind was on their side, and they started to quickly pull away in a controlled haste from the dock. They started to shoot at the men in the rigging, but everyone stayed as hidden as possible. It didn't take long to get out of range. Once he felt it was safe, Ben quickly assembled the men, making sure everyone was safe and unharmed. Then Ben went to Captain Hawkins to see how he was doing. Goliath was standing by, and Ben held out his hand to shake. Goliath looked at him hesitantly and grabbed hold of Ben's hand.

Ben said, "Thank you, Goliath. I really appreciated what you did back there. I'm not sure what we did was the right thing, and you being dark skinned, I'm pretty sure you will never be allowed back in Homeport without being hung."

Goliath patted Ben on the shoulder and smiled big. "Mistah Summit, sir, I never was allowed off the ship in Homeport. I have always been property of Captain Nelson. Now I'm pretty sure the way the law reads, y'all are now accessories to harboring escaped slaves." Ben hadn't realized it before, but Goliath wasn't on the payroll book. Goliath said, "That's why I took those two sailors overboard to escape. I didn't mean to cause everyone a problem, sir. It's just that with the share of treasure everyone got, I could afford to buy my own freedom."

Ben felt a hatred for slavery he never felt before. He always never agreed with it but watched it surround his everyday way of life. He held a tighter grip on Goliath's hand, reached up, and grabbed his arm with his free hand, saying, "Goliath, keep your money. I think we just set you free today."

Goliath walked away to his duties, saying, "Thank you, Mistah Summit. You's a good man."

Captain Hawkins was sitting on the bridge, Ben asked, "How are you doing?"

Captain Hawkins was rubbing the knot on the back of his head. "Oh, I will live, not that you need me though. That's a fine crew you have."

Ben looked around and saw his crew was amazing and taking care of everything. Ben could only add "Yes…yes, we do."

Just then, Squeaky came bounding up and smiling. "Hey, Captain, you look like shit."

Captain Hawkins looked up with a squinted eye and the other shut. "Tell me again…how were you chosen for first mate."

Ben interjected, "Nice work, Mr. Freewater."

"You're welcome, sir. And to answer your question, Captain, no one else was stupid enough to take the job."

Captain Hawkins shook his head and smiled a bit. "So where to, gentleman?" Captain Hawkins and Ben looked at each other.

Captain Hawkins said, "Go North. We're wanted men in the South."

Ben looked at Squeaky, shrugged his shoulders, then nodded agreement. As Squeaky turned to go, Ben asked, "Have you seen Jackie?"

"He said he had to stay and see his father and will straighten everything out."

Ben slapped his arms against his side. "Damnit, what if he gets caught?" he yelled.

Squeaky just apologized. "Sorry, sir, I thought you knew."

Ben realized his frustration and said, "No, it's not your fault, Mr. Freewater. It's mine. Carry on."

Squeaky nodded and took off to fulfill his orders. Ben's mind raced to his mom. *I hope she's all right.* Captain Hawkins started to walk away from the wheel and had to catch himself. Ben rushed to his side, propping him up under one arm.

Captain Hawkins said, "Help me to my room, will ya, son?"

Ben asked him, "Are you all right, Captain?"

"I will be. Just feel like lying down for a bit, that's all."

Goliath saw the two and came over to help. They got him to the cabin and put him down on his bunk. He thanked them. Ben said, "I will go see that things are working and be back in a little bit. Goliath, will you stay here with the captain in case he needs something?" Goliath nodded and agreed.

But Captain Hawkins said something about he didn't need to be looked after like some wet-nursed kid. And he waved at them to leave. Ben looked at Goliath, and he nodded, assuring Ben he would stay. Ben went about the whole ship, and once it looked like everything and everyone was doing well, he went to check on his share of the treasure. He climbed into the bilge deep and reached. It was still there. He came out and helped the crew secure the cargo back in order. He walked through the galley to see if it was in any shape. When he got there, he noticed Old Chef sitting in the middle of the floor. Ben rushed over to him shook him by the shoulder.

"Chef, you all right?"

Chef looked up at him, laughed a little, and said, "That was fun. We haven't had that much fun in years." His eyes rolled a bit as he spoke, and then he coughed a spasm cough, wincing in pain. A little blood came from his mouth, and he spit it on the floor. "It appears, my young friend, I caught one in the midsection."

Ben looked confused. "What do you mean, Chef?"

Chef leaned back a bit and pulled his left hand away from his belly. There was a large amount of blood soaking his shirt. "I'm not sure if it was ours or theirs."

Ben eased him to a lying position. "Hang in there, old friend. It'll be all right. I'll get some help." Ben started to jump up.

The old man held on to his shirtsleeve. "Don't bother, kid. I think it tore me up pretty good. I think it's my time."

A feeling of emptiness shot through Ben. Everything was out of their control. And it hit him…that damn treasure. It was a curse. It brought nothing but hate, discontent, death, and destruction. And as he was despairing over the treasure, he heard someone walking by. "*Hey, out there! We need some help!*"

A young sailor, not as young as Ben and Jackie, poked his head in. "You call for help, sir?"

Ben recognized him. "Yes, Robinson, please, Chef's been injured. Help me get him to his bunk." The young man could see now and came in and helped Ben lug the old man to his bunk. As they lifted him, he groaned with pain, and when they laid him out, he did again. Ben told him to stay with Chef for now. Mr. Freewater would relieve him with someone or let him stay, but he would tell him what has happened and where Robinson was. He made his way topside and told Squeaky what was happening and then went to his cabin. He pulled out charts of the area. He was looking for a small inlet or port that was nearby and was big enough for *Charee* but small enough to hide her. He chose one that looked good on the charts. It was only about twenty miles from Homeport.

Ben knew that Captain Nelson didn't get what he wanted and wouldn't give up that easily. He had the helmsman set the course and explained to the men what he was about to do. He gave them the choice. Anyone who wanted off at that time was welcome to leave the ship. He apologized for putting them in the predicament they were in.

One man yelled, "I've never been richer in my life, and for that you're apologizing?" The men all laughed.

But it didn't make Ben feel any better. Ben was right about Captain Nelson. He had put a party together and was heading North at a fast pace. Chef's dilemma was almost a blessing. Captain Nelson's plan was to intercept the *Charee* at one of the larger ports up the way and rode right past the small inlet Ben had chosen. It didn't take them long to reach the small inlet. They were afraid to go too far in for fear of running ground, and they watched it carefully as they approached. They wanted to get in far enough so they wouldn't be visible to passing ships. They dropped anchor and prepared a dingy to go into shore and easily maneuvered Chef into the small craft. Then a landing party was assembled and lowered into the water. Once on shore, they started to secure the dingy. They were met by a band of black men, all armed with machetes, clubs, pitchforks, and many other crude weapons.

Goliath immediately held up his hands in a gesture showing they didn't want any trouble. He spoke to them in a language Ben did not recognize, but it seemed to stop them where they were, and they didn't approach any farther. Then he spoke English. "We don't come to harm you."

They hesitated but were still very tense. One asked, "You hallin' slaves on dat ship?"

Ben started to say no and shake his head. Goliath said, "No, my brother, that ship does not haul slaves. The owner won't allow it."

One of them raised his machete, pointing at Goliath. "Me think you his slave and made to say things. Me thinks you all here to take us back."

Goliath held his hands up again as they all moved in closer, getting battle ready. He stared saying, "Wait…wait, my brothers. This man helped me to get free."

They all stopped for a second. "How he do this for you?"

"He helped me escape. He's takin' me North to freedom." You could see them all start to relax and think for a second.

A large man about the size of Goliath pushed forward. "Why you here? Why you bring dat big ass boat in here den if you ain't bounty hunters?"

Goliath pointed in the dingy. "We have a mate. Was shot trying to help me escape. He needs a doctor, that's all."

The large man pushed past the rest and looked in the dingy. He looked back at Goliath and said, "Dat man look dead ahready."

Goliath said, "Please, I feel I owe the man for trying to help save me. Please let me take him to a doctor."

The large man turned back to the crowd and motioned them to come back with him. They stepped away from the landing party and talked in a hush. Then they all turned the landing party's way all at once. The large man spoke again. "We help you, but you help us. You take us all North on that freedom ship."

Ben thought for a moment and realized what he just asked. Ben started to shake his head no and tried to get Goliath's attention. Goliath turned to him. Ben said in a low voice, "We can't do that. We could be hung for transporting runaway slaves."

Goliath's face lit up with a huge grin. He patted Ben on the shoulder. "Mastah Summit, you's already gona get on da hangman's list."

Ben thought for a second, and Goliath was right. He looked in the eyes of the men standing there and he knew he should help, for if these men didn't get help out of there, their blood would be on his hands. He gave in. "Fine, I'll do it."

The men put their weapons down and ran over and picked up Ole Chef carefully and started to carry him off, almost running through the brushy terrain. They came to a small clearing small that was not visible from a road or path. It had a small firepit and a few tents. They put a blanket down and then eased Chef onto it. They all got down on their knees, except one man, and he went to a small lean-to. Ben was confused. He wanted to take Chef to a doctor in town. Why was he stopping here? He reached down and tapped a man on the shoulder to ask him. He turned to Ben and put a finger to his lips to show Ben to be quiet. Ben swelled with frustration and was about to say something again, but Goliath put a hand on his shoulder, showing concern on his face and shaking his head no to Ben.

Right then, an elderly black man stepped out of the lean-to. He was badly crippled up and using two tree limbs for crutches. He hobbled over to where they were all standing. All the men fell forward, their chests on their knees, and put their faces into their cupped hands. The man was about forty. His nappy hair was short and gray on the sides. He was lean, but his body was muscular on his upper torso. He lowered himself down by Chef, looking him up and down. He put his two rustic crutches together and thrust them at Ben, who was standing close. Ben took them with surprised look. Their eyes met only for a second, but Ben could see in his dark brown eyes this man demanded respect even from a white man. He showed no fear. He then took off a shawl he had around him, and the one man took it from him as he handed it back without even looking, knowing the man was there and would take it. He then reached over to Chef and forced his eyelid open with his thumb and forefinger. He studied his eye for a second then other one. He moved Chef's hands from clutching his stomach and laid them at his sides. He opened Chef's shirt and gently poked around the wound. Chef groaned from the intrusion. It had stopped bleeding for the most part, and Ben wasn't sure if that was a good thing or bad.

This medicine man, as Ben was thinking of him, turned and said something in a language Ben had never heard, and he jumped up and ran off to the lean-to. He came running back and handed him a large rolled skin. It looked a lot like sheep. As he started to unroll it, Ben said quietly to Goliath, "Are you sure this is all right? I mean, do you think he knows what he's doing?"

The man shot a look at Ben that ran a chill up his spine, but he never said a word and finished rolling out his tools. He arranged them in an organized fashion. He then grabbed a tufted grass and held it in the fire. It started to smolder. As it did, all the other men, including Goliath, started to chant. It was a low mumble of words over and over. Ben watched with a curios eyes as the man ran the smoldering bunch around Chef back and forth from head to toe. As he finished, he threw it into the fire. They all stopped chanting right when it hit the flames. He reached over and picked up a small clear bottle and pulled a cork from its top. He pinched Chef's mouth open with one hand and poured two drops into Chef's mouth. His eyes fluttered as he showed a little life. He coughed a couple of times and reached for his wound because it hurt to cough. The medicine man would restrain his hands. And then he poured several drops into the wound itself. Chef groaned again reached for the wound. He said something else, and a man next to him poured hot water from a pot by the fire into a small bowl. The medicine man put a long shiny rod into the fire. He then took small rags and cleaned around the wound. He clapped his hands once, and four of the men jumped up and held one leg and one arm of Chef. He then reached his finger around in the hole with his eyes shut. He finally opened his eyes. Chef moaned a little but did not fight or kick. Ben thought it must be the drops. It must have something to do with it, and he kept watching. The medicine man then pulled his finger out and dropped a lead ball into the small bowl. It made a tinking sound as it was dropped.

He then took the hot rod out of the fire and applied it to Chef's wound. Chef arched that time, yelled a little, and writhed, but the men held him fast. The smell of burning flesh permeated the air. He moved cautiously as he worked then removed the tool. He looked closely in the hole reached over and put the tool down and took a small handful of leaves and rubbed them vigorously between his hands, rolling it into what looked like hemp rope. He poured a few more drops into the now charred hole and inserted the leaves into the hole. Then, taking a long piece of cotton bedding, he nodded once, and the men sat Chef up. His eyes opened for a second, and he groaned a bit but seemed to be sedated. Ben was feeling better that the old man was still alive. The medicine man wrapped Chef carefully, then when done, they laid him down again. One man took the tools and wrapped them up and took them back to the shelter. The medicine man turned to Ben, reaching out for his walking sticks. Ben understood what he wanted and handed them to him. He struggled to get up, and Ben stepped over to help him, touching his arm. The man pulled away harshly, almost falling over. In a very thick British accent, he said, "I don't need help from anyone...especially from a white man." He got himself upright and then told Ben, "Your friend will be fine. He needs a lot of rest. That bullet nicked his spleen, but I'm pretty sure I cauterized it. It missed any bowels, so we will see, but he should be fine. Now I was told you were willing to help my comrades, and I to find refuge to the north and escape this savage land of slavery."

Ben only stood still, a little shocked at the sophistication of this man's speech. He stammered, "Why...uh...yes, that was the deal." He remembered his lesson from Captain Hawkins: "if you want respect, then stand tall and give direct answers." Ben then looked this man in the eyes. "Where did you learn the medical trade?"

The old man gave him a sheepish grin. "Oh, that. I came from a very rich family in Nigeria. I had gone to medical school in England, and when I graduated, while making my trip home, I was kidnapped by a slave trade group and sold. When I would open my mouth to explain that I was a free man, I was beaten severely. For one talking so well and two demanding my freedom. Then one night, I decided to run, and they caught me and broke both my ankles to hobble me. That is why I walk the way I do. So, my dear boy, shall we get loaded and cast off? We are all surely being hunted as we speak."

Ben stood for a second, taking this in before he answered. And in those few seconds, Ben had finally realized what the slave trade had done to humanity. How it was all around him, and yet even though he was taught that it wasn't something they as a family agreed with, they learned to tolerate it as if it were a normal way of life. Ben even realized that if that had been a white doctor who helped out just then, Ben would have called him sir. All the things Ben had witnessed, the sale yards, the beatings, the way they were all unhappy, the way they all cowered to him even though he was not a slave owner but because they feared being caught not talking to a white man in any other fashion. Ben started to see slavery for what it really was. Ben snapped to his senses. "Yes, sir, do you need any help to load anything?"

The doctor looked surprised when Ben called him sir but answered, "No, we have meager belongings. We can manage." A wry smile came to his lips.

Ben asked Goliath, "Would you help me transport Chef back to the ship please?"

Goliath nodded, and they each took an arm and a leg and made their way back to the dingy. As they reached the dingy, Ben realized that they all wouldn't fit, so he decided to send the slaves and Goliath back to the ship. Ben told Goliath to send Squeaky and two white volunteers back and help him with Chef. He also told him to have them come with a stretcher. He wanted to get Chef to town. Goliath wanted to stay and help Ben, but Ben told him he didn't want him to get caught. Goliath tried again to tell him he was already in trouble, but Ben made the argument that Goliath would be hung on the spot.

COCKROACHES IN THE BILGE

Ben might get a trial, then Ben told him it was an order. He was not going, and Goliath shook his head, knowing in his heart Ben was right. Goliath put a hand on Ben's shoulder. "You're a good man, Mr. Summit."

Ben put his hand on Goliath's. "As are you, Goliath."

Goliath helped the other men into the boat, and Ben helped the doctor ease his way in. Ben held out his hand, saying, "Thank you again, sir."

The doctor looked at Ben's hand, laughed, and took Ben's hand. "I haven't shook a white man's hand in almost fifteen years, but it is I who will be thanking you when we are done."

Ben smiled back. "Let's hope so."

They rowed off to the ship, and in minutes, Squeaky and two volunteers came back. Ben instructed Squeaky to set sail before the next morning if they hadn't returned by then and head north to get those men to a safe area. Squeaky told Ben that the black man with the British accent said to get into the lean-to and take the clothes that were left behind. "He said, 'If they are looking for sailors, you guys wreak of saltwater and look the part.' He said the clothes aren't much, but you need to tell them your sharecroppers looking for work and nobody will pay you any mind."

Ben thought about this, and the doctor was right. They both agreed, and he made his way back to the ship. When Squeaky reached the ship, Captain Hawkins was now up and moving around. He greeted the boarding crew. Squeaky told the captain what Ben had said. Captain Hawkins was surprised to find they were only twenty miles from Homeport and they were harboring runaway slaves. He just shook his head and said, "You can't turn your back on that boy for a second, can you, Mr. Freewater?" Squeaky just squeaked out a laugh and shook his head in agreement. Captain Hawkins sat quiet for a minute and then said, "Tell you what, Mr. Freewater. I am not comfortable in this little bay. Put two men ashore and we will sail out of sight and hove to out in the open water. We will come back in and pick them up. We will give Ben more time. Tell the men if Ben is with them, light two lanterns from that large pine. If he's not, then light one. We will give him three days, but come back in and check each night. And tell the men to stay hidden and take plenty of provisions. And for God's sake, if they need to build a fire, make it small."

Squeaky snapped an "Aye, aye, sir" but stopped short. "What if there ain't no lanterns when we arrive, sir?"

"Then we sail north and hope Ben catches up to us later. Now go be quick. We're sitting ducks in this bay." Squeaky bounded off, giving orders and getting the men to get ready to sail.

* * *

Ben and the other men had made it to the main road. Ben was getting worried at the rate it would take to carry Chef twenty-some miles. They had walked about a mile, and he was realizing that he wouldn't make it back at the agreed time. He and the other sailors discussed it and decided they would drop off Chef and then head north to find the ship. Just when they were starting to panic about the time factor, as luck would have it, a man with a two horse-drawn wagon came along. He slowed as he came near.

"Good day, my friends. Looks like you have a bit of trouble on your hands."

Ben replied, "Yes, sir, we be tryin' to git my father-in-law to a home in Homeport. He be hurt from a huntin' accident. Needs rest, an we was told to take im thar."

The driver looked at the crew. The other two remained silent, looking on and trying not to look guilty. The man perked up. "Well, gentlemen, this is your lucky day. I happen to be heading to Homeport to pick up a bell for my church and some new pews so I have an empty wagon, and I feel it would be my Christian duty to help you fellas get to where you need to be. So why don't you load that poor fellow on and climb aboard."

Ben bowed his head. "Thank you, sir. That would be most kind. Are you sure it won't be too much trouble?"

"No trouble at all, son. Besides, I have been traveling for a couple of days and could use the company."

They climbed aboard. They had already worked on their story. The dark-haired brown-eyed sailor Charles would be Ben's brother, and the blonde blue-eyed sailor would be their brother-in-law, Johnny, married to Ben and Charles's sister. Ole Chef would be Johnny's dad, shot himself while cleaning his gun.

The story just flowed out of Ben's mouth when the driver said, "I'm Pastor Jacobson from the next county." He reached out to shake Ben's hand.

Ben shook it. "Nice ta meet ya, Pastor." Then Ben went into his speech of who was who and how they got there.

The driver looked back at Ole Chef and said after a while, "Your pa, son, must have had you at a later time in life."

Ben was amazed at how quick Johnny said, "Yes, sir. I was the youngest of thirteen, and it was his second wife."

The pastor turned and looked at him gruffly. "He wasn't a polygamist, was he?"

Johnny saw he struck a chord and corrected himself. "No, sir. His first wife died of the plague about ten years before I was born." This seemed to please the pastor, and he went on to telling biblical tales. He kept them all entertained while they traveled. Ben explained when they reached the road that would take Pastor Jacobson to town that they would get off at the junction, but the pastor would not have it and insisted it was his Christian duty to take these men to the home. He drove them right to the door, blessed them all, and said a prayer for Johnny's dad, and they all had to bow their heads and answer amen at the appropriate times. Then he was off.

As he pulled away, Ben's mom came out the front to see what was going on out there. She came across as angry at first. "Is there something I can do for you gentlemen?" She asked sternly then she saw Ben's face. Her eyes got big, and she gasped a large breath in, putting her hands to her mouth. Then her face went back to angry. The transformation was scary, even to the other men. "Benjamin Summit, what are you doing here? And who are these men? Do you know how much trouble you're in?" And as she said that, she quickly looked around then threw the door full open, waving her arm. She motioned them to get inside. She looked around again then quickly slammed it. She turned around and gave Ben a big hug. He returned it. Then once again, her face turned to anger. "What have you gotten yourself into? There were soldiers here looking for you, and I'm not so sure they aren't still here watching for you."

Ben reached up and pulled his mom to him again, and she hung on tight. "I will explain it all, Mom. But first, I have a wounded friend. He needs help and a place to stay. Ole Chef was shot. A doctor helped him, but he needs rest. He can't get that on the boat."

"Who are these men, and what's an Ole Chef?" She pushed away as she asked.

"They're all shipmates, and Chef is our galley slave."

She interrupted, "A what?"

Ben held up his hand to stop her so he could continue. "He's the cook. That's all, Mom. The cook." His voice had a hint of irritation.

She put one hand on her hip and wagged her finger in his face and said, "Don't you take that tone of voice with me, Mr. Summit."

The two sailors snickered under their breaths, and Ben felt his face blush with embarrassment. Ben had a pleading face as he said, "Mom, please, can we just help Chef? He needs a place to stay and mend."

She looked back at the grinning sailors and knew she had stepped on Ben's manhood. She pushed past Ben and took a look at Chef. "He does look pretty bad. Follow me, gentlemen. This way please." She marched down the hall. The two men followed obediently. She pointed to a single bed in the small room, and the two sailors transferred him from the stretcher to the bed. As they stepped out of the way, Mrs. Summit sat on the edge of the bed and undid Chef's shirt. Her nose wrinkled at the smell of burnt flesh and stale blood. She looked directly at Ben. "Go get some hot water and some towels from the kitchen."

Ben nodded and went off to get what he was told. The two sailors helped getting the rest of Chef's clothes off. As there was an awkward silence for a minute, one of the sailors said quietly, "You have quite a son, Mrs. Summit."

She looked sharply at the man and then snapped at him. "Under normal circumstances, as a mother I should thank you and be proud of that comment. But I'm not happy with the situation he is in because of that stupid ship. He was always a good boy, and now he is an escaped convict, thanks to the likes of you." She worked a little more aggressively as she spoke.

The sailor backed away, knowing he didn't want to be any closer to a mother's rage. He hadn't been around an angry mother for quite some time, but he did remember the best thing to do now was be quiet. Ben returned to the room with towels and water. He set them down and told the two sailors to leave him alone and go to the kitchen and help themselves to some food.

The two men nodded and one said, "Aye, aye, sir."

As they left the room, his mom blurted out in the heat of her anger, "Oh, what, are you the captain now?"

Ben interrupted her with a pleading voice, "Mom, please hear me out."

"What's to hear, Ben? You ran off to sea to become a criminal."

"It's not like that, Mom." Tears started to well up in her eyes.

"What is it like, Ben? You explain it then because what I know is if they find you, they are going to hang you." She sat staring at him.

Ben wasn't sure where to start now, so he quietly said, "I found one of the treasures." She looked like she was about to say something else to interrupt him, but her breath caught in her throat, and she exhaled slowly as he continued, "It's a curse, Mom. Nothing good comes of it. I can't change what's been done, but you have to trust me. I did nothing wrong." He explained more as they worked on Chef, and she listened without interruption. When he finished, he explained that he must go. He couldn't hang around. She knew that and knew he was in danger. He stood to leave, and she stood with him. They hugged so intensely that she was afraid to let go for fear this would be the last time she would ever get to hug him again. He pulled away, and she reluctantly let go. He pulled a sack and handed it to her.

"What is this?" she asked.

Ben smiled a sly smile. "It's part of the curse. There's more, but that should help for now. Careful where you spend it. Those coins are pretty recognizable. I will be back, Mom."

She had tears welling in her eyes again as she said, "Don't make a promise you can't keep."

Ben smiled back at her. "It's not a promise I make, Mom. It's a vow. And please take care of that old goat there. He's a good man. He saved my life. Oh, and by the way, he sailed with Great-Grandpa."

She took a long look at the old man lying there and whispered, trying to keep her composure, "I will, son."

Ben pulled her in close and held her tight as her whole body shivered. She let herself cry. "I'll be back as soon as I can, but now I have to go."

She pulled away and straightened her apron and patted him, regaining her strong appearance. She patted his shoulder and nodded to the door. Ben understood and knew she couldn't speak or she would start to cry again. As he reached the door, he turned to tell her he loved her. She again nodded, and without audible words, she mouthed "I love you" to Ben. Ben went to the kitchen and loaded some provisions in a bag. They snuck quietly out a back window just in case Ben's mom was right and someone was watching the home. They decided to check on Jackie and see if he was in any trouble and whether or not he wanted to come with them. He moved through town hiding in the shadows of evening till they found their way to the Huntington's house. They rapped lightly on a back-alley window. He waited a few minutes, and as he was looking around to spot anyone who might see him, the window opened a crack, and a rifle barrel was meeting his chest.

A voice said sternly, "What do you want?"

Ben recognized the voice. "Mrs. Huntington, it's me, Ben."

The gun dropped, and the window flew open. "Benjamin Summit, what do you mean scaring me to death like that... What are you doing here! Why, Ben, they'll hang you if they find you here."

Her voice was getting louder as she spoke, and Ben finally interrupted her by first shushing her and making a gesture for her to be quiet. "Please, Mrs. Huntington, please lower your voice." Ben was looking around nervously as if the whole neighborhood might look out. "I am aware that I shouldn't be here, but I had to see if Jackie was all right."

She puffed up again and yelled in a whisper, "You two boys are in so much trouble. What's a matter with you boys?" Ben knew that wasn't a real question he was to answer.

But he attempted. "Mrs. Huntington, we really didn't do anything. We have been set up. You see, Captain Nelson—"

That's all he got out before she interrupted Ben in a solemn tone, "I know, Ben. Jackie told me all about it."

Ben asked, "Is he here? I would really like to talk to him."

Her face dropped and she said, "No, Ben, he's not." She hesitated then added, "He and his dad went to join the Union Army and fight for the freedom of the slaves." Her voice cracked a bit. "As soon as he came home, they both felt the same way and decided to do something about it." Then she sobbed a bit while she said, "Oh, Ben, I'm not sure what to do. He said he would send for me and try to sell the shop, and who knows how long he will be gone?" She was crying openly. "What am I to do, Ben? I'm not even sure I understand what's going on. There's no telling how long they will be gone or...or if they will even come back." She broke up a little more, crying hard. Ben wanted to hug her like he did his mother, but he couldn't reach the windowsill. She fell forward out the window, which allowed him a stretch to give her a hug. They hung on for a second as she tried to regain herself.

Ben asked her quietly, "Mrs. Huntington, did Jackie give you some gold coins?"

She pushed back, wiping her face with her hands, answering him, "Yes, yes, he did. Do you need them?"

Ben said, assuring her, "No, but they were for Jackie to do what he wanted. But please be careful. If you try to spend them, they will know where they came from, and it could get back to the wrong people." He heard a faint whistle, and he turned to see a sailor waving at him form a lookout point by the corner of the building. He turned to her and whispered, "Someone's coming. I have to go." She leaned out. They hugged once more, and Ben kissed her on the cheek and said, 'I'm sorry for any trouble I have caused, Mrs. Huntington."

She patted Ben's face. "Mr. Summit, Jackie had never been happier than when he left on that ship, and I surely can't blame you for this war we're in. You just take care, and God willing we will see each other again." And with that, she shut the window.

* * *

Captain Nelson had assembled a group of soldiers and headed north. He was allowed to travel only so far and then return. After going to his higher command and trying to get permission to take troops farther north, he was denied, saying the *Charee* incident was a waste of time and an embarrassment to the unit and the Confederate states. He was bumped down in rank, and his hatred for Ben became a true obsession. He had other plans and took his troops into enemy territory where he was told not to. They followed him because he promised them riches beyond their dreams if they helped him find the ship *Charee*. His troops were overrun one day, and almost all of them were killed. He was wounded and taken prisoner. He lived out his days in a prison until one day, the south overtook the prison. He was found and then was incarcerated for being a deserter and was executed for treason.

* * *

The one sailor that spotted the approaching figures was on a fast run toward Ben, and Ben could see by how fast he was running that the intruders were not far behind. The sailor was gesturing without saying a word to get moving. Ben turned and ran just ahead of the sailor, and the other man at the other end of the building also figured it out. Just as all three met, two soldiers rounded the corner. They saw the three figures gathering at the far end of the building. One yelled, "*Halt!*" The other dropped to his knee. raising his riffle.

The three men pushed each other around the corner and heard a shot ring out, and a chunk of the corner wall blasted away right behind Ben's shoulder. The three picked up speed, and Ben took the lead, saying, "Follow me." Ben and Jackie had run this course before. In fact, many times. He and Jackie had to go this way. After a couple of turns, they came to a stairway leading up to a balcony on the second floor of a building. At the base of the stairway was a loose board. Ben pulled it open and allowed just enough room to squeeze into the hollow body of the staircase. Ben then eased the panel back into place. Unless you were a young curious type, you would never look twice at this fine hiding spot. They all held their breaths as they heard footsteps running up the alley and then stopped just feet from their hiding spot. They could see out a small slit in the panels, not enough to see a whole body but enough to make out they were Confederate soldiers. Several more joined them as they could hear them talking as if they were standing there and part of the conversation. All three were standing there, not breathing or blinking as they waited their fate.

One soldier said, "You check the alley to the north. You two go south. You two check that door up there. They had to go somewhere."

Ben's heart was pounding so hard he was sure if they stopped to listen, they would hear it. Then came the sound of someone on the stairs right on top of them. They ran up, and all their eyes followed the pounding above their heads. Then came the shaking of the doorknob. They heard him say, "It's locked."

The other one standing inches from them said, "Well, duh, it is now, you idiot. They problubly done locked it after they was inside."

Ben thought to himself, *As ignorant as that man sounded, that was a pretty good observation.* The man up at the top knocked hard on the door a few times. Then they heard him start to descend. He stopped at their head level. They could see his boots through the separation of the steps. The soldier on the ground said in an agitated voice, "What the hell you doin' now?"

"Rollin' me some tobacee, you ignorant hillbilly" was his reply.

"We ain't got time for that. Wees chasin' deserters. You heard the lutenant."

The other soldier sat down on the step, saying, "We're chasing ghosts and wastin' time." They heard him strike a match and could smell the tobacco.

"I'll just go without you then." And they heard the hillbilly start to walk away.

The other soldier stood right away. "Fine then, you little cry-baby. Lets' go chase ghosts. Besides, I can't leave you alone. You might shoot yourself by accident."

He bounded down the stairs. As he did, they all took a real breath after what seemed to be forever, and one said, "Shit, that was close. My god, I was scared."

As the men disappeared around the corner, Ben asked in a hushed whisper, "Can you fellas make it back to the cove all right by yourselves?"

They both looked at each other and nodded. Then one asked, "What happened to Jackie?"

Ben explained that he and his dad went to fight for the Union Army. Then he said, "They are looking for three men right now. Let's all split up and make our way back to the cove. Try to take your time. Don't look like you're running from something."

They all agreed and slid out of their hiding place, each going a separate way. Ben had a lot of time to think as he made his way back to the cove. He hoped mostly his mom would be safe from all this, and he wondered about Jackie and his dad going off to fight for what they believed in. Ben remembered one time he and Jackie wanted to witness a public lynching of a slave that had done something wrong. They had always witnessed beatings in town, but not a lynching. Ben's mom wouldn't let him go, so he and Jackie were going to sneak in to see it. Ben's mind was working hard as he remembered watching in horror as the man bounced and swung, how the crowd cheered as he hit the end of the rope. Ben and Jackie tried to be tough. They didn't cheer, but they tried not to show fear at watching such a display. Neither one of them saw Mr. Huntington as he came up behind them and put a hand on each one of their shoulders. His words still haunted Ben to that day, and he felt a cold rush even now as he remembered. Mr. Huntington had tears in his eyes and he said, "I think you young lads have seen enough today, and I think we should go home and talk about what you just witnessed."

They did go back and talked. He explained that they hung the man for running away, but he had tried to run because he lived on a plantation for years and had a wife and four children. He was sold because the plantation saw him as too old and wanted to make room for his sons to work now and didn't want to feed him anymore. So he took his sons and wife, and they tried to escape. That was his only crime, wanting to stay with his family. He turned away from the boys, trying not to shed a tear. Ben could hear it in his voice. "I would have done the same thing boys." He finished with that. He never did tell Ben's mom, and it was their secret from then on. Ben also wondered if his dad were still alive, would he have embraced slavery, or would he have been compassionate to their cause?

Ben got to the cove right at daybreak, hungry and tired. He was surprised when he was met by the two sailors he had left in town and by two others who explained the situation and what they were to do by orders of Captain Hawkins. They shared their food, and they all celebrated their successful endeavor. They all slept until night had fallen with the setting sun. The sailors climbed the tree and lit the appropriate lantern. It burned for about an hour, which seemed like days. Finally, off on the horizon, a lantern light could be seen coming in. As the ship got closer to the cove, the light disappeared and just the silhouette of the *Charee* floated into view. The men on shore quietly celebrated and readied the dingy and made their way to the ship. On *Charee*, they all celebrated quietly. And at the orders of Captain Hawkins, they made their way north.

The winds were strong, and the crew was in good spirits. They reached a safe port in a little over two weeks. During their trip, Captain Hawkins, Doctor Ahghona, and Ben had long discussions. They developed a strong friendship. The appreciation they received from the men as they set them free was so overwhelming that Ben and Captain Hawkins decided they needed to continue their work for the cause of freedom for the oppressed slaves of the south. They put their plea before the crew one day that anyone wanting to stay was very welcome, that pay would be small as for shipping illegal slaves did not pay much. They would respect any man's decision not to stay on, and they would deliver any man who didn't want a part of it back to his homeport when they could. Some with families from distant areas were the ones to abandon the ship, and some who believed that slavery was the right of a man who could afford it wanted no part of it, but there were only two of these, and they were hired on together just a few years back. With that decided and most of the crew willing, *Charee* became a freedom ship, hauling some goods for cover but getting slaves out from harm's way as the battle raged on between friends and brothers.

While in the Bahamas, Ben and Captain Hawkins found a jeweler eager to buy up Ben's jewels and gold. He gave him an extremely fair price so Ben had collateral. Then they loaded some supplies, stopped in at the cove, filled the rest of their cargo space, and headed north.

Ben and Captain Hawkins went into New York, which was about as stable as a northern town could get at the time, and found a reputable lawyer. When they showed up for their appointment, they were greeted by a younger man but very distinguished and had a great reputation.

Captain Hawkins introduced himself first. Holding out his hand, he said, "Good day to you, sir. My name is Benjamin Summit."

The lawyer shook his hand with a strong grip. "Well, sir, it is indeed a pleasure to meet you."

Then he turned to Ben and said, "Sir, I would like to introduce to you Captain Reginald Roach."

The lawyer, wanting to be very cordial, took hold of Ben's hand. "It is indeed a pleasure to serve you, sir."

Ben bowed at the waist a little, adding, "The pleasure is all mine." They sat down to business.

The lawyer started by looking at Captain Hawkins. "I understand you have personal business to discuss about a business you share with a Mr. Harsgrove from Homeport?"

Captain Hawkins nodded, saying, "That is correct, sir."

"Do you want to discuss this privately or with Captain Roach involved as well?"

Captain Hawkins smiled. "No, by all means, Captain Roach needs to be very involved with the process. You see, sir, Mr. Harsgrove was…let's say less than honorable as a partner in our business, so I would like it dissolved between the two of us. Any monies salvaged by the endeavor shall go to my sister, Ms. Summit, at the home at Homeport."

The lawyer interrupted, "Well, I will see what I can do, Mr. Summit. But you do realize there is a war on, and most all cash and bonds are frozen, but I will see what I can do."

They both nodded in agreement. Captain Hawkins, pretending to be Benjamin Summit, said, "Just do what you can, sir. That would be fine."

Ben had a bag of gold set aside for Mr. Harsgrove, but under the circumstances, he decided not to give it to him and buy his company and the *Charee* for himself under the name of Captain Reginald Roach.

"When the partnership is dissolved with Mr. Harsgrove, Captain Roach would like to purchase the shipping business and the merchant ship *Charee*, the ship I am sole owner of."

The lawyer looked at Ben and asked, "You, sir, are in agreement with this transaction?"

Ben answered, "Yes, we have discussed it and have reached an agreement."

The lawyer smiled a little and said, "You must excuse my rudeness, sir, but you seem so young to be a captain or have the funds for such an investment."

Ben had a small grin on his face. 'You, sir, appear to me to be too young to be a lawyer, but here we are. Besides, if it makes you feel better, my family has been in this business a long time. This ship and business is a present from my grandfather."

The lawyer, feeling a little embarrassed, looked down at his papers. "Well then, let's get on with this," he said, readjusting his papers. "Mr. Roach, you have up to thirty days to have the ship inspected and evaluated. Would you like me to handle that or would you?"

Ben answered fast and confidently, "There will be no need for that, sir. I have inspected her on my own and find her very sound."

The lawyer looked taken back a bit. "Well, I, uh, all right then. We can proceed. When the amount agreed upon has been delivered, we can get the paperwork started."

Ben then reached into his coat pocket and pulled out a large roll of money. The lawyer looked surprised and stumbled as Ben explained, "The amount for both the *Charee* and the business is all here, sir. The amount that Mr. Summit and I agreed on. The only thing that is not included is your fee, and we will put a security on that. And when the final paperwork comes back from Mr. Harsgrove, we will rewrite the contract so I am sole owner, and I would like it to be called the Gregoreouse Shipping Company. If this is all worked out in a timely fashion, I would like to consider you as a retained lawyer for the company. That is, if you would be interested?"

The lawyer, not taking his eyes off the large sum of money in front of him, nodded as he answered, "Yes, I think we may work something out."

Ben said, "Wonderful. We will be in port for the week. I hope we can get this worked out during that time frame. If not, I will be back in the area at the end of two months, at which time Mr. Summit and I will return to finish the transaction." Captain Hawkins was looking at Ben the whole time, realizing Ben had grown in the two years that he had known him and was well impressed at how he managed himself. Ben stood, saying, "If you've no further questions, sir, we will be on our way awaiting word from you."

The lawyer stammered a bit. "I, uh…no, well, maybe one. Are you staying in town or—"

Ben interrupted him. "I will be staying aboard the *Charee*. You may send word there."

The lawyer reached out his hand and bowed as Ben shook it, saying, "It is a pleasure to do business with you, sir. And you, sir." He turned to Captain Hawkins.

When the two men walked away that afternoon, Benjamin Franklin Summit disappeared off the face of the earth. Captain Reginald Roach took back the *Charee* as owner and operator. The Civil War raged on. The *Charee* worked as a merchant ship staying clear of southern waters except to pull in now and then and transport slaves to freedom to the north. Captain Hawkins and the doctor sailed together even after the war between the states had been won by the north. The crew took enough time to locate one more treasure. This left six more spots out there. Most of the crew that had sailed with them through the years took their share and retired from sailing. When Ben had made it back to Homeport and got to see his mother, he had found out that Chef lasted four years at the home and died peacefully in his sleep. Jackie and his dad, Mr. Huntington, had been killed in battle and buried in a graveyard befitting of the captured union soldiers. Ben got with Mrs. Huntington and paid to have them both exhumed and buried where she wanted them. This time, he got to go to the funeral and pay his respects. Ben's mom never wanted anything to do with any of the treasure, so she worked to her last days at the home. She was allowed to hire some help, so a couple of ex-slaves paid little or nothing helped her each day, and she died at the age of sixty-three. All the money that Ben would send her she gave to her hired help as a bonus.

Captain Hawkins met a woman, and shortly after they had found the other treasure, he made his way back to England and bought a small farm and settled down into a land lover's dream. Ben would see him every so often if the *Charee* happened to make its way to that part of the world. It didn't happen too often. And then when Ben was about fifty-two, he heard that Captain Hawkins had died, leaving a legacy of little sailors behind—three boys, all determined to join the Queen's Navy.

Squeaky or Mr. Freewater met his death on stormy seas off the horn of Africa. Ben went that way to get over and see the excitement of gold on the Pacific side of the world. Mr. Freewater was washed overboard with three other sailors into the cold and raging waters, never to been seen again.

Goliath abandoned ship after they found and divided the other treasure. He found his way home to where he came from, and on that eventful trip to Africa, he was dropped off at a port close enough to get home easily. And with enough money, he would live like a king.

Ben never did marry, nor did he have children of which he was aware. He did purchase a forty-foot yacht, a schooner that he lived on for quite some time. It was called *Jackie*. The *Charee* became old, and as time wore on, it also became a dinosaur. Ships were being driven with engines. The Gregoreouse Shipping Company had done so well that Ben now had half a dozen tankers, they called them. He had realized the new age of oil, and it had to be shipped just like everything else. He didn't spend much time on those ships. He didn't like the way they went through the water, and he didn't like the smell they took away from the fresh salt air. The captains he chose to drive these contraptions were of his picking, and they were the only ones aboard that would know or recognize him as Captain Reginald Roach. So he spent most of his years on his yacht from about the age of sixty on up.

One day, while on the docks, he suffered a stroke and lost most of the use of his right side and the ability to communicate very well. He was sent to a nursing home to rehabilitate. He was ninety-two and had seen his share of wars and suffering. The black man was declared free and equal in the eyes of the government, but not necessarily in the eyes of the white man himself. World war was fought, and another war was on the horizon. Ben had seen presidents come and go He saw large changes in society, some good and some bad. Ben's mind was still sharp, but his ability to communicate was hard. But he could type with his left hand, and with the help of the law office that worked with his business, he was able to finish what he decided he had started years ago. He worked diligently on writing his story, the whole truth, which made him feel better after all the years of deception. Every day he worked, typing away painfully slow. A young man would come in after school. He was always pleasant and would greet him as Captain Sir. He was very patient as Ben struggled to make conversation. Ben always looked forward to seeing him. He then found out a cleaning woman named Betsey was his mother. She worked in the early morning, and she was just as pleasant.

Gerard was his name. He was a strong tall black kid, handsome with strong features as most were to Ben. He reminded Ben of Goliath. He wasn't as big, but he had the same strong features and a deep voice. He was at work after school every day, and on weekends he worked a full day. Ben asked him once if he ever just played after school and what a young man like him was working so hard for. He didn't complain but explained that he was without a father, and his momma needed help. Ben asked Betsey one day what happened to

Gerard's father. She explained to him that Gerard's father was hung down in Mississippi for marching with a group that wanted blacks to have the right to vote. Ben thought this over for several days, and as his story came to an end, he had a copy made and had a long discussion with his legal advisor.

One day, when Gerard came to work and entered his room, Ben worked hard on his ability to speak and practiced what he wanted to say.

Gerard entered the room, saying, "Good day, Captain Roach, sir. How are we today?"

Ben managed to say, "Gerard, please sit down. I need to talk to you."

Gerard smiled a little, answering, "Captain Roach, sir, you know I can't be sittin' talking to you. They'd fire me, and I needs this job."

Ben smiled and added, "Gerard, for one, why do you talk like that? You're educated. Talk to me without that Southern hospitality shit." Gerard's eyes went wide. "Sit, son. What I have to tell you can change both of our lives."

Gerard looked around nervously toward the door, gripping his mop handle and wringing it in his hands. Ben pointed to the chair by the bed where he was lying. Gerard talked straight now. "I don't think I should, Captain Roach, sir. I really should get back to work."

Ben pointed again at the chair. "That is exactly why I chose you, Gerard. You're hardworking, and you have a conscience. That is important in life."

Gerard looked at him funny. "Chose me? What do you mean chose me?"

Ben, having a hard time with his words, spoke very clear today and said:

"The way to English riches are found through
my stitches
Not on paper or tablet or chiseled in stone
But carved into my hide down deep to the bone
Each dot and each dash or symbol you see
Will help you find the lost and hidden treasury

The cuts, the gouges are not just scars
But the legend and directions according to stars
It tells you directions and how many paces
And will take you to far off and mystical places
I've only found a couple but many remain
So get yourself going to find riches and fame."

Gerard stood still. He did not sit. A small smile came over his face. "Well, Captain, that was nice. Did you write that?"

Ben's frustration for not being able to talk came out in anger, and he threw a notebook at Gerard. Gerard almost dropped the broom as he managed to catch the book. Ben growled at him as he said, "I know you're busy, and you work too much for a boy your age. But I want you to read this and meet me here next week to talk about it."

Gerard saw that the old man was not joking. Gerard humbly started to say, "I...I don't know, Captain...I—"

Ben interrupted him. "Damn straight you don't know, and that's why between your studies and your work, you will read that and meet with me next week." He softened his tone a bit. He could see Gerard was getting a little scared at the way Ben was sounding. "Son, this could be the most important talk of your life next week. Please, son, don't let me down."

Gerard looked at the notebook and then at Ben. "All right, Captain, I will do as you ask."

Ben settled down a little and looked more relaxed. Gerard left with the book in his hands, mopping as he went.

The week passed slowly for Ben, but it moved right along for Gerard. He read the manuscript and finished the day before the meeting. Gerard showed up a little early for work to discuss whatever the captain wanted to talk about. He rounded the corner to the room and found two men in well-tailored suits sitting in chairs with an extra placed in front of them.

As he entered the room, one of the men stood and asked, "Are you Mr. Gerard Komunto Brown?"

Gerard nodded and quietly answered, "Yes, sir, I am." Gerard's heart started to pound. The story the captain wrote was an amazing story, but Gerard still had no idea what it all meant or what it had to do with him, and now he wasn't sure if the captain involved him in something that he was going to get in trouble for.

The man pointed at a chair. "Please, Mr. Brown, have a seat."

Gerard made his way to the chair the man pointed at, looking at both men in a curious and scared way. He asked as he sat, "What's this about, sir?"

The man reached over and held out his hand. "I am Jonathan Striker, and this is my colleague, Mr. Steven Benson."

Gerard shook his hand in a wary sort of way. As the man sat down, he explained as he arranged some briefcase on his lap. "We represent Captain Reginald Roach and the Gregoreouse Shipping Company. We, Benson and Striker attorneys-at-law, were asked to meet you here today and discuss."

Just as he got to that point, Gerard's mother came rushing in the room. She was a larger woman, full figured, they call it, wearing the cleaning house uniform. There was a look of despair on her face. Her hair was tightly wrapped on her head. She had strong features and large brown eyes. She was speaking already as she entered, "I don't know what you think my boy done, but he ain't in any trouble." She hesitated and looked at Gerard. "You ain't in no trouble, is you, boy?" Before anybody could respond, she was pointing a finger at Gerard and shaking it. "You ain't so big, boy, that I can't whop you a goodin'."

She would have kept going, but Mr. Benson stood holding his hands up and saying, "Please, Mrs. Brown, no one is in any trouble here. There is just something we want to talk to you and your son about."

She took a breath between ranting but didn't seem too convinced. She didn't need her guard up. Mr. Striker pulled a chair over, and they asked her to sit. She sat, and Mr. Benson started in. "We represent Captain Reginald Roach and the Gregoreouse Shipping Company. Mr. Roach has a lot of admiration for your son, Mrs. Brown, and he decided to make you and him an offer. Being how he is not eighteen yet, we need your assistance in any decision he makes, Mrs. Brown."

She interrupted, "What decision about? What are we talking about?"

Mr. Striker smiled, adding, "Please, Mrs. Brown, let Mr. Benson finish, and it will all make sense."

She sat back with a huff and shot a look at Gerard that said "you better not be in trouble." Gerard just shrugged his shoulders at her as if to answer he didn't know.

Mr. Benson started again. "Gerard and Mrs. Brown, Captain Roach is a very wealthy man and has a net value of over two million dollars. Most of it is in assets of ships. He owns four freighters. He also owns the shipping company Gregoreouse Shipping Company, which is worth three million." Mrs. Brown knew that. Most of the white folks who lived in this home were well to do, but she had no idea he was worth that much. "Captain Roach has asked us to propose a deal with your son. He has no heirs to his businesses, and providing Gerard stays in school and finishes high school, he would then be hired on as a crew member on one of the merchant ships. After one year of learning this trade from the bottom up and if he still would like to continue, he will be sent to college to earn a business degree. And after completing that four-year degree, he would become sole heir to the Gregoreouse Shipping Company, owner of the Reginald Roach fleet, and all of Captain Reginald Roach's belongings, of which I have a list of here with their values."

He didn't get to say much more as Mrs. Brown was starting to slide out of her chair, nearly fainting as she realized what they were saying. All three men reached over and stopped her from falling out of her chair. She shook her head, a little embarrassed, and got control of herself, apologizing the whole time and fanning her face. She sat back in the chair. "Oh my...oh my, I don't know what to say. Can we talk to Captain Roach? I think we have some questions for him."

The two men looked at each other with a solemn look. Mr. Benson said quietly, "No, Mrs. Brown, I don't think that's possible. You see, Captain Roach passed away two days ago."

Gerard and his mother sat in quiet shock. Finally, Mrs. Brown asked, "Why Gerard? Why my boy?"

"Mrs. Brown," Mr. Benson started to say again. "He has no heirs to the fortune, and he chose your son on merit and other personal reasons."

Gerard finally spoke. "He was a sympathizer, Mom, in the Civil War. He helped slaves to escape to freedom, and that's why he chose me, Mom. He told me it was because I worked hard and cared about my education. But that's about all he said. The rest I think is written in this notebook he gave me." Gerard left out the part about the treasure. Something inside told him not to bring it up.

Mr. Striker interjected his talk, "Regardless of why Captain Roach decided to propose this to your son is really less the issue as is the proposal, and your decision now is the important one."

Gerard asked, "What if I don't finish high school or make it in college? Then what?"

Mr. Benson smiled at Gerard. "Captain Roach said you would be worried about that and would ask that very question the last time he and I talked." He reached down and pulled a sheet of paper out of his briefcase. "This is what I was to read to you if you asked. 'Gerard, you are a bright young man, and I don't blame you for being suspicious or worried. If at any time you want out of this deal, you will be given one hundred thousand dollars to get you on your feet at anything new you want to do. But I want to ask you this question. When was the last time you really felt there wasn't anything you could do? When was the last time you were told you couldn't do something and you agreed in voice, but in your mind you were saying yes, I can, and you can't stop me? Give it a try, Gerard. You have nothing to lose. If it doesn't work out, the company will be sold. You will get your money, and the rest will go to prechosen charities. It is all up to you, Gerard. Good luck in life, my friend, and never lose that charm of yours. You have a good heart.'" Quiet fell over the room for more than seemed comfortable.

Mr. Striker finally broke the silence. "I think you two need to talk. Just remember, this isn't even a once in a lifetime offer. This is like a fantasy, the kind that movies are made of." With that, they both stood and left Gerard and his mom in the room alone.

They sat looking at each other quietly. Gerard's mother started to grin, and then she had to cover her mouth from bursting out laughing.

Gerard started to smile a little now, and he asked her, "What do you think about this?"

Mrs. Brown composed herself from laughing out loud. "Truthfully, son, I think the old guy was crazy, but I'm sure glad this wasn't a problem with you bein' involved with the law." She reached over and patted his face. "We've come so far, and you have done so well. You make me so proud, but this, I don't know what to think about this. You know what I think, son? We need a day to think about this and do some checking, make sure what these men say is the truth. Even if the old man is dead now, what's to say these fellas haven't got some scheme where they hand you a company that is legally a mess and they need a fall guy or somethin'?"

Gerard was getting kind of excited for a second. That just wiped the smile off his face, and he asked, "How can we make sure, Momma?"

"Well, we'll tell those gentlemen that we need a day and take as much information that they'd give us, and then we go ask our own lawyer."

Gerard looked confused. "We ain't got a lawyer...do we?"

Being a mom, she said, "Honey, we don't have a lawyer. Don't they teach you anything in that school? But no, we don't. But I think I know where one might be. My cousin Trixy used to go out with one. I still remember his name and where he works. So that's what we'll do, son. That's our plan. If he don't see nothin' wrong with it, I say if you want to, do it."

Gerard called the gentlemen back into the room. They explained what they wanted to do, and both Mr. Stryker and Mr. Benson said that was a good idea and gave her their phone numbers in case her lawyer had any questions. But they reminded her that time was essential. Mrs. Brown assured them they would get right on it. The very next morning, Mrs. Brown went to the office, and he did remember Mrs. Brown. He invited her in and had time to talk to her about her problem. He was in disbelief also as she explained what the two men had approached her with. He told her he needed a couple of days but would look into it and get back to her. She asked how much she owed him for his services today. He smiled and said, "Mrs. Brown, today and tomorrow are free, but if this thing is real, it doesn't sound to me like you will have any problems paying me for my services." She gave him the information the other two men had given her, and she walked away feeling worried about who she should trust now.

Three days passed, and Edward Sinclair, Mrs. Brown's lawyer, finally met with Gerard and her. He apologized for taking so long, but the other law office took him on a tour of the facilities, one ship that was in dock, and went over the books with him. He told Gerard and his mother this was a great opportunity, and he saw no problem at this time. Gerard started to get that excited feeling again, and so did Mrs. Brown. They met with the other men from the law firm, and they put things into motion. They also took them on a tour of the business and the one ship waiting to be loaded. They made sure to show Gerard the ship and introduced him to the captain so he would know what he would do when he went to work on one of these big ships.

They took him for a sail on the forty-foot yacht, and he really got excited. He told his mom they should move aboard it instead of the apartment they rented, but Mr. Stryker said, "No need for that if you don't want to." And he took them to a large house where they could live. It was Captain Roach's, but he never stayed there. When they got there, they met the staff. Many were black and looked with a very curious eye at the two black people that were to be the owners. Gerard and his mother both felt a little weird meeting the staff and having them call her madam and him sir. The lawyers were getting a kick out of watching them as they tried to make this transition. It was like a dream, and Gerard kept waiting to wake up on the drive back to the law office.

Gerard asked, "How come Captain Roach never stayed in the house?"

Mr. Benson smiled. "He preferred to stay on the ship. The house was mainly for guests involved with the shipping business, so for you to want to stay on the yacht tells me he chose you very well."

When they got back to the law office, they went over hours of paperwork. They were fed a terrific lunch, and as they finished, with all the directions to the contract completed, Mrs. Brown thanked the two gentlemen for being so kind. Mr. Stryker pointed out Captain Roach was one of their largest accounts and this was his last rights and wished they had better be nice as they were hoping they would remain a customer. And in any event they were not feeling they were being treated well, they should call on Mr. Benson or himself, and they would do everything in their power to correct it.

Mr. Benson came in carrying a chest. He said to Gerard, "Mr. Brown, this is the last thing on our list. I am instructed to have you take this home and open it privately."

Gerard looked curiously at the box. "What is it?"

Mr. Benson grinned. "I have no idea, sir. I am told to give you this box and this key."

He held out an old skeleton key and handed it to Gerard, and then the box. It was a sturdy box and looked like an old treasure chest described in books. It had ornate hinges and metal straps with carvings engraved in them. Gerard went to open it, but Mr. Stryker stopped him. "Not here, Gerard. For some reason, he made it clear it was to be opened privately at your home."

Gerard felt a rush of fear and curiosity run over him but said nothing and put the key in his pocket. Mrs. Brown asked shyly, "Which home would that be?"

Mr. Benson patted her shoulder and said, "Mrs. Brown, your son is today a very wealthy man. You may live in the big house, move on to the boat, or stay in your apartment. Why, you may want to buy a house just for you on your way home." They all laughed out loud as the tension started to ease. They were both walked to the front of the building, and a large car pulled around and drove them back to their apartment. Gerard's mom wanted to pack some things up and explain to her neighbors they were moving. Gerard and his mom decided not to share the news of great fortune with the neighbors at this time to see if it all worked out first. Or they would be hounded by all the less fortunate folks for loans and moneys. They did decide to go back and choose some who really needed a hand and made donations anonymously.

Gerard went to his room and set the chest on the floor. He expected to open it and there would be a note: "Ha, ha, ha, quite a joke. Are you laughing yet?" Or something to that effect. But a hoax like this was pretty elaborate, and he was sure none of his friends or relatives could do such a thing or afford it either. He slipped the key in the lock and slowly turned it. As he felt the lock release, he slowly opened it. There was only a note and a stack of papers in it. He read on to find they were the maps to the treasures left. Three of the maps had *Found* written across them. The note went on to explain how the maps worked, and there was a small note at the bottom of the paper:

Beware, the treasure can be more curse than opportunity. If I were you, I would throw the whole thing away and enjoy the riches you have. Thank you for taking on this adventure. I know you will do well, Gerard, and my company is in good hands. Do well with the money, my friend.

Signed,
Captain Reginald Roach
Benjamin Franklin Summit.

The End

ABOUT THE AUTHOR

Mitchell Perry has lived in the state of Washington all his life. He has sailed the Salish Sea, the Caribbean, and the Celtic Sea. He worked as a cowboy in Eastern Washington. He is married with four children and twelve grandchildren and still lives in the evergreen state.

CPSIA information can be obtained
at www.ICGtesting.com
Printed in the USA
LVHW051455210421
685124LV00017B/157